KEITH R. FENTONMILLER

KASPER MÜTZENMACHER'S

CURSED HAT

LIFE INDIGO
BOOK ONE

CURIOSITY QUILLS PRESS

A Division of **Whampa, LLC**
P.O. Box 2160
Reston, VA 20195
Tel/Fax: 800-998-2509
http://curiosityquills.com

© 2016 **Keith R. Fentonmiller**
http://www.keithfentonmiller.com

Cover Art by Eugene Teplitsky
http://eugeneteplitsky.deviantart.com

All rights reserved, including the right to reproduce this book or portions thereof in any form whatsoever. For information about Subsidiary Rights, Bulk Purchases, Live Events, or any other questions - please contact Curiosity Quills Press at info@curiosityquills.com, or visit http://curiosityquills.com

ISBN 978-1-62007-273-8 (ebook)
ISBN 978-1-62007-285-1 (paperback)

PART ONE

CHAPTER ONE

1923

Borough of *Schwarz Boden, Berlin.*

Kasper Mützenmacher set his cornet on the cutting table, slung on a herringbone overcoat and matching fedora, and locked the hat shop behind him. He crossed Mauer Street and entered Kiegel Park, where his father used to push him on the center swing until that tickly feeling nearly exploded from his guts. He emerged on the elm-lined Hufeisendamm.

The grand boulevard swarmed with hansom cabs and Model Ts, alfresco diners, queuing cinema-goers, overzealous fiddlers, mustachioed accordionists, black-tied men, and cloche-hatted women. A flapper in a chemise dress tapped her foot impatiently, arms akimbo, as a policeman measured her hemline for a third time "to make absolutely sure" it conformed with regulations. Ex-military men dotted the sidewalks, most with a rolled jacket sleeve (or two) pinned to the shoulder, others leaning on crutches in place of absent legs. Some appeared whole until closer inspection revealed their copper facemasks, meticulously painted with their pre-battle likenesses to conceal the jagged-edged voids where noses, chins, and eyes had been. When a wind gust liberated a five-Mark note from a sausage vendor's cashbox, he didn't bother giving chase. A veteran, little more than a one-armed torso propped on an apple crate, caught the worthless bill and blew his nose in it.

Hyperinflated currency wasn't the only worthless paper to have infiltrated Schwarz Boden. The Nazis had plastered every building, storefront, and kiosk with their propaganda posters—the stern-faced portrait of Adolf Hitler, of course, but also Klaus. A cap, pulled low, enshadowed the feared interrogator's eyes, while a bandage-like veil obscured everything from his nose to his shirt collar. "One People, One Empire, One Face," the posters paradoxically proclaimed beneath the invisible face.

There was no shortage of conjecture about the face behind Klaus's veil. Some believed a toothless, lipless maw occupied the space where a mouth should have been. Others insisted that even the inscrutable Klaus needed a mouth to survive, and instead speculated that row after row of needle-like fangs poked from his festering gums. (A rumor that the veil was simply meant to muffle Klaus's severe gingivitis was quickly discredited as propaganda by a nascent dental association on a membership drive.)

Regardless of Klaus's facial topography, there was no dispute about why the residents of Schwarz Boden had dubbed him the "Stealer of Faces." Klaus reportedly had kidnapped scores of women, only to release them unscathed except for the inability to see their own faces. Kasper wondered whether the kidnappings—and perhaps Klaus himself—were a product of mass hysteria, or, more cynically, a myth that opportunistic housewives had invented to take vacations from their cocaine-addicted, borderline-syphilitic husbands. These were the Roaring Twenties, after all.

Kasper cut through Schwarz Boden Platz and passed the war memorial, his mood darkening as he brushed his fingers along the chiseled letters of his father's name. He brightened after emerging on Teilung Street and reading Club Zola's marquee: "Queenie Coquette and Fats Philadelphia." *Metronome*, the English-language jazz magazine Kasper read religiously, had run a feature on this bawdy American duo from Detroit's Black Bottom, describing them "as a gender-bending, rule-smashing, note-twisting, quaking font of musical iniquity."

Kasper had been enthralled with Black Bottom's music since age sixteen, when Uncle Axel (technically a first cousin, once removed) took him to the Kabarett de Karneval to hear Moses Muznick, a half-black, half-Jewish, cross-dressing cornetist. After the final set, Moses gave Kasper a spare cornet, and for the next seven years, Kasper attempted to emulate Muznick's distinctive phrasing and harmonics, with little success. Still, Kasper kept at it, even when his cornet teacher at the University of Grünwald threatened to expel any student caught playing "nigger-Jew ragtime." Kasper simply retreated to the school's boiler room and practiced the *verboten* music with a mute in the cornet's bell. He occasionally dreamed about stuffing a giant mute in the professor's ass, causing the old fool to belch out ragtime whenever he broke wind.

Kasper smiled at the memory as he entered the club.

The maître-d' sat him at his usual two-top table, and the waitress promptly delivered him his usual drink: Bushmills whiskey on the rocks. The audience laughed and cheered as the cornet and saxophone traded musical calls and responses. When they finished, a heavyset black man came in on the piano—Queenie's cue. The slender, black flapper sashayed on stage in a blood-red dress and began to sing:

My Fats been actin' funny, ever since he met that guy.
Eatin' with his friend, 'stead of feastin' on my pie.

Queenie's chocolate legs were so smooth and flawless, they looked artificial, like a mannequin's. Her eyes had the time-hardened look of a woman in her forties, but her full lips, painted red, and broad smile lent her a timeless sensuality.

Last night I went to bed. I was feelin' kinda antsy.
Found Fats in the sheets. He was sleepin' with a pansy.

The waitress delivered Kasper another shot. Fats was singing now.

My sweet Lang and his thang have set me free.
Come join us tonight. It'll just be us three.

Queenie threw a leg on a table occupied by four men. The crowd hooted when she shook her bobbed, shiny black hair. One man reached up Queenie's dress and rolled a garter belt down her thigh. The crowd hooted again. Kasper couldn't discern the next few lines because Fats played with such a heavy left hand and his hoarse singing voice elongated and stretched the words into incomprehensibility. Kasper was fluent in English but not *Jazz* English. He didn't care, though. Only the energy behind the words mattered, and the pound, pound, pound of the ivories, which set his bones and brain a-rattling.

After the set, Kasper approached the maître-d' and asked whether Queenie and Fats had phonograph recordings for sale, but a woman interrupted before the maître-d' could answer. The diminutive flapper stood five foot four in heels, even with a bell-shaped cloche hat adding more than an inch to her dark bob. The tight pearl choker made her head look detachable. If she really could've popped off her noggin, Kasper was happy she, or the divine doll maker who'd assembled her, had selected that particular head. The nose, too. It was a delicate nautilus shell, unlike Kasper's broad cockleshell of a schnoz. Yet she wasn't pliable like a doll. Her irreverent smirk and three-quarters-open blue eyes exuded intractability. Her expression seemed to say, "Come on, big fella. Impress me."

"Sorry, Papa Bear," she interjected. "I just bought the last one." She winked at the maître-d', who bowed his head then departed. "Buy me a drink, and we can give it a whirl back at my place."

"Sure you can trust me?"

"You're the cat's pajamas."

"How do you know?"

"By that big ole nose of yours."

"You're putting a lot of faith in a nose."

"Don't need faith. I can see it right on your face. Most things people believe in, they can't even see."

"Good point."

"How 'bout that drink? I go by Isana."

Kasper signaled to the waitress. Isana ordered a pint of Doppelbock.

"Kasper."

"If it's all right with you, I'll call you Papa Bear."

"Guess that's okay."

"I should warn you. I'm not so good at telling the truth."

"You don't really like my nose?"

"You kidding? I love that honker. But that scar on your cheek's another story. You ain't a Brownshirt, are you? 'Cause if you are, I may have to slit your throat."

"You tell me."

Isana scrutinized him through heavy-lidded eyes. She then gulped half her beer and dabbed the froth from her upper lip with the back of her hand.

"Nah. You're the bee's knees."

As she regripped the glass, Kasper noticed a crescent-shaped burn mark on her palm.

"I see you're no stranger to scars."

Isana retracted her hand as though the glass had caught fire and hid it under the table. She fixated on her beer, silent and expressionless. Kasper could've kicked himself for violating the first rule of flirtation: Never mention a woman's flaws. Only weeks earlier, Helga Howland had impressed this rule upon him (literally, with an open-handed face slap) in response to his drunken, improvised sonnet that compared her oblong rear-end to a zeppelin. And now Kasper had stumbled into the rule's obvious corollary: If you mention a woman's *immutable* flaw, you're an incorrigible jackass and can abandon all hope of female companionship. Kasper envisioned a celibate future, cloistered in a remote, alpine monastery, his nether parts recoiling from the cold updrafts.

But then Fate granted Kasper a reprieve. Isana's lips—those lips!—curled into a smile, and she said, "I lied to you, Papa Bear."

"About what?"

"The record. I didn't buy the last one. I don't even know if they're sold out."

Kasper sighed, relieved that he could stuff the monk robe back into his subconscious closet.

"I forgive you."

Over more drinks, Kasper learned Isana was a Jew and a rabid Communist, though her party leanings were grounded in jazz, not political philosophy. Jazz represented the ultimate in communal creative effort. Hormones also had come into play, as she'd dated two Communist musicians—a base player with strong fingers and a saxophonist with soft lips.

"Ever date a cornet player?" asked Kasper.

"You have a good recommendation?"

"I might."

Isana cocked her head. "Have we met?"

"You don't need to use that line on me."

"No, you really remind me of someone." She snapped her fingers. "I got it. Chess! My Clydesdale."

Kasper choked on an ice cube. "Should I be offended?"

"Chess had a big nose like yours. Loyal to the bone. Never ran away on me. Never threw me."

"Sounds a little dull."

Isana opened her eyes fully. "But he was thunder between my legs."

The band took a break, leading to an awkward silence. Kasper swigged the rest of his Bushmills. As he signaled for another, there was a commotion at the door. Ten men entered, all decked in tan shirts and high-waisted pants tucked into black boots, thin black ties, and swastika armbands.

"Fucking SA!" swore Isana, under her breath. She swigged the rest of her beer.

The Brownshirts strode to the stage and unleashed a barrage of insults at the musicians, calling some "dirty Jews," others "dirty Niggers," and the one whose genetic identity they couldn't discern, a "dirty Nigger-Jew." One SA hung back from the others, silent. He was a short man with narrow shoulders, clearly the meekest of the bunch. The burly gang leader, a sweaty bratwurst of a man the others called Grosse, turned toward his wallflower companion, whom Kasper now recognized as an officious twit named Dieter Daimler.

During Kasper's second year at university, Dieter had lobbied the administration to crack down on sword fighting, arguing that the extra-curricular practice not only violated the school's code of conduct but also represented a form of sexual deviance. Kasper subsequently "convinced" Dieter to withdraw his campaign against the "man-on-man blood lust" after dragging his slight, five-foot-three frame to the boiler room for a "talk." That evening, during another unsanctioned sword fight, Dieter's brother Max carved a deep gash in Kasper's cheek. Depending on one's perspective, the resulting scar resembled a sideways sombrero, a golf flag, or the Runic symbol for Thor.

"Dieter! You are too quiet," Grosse admonished. "You haven't uttered a single insult."

"I believe you said everything I could have said, my leader, and much better, too."

Grosse got in Dieter's face. "If you can't instill fear in these degenerates, there is no place for you in the SA. Tonight is your night, Dieter. Prove me wrong." Grosse gestured to Kasper, who stood in profile. "See him? The one with the big nose? Probably a kike."

"What would you have me do?"

Grosse poked his stubby finger into Dieter's chest for emphasis. "Prove... me... wrong."

Dieter sighed and took a wide berth around Kasper's table before tapping his shoulder. His touch was so light, Kasper thought it was the brush of a passing barmaid. Dieter cleared his throat and tapped harder. Kasper turned around. Dieter turned white.

"Ahh. Daimler."

"K-k-kasper?"

"What the hell are you wearing?"

"What? Oh... it's the uniform."

"I know it's the uniform. Why are you wearing it?"

Dieter puffed out his meatless chest. "It is Germany's future. We are purifying the Fatherland."

Isana trembled with rage. "You jack-booted piece of shit."

"What do you want, Dieter?"

Dieter shifted uncomfortably. "I am under instructions..."

"Instructions?"

"I am required to instill fear in you."

Kasper laughed. "You make it sound like a medical procedure. Shall I disrobe?"

"No, that won't be necessary," said Dieter, too nervous to grasp Kasper's sarcasm.

"Then how do you intend to accomplish this feat?"

Dieter was perspiring. "Please, Kasper. I'd like nothing better than to walk away, but I have my orders. Perhaps we could pretend... as a favor... between chums... for old times?"

"You want me to feign fear, make a big scene, so you can impress your Nazi boss?"

Dieter nodded. "I'd be most appreciative."

"What are you all planning?" asked Isana.

"I... I'm not supposed to say."

"So you are planning something."

Dieter looked away.

Isana leaned into Kasper. "This doesn't smell right, Papa Bear. We need to sniff out their plot. I say play along with the little Nazi and get the scoop."

"All right, Dieter," said Kasper. "I'll do you this favor, and then we will talk. Go ahead. Make me quake in my shoes."

Dieter was at a loss. "Do you have a suggestion?"

"Good God, Dieter! You're a terrible Nazi."

"I'm still in training."

"Here. I'll put my arm behind my back. You take it and shove me out the door. Shout a few colorful insults on the way."

Dieter rehearsed the blocking in his mind, grabbed Kasper's arm, and pushed him toward the exit. His insults were a mixed bag. He invoked the standard invectives: "Foul, stinking Jew... Degenerate... Enemy of the Fatherland... Black swine..." But nerves got the better of him, and he mangled some insults: "Stinking Fatherland... Enemy of the degenerate swine..." Once outside, Isana led them to the alley, where they spoke in private. Dieter revealed that Grosse had heard an unconfirmed rumor the SA was plotting a putsch that very night. Grosse was determined to be the first unit to march on the Reichstag, where he expected Hitler himself to make a stirring speech for the Republic's overthrow.

Isana's eyes lit up. "I know what to do."

As Isana elaborated on her plan, Dieter's frown sagged in inverse proportion to Kasper's expanding smile.

Dieter backed away. "No. Please."

"You heard the lady," said Kasper. "Strip."

After Dieter disrobed, Isana put on his SA uniform, which fit her slight frame well. With her bobbed hair, and, after wiping off the lipstick and blush, she looked androgynous enough to pull off the deception.

Dieter shivered in his drawers and socks. Kasper had seen skeletons with more flesh on their bones than this scrawny, denuded tadpole of a Nazi. Dieter rejected Isana's semi-serious offer to put on her flapper dress and cloche hat, so Kasper removed his overcoat and draped it over his old nemesis. He grabbed Dieter by the lapels and pulled him close.

"Go home, Dieter, and think about the man you want to be. You'll always be short, but jack-boots won't make you any taller."

Kasper was about to release him when he recalled an incident from philosophy class during senior year. Dieter's brother Max had just argued that "Sodomites and filthy kikes" shouldered the blame for Germany's defeat in the Great War and should be exterminated. In a seeming "fuck you" to his brother, Dieter responded with this Nietzsche quote: "The great epochs of our life come when we gain the courage to rechristen our evil as what is best in us." As Dieter exited the classroom, ignoring the professor's order to sit back down, Kasper realized how dramatically Dieter had changed since his failure to ban swordfighting sophomore year. Dieter hadn't flashed his supercilious smirk in months, and it had been more than a year since he'd jotted a rule infraction in his special green notebook or threatened to report Kasper and his friends for spinning ragtime records in the boiler room. Kasper should've been quietly celebrating the demise of Dieter Daimler, school nudnik. Instead, he felt horrible. He'd failed Dieter. His strong-arm tactics hadn't rechristened anything in the pitiful fellow, only sapped his will. Kasper had become what he most despised—a bully.

Kasper unhanded Dieter and then smoothed the coat's lapels while uttering the Nietzsche quote. "Do you remember saying that, Dieter? Because I sure do."

"You do?"

Dieter seemed surprised but also flattered.

"I'll never forget it. Beautiful, powerful words."

"Not my words."

"But they can be your creed. You're not your brother, and that's a good thing. Embrace it."

Dieter stayed silent.

"At least think about it. Will you do that much?"

Dieter shrugged.

"If that's the best you can do, Dieter, you'd better get the hell out of here before I take back my coat."

Dieter trudged into the alley's shadows, his naked ankles and feet exposed to the elements, the same way he'd entered the world.

"All right," Kasper said to Isana. "Now what?"

"Now comes the fun part."

Isana re-entered Club Zola, striding with the stiff arrogance of the Nazi elite. Kasper followed a few moments later and spoke privately to the band. Isana then took the stage and shouted, "*Achtung*" in her deepest, gruffest, dictatorial voice. The SA gathered before her.

"Who the hell are you?" asked Grosse, the talking sausage.

"I am Herr Hitler's personal emissary from the Ninth Precinct."

"The Ninth Precinct of what?"

"If you do not know the Ninth Precinct, then I am not authorized to say more. Suffice to say, the Ninth Precinct is the brains of the operation."

"What operation?"

"Why, the putsch, of course."

Grosse's face widened into a vindicated smile. "I was right. The rumor is true."

"As true as the sauerkraut stuck in your teeth."

Murmurs of "Herr Hitler" and "Der Führer" passed from the Brownshirts' lips. Grosse shut his mouth. His tongue probed his teeth for the sauerkraut that wasn't there.

Isana continued. "Herr Hitler demands that his troops be in the correct state of mind before his arrival here."

"Herr Hitler is coming here first?" asked Grosse. "But we are to meet him at the Reichstag."

"Who sets the plans? You or Herr Hitler? Are you placing yourself—your flabby self—above the party's führer?"

"No, I..."

Grosse looked to his colleagues for support. They responded with disapproving stares.

"Remember, Grosse, you are but an organ of the body. Most likely the fatty liver. Herr Hitler is the head. You will now be silent and listen, unless you want to end up an appendix—vestigial, ready to be cut out."

The other men stepped in front of the chastened Grosse. They were eager to hear their new orders.

Kasper was astonished that so much strength could emanate from someone so slight. Isana was a torrent, inundating the Brownshirts with a force of personality matched only by their maniacal leader. He was in love.

"Now, who can tell me how the Nordic man gets in the revolutionary state of mind?"

"Spilling the blood of the Jew!" shouted one Brownshirt.

"I like your spirit, but no."

"Smashing their shops!" shouted another.

"Too messy. Anyone else? No? Men, the answer is all around you. Beer! Beer is the Nordic man's lifeblood. We must drink. Barkeep, set up my good men at once! Put it on Grosse's tab."

The Brownshirts cheered. The waitresses served the men beer in pints, yard glasses, and steins. They imbibed with relish, working themselves into a drunken lather of untucked shirts, yanked neckties, and urine-spotted trousers, after which Isana re-took the stage and announced the next phase of Herr Hitler's purported plan.

"Achtung! Achtung, soldiers! Gather around. It is time to learn a new song to announce the coming of the Third Reich. Who here speaks English?"

The Brownshirts were stupefied. These poorly educated working stiffs were barely literate in their native tongue.

"No one? Well, you can still learn to sing the words."

"Why would Herr Hitler want us to sing an English song?" asked Grosse.

"Ahh, more grumblings from our bratwurst friend!"

Two Brownshirts pushed Grosse from behind, telling him to shut up.

"Our leader was very clear on this point. The song must be in English, to send a message to the British and the Americans that our revolution extends beyond the Fatherland. It begins in Berlin. But it will spread to Frankfurt and Munich. Then, to Warsaw, Paris, London, and Washington, where Herr Hitler himself will chisel away Lincoln's marble beard into a proper toothbrush mustache!"

The Brownshirts cheered.

Isana then taught them a modified version of Bessie Smith's bawdy anthem, *I Need a Little Sugar in My Bowl*. She also choreographed a sequence of shuffles, sliding steps, and hip gyrations. The sequence culminated with the Nazis bending over and shaking their asses while they sang, "We need a little hot dog between our rolls."

"Troops, it is time for the revolution!" Isana announced after forty-five minutes of rehearsal.

"But Herr Hitler is not here," said Grosse, confused.

"Our leader has changed his plan. Do you wish to countermand his order?"

"No. I... No."

Isana led the noisy procession of slovenly Nazis from Club Zola. They meandered through the streets, creating an ungodly ruckus. Apartment lights switched on. Windows shot open. Ornery Berliners shouted for silence. But the Brownshirts were undeterred. This was their revolutionary march, though they would've fit better on New Orleans' Bourbon Street instead of parading in front of the staid Reichstag.

Kasper took a position behind a low wall leading up the Reichstag's steps, thirty feet from Isana. He figured the prank was over, Isana would sneak away, and they would head to her apartment, where he'd peel off her SA uniform and make frenzied love to her. It was not to be.

A black Lincoln sedan pulled sharply in front of the jubilant gaggle of Nazis. Several Brownshirts braced themselves against the car to avoid falling under the wheels. The driver exited the car and opened the rear door for a highly-polished Nazi official, an Oberführer. Kasper waved to Isana, beckoning her to get the hell out of there. Isana nodded. She rounded the car, striving to stay out of the Oberführer's view.

Grosse approached the Oberführer and delivered a wobbly military salute. "You can see we have learned Herr Hitler's revolution song to perfection. When will our leader arrive? Is he in the car?"

"You fool, Grosse. You've embarrassed yourself and the SA with this perverse dance through the streets."

"But this is Herr Hitler's song. His personal emissary taught it to us."

"What personal emissary?"

"From the Ninth Precinct."

"Idiot!"

The Oberführer unholstered his pistol and whipped Grosse's cheek. Grosse fell to the ground, cradling the welt crowning under his left eye socket.

A slight figure in a black uniform emerged from the Lincoln's left rear door. A close-fitting veil obscured his face. Kasper shuddered. *Klaus?* The masked man took five fluid strides toward Isana, who had stopped to relish Grosse's humiliation. In moments, Klaus had Isana by the elbow and was guiding her into the Lincoln. The Oberführer reentered the car, which then drove through the confused group of Brownshirts.

Isana had stalled the Nazis' revolution for the time being, but now she was Klaus's prisoner.

CHAPTER TWO

The ten incandescent bulbs dangling from the ceiling transformed the eight-foot square room into high noon in the Sahara.

At 12:15, an SA guard entered with a tall drinking glass and a plate of bread and sausage and set it on the table in front of Isana. She was famished and ate quickly. The salty sausage made her thirsty, but the glass was empty. She tongued the inside of her mouth for a trace of moisture.

Klaus entered with a thick dossier in one black-gloved hand and a water pitcher in the other. He set the papers and the pitcher on the table and then sat opposite her. Isana had been stripped of Dieter's SA uniform and given a pair of trousers for someone six inches taller and fifty pounds heavier, and a shrunken blouse with sleeves reaching to the middle of her forearms. The bulbous pitcher, sweating like a fat man in a public bathhouse, rested mere inches from her fingertips. She raked her tongue over her parched lips while glancing at the wall clock, which now read 12:45.

Odd, she thought. *I must have misread the clock before eating.*

Klaus filled the glass and began to speak. His voice betrayed less color than that glass of water, sounding neither male nor female, neither young nor old. The timbre was clean and unaffected, as though filtered through a fine mesh that stripped all idiosyncratic grit. He ran through a litany of "undisputed facts." Isana was a Jew. She'd had trysts with Communist musicians, including one named Ursula. Yes, Isana was a true deviant. There was no question where she stood relative to the Fatherland. She hated Germany. She was an enemy of the Nordic man. She was impure. But there was hope—even for a defiled, bisexual, Communist Jewess.

"You're not the Schutzpolizei," Isana protested. "You have no right to hold me."

"Yet here you are, being held."

Klaus gestured to the glass, granting Isana permission to drink. The water was cool and sweet. Klaus advised her not to drink too much too fast. It wasn't an order, more a friendly admonition—a concerned mother warning a child against the possibility of a cramp.

There was a knock at the door. An SA guard entered with a plate of bread and sausage. Isana was confused. She'd eaten only minutes earlier, hadn't she? She could still feel the gristle in her teeth. Yet, the clock didn't lie. It was now 3:30. Hours had passed. She should've felt hungry, so she decided she was hungry. Klaus told Isana to eat her "hot dog in a roll," adding, "Be sure to have a good drink of water but not too big a drink."

Isana took a small sip, sipped some more, and then gulped every last drop. Klaus circled behind her chair. Isana set down the glass and sat stock-still. Only her growling stomach and the electric whine of the overhead lights broke the silence. Suddenly, an empty leather glove landed on the table. Seconds later, cool fingertips touched her neck and gently worked into the base of her skull.

"You are tense."

"I wonder why."

Klaus pressed harder into Isana's flesh. His fingertips warmed, radiating heat into her muscles. As much as Isana resisted, she couldn't deny his deft touch felt good. The stiffness in her neck melted in seconds.

No, she told herself. *Don't relax. Don't let your guard down.*

Isana tried to clench her muscles, but Klaus's heat had already penetrated deep into her spine. He seemed to have latched onto her nerves, holding them like a marionettist would grasp puppet strings. Isana should've felt panic, relinquishing her volition to this monster, but his touch had suppressed that reaction as well. She was sleepy and light. Her body had lost substance. She had dissolved into the hot, stale air, or evaporated into the overhead lights. She was nothing at all.

When Klaus unhanded Isana, her corporeal nature returned. In her bewilderment, she momentarily worried her chair might give way under the weight of her body.

Klaus rounded the table, plucked the empty glove with the thumb and forefinger of his gloved hand, and then turned his back to slip it on. He lowered his hat, shading his eyes, and sat opposite Isana.

"I apologize for your lengthy incarceration, but we should be done soon." He picked up the pitcher and refilled the water glass. "You look no worse for the wear. Typically, after three days, you people are scratching the walls to get out."

"Three days? I haven't been here even three hours."

"Don't be silly. We've had numerous discussions."

"We've never spoken before."

"I am hurt, Fraulein. You've shared so much over the last three days. About your childhood on your grandparents' farm. About your lovers—the men... and the women. About your horse, Chess."

"I never said anything about those things, certainly not to you. What have you done to me?"

"You are unwell. But, as I said, there is hope."

Isana looked at the empty water glass. "Poison? Why not just shoot me and call in the Sod Buster?"

"Sod buster?"

"The grave digger."

"I don't want you dead."

"What then?"

Klaus opened a drawer on his side of the table, retrieved a hand mirror, and set it before Isana.

"It took a full day for your nose to disappear. That was a lot of work for such a small feature. But then the rest of your face fell like dominos. Your right cheek, two hours later. Your left, three hours after that. Your chin and eyes went this morning. Your mouth has been most stubborn. That's not unusual."

Isana felt her face. She panicked for a moment, thinking Klaus had performed surgery, removing bits and pieces of her face as she slept. But her fingertips told a different story. Her features were all there—nose, cheeks, chin. What the hell was he talking about?

Isana picked up the mirror. She saw the outline of her head, her short black hair, and round ears. Her eyes, however, were voids, as were her chin and nose. Those areas were blank, as though portions of her retinas had burned out, or the transmission lines between her eyes and brain had gotten kinked.

Klaus had tricked her, probably something he'd picked up from an illusionist on Lutherstraße. Yet, when she turned the mirror left and right, the wall behind her came into full view. She picked up the water glass and brought it to the blank spot where her nose should've appeared in her reflection. The glass didn't vanish. This was the most devastating trick Isana had ever experienced. She set down the mirror and gulped the water, trying to swallow her dread with it.

"What's the matter, Fraulein? You don't seem as confident as before."

"I'm sick of being Edisoned."

"What is this word '*Edisoned*'?"

"Questioned. Just tell me what the hell you want."

"I want to know if you see your mouth in the mirror."

"Yes. Of course, I do."

"I wish I could take your word for it. In order to be scientific, I'll need you to identify the color of your lipstick."

"I wiped it off."

"We painted your lips while you were sleeping."

Isana touched her lips, alarmed. What else had they painted or manipulated as she slept?

"I am no expert in these matters," Klaus continued, "but I'd venture to say we used a much more tasteful color than your usual 'passion red.'"

Jesus, he knows my lipstick color.

Klaus pulled ten metal cylinders from the drawer and set them before Isana. Some were jeweled; others etched with ornate patterns. Some were round. Some square. One was octagonal. Klaus extended each stick, exposing a spectrum of reds, plums, browns, and oranges.

"The color is among these ten here. A rather wide selection, don't you think? Maurice Levy. Helen Rubinstein. Max Factor. My goodness. They're all made by Jews. Why are you people so obsessed with covering your faces?"

"There ain't no cover-up. Munitions—that's flapper-speak for makeup—is just how we draw attention to our faces, to say to the world, 'Look at me! Ain't I just the cat's pajamas?' It's the opposite of a cover-up. It's advertising."

"It's pitiful. An elaborate self-deception because you can't stomach the way you look."

"You're one to talk."

Klaus paused but let the comment pass. "You have a one in ten chance of guessing the correct color."

"I don't need to guess."

"Of course, you don't. Just look at your reflection and tell me the correct color."

Isana picked up the mirror. She studied the lipstick colors and glanced back at the mirror. After a minute, she sat back and stared into Klaus's eyes.

"I take it your mouth has vanished?" asked Klaus.

"Your little experiment failed. My lips are there in all their glory."

"And what is their glorious color?"

Isana hadn't a clue, and one-in-ten were horrible odds. The answer was in her brain somewhere, huddling in her subconscious, waiting for permission to leave the shadows. If only she could throw the answer a rope—a memory or an association—and haul it into the light.

She detected an odor, like an animal smell. Perspiration, maybe. The scent reminded her of her grandparents' farm, her horse Chess... and something else. No, *someone* else—who, she couldn't have said. She grew faint, and, as she faltered, she had a vision of crimson lips. Those lips then morphed into the gunshot wound between her horse's eyes. How distinctly the blood had pooled. Like a flower. Like a perfect red orchid. *Yes, a red orchid*. She'd found a rope. Was it strong enough?

Isana reached for a lipstick and handed it to Klaus.

Klaus sighed, defeated. "Obviously, we have more work to do."

"I've heard your face is horribly disfigured. No lips. Just a hole and a few fangs. But that's stupid. You wouldn't be able to talk. I'd bet you have a beautiful face. Flawless skin. Not a wrinkle or a scar."

"My face is irrelevant. Only one face matters—our future Führer's."

"Come on. Show me that mug. Let me plant a kiss on it. Have you ever kissed a girl? Never kissed *this* girl, anyway."

Klaus rose. "You will be silent."

"Crud. I'm such a tomato. I've touched a nerve in ya." Isana laughed and added, "There I go again. I shouldn't laugh at your pain. It's a defense mechanism, I suppose. Kind of like your veil."

"Careful, Fraulein."

"Rumor has it you steal only women's faces. Is it true?"

Klaus didn't answer.

"Maybe you ought to check my pants, make sure I ain't hiding the goods."

"Silence."

"You don't scare me. I'm way more of a man than you'll ever be."

Klaus slapped Isana's face, opening a cut on her upper lip. She tongued away the blood as though it were a spot of spicy mustard.

"No hard feelings, fella. We all have our off days."

Klaus went to the door and paused. He brought his fingertips toward his ear and motioned as though sweeping away a few errant, invisible hairs from his closely cropped head. He gathered himself, stiffened, and left the room.

The clock read 9:30. Isana rested her head on the table, convinced she wouldn't leave that cell alive. How the hell had she ended up there? She'd promised to take it easy that night—a few smokes and brews at Club Zola, that's all. But those plans went out the window the second she'd spotted Kasper. Although he had a big nose and a strange scar, his eyes exuded the wisdom of someone who'd seen a lot of the world, far more than the typical fellow his age, perhaps more than any man should see in one lifetime. And he was thick and muscular, oddly reminiscent of her horse Chess.

Was it stupid to fall for a man who reminded her of a dead horse? Definitely. Yet, Isana couldn't control her feelings, as though her love for Kasper was automatic, pre-ordained even. Fate had etched it in her soul at birth, like grooves in a phonograph. But something had gone wildly wrong during the playback. The needle had slipped from its groove and skipped to the end. The music was fading.

CHAPTER THREE

1922 (One Year Earlier)

Hermann Mützenmacher hadn't trusted his son to dispose of the hat shop's rubbish, let alone steward the cursed heirloom inside the wall safe. Before heading off to war in 1916, he'd instructed Elsie to withhold the combination until Kasper turned twenty-two, assuming six more years of life experience, including four at university, would mold their child into a semi-responsible adult. If Hermann's assumption proved incorrect, Kasper likely would end up mad or dead within six weeks of getting the combination.

Hermann's assumption did, in fact, prove incorrect. It took Kasper only four weeks.

Kasper gave his mother every reason to believe he'd matured. He'd graduated, albeit with a music degree of dubious value to the family hat business. Still, he'd come home straight away and immediately went to work in the shop. He put in long hours without complaint. He hummed while assembling wire frames, and displayed a beatific smile as he weaved and braided Leghorn straw. He showed up promptly for dinners and awoke at seven each morning to begin the day anew. He even prepared meals twice a week, purportedly to give a well-deserved rest to his "hard-working mother, who'd sacrificed so much" for him.

Kasper had transformed into the perfect son. That's what worried Elsie. Nevertheless, per her husband's instructions, she handed Kasper the safe's combination on the morning of his twenty-second birthday. He accepted the numbers indifferently, stuffing the slip of paper in his pants pocket while inquiring about the shop's burlap inventory.

The front door squawked open. Elsie swallowed her reservations and exited the cutting room to greet the customer.

With his mother occupied, Kasper rushed to his father's portrait hanging over the wall safe. He unmounted the painting and propped it against the armoire, which held various ribbons, trophies, and medals his father had won for millinery excellence. Hermann's scrutinizing gaze seemed to burn a hole in Kasper's forehead, so he turned the portrait around.

Kasper read the numbers on the slip, spun the dial left, right, and left, and then cranked the lever, liberating a waft of stale, tannin-laced air. In his excitement, he swung the door open with too much verve, and it clanged into the wall. A chunk of plaster fell to the floor and exploded into tiny particles. He froze, holding his breath, certain the noise had attracted his mother's attention.

Kasper peered through the curtain separating the front and back of the shop. Elsie was engaged with Frau Schwellen, their fussiest, most indecisive customer. That was good.

There was no time to waste. Kasper plunged his hand into the safe's darkness. He pushed aside the large gold coin bearing Hermes' face, passed over Lorenz Mützenmacher's three-hundred-year-old "family bible," and retrieved the hat. When he put it on, the warm scaly leather conformed to his skull like a blanket of heated wax. He closed his eyes and recalled his father's instructions: *First, think of the place. Then make the wish. Not the other way around.* Kasper breathed deeply and then exhaled as much air as he could, a precaution to stave off the overwhelming nausea that surely would follow. Before the next inhalation, he thought, *Take me there.* In an instant, he was compressed to a point, drained of all material substance. The world went dark and silent. He felt only a sensation of impossible acceleration and then nothing at all.

—o┼o—◇◇—●—◇◇—o┼o—

Kasper wished himself from cabarets to booze cellars, concert halls, and boxing venues all over Europe and North America. Although hat travel made him queasy and headachy, whiskey took the edge off. Then, after a week of around-the-clock hat travel, the nausea and head pain receded, and he began to enjoy the rush of compression, expansion, and acceleration.

Well, labeling the experience "enjoyable" would've been a vast understatement. The nascent drug addict doesn't merely "enjoy" a shot of heroin or a puff of opium; he relishes it, embraces it, becomes one with it. Using feels like an act of self-creation—conception, gestation, and birth wrapped into a singular, lightning-strike moment.

So it was with Kasper. With each wish, his eyes rolled into his skull, and pleasure waves rippled through him, culminating in orgasmic spasms, both psychic and physical. He craved wishing for wishing's sake, not for the destinations the hat could take him. He couldn't fathom his father's admonition against using the wishing hat for fun. He saw no serious danger to life and limb. As far as he could tell, the greatest risk was embarrassment, like when he'd appeared in crowded Red Square, wobbly-kneed, wailing in ecstasy like an oversexed hyena.

But soon Kasper couldn't ignore the side effects of so many trips over such a short span, or the inevitable truth that he was sowing the seeds of self-destruction. First came the blue-tinged vision—annoying but not debilitating. Then the tinnitus, which loud music exacerbated, so he stopped frequenting cabarets. Shortly thereafter, he gave up boxing matches because the mere sight of punches sent sympathetic jolts through his head. Soon, he couldn't tolerate even basic human interactions. A perfunctory hello was a slap in the face. A cough was a knife to the kidneys. A smile was an arc lamp shone in the eyeball. Even the sound of his own breathing set his teeth on edge.

Things rapidly degraded in Miami. A black speck appeared in his dream world, like a persistent smudge on the window into his unconscious mind. In Paris, the speck swelled to the size of a dime and sprouted teeth around its circumference. In Vienna, the jagged dime began spinning like a buzz saw. Then, inside a stuffy London hotel room, his dreams went dark, as though the saw had cut the power to his subconscious.

Kasper shot awake with an intense itch in his brain. Stupidly, he assumed that scratching his head would alleviate the discomfort, not comprehending that the itch was far beneath his scalp, between his ears, inside that twisted mass of neural tissue that had put him in this predicament. He fantasized about a steel auger drilling deep into his brain and boring out that flaming nettle, that cruel burr, that angry urchin, that spiky caterpillar. The crude surgery would kill him but not before delivering a moment of profound, exquisite relief.

So delirious had Kasper become, he formulated plans for the barbaric procedure. *Where can I find a steel auger at this early hour and an unscrupulous auger operator to drill into my head? I'll place an ad in* The Times. *No, an ad will take too long—a day, possibly a week, for someone to respond. Do auger owners read* The Times? *Do they even read? Jesus, it's hopeless.*

Kasper eyed the wishing hat on the bedside table. He couldn't discern the scales from that distance; the deep black gryphon leather just looked like ordinary cowhide. Without a head for support, the hat had crumpled in on itself like a deflated pig's bladder. Although the gryphon who'd donated its flesh was long dead, the hat's leather remained very much alive; hence, its constant temperature of fifty degrees Celsius. But now the hat was manifesting traits Kasper's father hadn't mentioned—a mind of its own and a voice to match. The casual observer, had there been one, would have heard nothing, because the voice emanated from inside Kasper's head.

"Put me on," the hat teased. "Scratch that itch."

Kasper looked away.

"I still see you," the hat said playfully. "Let's go for a ride."

Kasper laughed, attempting to mock that inner voice into submission.

"Laugh all you want. The itch will only get worse. You feel how it burns? Imagine an hour from now. Two hours. It'll be unbearable, I'm afraid. I predict you'll throw yourself from the balcony."

"You can't predict anything," Kasper shot back. "You're a hat."

"A *god's* hat."

"A *dead* god's hat."

"Hermes isn't dead."

"Might as well be dead."

"He'll resurface. He'll reclaim me."

"He blew his chance three hundred years ago."

"He was destined to fail. Daphne's sisters weren't yet born."

"When's that gonna happen?"

"Haven't a clue."

"Meaning I'll make hats for the rest of my life."

"Probably."

"It's not fair, goddamnit! I didn't steal you."

"That's the way curses work. Might as well accept that."

"Or what? What if I never return to the hat shop?"

"You'll die. You're nearly dead already."

"Ridiculous! I'm in excellent health."

"You're delusional. You're succumbing, just like the others."

"What others?"

"The Mützenmachers and Petasoses that came before. You all share that same emptiness. If you're not filling the void with booze or opium, you're wishing yourselves away from it. But you can't get away. It's in your blood."

"I can stop wishing myself places anytime I want."

"Then stop. Lock me back in the safe and start making hats like an obedient little Mützenmacher."

"Go to hell."

"Put me on, and we'll go together."

"Hell's not a real place... *is it?*"

"Only one way to find out."

Kasper winced from the itch searing into his brain.

"Maybe you're already there," the hat added.

"I'm fine."

"Come on, Kasper. Just one puny, little wish. It doesn't have to be far. The street corner will do. It'll scratch that itch. I promise."

"How the hell can a hat promise anything?"

"Asked the man arguing with his hat."

Irritated, Kasper plucked the hat from the table and stuck it on his head.

"Yes. Good," the hat said encouragingly.

Kasper envisioned the street corner. He saw the Victorian gas lamp dangling from the gooseneck post, the fixture resembling a giant Chess pawn giving birth to a glass bubble. He pictured its warm light puddling on the impractical cobblestone sidewalk. He didn't need to be that specific with his wish, but he wouldn't leave anything to chance. He had to scratch that inner itch.

Take me there. And the hat did just that.

No sooner had Kasper appeared in the flickering yellow circle than the fire inside his mind extinguished. At last, his head was clear. He removed the hat and returned to his room the conventional way, slogging up three flights of a dank stairwell while his thigh muscles and straining heart cursed gravity. An hour later, the itch returned with a vengeance—the nettle engorged and prickly, the spiky caterpillar straining at its insect-sized yoke. Again, Kasper wished himself back to the lamppost and trudged back to his room, relieved.

And so it went every hour, day after day. When he wasn't making a wish, he was anticipating the next one. He stopped eating and drinking. His personal hygiene, which already had become sporadic, became nonexistent. He reeked of stale sweat, bile, and decay. Malnutrition and dehydration turned his skin the color of cigarette ash and caused his eyeballs to recede in their sockets like two proto-humans slinking into their caves. His next wish, or maybe the one after, would kill him. That was fine. Finally, there was something he craved more than the next wish.

With the matter of his mortality settled, Kasper put on the wishing hat and contemplated the location for his final wish. But his thoughts soon drifted into incoherence, and he fell into a black dream. He lost his sense of time and space, the same disorientation he'd experience during journeys with the wishing hat, although with hat travel, that bewilderment didn't last more than the split second it took for the atoms in his body to compress into nothingness. Now, however, he seemed trapped in this amorphous state. Would this be his existence for eternity? A disembodied mind in the darkness, with only the memories of a short, useless life on which to cogitate, while that incessant itch suffused his world like the stench of raw sewage or the squeal of a broken bow dragging across a warped violin string?

There was a tearing sound. A sliver of indigo light pierced the void like a rent in a heavy theater curtain. *Are those talons?* The claws pulled and stretched the edges of this mysterious slit, ripping it wide open and flooding his dream world with a dazzling blue-purple light. A bird's head poked out, and its feathered body shimmied through. The beast bore the head and wings of a giant eagle and a lion's body and tail. A gryphon.

According to legend, a mountain nymph had harvested the voice box of a dead gryphon to fashion Hermes' wishing hat, thus the characteristic squeal that accompanied each wishing hat journey. Was the beast back from the dead? Was it seeking to reclaim its voice box? Would it kill Kasper for it? The gryphon unfurled its wings and released a shrill, thunderous peal. Clearly, this particular gryphon's voice box was quite intact.

The beast drew closer and squawked again. Its indigo pupils widened into their black irises, seemingly ready to suck Kasper inside. His instinct was to turn and run, but turning and running assumed a sense of place, and he was no place. A pair of legs would've been as useful as a ladder in a two-dimensional world. Yet, he had to get away. He thought of the safest place he knew, the place he was supposed to be, the place he never should have left. Home.

Take me there.

—o╂o-◇◇-◯-◇◇-o╂o—

Kasper collapsed into the foyer when Mama Elsie opened the door. Hermann had prepared her for this very scenario. She removed the wishing hat, dragged Kasper's feverish, emaciated body inside, and locked the door. She put Kasper to bed, where he drifted in and out of a delirious sleep, while she dabbed his forehead, arms, and chest with a damp cloth. Whenever his eyes popped open, she forced thin broth down his throat. He survived the night. That was promising.

As Kasper's body reinvigorated, excruciating withdrawal symptoms set in. First came dry heaves, shivering, diarrhea, and cold sweats. Next, strobe-like flashes of indigo light, random buzzes, clicks, and squeaks, delusions of a gryphon perched over his bed, and an incessant sensation of falling, decelerating, and falling again. All the while, that infernal, internal itch wriggled between his ears. He was mostly conscious during the day, but his moods were mercurial and rabid. He begged Elsie to fetch the wishing hat, and when she refused, he pounded the walls and called her a "cruel bitch" and a "dried-up old whore."

In lucid moments, he lamented his abominable behavior by pulling his hair and pacing obsessively. But the dark cravings invariably returned. At one point, he announced he couldn't take it any longer and would fetch the wishing hat himself. Elsie told him not to bother, as she'd locked the hat in the safe and changed the combination. Kasper threw a fit, knocking over an end table and tossing couch cushions. When he got in Elsie's face and demanded the combination, she grabbed the copper flower vase and threatened to brain him. Although Kasper relented that time, he repeated the rampage two days later, insisting he'd hire a locksmith to open the safe for him. He knocked Elsie into the sofa and made it all the way to the door but no farther. He awoke with an ice pack on his head. The copper vase, now featuring a semi-circular dent, smirked at him from the nightstand.

He wasn't going anywhere.

That night, Kasper drifted in and out of a twitch-filled sleep, muttering about a rip in his mind.

"I must repair it, but there is no needle and thread here."

Desperate to calm him, Elsie pretended to hand him those implements. "Here are the tools you need. I've already threaded the needle. You can start the repairs."

It took the sleeping Kasper a moment to register the outside influence, but when he did, his hands started miming a sewing motion. "It's working, Mama," Kasper said hopefully. "It doesn't itch as much. But I will need more thread, the sturdiest we have."

Elsie answered, "We have all the thread you need. When you run out, hand me the needle and I will rethread it."

Kasper smiled and then asked, confused, "Mama, why does my head hurt?"

Elsie eyed the dented vase. "I... I... Keep sewing, my son, and the pain will go away." She then rose from his bedside, grabbed the vase, and flipped the light switch.

Kasper snored softly while his hands continued to fidget with the imaginary needle and thread.

Kasper regained weight, and the color returned to his cheeks. The inner itch receded to the back of his thoughts. But his hands remained restless, compulsively so. He fixed the teakettle's handle, re-plumbed the kitchen sink, and fashioned bedroom window curtains from an old velvet bedspread. He decorated the cathedral style radio with paint, fabric, and decoupage glue. He did the same to the grandfather clock and the commode. He deconstructed three of Hermann's dusty suits and re-altered them to fit the icebox, sink, and stove. It looked like the kitchen appliances had joined the Sicilian Mafia. Elsie had to roll up a sleeve to get water from the tap, unzip the icebox door, and reach through a fly to turn on a gas burner. Although pleased her son was on the mend, she felt unclean having to fondle the stove every time she needed to boil water. She had to get Kasper out of the house.

"Come on," Elsie ordered her son.

"Where are you going?"

"You need fresh air."

"But I'm not done with the radiator's neck warmer."

"Radiators produce their own heat."

"It looks cold."

Elsie took Kasper's knitting needles and set them on the radiator. She extended her hand.

"It's a beautiful day."

"You sure it won't get cold?"

Elsie cranked the valve, and the radiator clanked to life. Satisfied, Kasper walked through the apartment door for the first time in two weeks. Elsie, sans flower vase, followed behind him.

They strolled to the River Spree, where young girls sunned, fathers taught their daughters to swim, and teen boys engaged in raucous horseplay. The air was filled with the smells of sizzling sausage and roasted nuts. Kasper's stomach growled.

"How about a sausage?" asked Elsie.

"It'll cost a small fortune."

"Consider it a celebratory sausage."

Elsie shelled out three thousand Marks for two sausage rolls and beers. They clinked their rolls in a toasting motion and then turned right on Mauer Street, home to Schwarz Boden's garment district. The big fabric producers were concentrated nearest the river, where they churned out bolts of linen and wool in two twenty-story buildings. Boys with pushcarts filled with fabric emerged from the buildings like a chain of picnic ants, zooming around, through, and sometimes over, pedestrians. Farther up the street, frustrated bicyclists attempted to bypass the double-parked trucks that the major fashion houses, like Klempner's, Hockner's, and Weinstock's, were loading with flapper dresses, shifts, and chemises.

Beyond the fashion district, Jewish butcher shops and delicatessens bustled with customers buying briskets, liver, and kishkes, while hat shops and haberdasheries stocked their display windows with cloche hats, straw boaters, men's suits, silk scarves, and neckties. Across the street, Kabarett de Karnivale lay dormant but later would be teeming with jazz musicians, bobbed-hair flappers, and slick-haired gents.

The next block was home to an apothecary, two tobacco shops, an optician, a hardware store, and Kimball's toy shop. Kimball's had the distinction of being the only structure in Schwarz Boden with a giant moon on its roof. Herr Kimball's father had been so taken with the 1902 film *A Trip to the Moon* that he'd built his own replica of the man in the moon with a rocket ship lodged in his eye. He coated the sculpture with phosphorescent paint and illuminated it with a spotlight for night viewing.

Kasper pointed to the island of green space across the street, Schwarz Boden Platz. "Is it finished?"

"Two weeks ago."

"And all the names are there?"

"Yes."

They entered the park, the site of a memorial sculpture for local men who'd perished in the Great War. Originally, the sculpture had consisted of a small soldier figurine surrounded by a giant ellipse, but just before the public dedication a stray Doberman plucked the man from his base, gnawed off his face, and buried him with a previously purloined saucepan, ladle, and ham bone. With no time to cast another copper soldier, the sculptor created a plaque explaining that the empty ellipse "represents the moral oblivion from which war is spawned, the cruel void that resides inside each of us, not just the men who wear the uniform."

Chiseled into the memorial's limestone base were the names of Hermann

Mützenmacher and the thirty-one other "*Schutz des Vaterlandes*" (Protectors of the Fatherland). Kasper mentally revised the phrase to read "*Scheiße des Vaterlandes*" (Shit of the Fatherland), because the military had flushed these men away. Literally. During the Battle for Perdeau Valley, General Friedrich von Tannenberg had ordered a mock surrender to draw out the American Marines. When the Americans took the bait, the general blew the dam holding back Lake Perdeau, drowning everyone in the valley, including two hundred of his own men. The general's court martial fizzled in the confusion of the Armistice. He returned to his Munich farm with a full military pension, while the army delivered Elsie a package containing Hermann's right boot and an invoice for a "suggested" three-Mark donation to cover shipping charges.

Kasper located his father's name between Bernd Münch and Karl Nacht. He traced the letters with his fingertips. Hermann's death felt more real now than five years earlier. The single empty boot had left open the possibility, however remote, his father was alive somewhere and wearing the left boot. Perhaps he'd hit his head in the tumult of the great flood, lost his memory, and then wandered the Alsace countryside until a beautiful widow took him in, and he began a new life with a new right boot. Letters in limestone quashed such fantasies.

"He was a good father," said Kasper.

"And a good husband."

"And a brilliant hatmaker."

Elsie shrugged. "Meh."

"What do you mean, 'meh'?"

"Your father was a serviceable hatmaker. Brilliant? No."

"But he won all those awards. First prize in the Art Nouveau Exhibition for the bowler with the ostrich feather."

"I made that bowler. He accepted the trophy."

"What about that silk top hat with the reflective grosgrain ribbon? That got him second place in Düsseldorf."

"Also my creation."

"Don't tell me he didn't make the straw toque. That was practically all we sold in Aught Seven. He made tons of them."

"True, he wasn't bad with straw, though it took him twice as long as it should have. Mostly, he took care of the shop's basic tasks—cutting, bending the wire, stuffing hats in boxes for shipment, running the register. The mundane stuff."

Kasper shook his head in disbelief. "That can't be." But the more he thought about it, he couldn't remember a specific occasion when his father did fine craftwork. He recalled only his mother's thin, strong fingers brocading the silk or fashioning bows around brims. "How could I've been so blind?"

"Boys worship their fathers. They see what they think their fathers want them to see."

"I obviously should've been worshipping you."

Elsie extended her left hand in a show of mock regality. "Kiss my ring."

"Papa was lucky to find you."

"He'd inherited the hat shop but no ability. Klempner's was paying me a pittance for designs they produced by the thousands. It was a good deal for both of us."

"A 'deal'? What about love?"

A wind gust blew a stray newspaper across the brick walkway, and it wrapped around Kasper's leg. He peeled it off and refolded it into a neat square.

"He was smitten right away. It took me a bit longer. I had to get used to that big Mützenmacher nose."

Kasper pressed the square of newspaper into a triangle and then bent the outer corners downward and toward the center.

"There's something I always wondered about Papa. Why did he re-enlist for the Great War? He was no fan of the Kaiser, and he was kind of old, wasn't he?"

Elsie looked to the distance. "Yes, he was."

Kasper continued to work the newspaper, barely glancing at the intricate creases and folds he was making. "Clearly, he loved his country more than he'd let on."

"I swear, Kasper. Sometimes you can be positively thick in the head. He enlisted to spare your life."

"What?"

"You would've been sent to the front otherwise."

"No, I had flat feet, remember? That's why they put me on three months of trash collection for the Ersatz Reserves."

"'Flat feet' was the official reason. The truth is, the fellow who ran the mustering office—Captain Burgdorf, I think—let Papa take your spot in the infantry."

"Papa traded away my spot in the army?"

"He also had to throw in a velvet fedora and a silk bonnet, but yes."

"Why?"

"To save your life."

"But I should've gone to war."

"Papa was never going to let you go, not after what he'd gone through in Africa. The uprisings. The slaughter. He always said the military broke something inside him."

"But it was my duty to fight, not his. He died because of me."

"He died because of General von Tannenberg."

Kasper wept while his hands folded the newspaper into its final form, an elegant top hat with a taut, cylindrical crown and gently curved brim. He'd managed to center that day's headline about Togoland at a jaunty angle on the crown's front.

A young girl skipped over to Kasper and pointed at the paper top hat. "Mommy, hat."

"Yes, Frieda," her mother agreed. "It is very beautiful." The plump woman, her face framed in blonde sausage curls, smiled at Kasper and asked, "Did you make it?"

"Make what?" Kasper glanced at his lap. "Oh." He looked at Elsie, befuddled, and then at the apple-cheeked girl. "Would you like it?"

"Yes!"

Frieda reached for the hat but pulled back when her mother admonished. "Ahh. Ahh. Yes, *please*."

"Yes, please!"

Kasper placed the hat on Frieda's head. "A perfect fit."

"Isn't that lucky, Frieda?"

Frieda toddled off toward the sculpture. She removed the hat and stuck it through the ellipse a few times, probing the empty space. She then bowed deeply, stuck the hat on her head at a crooked angle, and pirouetted away.

Kasper and Elsie laughed at the diminutive dancer.

"Frieda!" her mother called. "Don't get too far ahead!" She thanked Kasper and then hurried off.

Elsie stood. "I need to stop at the shop for a delivery. You feel up to it?"

"Sure."

They headed two blocks north on Mauer Street, but Elsie stopped short of the shop upon spotting a corpulent older woman in a hobble skirt. She was holding a parasol in one hand and a straw garden hat in the other.

"Ugh," said Elsie. "Frau Schwellen. She's gone back and forth between the garden hat and the cloche three times. Looks like she's changed her mind again. I'll stop at the store later. Let's cross the street and hurry before she sees us."

Elsie didn't take two steps before Frau Schwellen beckoned with her parasol.

"She sees me. Well, I'll have to deal with her. Do you mind checking the alley for the delivery? There should be a silk, a velvet, a chiffon, and three worsted wools. Oh, and a box of Leghorn straw, too. Here's the key."

Kasper headed into the alley separating Mützenmacher's from Gottfried's Wig Shop. After accounting for the bolts of fabric and box of straw, he opened the rear entrance and hauled the materials into the cutting room. He propped the bolts against the wall, underneath his father's portrait, and set the straw on the cutting table.

Although he'd been in this room hundreds of times before, it seemed larger that day. Had Mama Elsie moved out a table or a cabinet? No, everything was in its place. Was the room illuminated differently? Had his mother changed the light bulbs in the fixture? No, they were the same three Edison bulbs as always. The smell, then. That was different. Like sweet clover. But there was no greenery in the room. What the heck was different?

Kasper unwrapped the bolt of black velvet and pushed his fingertips through the plush pile. A surge of tingles coursed up his arms and into his chest, stimulating his heart into an excited patter. A design flashed in his mind's eye like the afterimage of a lightning strike. He saw each shape, measurement, and stitch as if perusing a detailed map. He picked up scissors and cut the fabric into squares, triangles, and rectangles of different dimensions. He threaded a needle and began joining the pieces into the millinery representation of a gryphon. He incorporated a subtle swale in the crown to suggest the beast's broad chest, and arranged chiffon "scales" into a ribbon to represent wings. He dug through the drawers of the small parts storage cabinet until he found a broken starfish ornament that resembled talons, which he glued to the ribbon.

Elsie entered the cutting room, exasperated. "Frau Schwellen is simply impossible. She finally settled on both hats." She eyed Kasper's creation. "Oh my. Did you just make that?"

"I did."

"In a half hour?"

"I... I guess so."

"It's brilliant, Kasper, but we should go. You need rest."

"I'm not tired at all. I'd like to stay."

Kasper worked another six hours, cranking out fedoras, cloche hats, and straw boaters. The next day, he worked for eleven hours, and the day after that, thirteen. *It's okay*, he told himself. He wasn't succumbing to the curse he'd inherited from his forefathers. He was embracing it. He wasn't a prisoner of the cutting room. He was an artist in his studio. He had his mother to thank for that.

CHAPTER FOUR

1923

Kasper had no idea where Klaus was holding Isana. He figured Dieter would know, and if past was precedent, it wouldn't take more than a flash of Kasper's scar for that coward to cough up the information. But there was a much bigger problem. Even if Kasper learned the location, what could one man do against a (presumably) well-fortified Nazi hideout?

Kasper considered going to the police but then recalled their indifference to the other reported kidnappings (dismissing them, as he had, as mass hysteria). Plus, the police were incompetent, if not blatantly corrupt. He recalled his father going to the Schutzpolizei after a series of break-ins at the hat shop. Two disinterested eyewitnesses had seen the perpetrator leaving the store and described an older male, dressed in a ripped yellow coat, with an exaggerated side-to-side limp from one leg being shorter than the other. Even though there was only one individual in Schwarz Boden who fit that description—Josef Deller, a vagrant who'd lost a chunk of his hip during a fishing boat accident—the police deemed the evidence "too circumstantial" and made no arrest. Captain Gustav Deller, head of the precinct and, coincidentally, Josef Deller's brother, had advised Hermann to notify him immediately should he find a more solid lead.

No, there was only one reliable means to pull Isana from Klaus's clutches unscathed—the wishing hat, and that was locked in the shop's wall safe. A year earlier, as Kasper lay in bed, delirious with addiction, Elsie had returned the wishing hat to the safe and then hired a locksmith to change the combination. Following his recovery, Kasper instructed Mama Elsie not to tell him the new combination. He didn't trust himself. He had no idea if or when the itch in his head would return, and he was quite sure if he relapsed, he wouldn't make it home again. He'd kill himself, or worse, that winged chimera would shred his mind to ribbons, rendering him a drooling idiot. Thus, Kasper now had to answer a most dangerous question: to wish or not to wish.

Was this feisty Jewish flapper whom he'd just met worth the risk of relapse? He wasn't to blame for her predicament. The practical joke had been Isana's idea. Kasper had done little but encourage her. He had no moral obligation to intercede. Also, if the rumors held true, Klaus would release Isana in a few days. She might be unable to see her own face but otherwise would be no worse for the wear. Moreover, Isana might not even have feelings for Kasper. He might not ever see her again. The more Kasper thought about it, Isana wasn't that beautiful, not in the classical sense. She was short, small-breasted, and mouthier than a crew of drunken sailors. Heck, they probably wouldn't get through a single date before she'd jitterbug off with some other sucker with a big nose. For all these reasons, it would be absolute stupidity for Kasper to don the wishing hat again.

Kasper roused Mama Elsie and got the numbers to the safe.

Dieter claimed not to know where Klaus was holding Isana. Kasper believed him, a conclusion based mostly on the size of the puddle around Dieter's shoes. Dieter did, however, know a man who knew a man who might know. As it turned out, Dieter knew a man who didn't know, but that man knew a man who knew a man who knew a woman who knew the location. Following that trail of ignorance consumed two precious days, but Kasper had no other choice. He had to know Isana's precise location. He couldn't simply wish himself to Isana, for the wishing hat would take him only to places, not people.

Kasper unlocked the safe. He plunged a shaky hand into the darkness and gripped the floppy, wide-brimmed hat. He hesitated and then put it on, allowing the animalistic heat to nestle onto his skull. He was relieved he felt nothing else. No temptation. No itch. Just a sense of clear purpose. He closed his eyes and fixed the holding cell's location in his mind. His heart was racing. He envisioned his mental scar. There was no sign it had buckled or torn in the last year. But would it survive the extreme compression and expansion? Would the scar's thickness and rigidity render it too inflexible to withstand the shearing forces of corporeal extinction and recreation? He couldn't know for sure. He had to have faith. At worst, he'd die an unselfish death. His father would approve of that.

Right, Papa?

The last time Kasper had spoken with his father was in that very room, on that very spot, in 1916. A nasty head cold had forced Hermann to breathe through his mouth, and the essence of his breakfast (black bread and gin) had permeated the cramped cutting room.

"You remember what I taught you, Kasper?"

"Yes, Papa. Think of the place *before* wishing to go there."

"That's right. It won't work the other way."

"What if I want to go somewhere I've never been? What about a place I've only read about or seen on a map?"

"As long as you think of a real place, the hat will take you there. If it's a city or town, think of a specific spot—an address or a park. At the very least, wish for dry land. You don't want to arrive in the middle of a lake or an open sewer, ear deep in shit."

"Anything else?"

Hermann loosed a high-pitched sneeze.

"Be decisive when you wish. *Want* to go to that place with every ounce of your being."

Hermann blew his nose into a handkerchief.

"Got it, Papa."

"And for God's sake, don't ever—and I mean ever—take the hat off mid-wish. Once you think or say 'I wish' or 'Take me to,' the hat locks onto your soul like a bear trap."

"What'll happen?"

"I wouldn't want to worry you."

"Too late."

"My great-great grandfather Ludwig started a wish while on horseback. A squirrel spooked the horse. The hat flew off Ludwig before he could think the location and landed smack on the horse's head. Next thing Ludwig knew, he and the horse were inside the barn. Evidently that's where the horse wanted to go, so the hat took them there."

"What's so bad about that?"

"Nothing, until Ludwig began having visions of eating oats from a feedbag and exercising in the paddock. Only they weren't visions. See, when the hat blew off, it ripped off a piece of Ludwig's soul, and it found a new home inside his horse. He lived the rest of his days part-man part-horse."

"How awful."

"Grandma Sara said Ludwig was happiest in springtime."

"Why?"

"Breeding season."

"Oh. All right. I'll be sure to keep the hat on. Anything else?"

"Exhale before you wish. Staves off the nausea. Most important of all, remember the hat's not a horseless carriage. You can't just take it for a spin on a whim. Promise me you'll use the hat only if you're in mortal danger. Otherwise, the only other soul who should touch the hat is Hermes himself."

"Do you think he'll come for it?"

"Some day."

"Soon?"

"It could be tomorrow. It could be a million tomorrows from now. That's why, whatever you accomplish in this life, it won't matter one whit unless you pass the hat to the next generation. The hat sustains our family. It *is* our family. Lose it, and we lose everything—what we were, what we are, what we could have been. Understand?"

"Yes, Papa."

"Don't let your forefathers down. Don't let me down."

"I won't, Papa."

"Mama Elsie will give you the combination when you turn twenty-two. Hopefully, you'll have enough good sense by then."

"Why won't you give it to me?"

"I will. I'm just saying, in case I'm not around."

"Where would you be?"

"Fate's unpredictable. We live in a dangerous world, people get sick, or... why are you crying?"

Kasper threw his arms around his father and cried into his shoulder. Hermann habitually resisted such intimacies, but this time he kissed Kasper's taut brow, impressing his son's skin with the salivary essence of black bread and gin. That would be the last time father and son would ever touch.

—o╂o—◇◇━●━◇◇—o╂o—

Kasper pushed aside the painful memory and focused on the task at hand.

He expelled the air from his lungs and imagined an interrogation room on the particular floor of the particular building on the particular street where, according to Dieter's contact, Klaus was holding Isana captive.

Take me there.

Isana heard a squeal just as the clock in the interrogation room struck midnight. A hawk? No, that was impossible. She was in a windowless room, with no access to the sky or the creatures that lived there. Yet, there was something, or, rather, a someone, who hadn't been there before, and he was wearing a most peculiar hat. She assumed he was an illusion. There was no way Kasper could've gotten into the room undetected or unmolested. He was a figment of her sausage-saturated, dehydrated imagination. He was the face the Grim Reaper had chosen to wear to make her more compliant on the way to Hell.

Isana allowed the figment to embrace and then kiss her. *This is how death should be*, she thought. *Welcomed with a kiss.*

Footsteps echoed in the hall. The door creaked open. Before Klaus entered (perhaps as he entered, they couldn't be sure), the Stealer of Faces announced, "I'm afraid our time is up, Frau—".

That was all they heard before the squeal pierced their eardrums, the dazzling, indigo flash consumed them, and they vanished.

CHAPTER FIVE

1925

Though not a practicing Jew, Isana had insisted she and Kasper marry under a chuppah to honor her dead grandparents, the only time she'd ever spoken of the people who'd reared her. Kasper crushed a glass under his foot to conclude the ceremony. For Isana's ancestors, the break symbolized the destruction of the Temple of Jerusalem. For Kasper, it represented the psychological destruction Klaus had wrought on Isana and his frustration over his inability to restore the blank in her self-identity.

Isana had spent fruitless hours staring at photographs of her face, attempting to superimpose a static, black and white image over the perceptual void. She resigned herself to the loss until giving birth to Duke a year later, when she began to detect hints of infantile features in her reflection. Then, as her love for the child matured and deepened, those hints took on contour and color. Eventually, Duke's visage completely filled the void. Although disturbed at first, she grew to appreciate the surge of maternal warmth that accompanied each hair brushing and face scrubbing. The only downside was the inability to detect stray pimples on her chin or the occasional chive stuck on her front tooth.

They named their son after Duke Ellington. The jazz great had been especially prolific during Duke's birth year, releasing eight albums in 1924, which also coincided with the birth of commercial radio in Berlin.

The growing family listened to VOX House on Kasper's new Telefunken radio set. At first, the programming was mostly weather and stock reports and time signals, but it slowly incorporated more music. The sounds from the strange box drew Duke in like a magnet. The second the radio was flipped on, his face would go blank, and he'd meander toward the radio in his turtle-like shell of chub. So powerful were these electromagnetic tentacles, they'd tear him away from breast-feedings, triggering something in his infant, reptilian brain that overwhelmed his sensorial pangs. Caresses and milk were merely means for survival. Radio was an intangible opiate. Duke would sooner wither in his diaper than allow his smacking lips and gurgling intestines to interrupt the sounds from the radio.

As a toddler, Duke learned to adjust the dials to tune in the many new stations. Isana tried engaging him with books, coloring, and meal preparation, but the radio, which had to stay within reach, divided his attention. For a while, Isana diverted him with strolls through the Tiergarten and along the Kurfürstendamm and Hufeisendamm. That worked until they entered Heider's Electronics. Duke wouldn't leave even after exploring the different radio sets for two hours. When Herr Heider announced he was closing, Duke didn't seem to understand—or didn't want to understand—that he and his mother had to leave. After fruitless pleading, Isana dragged him to the sidewalk, where he crossed his arms and stood defiantly next to the pram instead of climbing in. When she tried to place him in the seat, Duke adopted the "stiff as a board" technique, locking his joints so Isana couldn't articulate his limbs. Frustrated, she scanned the street for something—anything—that might distract Duke out of his obstinacy. Perhaps a candy kiosk or an organ-grinder... or a good, stiff club for cracking heads. But she saw only Onkel Frank.

Onkel Frank wasn't really Isana's uncle, nor did she know if Frank was his actual name. That was just what she'd named the man who'd been surveilling her since 1923; he had the same egg-shaped body and loose turkey neck as her real Onkel Frank. The faux Frank occasionally jotted notes but otherwise kept his distance.

The first time Isana had noticed Onkel Frank, a few weeks before her wedding, she'd assumed he was Klaus's henchman and worried that the Stealer of Faces intended to re-arrest her, perhaps to confirm he'd erased her entire face, perhaps to solve the mystery of her escape. She was relieved when Onkel Frank didn't escort her into a black sedan or even approach her. Kasper wasn't surprised. If Klaus truly had wanted Isana in custody, he could've re-captured her within days of her escape. She hadn't changed her name or made an effort to conceal her whereabouts. Such measures were unnecessary, Kasper had assured her, because if Klaus were to arrest her again, Kasper would use the wishing hat to whisk her away.

According to Kasper, Klaus had either concluded that Isana had been lying about the visibility of her lips or decided to cut his losses and move onto his next face. As to her means of escape, Klaus must not have seen Isana and her black-hatted rescuer vanish before his eyes. From Klaus's perspective, he'd entered an empty interrogation room, and the only logical conclusion was that Isana had taken advantage of the guard's inattention or incompetence to slip away.

Onkel Frank was just one of those run-of-the mill, plainclothes Nazis who kept tabs on Berlin's so-called "communist subversives." These buffoons were everywhere and obvious. The scrutiny didn't trouble Isana. She'd long since lost her copy of *Das Kapital* and kept *The Communist Manifesto* around only because the edition's oversized pages made for an ideal fly-swatter. Indeed, Isana was oddly flattered anyone, including the deranged Nazi party, would think she had the power to destroy a society.

Isana nodded to her faux uncle, who pretended not to notice by checking his wristwatch and adjusting his necktie. She then pushed the empty pram ten blocks home, dragging the petulant Duke by his arm. When their apartment building came into view, Duke crawled into the stroller and fell asleep, despite Isana's admonition that she would have to wake him in two minutes, which she did. The ensuing struggle to drag her hellion child up three flights of stairs generated so much yelling, wailing, and threats of bodily harm that a panicked tenant fetched a policeman, who briefly placed Isana under arrest. After Duke stripped off his clothes and began tossing pots and pans around the kitchen, the cop commended Isana for her self-restraint and made a quick exit.

When Kasper came home that evening, he tripped on the radio, which Isana had set at the door. Isana insisted they get rid of the machine, sparking the first significant argument of their young marriage. Kasper agreed there was a problem but argued that avoiding radio wasn't the answer. Radio was the future of communication, and there would be no way to shield Duke from its ills without also depriving him of its benefits. Isana quoted from a newspaper editorial that described radio as a prideful attempt to overcome the natural limits of a human life.

"Listen to this part, Kasper. 'Another age would have hesitated to annihilate space and time the way we grind them up in our machines. They would have feared the envy of the gods.'"

"Since when do you fear the gods?"

"Ever since you whisked me away with that magic hat. If I were a god, I'd want it back, and I'd be awful pissed that a dinky human swiped it from me. Better watch yourself, Papa Bear."

"Well, I didn't steal the radio. I have the receipt to prove it. I'll move it to the study. We'll only play it low, after Duke's asleep. We'll tell him it broke, and we returned it to the store for credit."

"In short, we're gonna lie to him."

"Pretty much."

"Works for me."

1927

During her long second labor, Isana bore down like Louis Armstrong trying to eject a stuck turd from his trumpet. Her blood pressure fluctuated wildly, leading to bouts of throbbing headaches, followed by periods of blissful lightheadedness. Finally, at hour sixteen, Isana settled on a mantra to control the delivery, replaying Jelly Roll Morton's *The Pearls* in her head and pushing each time the tuba's refrain began to build. Within five minutes, she birthed Bessie, her precious pearl.

The nurse sponged off the birth slime and swaddled the child. Isana was asleep. "She has her mother's lips," said the bespectacled nurse in an affectless voice. "Like the petals of a beautiful red orchid."

Kasper cradled the child, whose rosy cheeks, flaming lips, and long fingers captivated him in a way that Duke's boyishness hadn't. She was an impossible creature, a series of contradictions wrapped into a plump, fleshy package. She was delicate and powerful, wrinkled and young, pungent and sweet. And when he gazed into her blue eyes, he became hopelessly lost in their roiling seas. She was jazz incarnate. She was Bessie.

Kasper and Duke left the hospital for a few hours to check on Mama Elsie at the hat shop. When they returned, Isana's room was empty. The delivery nurse said the hospital had moved Isana to a quarantine wing for "protective observation," explaining that Isana was very ill with infection and likely contagious. What type of infection, the nurse couldn't say. And if Isana were contagious, queried Kasper, wouldn't he have been exposed, too? The nurse deferred to the doctor. Could he see the doctor? No, the doctor had left for the evening and had given strict instructions against visitors under any circumstances. What about Bessie? The baby was fine, the nurse reassured him. She was in the nursery. She recommended that Kasper go home and get some sleep and then return in the morning. Hopefully, by that time, the doctor would know more about his wife's condition.

As instructed, Kasper returned to the hospital in the morning with Duke. A Dr. Steinholz greeted them with news that Kasper's wife had passed in the night. She'd suffered an extremely virulent hemorrhagic infection, something they'd never seen before. Her lungs had filled with fluid. She bled from her nose and mouth, and soon lapsed into a coma. Death followed. Normally, the doctor explained, they would've waited seventy-two hours (and certainly would've notified family) before cremating her, but new pandemic protocols called for immediate cremation. Dr. Steinholz expressed his condolences as he scrawled a signature on his clipboard and tore off a pink slip with which Kasper could claim Isana's ashes at the Gerichtstraße crematorium.

Dr. Steinholz had spoken so rapidly and excused himself so quickly that Kasper barely had time to process the information, let alone ask questions. All he could absorb was his wife was dead, and he had a paper in his hand to prove it. It looked remarkably like the receipt for his radio set. But unlike the radio, there would be no lie he could tell Duke about his mother's whereabouts. He couldn't say he'd returned Isana to the store for credit. He couldn't rest easy, knowing Isana was secretly lurking in the study, to be enjoyed after Duke went to bed. She wasn't anywhere Kasper could get to with the wishing hat. Not even radio, which annihilated space and time, could reach her.

Kasper chided himself for not having stayed overnight at the hospital. He should've challenged the nurse's claim that Isana was contagious. He should've recognized the oddness of the hospital's decision to move Isana during his brief absence. It would've been so simple to have wished himself into the quarantine wing and find Isana, if that was in fact where she'd been. But he'd dismissed the idea, more concerned about exposing himself to influenza or typhus. Sickening himself would've been irresponsible with young Duke and Bessie. In his fatigue, he'd given the hospital the benefit of the doubt, and now Isana was nothing but ash.

Kasper refused to explain Isana's absence with euphemisms. He told Duke flat out that his mother had died and death is a one-way trip from which there's no return. The boy asked whether mommy didn't love them anymore or he'd been bad. Kasper answered no, and that response seemed to reassure the boy for a time. Nevertheless, in the following weeks, Duke periodically asked when mommy was coming home, and Kasper would answer, "She's not."

"Because she's dead. Right, Pops?"

"That's right, son."

"She went on a one-way trip."

"Yes."

"And she can't come back."

"No."

"Not ever?"

"Not ever."

"Not ever," Duke repeated.

Since there was no corpse, and because he was overwhelmed with the care of two young children, Kasper hadn't held Isana's funeral right away. But after the fifth such interchange with Duke, he couldn't hold off any longer.

One Sunday morning, Kasper grabbed his cornet, gathered every musician he knew, and led a procession of trumpets, trombones, saxophones, clarinets, cymbals, and a Jew's harp down Teilung Street. Duke walked behind his father, holding Isana's ashes in a box he'd decorated with seashells. The music began in a traditional way, with Chopin's *Funeral March*. After a few staid measures, the "jazz spirit" overtook Kasper, and he was bending the tune and syncopating the notes. His hodgepodge of a band followed suit. Soon, the entire procession was foxtrotting, while Duke toddled along in a jazzified way.

A major from the *Schutzpolizei* stopped the procession abruptly at Mauer Street. He admonished Kasper for turning the solemn funeral march into something profane. Kasper explained that his wife wouldn't have wanted a solemn affair. Ignoring her wishes would've been profane. The major wasn't an uncaring man, nor was he unreasonable. Still, the upper-level brass had ordered him to crack down on Berlin's "jazz element." The tipping point had been a complaint from Johann Strauss II's widow about the jazzification of her husband's music. Frau Strauss had marched into the precinct with a blowhard music critic, arguing that jazz players weren't true musicians and "the brains of the whole lot of them put together would not fill the lining of Johann Strauss's hat." Kasper said that was wrong, because in 1910, his father had sold Johann Strauss a homburg hat without any lining whatsoever.

The major laughed. He compromised and asked Kasper to shift to a less syncopated cadence and perhaps play more quietly. Kasper understood the major wasn't really asking. He put the cornet to his lips and played the march more softly. He still twisted the notes. He still played a syncopated meter. But instead of vaguely conducting twenty-five musical currents that weaved and mixed haphazardly, he organized the sounds into one direction, forming a swirling confluence of harmonies. The musical vortex surrounded the throng, with Duke and his mother's ashes at the center. The eye of this private hurricane ambled to the Spree River, where Duke opened the box and released his mother into the flow.

"How far will she go, Pops?"

"Very far."

"Too far to visit?"

"'Fraid so."

"Farther than France?"

"Much."

"Farther than America?"

"Yep."

"How far is it?"

Kasper pointed to the crescent in the sky. "That far."

Duke gazed at the moon and marveled at its similarity to his mother's hand scar. She'd once told him all pure-bred "Moon people" were born with one. That was why she liked cheese so much, she'd added with a laugh. At the time, Duke had assumed she was joking, but now he concluded his mother was telling the truth. His father had just confirmed it. But how would the river carry her ashes to the moon? He didn't see a water current in the sky. He figured it was an invisible stream, like the unseen waves that carried voices into their radios. Duke vowed to see his mother again. He'd ride an invisible wave all the way to the moon.

CHAPTER SIX

1933

The Weimar Republic's prior governments had turned over every year or two, so Kasper assumed the National Socialists would be out of power before 1934. In the meantime, they were a damn nuisance. Several of Kasper's Jewish customers had been fired from the civil service. Two Jewish lawyer friends had been expelled from the Bar. New German laws restricted the number of Jewish students at public schools. The Reich deemed Duke and Bessie Jews because of their Jewish mother. Fortunately, their primary school had far less than its quota of Jews, and their friends and teachers treated them no differently for the time being. Consumers weren't discriminating either. The Nazi boycott in April 1933 had been a major flop, especially in Schwarz Boden. Customers shrugged off the Brownshirts loitering outside the department stores, tailor shops, and shoe stores with their "The Jews Are Our Misfortune" signs. Even the threat from Klaus seemed to be waning. Reported face-stealings had dwindled to a trickle, though the Klaus posters remained omnipresent. Overall, Kasper felt confident the German people's fundamental goodness and the civil rights embedded in the Constitution would trump the Nazis' outrageous rhetoric and macabre propaganda.

The Nazi threat was an abstraction compared to the day-to-day demands on a single father. Although Mama Elsie prepared meals, Kasper insisted on dressing Duke and Bessie in the mornings and bathing and entertaining them in the evenings. And, with Duke nearing nine, Kasper took on a new duty—millinery taskmaster. Unlike Bessie, who tagged along, Duke was a reluctant apprentice. He'd flip on the radio the second he entered the cutting room, which irritated Kasper, who'd have to shout over the weather reports and military marches to communicate instructions. Nevertheless, Kasper permitted the radio—at a reasonable volume—because the alternative was a petulant son who'd take a half hour to slip on his sewing apron and then perform "work" in only the most liberal sense of the term.

Like his father before him, Kasper wouldn't permit his son to touch blade to fabric until he learned to make the hat's form out of wire, which meant Duke first would have to master the simple act of cutting thin metal. For the initial lesson, Kasper handed Duke a three-foot length of scrap wire and told him to clip off neat, two-inch bits. Duke's first clipping was a perfect two-inch segment with a square face. But the next seventeen either had jagged, off-kilter faces or were too long or short. Bessie got it right on the fourth try and all subsequent attempts. Kasper then demonstrated how to bind segments with a tie wire. Despite explicit instructions not to twist the tie wire more than once, Duke twisted it four times, rendering the binding loose and bulky.

"Look, Pops," exclaimed Bessie. "Did I do it right?"

Kasper grunted. Yes, she'd done it perfectly, but her achievement merely made his son's inadequacy all the more stark.

A few lessons later, Kasper moved to hat frame construction. The task was to construct a one-piece circular frame with a short crown. After two hours of frustrated cutting, twisting, and bending, Duke produced a massive pinched oval with a sharp triangle for a crown. If covered in fabric, Duke's frame would've looked less like a hat and more like a diorama of a reef shark surfacing through a gigantic peanut.

"What happened here, son?" asked the wide-eyed Kasper.

"It's finished."

"I'll say."

Meanwhile, Bessie had constructed a reasonably circular frame with a low crown. Not perfect, but it at least approximated a hat shape. She poked the frame into Kasper's arm.

"I finished, too, Pops."

"That's fine, Bessie," said Kasper dismissively. "Duke, were you rushing?"

"Maybe a little."

"You can't hurry the creative process, especially when you're learning."

"We've been doing nothing but cutting and bending wire for days on end.

Can't we cover the frames?"

"If you build a house, wouldn't you want a strong foundation and good, sturdy beams to keep it upright?"

"Yeah. So?"

"So, if you build a rickety house, it makes no sense to plaster and paint the walls, which will just end up crumbling. After you've mastered the frames, we'll move onto the stitching."

"I wish we could go straight there... you know, do it all at once."

Bessie waved her wire frame in Kasper's face. "See, Pops? See?"

Kasper pushed it away. "Bessie, you're being rude. I'm talking to Duke."

"You're *yelling* at Duke."

"I am not yelling, Bessie. My tone is perfectly calm."

"You're upset he made an ugly frame. Well, here's a pretty one. Mine."

"Stop interrupting." Kasper turned back to Duke and continued. "You must master each step. Otherwise, you end up repeating steps or doing them poorly. You can't 'go straight there' with a finger snap. Nothing in life works like that."

"The wishing hat does. You think of a place, and there you go. The radio, too. You flip a switch, and the radio waves change to sound... instantly."

Kasper stammered. "Well, it doesn't work that way for hat-making."

"Duke stinks at making hats!" Bessie announced with glee.

"Shut up, Bessie!" yelled Duke. He tugged on her long pigtail.

"Ow!" Bessie shrieked.

"Quiet, the both of you!" As Kasper separated the children, his right latissimus dorsi muscle went into spasm. "Duke, sit at the desk," he said through a clenched jaw. "Bessie, by the cutting table." His back spasmed again, this time sucking the air from his lungs. "Not a peep from either of you until Mama Elsie comes." He walked stiffly to the radio set and flipped it off.

Kasper didn't limit Duke's "education" to hats. After he'd put Bessie to bed, Kasper required Duke to sit through a course on music appreciation. He'd pour the sleepy boy a glass of milk and prop him in a leather chair opposite his own. Kasper would play the cornet along with recordings of Jean Goldkette's orchestra and McKinney's Cotton Pickers. Duke struggled to keep his eyes open as Kasper pointed out musical phrases and reveled in the ear-splitting solos. Once, as Kasper was tuning in Radio Luxembourg, the radio briefly locked onto a Berlin station playing *The Watchguard on the Rhein*, an old war anthem. Duke perked up, announced he liked the song very much, and asked his father not to change the station. Kasper, insulted, told the boy to sit back down. Within minutes, Duke had dozed off completely and dropped the half-full glass of milk on the Oriental rug, drawing the full force of Kasper's ire, his scar glowing orange like a fresh brand.

Despite the boy's clear lack of interest, Kasper also assigned Duke "jazz homework." After completing his duties in the hat shop, Duke would spend an hour listening to one or two albums from Kasper's extensive collection. Then, at dinner, Kasper would quiz him about the songs' time signatures or whether the clarinet or cornet played the solos. Afterward, Kasper inspected the 78s for smudges, while Duke squirmed in his chair, agonizing over whether he'd accidentally grazed one of the records.

Duke had a break from jazz on the weekends. That was when Kasper gave him boxing lessons. The leather gloves weighed down the boy's feeble arms, making it a struggle to hold up his hands during sparring sessions. Thinking Duke was just being lazy, he "incentivized" the boy by lightly jabbing him in the face whenever he let his guard down. It didn't work. The disappointment was written all over Kasper's face (and, indirectly, in the contusions on Duke's cheekbones).

Kasper didn't care that Bessie was proving herself a precocious hatmaker. He was rearing her as his ancestors had reared their daughters. Like him, they'd believed that the curse didn't bind females. Which isn't to say Kasper ignored Bessie outside the hat shop, not completely anyway. At home, he participated in her fashion shows, permitting her to adorn him with scarves and jewelry and paint his face with copious pancake makeup and rouge. He dutifully sat for teas with her family of porcelain-headed dolls. Ever the respectful guest, Kasper always asked Bessie for permission to play a jazz record in the background, and she'd always answer, "Sure, Pops. We'd all like that very much. We love jazz." Bessie would then carry on an entire conversation with her dolls.

After a few minutes of Bessie's lilting banter, Kasper's mind invariably drifted toward the horns and drums spilling from the study. He'd feel himself floating toward the turntable, then skating around the spinning vinyl, coasting inside the grooves until, before he knew it, he'd fallen into a deep trance. Bessie noticed his absence, and to draw him back, she'd direct a question or comment to him. He'd respond with a grunt, sometimes accompanied by a trickle of drool. Bessie then would sing along to the music, precisely mimicking the rhythms and syncopations, hoping to astonish her father into a wakeful state. Kasper, however, would continue to stare off into space, non-responsive.

One time, Bessie got so frustrated with her father's detachment she grabbed the boxing gloves off Duke's door and demanded he teach her to jab and throw crosses and uppercuts. When Kasper obliged, albeit in a timid, non-serious manner, she punched him hard in the gut, knocking the wind out of him. She then turned on her dolls, propped courteously behind their teacups, and pummeled them with vicious rights and lefts, as well as a solid hook, which Kasper hadn't even showed her. After Kasper removed her gloves, Bessie returned to her sweet self, singing "It don't mean a thing, if it ain't got that swing" while tightening loose doll heads and reattaching severed limbs.

"The child has spirit," Elsie commented later.

"More like she's possessed by a spirit."

"She gets it from her mother and her grandmother."

"You beat up your father, too?"

"My uncle. He's the one who taught me to box."

"Seriously?"

Mama raised her fists. "Let's go a few rounds."

"Maybe some other time. I think Bessie bruised a rib."

"You deserved it."

"Why?"

"You ignore that girl's talents. You put all your energy into Duke."

"Duke's got a lot more at stake. He is cursed, after all."

"So is Bessie."

"You know perfectly well that's not true."

"I'm talking about the curse of chauvinism. It's the reason my parents paid for my dim-witted brother's law school, while I went to finishing school. Never mind my higher marks. Never mind that my arguments twisted his tongue into knots."

"I'll support Bessie in whatever she wants to do."

"Except running the hat shop."

"Right. Except that."

"Duke doesn't have a knack for hats. What possible harm could come from allowing a competent woman to run things?"

"Fate won't allow it."

"Have you forgotten what I was doing while you were at university?"

"That was temporary, until I could take over."

"Why would Fate, a female Herself, discriminate against Her own kind?"

"You're looking at it the wrong way. The men are cursed. We're the victims of discrimination."

"Interesting that the victims in this family always end up in charge."

"And when they're not in charge, they die like Papa. Fate punished him for leaving the hat shop behind."

"Hundreds of men drowned on that battlefield, not just Papa."

"He shouldn't have been there in the first place. If I'd gone to war instead, Fate would've protected me, so I could carry on the hat business."

"You really believe that?"

"I have faith, Mama."

Mama Elsie shook her head. "Maybe I'll open my own hat shop. Bessie can be my apprentice and then take over when she's older."

"Are you serious?"

"Hell yes." After a pause, she added. "Of course not. We don't have the money, and my damn arthritis is turning my hands into lobster claws."

"Look, I'll pay more attention to Bessie. I'll even encourage her to make hats. But she'll never run the business. I wish it could be different, but Fate sets the rules, not me. You know this. You've read Lorenz's letter."

"Yes, I have. Very recently. He quotes the prophecy word for word, and you remember what it says? The curse applies to 'the kin' of the boy who stole the wishing hat. It doesn't say the *male* kin."

"It's implied."

"Really?" asked Elsie, incredulous.

"Also, the beginning of Lorenz's letter says only the men are cursed, and it's been that way for over a thousand years."

"Those are *his* words. That doesn't come from the prophecy itself."

"You think he made it up?"

"What was Lorenz basing it on? For all we know, he had a flimsy reason or no reason at all. Just one generation after another mindlessly disenfranchising their daughters until the practice fossilized into a sacrosanct tradition."

"I don't know how or why the women aren't cursed, but I'm sure there is a very good reason."

"Why are you so sure?"

"I have faith in my forefathers."

"And there's nothing your fore*mother* can say to change your mind?"

"We shouldn't abandon our traditions just because we don't understand them."

"Your father was prepared to."

"I doubt that."

"Well, it's the absolute truth. You were born with a very small penis and a separated scrotum. Your testicles—"

Kasper ushered his mother away from Bessie's bedroom door. "Mama! Have you gone mad? Are you having a stroke?"

"I'm fine." Elsie continued in a loud whisper, "Your testicles didn't descend until the third day. Before that, your parts looked like a girl's. We even named you Beatrix."

"What the hell does this have to do with the curse, and why am I just hearing about this now?"

"We thought the truth might scar you."

"You were right."

"My point is, after you were born, I couldn't have another child. For three days, Papa thought he'd bequeath the shop and the wishing hat to a daughter. He made peace with that future."

"A future Fate didn't let happen."

"Please just think about what I said."

"I'm not sure I can *un*-think it."

"At least let Bessie share the hat business with her brother, if that's what she wants."

"I'll think about it."

"You won't. You're just saying you will."

"Good night, Mama."

"Good night... Beatrix."

After Kasper read Bessie a bedtime story, but before he flipped off her light, she asked why he and Mama Elsie were arguing about "tesstinkles." Kasper suggested that Bessie had misheard them, that he and Mama Elsie had been discussing "festivals." He flipped the switch and closed the door firmly behind him. He then went to the kitchen, wrapped a towel around an ice chunk, and stuck it against his throbbing rib.

CHAPTER SEVEN

Kasper closed the shop early and went home to collect records and booze for that night's meeting of Mooch's Minions. The Minions was a group of ten misfits—Jews, communists, a Roma, and one (possibly two) gays—who'd gather in the back of Kasper's hat shop, sip whiskey, and play records or listen to Radio Luxembourg. This regular Friday evening gathering was Kasper's sole respite from the demands of the shop and his family. As he flipped through the albums in the study, Kasper noticed several Ellington RCA Victors were missing—*Bugle Call, East St. Louis Toodle-O*, and *Shout 'Em Aunt Tillie*, among others. A few Brunswick records were missing also, including his most prized recording, *Black and Tan Fantasy*, which Isana had bought for him only days before her death. He thumbed through the albums to see if he'd misfiled it. It wasn't there. He felt panic, the panic he should've felt on the night Isana died while he slept at home, oblivious.

Kasper burst into Duke's bedroom. His anger turned to shock, however, when he saw Duke's face. A giant albino spider appeared to have latched onto his son's nose.

"What the—?"

Startled, Duke quickly peeled the "spider" from his face and wadded it in his hands. But there was no sense in Duke denying anything. He opened his hand, revealing a harness.

"Are you injured?" asked Kasper.

"Not exactly."

"Then what the hell's it for?"

Amazing Stories magazines were stacked on Duke's bed. Duke sorted through the issues, pulled out one with a purple cover and an illustration of a man in a white robe shooting a ray gun at a fierce-looking flower creature. He flipped through the pages and then handed the open magazine to Kasper. The page was littered with advertisements. One ad promoted the McSweeny Electrical School, which offered a twelve-week training course in motors, generators, and house wiring that supposedly would lead to a high-paying job ($50 to $150 weekly). Other ads promoted business opportunities in cartooning, operating a telegraph, flying airplanes, managing automobile traffic, and playing the banjo. The only ad on the page that didn't promise "big bucks" was the one captioned, "CORRECT Your NOSE." Next to the cartoon image of a man wearing a nose harness, the ad touted the ANITA Nose Adjuster, which "[s]hapes flesh and cartilage—quickly, safely and painlessly, while you sleep."

"What's wrong with your nose? Don't you like it?"

"Boys at school make fun of it."

"Who?"

"It doesn't matter."

"You and I have the same nose, so if they're making fun of yours, they're making fun of mine. You need to stand up for yourself."

"There's more than one of them, and they're all way bigger."

"Ach. Size is overrated. I've seen a Great Dane cower before a Siamese cat. It's all about attitude."

Kasper felt Duke's skinny arm and added, "Though in your case, it may be a little bit about size. Your nose doesn't need reshaping. Your muscles do. Anything in this magazine about muscles?"

"Actually, yes, but that's not why I—"

Duke reached for the magazine, but Kasper pulled it away and flipped through it. Duke winced, worried his father's thick fingers would rip the pages. The inside cover pictured a sculpture of Jules Verne bursting from his grave, reaching for the heavens at a forty-five-degree angle. A quirk in the printing process made the wrinkles in his burial shroud resemble the bosoms of an eighty-year-old grandmother. The next page advertised the ten-volume *Sexual Education Series*, claiming that most misery and suffering in human life could be directly attributed to sex misinformation. The ad touted the books' "excellent anatomical drawings" that were so "mechanically treated that they [would] never arouse the sensibilities of even the greatest prude, yet, they

[were] an education in themselves." The subsequent page promoted a collection of photographs that demonstrated the "techniques" of lovers from France, Spain, the United States, and the South Sea Islands.

"What the heck kind of magazine is this?"

"Science fiction."

"More like sexual fiction."

"Can't judge it by the ads."

"I disagree. Obviously, the people running this magazine are all big-nosed, unemployed, sex-starved perverts, or at least their readers are. Why do you read this junk?"

"You said I had to learn English. School teaches a little. *Amazing Stories* fills in the rest."

Kasper harrumphed and flipped another page. Suddenly, he looked pleased.

"Here we go. Charles Atlas. 'Don't be an underweight, always-tired weakling that nobody fears or respects!' He's talking to you, son. He'll make you a muscular giant in ninety days. I'm going to order it for you."

"No, Pops. Really. I don't—"

"Do you want to end up with old lady boobs like Jules Verne? We're getting that booklet."

Kasper turned to leave but then stopped himself. "Oh, I almost forgot why I came in here. Some albums are missing—all Ellington stuff. What'd you do with them?"

"I don't know."

"You don't know what you did with them?"

"I don't know why they're missing."

"You're denying you took them?"

"Yep."

"We're the only two people in the apartment who have any business handling those records. I know I didn't lose them."

"Maybe you filed them out of order."

"No, they're just gone."

"You took them to the shop, then."

"No."

"Then it was either Mama Elsie or Bessie."

"Mama Elsie's hard of hearing, and Bessie's only six."

"Uh-huh," agreed Duke, disinterested.

Duke's indifference irritated Kasper. His son wasn't making eye contact.

He was barely listening as he lay on his stomach, studying a magazine's cover that depicted a bug-eyed robot grappling with a lion. The magazine's price, twenty-five cents, converted to about one Mark. As an American magazine, however, it cost several times that in Berlin.

"You buy these magazines yourself?"

"Yep."

"Must have set you back quite a few Marks."

"Yep."

Heat welled around Kasper's collar. He closed his eyes and rolled his bottom lip over his teeth to contain his urge to dive on the bed and throttle the boy.

"Where did you get the money?"

"Odd jobs. Mostly for Herr Kimball. Some deliveries. Some sweeping."

"What nine-year-old has a job?"

"I work in the hat shop. That's a job. You just don't pay me for my labor."

"Have you seen the quality of your labor?"

"Maybe it would be better if you paid me."

"My father never paid me. His father didn't pay him. That's the way it's always been. It's a son's obligation."

"And that's why I also work for Herr Kimball."

"So when I ask him, he'll confirm what you're saying, right?"

"Right."

Kasper thought he'd called Duke's bluff. He'd been sure the boy would cave once he'd threatened to check with Herr Kimball. Yet, Duke hadn't even glanced from the damn magazine.

"Put that down and look at me."

Duke complied.

"What the hell is so important about these magazines you can't look me in the eye?"

"It's research."

"On what?"

"The moon."

Even a cursory glance at the wall would've revealed his son's lunar fixation. He'd hung paper maché models from the ceiling and posted several moon maps on the wall. The largest map—a four-by-four-foot square—showed the craters and "seas" in great detail, including Mares Imbrium, Tranquillitatis, and Fecunditatis, and Craters Tycho, Copernicus, and Plato. Duke had marked the map with red Xs, blue circles, and yellow triangles, as though tracking down buried treasure.

A similar-sized poster hung next to the moon map, but this one was entirely hand drawn and forebodingly labeled "The Dark Side." Unlike the Latin names of the features on the other poster, these seas and craters had German names like Elsie, Kasper, Isana, Bessie, Gustav, Otto, and Adolf. Duke also had marked potential locations for cities. According to the key, several were underground. One was an above-ground, domed city in an equatorial crater labeled "Mare Isana."

"You're not gonna learn about the moon from that trash."

"I know they're just stories. But since no one's been to the moon, it's all I have if I want to know what it's like up there."

"It's nothing but gray sand. Don't even need a telescope to see that."

"What about what we can't see? Some say an advanced race of creatures lives under the moon's surface or under a big glass dome on the dark side."

Duke's eyes darted toward "The Dark Side" poster. Kasper moved in for closer inspection.

"Interesting names you've given these features. Who's Gustav?"

"A fat kid in my class. He's always hovering around me at lunch, begging for scraps, 'cause his mother put him on a diet. That's why I named that big mountain after him."

"If there's an advanced race on the moon, don't you think we'd see evidence? Even if they live underground now, we'd see old ruins above ground, irrigation channels, stuff like that. Heck, we'd probably pick up their radio broadcasts."

"Unless they live only on the dark side."

"Why would they live only on the dark side? We don't live only on one side of Earth."

"Maybe they don't want us to know about them."

"Then I guess we'll never know."

"This guy—Schlossel—his idea is to send a robot to the moon. He'd control it with a special radio. And look at this page, Pops. It's an ad for an actual mechanical man called Televox. Westinghouse makes it. You use your telephone to make the robot start the carpet sweeper or open and close windows."

Kasper shook his head, befuddled. "Westinghouse built a robot to vacuum carpets on the moon?"

"No. No. The moon robot is from a story. The Westinghouse robot is here on Earth. All I'm saying is someday we'll find out what's really on the moon, either with robots or we'll go there ourselves."

"Maybe."

"You and I could go there right now, if we wanted."

"What?"

"With the hat. All we have to do is put it on and make a wish."

Kasper grabbed Duke's shoulders. "Don't you ever even *think* that idea again! You hear me? It's suicide."

"But it would work, right?"

"It doesn't matter if it would work. It's never going to happen."

"With a special armor, like a suit for diving deep in the ocean, I bet it'd be safe."

"Stop! Stop talking! That's stupid. Just plain stupid."

Tears welled in Duke's eyes. "One day… when I'm grown up… and the hat is mine, I'm gonna do it."

"Not gonna happen."

"Yes, it will."

"No, it won't because… because I destroyed the wishing hat."

"How?"

"Doesn't matter how. That thing was too dangerous, and now it's gone. So just forget about the moon."

As tears streamed down Duke's cheeks, Kasper recalled the boy pouring his mother's ashes into the Spree River and asking if they'd be able to visit her. Kasper had answered that she was too far away, as far away as the moon. But Duke's three-year-old mind had processed the response without the simile. As far as he was concerned, his mother was living in the night sky, and all he had to do was bide his time, and he'd see her again.

"I know this is hard to accept, and I certainly don't like being the one to remind you, but your mother is dead, son. She's not on the moon. She's not anywhere. She's ash and water."

Kasper sat next to his weeping son.

"Have yourself a good cry. Take a day, a week, however long you need to shed the very last tear over your mother. Cry every last drop of the childish fantasy your mind concocted, and when you're done, you'll be one step closer to manhood. And then we'll turn to something real, like big noses and little muscles and school bullies. We'll make you strong, like a man. Does that sound like a good plan?"

Duke wiped the snot from his nose and nodded.

"Good boy."

Kasper slapped the boy's knee and rose from the bed.

"I think maybe I'll say hello to Herr Kimball."

Kimball's toy shop sold an eclectic mix of practical things, like rope, canned tomatoes, and matches, and impractical things, like rock candy, kites, and toy trains. The store also traded in used goods—old phonographs and radio sets, books, lamps, picture frames, records, and jewelry. To accommodate his child customers, Herr Kimball kept the most durable and fun merchandise on the lower shelves and set out tables and chairs, where little hands could explore it. Though Herr Kimball's prices were higher than department stores', parents appreciated being able to shop without hovering over their children every second.

Kasper inspected Kimball's record collection and found the missing six Duke Ellington albums. He was stunned Duke had lied straight to his face. His mind raced with potential punishments, ranging from a simple grounding to an elaborate humiliation involving a pillory (which Kasper would have to build) followed by a ride along Mauer Street in a manure cart (which had become increasingly rare in the city since the automobile's rise).

Herr Kimball greeted Kasper, interrupting his macabre contemplations. He was a portly fellow of indeterminate age because his rotundity stretched the wrinkles from his fat red face. He had a crazy mop of onyx black hair, with only one gray splotch indicative of middle age. He reminded Kasper of a neighbor's garden gnome he'd coveted as a child. Herr Kimball immediately recognized Kasper as Duke's father, praising Duke as a kind boy and a hard worker. He confirmed Duke had been performing odd jobs and used the income to purchase several issues of *Amazing Stories*.

How, then, had Kasper's Ellington records ended up in Herr Kimball's store?

Herr Kimball smiled broadly. "Have you forgotten? Your sweet daughter Bessie delivered them yesterday with your note."

"What note?"

"The note explaining your situation."

Kasper stared back blankly.

"You know," continued Herr Kimball, "the situation with your shop—business is slow, and it being Bessie's birthday but not having enough money to buy her a Gretchen Doll. You asked for a fair price for the records in light of the circumstances. I think twenty Marks was more than fair—well, fifteen Marks. The doll cost five."

"Are you completely insane?"

"Not completely, no."

"I wrote no such note. Business at the hat shop is booming. Bessie's birthday is not for another four months."

Herr Kimball rounded the counter and opened the cash register.

"Here. I still have the note."

He handed the paper to Kasper.

"The handwriting is uneven. There are numerous misspellings and hardly any punctuation. It's obvious a child wrote this."

"Maybe your clientele are all men of letters, but I cater to all classes, including the imbeciles."

"An imbecile did not write this note."

"How do you know?"

"For one, it's written in green crayon. What adult writes a note in crayon?"

"An imbecile will use any implement that's handy. I once received an IOU written in snot."

"Disgusting."

"He paid it off."

"If you flip the note over, you'll see the words 'kindergarten' and 'Lesson 6: Writing Your Letters.' This is clearly a child's paper from school."

"Herr Mützenmacher, I don't have time to play detective with every scrap of paper. You may have the records back for twenty Marks."

"But the records are mine. She had no right to sell them."

"Yet, she did. And she struck a very good bargain, too. You should be proud of her."

"I would be, if I were Al Capone," said Kasper as he peeled two ten-Mark notes from his billfold.

—o┼o-◇◇-◯-◇◇-o┼o—

Kasper hurried home, preparing to confront Bessie over the theft. Her bedroom door was open a crack. He paused and listened to the girl's animated conversation with her dolls.

"I agree, Gretchen," said Bessie. "These teas are so much better without that noisy trumpet music."

Bessie might as well have punched her father in the gut again. Not only was she a thief and a forger, she'd lied about liking jazz.

Kasper burst in, brandishing the recovered Ellington albums. "You little criminal! How dare you sell my records, especially my Ellingtons. You wicked, wicked child!"

Never had he spoken to Bessie so harshly. He fully expected the girl (and possibly a doll or two) to melt into tears. But she'd remained stone-faced throughout the tirade, and when he finished, she turned to the doll she called

Melinda and politely asked her to leave the table. Bessie removed Melinda from the chair and gestured for her father to sit in the little chair, which he did. Bessie then poured him a generous cup of pretend tea.

"It's okay to drink, Pops. Melinda didn't use it," she reassured him. "Now, Pops," she continued in a didactic tone, "you said I could sell the Ellington albums to Herr Kimball."

"I did no such thing."

Bessie nodded vigorously. "Two days ago, you said, 'Bessie, my sweet little girl, you may sell my Ellington records.' You said that. You did. As long as I got at least fifteen Marks for them. Anything more, I could keep.'"

"I said that?"

"Not out loud, but you nodded when I asked. A nod means 'yes,' doesn't it?"

"It does, but…"

Kasper felt like he was trapped in a dream, where individual words made sense, but the sentences they formed did not. He didn't recall this conversation with Bessie, and he couldn't imagine a reality in which he'd so cavalierly part with his Ellington records. Yet, her story was specific, and he couldn't deny his tendency to drift off during her teas. Maybe he had agreed, like a sleepwalker signing a contract. Or perhaps she'd misinterpreted his nodding to the music as ascent to her plan. Either way, Kasper had no one to blame but himself.

Kasper reflexively sipped the pretend tea and then chided himself for thinking it tasted pretty good.

Bessie began to cry. "I'm sorry, Pops," she said over and over.

Kasper felt terrible. He was responsible for the whole mess because he'd focused on the jazz music instead of engaging with Bessie during tea time. He couldn't stand the tears. She was like a miniaturized version of his dead wife, a sad little Isana doll.

"It's okay, my sweet girl," he said while wrapping her in his thick arms. "Pops just forgot. Give me the fifteen Marks, and you can keep the Gretchen doll."

After Kasper wiped Bessie's tears, she returned twelve of the fifteen Marks, confessing that she'd spent three Marks on tea for her dolls. Her chin quivered under Kasper's skeptical gaze. But just as he opened his mouth, Bessie launched into a frenzied lamentation, promising to pay her father back, even if it meant selling some of her dolls, the only toys she played with and, really, her only true friends in the whole wide world, and so she might as well sell all her dolls because there was no point holding sad teas where everyone was crying over their innocent friends they'd sold like slaves. Overwrought and breathless, Bessie fell back on her bed like a Victorian lady collapsing onto a fainting couch.

Kasper rushed to her bedside, stroked her cool forehead, and forgave the three-Mark debt. Bessie promptly sprang from the bed, kissed her father's cheek, and excused him from the room so she and the dolls could finish their tea.

Kasper retreated to the balcony with a glass of whiskey. When had he stopped knowing his children? His son was obsessed with finding his mother on the moon's dark side, and his daughter was striking crooked bargains with her hypnotized father. He looked to the night sky for answers. The turbid upper atmosphere made the full moon pulse like a giant radio beacon. He imagined tuning his brain to its lunar frequency, so he could discern some celestial guidance.

He raised his glass to Fate and said, "I'm ready." For what, he did not know.

After gulping down the whiskey, Kasper pulled the wad of bills from his pocket and began arranging them in the same orientation. He stopped when he realized that Bessie had suckered him out of those last three Marks. Last he checked, pretend tea was free.

CHAPTER EIGHT

1934

The newspapers' jazz reviews had become increasingly racist since Hitler's ascension in 1932. The epithets "Nigger Jazz" and "Nigger-Jew Jazz" were now standard terms in the reviewers' parlance. They condemned the "jungle cries," the "music of the howling cat," and the "dark aphrodisiac promoted by the Jews," in favor of clean, unadulterated Nordic music. "Clean" music referred to the likes of Strauss and Beethoven, as well as to the Nazified version of jazz exemplified by the Golden Seven orchestra. The Golden Seven's vanilla arrangements of jazz standards nauseated Kasper. The musicians memorized each note of the solos and reproduced them with absolute fidelity because they feared mistakes, unlike true improvisers, who embraced unexpected turns. They had sanitized and standardized that which was unsanitary and idiosyncratic at its core. They had transformed jazz from a whirling vortex into a gentle slope. Instead of shaking the listener in multiple directions, their music was a monotonous ride to an obvious destination.

The ubiquity of the reviewers' racist jargon had one surprising benefit, though. It provided cover for the stealth jazz lovers employed at the Nazi-dominated newspapers. By all appearances, Norbert Klingle was the ideal representative of the new Germany—young, blond, blue-eyed, and fierce in his rhetoric. But those who really knew him—the patrons of smoky jazz joints, the attendees of 3:00 a.m. "cutting" sessions where piano players engaged in musical duels, the few who'd seen his complete collection of *Der Eigene* magazines, replete with gay erotica—understood he was a friend of jazz. They knew how to interpret his reviews. The more racist and anti-Semitic language he employed, the higher his opinion of the particular jazz band.

For example, an excerpt from Norbert's review of the Stuttgart Syncopators' appearance at Club Zola in February 1933 stated, "The cacophony known as jazz continues to echo through the streets of Berlin. The Stuttgart Syncopators, an ensemble of five, managed to attract a thin crowd of masochists who'd rather spend an evening listening to jungle noises than an overture by our Aryan brethren." This tepid review, betraying only minimal bigotry, signaled to those in the know that the band was not very good.

By contrast, the vitriol in Norbert's review of the Chocolate Kiddies Negro Revue, an all-black eleven-piece band, was palpable, which meant they were not to be missed. Norbert spilled three hundred words decrying the "profane Nigger music," compared to the seventy-five mostly recycled words he'd written on the Stuttgart Syncopators. Norbert wrote of their

> ... schizophrenic rhythms, which mixed the savagery of the Savannah with the hopelessness of Harlem. The trombones growled like lions and the trumpets shrieked in pain, while the drums throbbed like broken heartbeats, and the saxophones cooed like streetwalkers along 125th Street. But we should not avoid the Chocolate Kiddies. Nay, I urge you all to attend and witness the profound degradation taking place under our perfectly-shaped Nordic noses. I, for one, shall be attending every night of the ten-day run. You will find me seated front and center, stone-faced, bravely absorbing the nauseating tones for the Fatherland. Admission is five Marks, with ladies admitted freely on Tuesdays.

In October 1934, Norbert published a review in *Der Rein*, which Kasper picked up from the corner newsstand. Club Zola was presenting dance routines, and Kabarett de Komiker was showing comedy sketches. The only jazz worth noting was a swing band at the Delphi. The Delphi attracted a younger, less-moneyed crowd. Although Kasper didn't mind a more middle-class mix of people, the Delphi's younger set might be a problem. They'd be mostly kids in their twenties. Kasper was well into his thirties and had two school-aged children. The patrons would be dancing to the jazz, instead of sitting at their tables, tapping their feet and puffing cigarettes to the syncopations. Jazz had become less about listening and more about "swinging." Swing was progress, evolution, though a bit too orchestrated and sanitized for Kasper's tastes. He would've passed on the Delphi, but Norbert Klingle's review, which referred to "a fat, hook-nosed Jew blasting inhuman notes on his cornet," convinced him to go. Big-nosed cornetists needed to stick together.

Kasper walked the half mile under a moonless sky. Was it already the new moon? He'd expected at least a crescent, at least a sliver of shiny grayness. For a second, he fancied the moon was actually full, only it had rotated 180 degrees, revealing its previously unseen dark side. But he immediately realized his fantasy's deep flaw. For one, the moon couldn't spontaneously rotate. Even if it did, the moon's dark side wouldn't remain dark. Sunlight would illuminate whatever mountains and craters lay on that side. The more familiar side would become the new dark side. Kasper wondered whether the Earth's telescopes would be powerful enough to see evidence of intelligent life. Would they see vast domed cities occupied by turtle men or worm creatures, as the science fiction writers posited? Would they see a short, Jewish, ex-Communist ghost floating about Mount Kasper or Gustav Crater in a shimmery flapper outfit? The answer to these questions was no, no, and no. The moon was utterly lifeless. Not even the memory of Isana could survive there.

The Delphi's young Lindy Hoppers swelled the dance floor. Kasper sat at a two-top and ordered a Bushmills. What was he doing there? What was he looking for? A wife? Not in this place. These women had barely slipped into adulthood. He didn't need another child in his life. After the waitress brought Kasper's whiskey, he downed it, threw a few Marks on the table, and got up.

Just as he made for the door, a coldness saturated his chest and spread down the front of his pants. His penis instinctively recoiled toward his body, but the crushed ice sliding down his abdomen made the crotch area a dubious sanctuary. He winced and jitterbugged in an attempt to dislodge the crystals from his underwear. His nostrils filled with the distinctive vanilla overtones of the Bushmills whiskey in which this clumsy woman had bathed him. She may have been an oaf, but she had good taste.

"I am sorry. I am so, so sorry!" the woman shouted over the music. "I tripped and... oh... look. You're soaked."

Kasper was supremely irritated. Yes, it was dark. Yes, it was easy to trip. Yes, it wasn't unheard of to have a drink spilled on you. This was all within the realm of probability. But he didn't want to be that statistic. Not then. He shouldn't have been there at all. He was already leaving, so why should Fate punish him with a blast of cold between the legs?

Kasper had his answer after he glanced up from his soaked crotch. She was the most stunning clumsy oaf he'd ever seen. Her gaze was sexy and dangerous, with just enough vulnerability to give Kasper hope he could squeeze his way inside. A clutching sensation in his chest made him catch his breath. Suddenly, he was more than willing to embrace the wet and the cold, as long as this woman's husband or fiancé wasn't lurking in the crowd. He prayed the spilt drink was Fate warning him, *Kasper, you fool! You're leaving too soon.*

"I must buy you a fresh drink." She gestured to an aproned man near the bar. "Waiter!"

"It's not necessary."

"I insist. You shall sit and drink long enough for your pants to dry," she ordered with a friendly smile.

"That could take a while."

"I have all night," she answered, though not in a furtive tone, as her words might have suggested. Her affect was factual, business-like, with less sexual innuendo than an adding machine catalog. "My name is Rosamund."

Rosamund was tall and thin, with long blonde hair pulled into a tight, orderly braid. Arching eyebrows capped her deep green eyes like the roofs of two A-frame chalets. Only one aspect seemed untidy. She'd drawn her red lipstick about an eighth of an inch too high on the right side of her upper lip. Perhaps she'd dressed in the dark, or in a hurry. Perhaps she'd been smooching with the saxophonist, whose thick lips could've cradled the entirety of Kasper's bulbous nose.

"Where's the fellow you came with?"

"What makes you think I came with a fellow?"

"It usually works that way."

"Evidently, I'm unusual." Rosamund stared into Kasper's kind, drooping eyes and then added, "Have we met?"

A weight sagged in his gut. Years earlier, Isana had posed the same question in her nasal flapper-speak.

"I hope to hell you're not gonna say I remind you of the horse you rode as a child."

"What a strange thing to say."

"Believe it or not, someone once told me that."

"He must have been quite peculiar."

"*She*, and yes, she was... very. That's why I loved her."

"I see." Rosamund's eyes softened, seemingly sensing his profound sadness.

Then, she exhaled and uttered, "Anyway, you look nothing like Chess."

Kasper shivered. "You're kidding, right?"

"Other than the dull brown eyes, you two look nothing alike."

"You're telling me you had a horse named Chess?"

"Yes. Why?"

"My wife... that is, my late wife... she had a horse called Chess, too. She said I looked like her horse the night we met."

"And you married her? Boy, you're easy."

Kasper laughed hard. It hurt but in a good way. He hadn't exercised his laugh muscles like that in years.

"What's your story, Rosamund? How is it such a handsome woman is at the Delphi all alone?"

For a split second, Kasper mistook the black pearl on Rosamund's silver pendant for a third eye in her neck's suprasternal notch. His gaze darted back to her face.

"I never said I was alone, just without a fellow."

Rosamund waved to a fair-skinned woman shaking her velvety black hair on the dance floor. Kasper wondered whether she was Rosamund's friend or love interest. He didn't ask, because it didn't matter to him, as long as it didn't matter to her, just as it hadn't mattered to Isana. Over successive whiskey shots, Rosamund explained that she was celebrating her release from a political prison. Unlike her Communist comrades, two years of prison camp hadn't deepened her commitment to the cause. The opposite, actually. The lousy food, cold showers, and interrogations had obliterated the idealist in her.

"I just want to live a normal, boring life."

"You deserve an easier time after what you've been through," Kasper concurred.

"It hasn't been so easy without a job. At least in the camp I could count on a steady supply of moldy pumpernickel."

"I've got some moldy rye in my pantry. You're welcome to it."

"You're too kind."

She patted Kasper's hand as a mock thank-you. The touch of a woman's fingertips sent electricity up his arm. *No*, he thought. *She's not just any woman.* There was magnetism, as though they'd been drawn together, or perhaps Fate had pushed them together.

"What skills do you have?"

"I'm good with people. They listen to me. I can be very persuasive ... in a polite way, mind you. I suppose I'm qualified for a sales job."

"How are you with the needle?"

"As in poking a person with one?"

"As in sewing fabric."

"I'm no seamstress, but I'm a quick learner, and I think you'll find I have very agile fingers."

"Will I?"

Rosamund placed her hands on the table, palms open, and then flipped them over. "Give me your hands," she said flatly. Kasper complied, laying his hands palms down, just short of her fingertips. Rosamund coiled her long, thin fingers around his hands. Farther and farther they reached, easily crossing his palms, extending beyond his thumbs, before remerging on the backsides. She pressed firmly into his flesh, leaving no doubt about her finger strength. She palpated his delicate muscles, transmitting equal parts pleasure and pain, not only into his hand but to a far deeper place, as though she were tickling his soul. Kasper felt uneasy, yet he didn't want to let go. She did, instead. She then checked the time on her wrist. She was wearing the same UG Tri-Compax wristwatch he owned. What a coincidence! Or was it? His wrist was suddenly bare.

"Missing something?" asked Rosamund innocently.

"How'd you do that?"

Rosamund unfastened the wristwatch and handed it back to Kasper. "As I said, I have very agile fingers."

Kasper leaned in. "Come work for me."

"What exactly do you do?"

"I've got a hat shop on Mauer Street. Mützenmacher's. You know it?"

"Of course."

"Are you a customer? Perhaps that's why I looked familiar."

"No, I've never been, but your reputation precedes you."

"Hell. Last thing I want is a reputation in this town. Attracts too much attention from the wrong type."

"I might be the wrong type. After all, I just stole your wristwatch."

Rosamund stared at Kasper hard. Was she smiling or leering? Kasper felt like an idiot. He'd offered her the job based on a thirty-second interview in a loud dance club. On top of that, she appeared to be some kind of master thief. Then again, she was the closest thing to a potential sex partner since he'd renewed his *Vogue* subscription, which was a terrible justification for a new hire and probably illegal. But Kasper had dithered too long and allowed the brief window to revoke the offer to slam shut.

"I accept," Rosamund declared.

Kasper handed her the shop's business card, figuring nothing prevented him from firing her after her first day.

"Wonderful. Be there at nine sharp. Thank you for the drinks and the shower, but I must say goodnight."

"Aren't we going to dance?"

"I have two small children who insist their muesli be on the table promptly by 8:00 a.m. If I sleep through muesli time, there's no telling what they may plot against me."

"I understand. Give them an extra kiss for me when you get home."

"I will."

"You promise?"

Rosamund's insistent tone took Kasper aback. It sounded like more than a mere nicety. She seemed to be demanding he kiss Bessie and Duke for her. He tried to discern her motive, but the dim lighting and smoky ambiance obscured her face. She was a blank, except for the overdrawn lipstick. Kasper shook off his concern. He was tired, and fatigue made him view the world suspiciously. He nodded, allowing Rosamund to interpret the gesture however she wanted.

"So I can get a jump start on the paperwork, what's your last name?"

"Lux."

Kasper got light-headed but not from the whiskey in his empty stomach.

"I'm sorry. What?"

"Lux. L-U-X. Is that a problem?"

"No, no problem. It's... Lux... Magnificent."

"It is? Why?"

"Because... because it's so easy to spell."

Rosamund scrunched her face. *Jesus,* thought Kasper. *I sound like a complete moron.* He had to leave before he scared her off.

"I... I'll see you tomorrow."

Kasper hurried home. He hadn't felt this exhilarated since Bessie's birth. He hadn't felt this nauseated since he'd last used the wishing hat. He stopped near a kiosk to catch his breath. After taking in the sweet night air, he turned and vomited ten Marks of whiskey on a Klaus poster.

CHAPTER NINE

Kasper typically didn't spend much time fiddling with his appearance. He'd apply a thin lather to his face and drag a newfangled safety razor over his stubble in a perfunctory manner because a shadow invariably returned by three in the afternoon anyway, so there was no sense risking a nick. He'd wet his slept-on hair and mold the semblance of a part with his fingers. He'd squirt a dollop of Tanagra on his toothbrush and scrub his teeth for thirty seconds. He'd put on a rumpled dress shirt. (Mama Elsie had a standing offer to iron his shirts, but Kasper didn't see the point, given they'd rumple after a few hours of wear.) He'd slip on a dark tie and a single-breasted suit, slide on his dulled wingtips, and head out the door.

Today was different. Kasper worked the shaving mug's contents into a thick froth and applied it to his face with great care, as though frosting a cake. He mentally divided his face into quadrants and shaved in small sections, applying more pressure than normal for the closest possible shave. He finished off by slapping his cheeks with menthol-scented Vigoroso, momentarily setting his skin aflame. He gave himself two minutes to brush his teeth and then scrubbed his tongue and gargled with Listerine. He applied pomade to his hair and used a comb to define a neat part on the left. He ironed his dress shirt's collar (the body wouldn't be visible under his suit coat) and polished his wingtips before slipping on a red necktie.

Mama Elsie choked on her coffee when Kasper entered the kitchen,

"Good Lord. Who died?"

"No one. I just think I should present myself more professionally. We sell the finest hats in Berlin. My slovenly appearance shouldn't detract from them."

"What suddenly inspired you?"

"Nothing in particular."

Elsie nodded skeptically. "Oh."

"Where are the kids?"

"Getting dressed. We'll leave in a few minutes."

"By the way, I've hired some help for the shop. Someone for the sales floor while I'm in the cutting room."

"That's a good idea."

"She can also help with hat construction. She has very agile fingers."

Elsie raised an eyebrow. "Does she?"

Kasper poured himself a coffee and brought it to his lips.

"Which service did you use to find her?" asked Elsie.

Kasper brought the mug down without drinking.

"I met her last night at the Delphi. I interviewed her, if that's what you're worried about."

"I'm not worried." Elsie sipped her coffee. "I hope she works out for you."

"Not just for me, Mama," Kasper urged with a tinge of irritation. "For us. For the shop."

"Right."

Kasper again brought the mug to his lips but then realized he didn't want coffee breath. He set the mug on the counter.

"I should get going. Rosamund will be there at nine."

"Rosamund's a nice name."

"Isn't it?" Kasper said dreamily before catching himself, clearing his throat, and adding, "Not that her name matters for her position. But objectively, I agree, Rosamund is a fine name. Rolls off the tongue. And it has a sturdy sound to it, don't you think? Like cast-iron."

"Just the image every woman wants to evoke," Elsie said sarcastically. "What's her last name? Griddle?"

"Lux."

"Are you serious?"

Kasper nodded. "First, I've got to figure out if she belongs to *that* Lux family."

"Don't get your hopes up. Your father and grandfather came across a couple Lux women over the years. They never panned out. Didn't know a thing about the prophecy, and they didn't have a twin sister anyway. It's a fairly common name."

"You're right. Probably just a coincidence."

Elsie studied her son coyly. "Uh-huh."

Kasper kissed Duke and Bessie goodbye and then left the apartment. Although he hadn't even sipped his coffee, he was giddy the entire way to the hat shop.

Kasper flipped on the radio in the cutting room. Duke had left the dial tuned to Radio Schwarz Boden, which, in Kasper's opinion, delivered too much talk and too little music. Kasper paused, however, before changing stations. Heidi Geissmütter had a soothing voice. She conveyed a sense of familiarity, which invited the listener in, as though she were chatting one-to-one over tea. But when she addressed her audience as "girls," which ostensibly excluded Kasper, he worried that continuing to listen would make him an eavesdropper or a deviant. He tuned the dial to Radio Luxembourg. Seconds later, he tuned it back to Radio Schwarz Boden. He was being ridiculous, he told himself. This was public radio. Anyone could listen in… at least for a little while… in private.

> Good morning, fellow citizens of Schwarz Boden. Girls, I hope you enjoy the sunshine today, but be sure to wear a good hat. We wouldn't want our fair German skin turning brown. A good hat is a girl's best friend. I suggest you frequent one of the many fine hat shops on Mauer Street, if you don't already have one.

Kasper liked this woman already.

> I want to talk to you girls about something much more important than a little sunburn. If there's one thing that defines the Nordic woman, it's her scrubbed face, neatly-trimmed, unadorned fingernails, and line-fresh clothes. This is how the Nordic woman has lived for thousands of years. This is the only way she can live for the next thousand. Girls, that is why it is so important you focus on cleanliness.
>
> Most everyday clothes are made of fabrics that can be washed with any old soap and some elbow grease. But like you, I occasionally dress in a smooth silk or a delicate taffeta, and the old ways of cleaning won't do. We need to dry clean these fabrics. Girls, there are twenty-one dry cleaners in

Schwarz Boden, but they're not all the same. I learned this the hard way. I won't name names, so I'll refer to one particular dry cleaner as Rosenberg's. Herr Rosenberg and his wife have run the business for decades. They are friendly enough and happy to accept all business. I've taken my delicates to them for years, until now, that is.

You see, eleven days ago, I discovered that my chiffon blouse, which I'd planned to wear to an art gallery opening, had a wretched stain. It was a Friday afternoon. Rosenberg's said they could clean it, but it wouldn't be ready until Sunday, because Saturday was the Jewish Sabbath, and they couldn't work. That did me no good, as the opening was set for Saturday. So, I took my blouse to Schmidt's. I was nervous going to a new dry cleaner, but Herr Schmidt put me at ease with his kind blue eyes. What's more, he cleaned my blouse brilliantly. It looked like new, girls!

How was that possible? Was it magic? Of course not. He uses Perc, like everyone else. But Herr Schmidt let me in on a dirty industry secret. Girls, come closer, and I'll share it with you.

Kasper leaned toward the radio.

To save on labor costs, many established dry cleaners don't regularly clean the filters in their machines, resulting in dirty solvent that redeposits dirt and odors on clothes. Dry cleaners like Herr Schmidt put the customer ahead of a few extra pfennigs. They understand the sacred trust they hold. They understand cleanliness. They understand the Nordic woman. Remember, girls. If you have a choice, always pick a Schmidt over a Rosenberg.

This has been Heidi Geissmütter with today's words of wisdom. Don't forget your hats!

Kasper was dumbfounded. *Always pick a Schmidt over a Rosenberg?* It sounded like a veiled dig at Jews. Heidi had spoken with such earnestness. She seemed so nice. Surely, that couldn't have been her intent. He cranked the dial to Radio Luxembourg, which was playing Benny Goodman's *Moon Glow*.

Kasper checked his wristwatch. It was 9:00 a.m. He stepped onto the sales floor right as Rosamund entered. They exchanged Guten Morgens. Rosamund had dressed smartly, in a gray wool suit. The skirt's hem grazed the middle of her well-formed calf muscles. She smelled clean but not perfumed. Kasper was happy about that. Hats were odor sponges. Some might sit on the shelves for months—like the mourning bonnets with oversized coronet brims—and extended exposure to heavy perfume made them smell like a French whorehouse. (Or so Kasper imagined. He'd been in only a German one, and it smelled like pickled herring.) No woman in mourning wanted to reek of a streetwalker, unless, perhaps, she happened to be one.

"Did you bring your identity papers?" he asked.

"I'm afraid not." Rosamund gave a crooked smile. "Forgive me. It has been years since I've had a job. You see, I was in the camp… and then Klaus…" She trailed off.

"Klaus was there?"

"He interrogated me repeatedly."

"Your face. Did he…?"

"Yes. He stole it."

Kasper felt like an ass. *This poor woman shivered herself to sleep every night with the acid taste of moldy pumpernickel on her tongue. Klaus stole her dignity and then her face. Now comes the heartless Kasper Mützenmacher, demanding she produce a few flimsy identity papers!* Kasper wanted to shrink to the size of his fountain pen, climb under a hat, and slink away.

"It's quite all right," Kasper said softly. "Bring the papers another time. In the meantime, if you're up to it, we can complete the identity verification form."

Kasper guided her toward the roll-top desk in the corner of the cutting room where Mama Elsie did the bookkeeping, paid supplier invoices, and logged customer orders. He pulled out the desk chair and set up a wooden folding chair for Rosamund. He'd already laid out the appropriate forms on the desk, along with a fountain pen, which he uncapped.

"Let's see," he said, while bringing pen to paper. "Name? Rosamund Lux. Again, that's L-U-X?"

"Yes."

"Address?"

"Nothing permanent. I've been staying with a friend since—"

"Right. The camp. Well, I suppose we can list the shop's address until you get settled."

"Birth date?"

"Four July, 1901."

"Just like America. Parents' names. First, your father?"

"He was estranged. My mother never told me who he was."

"Your mother's first name?"

"Tesse."

"I take it she's deceased?"

Rosamund looked down. "Yes." She bit her lower lip. Kasper capped the pen and set it on the paper.

"That's enough for now. Let me show you around."

Kasper started with a tour of the cutting room. He pointed out wooden hat blocks of various shapes and sizes, a drying cabinet, and a long worktable (the "cutting table") with thimbles, chalk, thread, sewing needles, linen dolly heads, scissors, tape measures, drawing pins, metal pins, sketch pads, and pencils. A smaller table, parked under Hermann's portrait, held irons, wire cutters, pliers, brushes, and hat wire.

They exited the back room and roamed the shop's front. Kasper gestured to the large plate glass windows, three on one side of the door, and one on the other. A solitary hat stand stood behind each windowpane. Kasper had set each stand's height progressively higher than the one to its left to create a sense of ascension.

Rosamund eyed the flamboyant hats skeptically, as though she were a military commander giving her troops the once-over. The first hat featured a Brazilian plover feather attached to a square lid of burgundy felt. The second hat was a dark green silk lid from which an Australian miniature stork feather protruded. The third hat, made from black patent leather, was shaped like a man's dress shoe, though the pink ribbon "shoelaces" indicated the hat was intended for a woman. The hat behind the fourth window was a staid man's fedora made of brushed chestnut suede; a thin lip of dark brown leather circumscribed the brim's edge.

Built-in mahogany shelves displayed the millinery mainstays, including beaver hats, bowlers, fedoras, homburgs, and porkpies. Rosamund ran her fingertips along the shelves and inspected the dusty residue. Embarrassed, Kasper quickly ushered Rosamund to four display areas, which filled the remainder of the shop floor. He'd devoted the first stand to the latest in ladies' hats. The styles tended toward the small and compact, making it easier for a woman to sport them at a jaunty angle. They had little or no brims and were modestly dressed with a ribbon or bow. There also was a collection of snoods, which were less hats than a decorative means of keeping a woman's hair out of her face. The second stand displayed formal top hats. A third featured the signature Mützenmacher straw hats—boaters, panamas, and even two-tone fedoras woven from the finest Leghorn straw, reminiscent of the traditional hats worn by the indigenous people of Colombia. The fourth and final stand held an assortment of wallets, belts, and cufflinks. They were the only items not manufactured in-house.

Rosamund didn't seem impressed, even when Kasper asserted he had the richest variety and best quality of hats in Berlin. She didn't disagree, nor did she agree. She merely took stock—counting the hats, noting their arrangements, inspecting for dust—as though Kasper were selling canned tomatoes and green beans.

Rosamund moved to the heavy black velvet drapes framing the windows. She shook them, releasing a dusty mist. She went to the cash register and hit the "No Sale" button, releasing the drawer. She rearranged the bills in ascending denomination and facing the same direction. She separated a few copper and bronze pfennig coins that were inappropriately mixed with their silver Reichsmark brethren. She shut the drawer, sighed, and then remained in a contemplative silence.

"Well?" asked Kasper with apprehension.

Rosamund turned her probing green eyes on him. He felt small, insignificant. The ground underneath had shifted, and he was falling into her pupils. He didn't know if he felt fear or love. Finally, she smiled.

"You made the right decision hiring me. But we need to make some changes. First..."

Rosamund didn't ask permission for her proposed changes, nor did Kasper explicitly grant it. She didn't demand anything. Not explicitly. She framed every decision as a question that, at least semantically speaking, Kasper had the right to reject, a right he didn't exercise because she invariably answered for him: "There are too many fedoras here, yes? Yes, of course... The mahogany shelves should be oiled weekly, yes? Yes, it must be done... You don't disagree you shouldn't display so many ostentatious designs? No?" Even if Kasper had harbored an opinion on that question, he would've had no idea how to answer the triple negative, or was it a quadruple?

The essence of Rosamund's proposed changes was cleanliness, both literally and atmospherically. It was a given there should be no dust on the shelves, hats, or drapes. Moreover, the display space should be clean and uncluttered. She would eliminate the display rack for the wallets and belts. The other three racks would be spaced equidistantly, with an empty space in the middle of the store. There, the customer could behold the wares from the center of the universe, as it were. The customer was the sun and the hat his planets. Like the sun, the customer would wield life and death power over the wares. His or her choices would determine which hats survived in the marketplace and which turned lifeless, cold, and extinct.

Finally, the designs on display should be clean. She instructed Kasper to heavily discount the hats with large plumes and plover feathers, billowing silk, and enormous brims, to make room for the neat, compact, and unadorned bowlers, fedoras, and homburgs. The overdesigned hats were at odds with women's roles as the nation's mothers, farmers, and laborers. Again, simplicity was the rule.

Rosamund explained that, as the Fatherland prepared for an inevitable war, the *Volk*—that is, the people—would desire clean, simple styles over the flashiness of the Weimar years. Rosamund said she hated the National Socialists more than anyone, but the Nazis were correct about the *Zeitgeist*, defined by the societal clamor for purity after the blood of the Great War and the booze of the twenties. The soap company Henkel already had tapped into this ethos with images of dirty, hook-nosed Jews delighting in their financial war against Germany, and African savages cleaning off their blackness with Persil detergents. To be sure, Henkel had taken it too far by drawing on the Nazis' interpretation of the Zeitgeist. She wasn't suggesting Kasper go in that direction at all. To the contrary, he should create a counterbalance. He should show the people the positive, inclusive alternative to the Volk's need for purity.

The wall clock read 10:30, which Kasper thought wrong. Rosamund had arrived not fifteen minutes earlier, hadn't she? He checked his wristwatch. It, too, read 10:30. He'd been so rapt in her diatribe, he'd lost track of time. She'd mesmerized him. She'd also subverted his will. He'd agreed to all her "recommendations," though he couldn't recall any particular instance of doing so, like one of Bessie's tea parties, only on a much grander scale. What else had he conceded or given away during this lost hour and a half? He checked the cash register, which was full and orderly, just as Rosamund had left it.

"One more thing," said Rosamund. "I require a place to live."

"I suppose you could stay upstairs," muttered Kasper.

There was a spare room above the shop, with a bed, toilet, and bathtub. Kasper occasionally slept there when he worked late on a new design. He also favored the toilet up there because of its southern exposure. The light was excellent for reading *Melody Maker* magazine's tiny print. He despaired that the bed and the toilet would be *verboten* once Rosamund moved in. He'd need an invitation to use the bed. The toilet, he could forget about entirely. He'd relinquish dominion over his haven of relief and music education for as long as he employed Rosamund, which he hoped would be for many years.

"That will do fine."

Christ, Kasper thought. *I better clear out those racy Vogues, too.*

CHAPTER TEN

Rosamund's first day on the job exhausted her. She retired upstairs without dinner. Kasper remained in the cutting room for a while, in case she changed her mind about eating with his family or decided she wanted companionship (not upstairs, naturally... unless invited, and even then...). He stared at the ceiling, listening for creaking floor planks and squeaking bedsprings but heard neither. Curious. Had Rosamund stopped cold at the top of the stairs? Had she transformed into a ghost, enabling her to float about the room? After a silent twenty minutes, Kasper deduced that Rosamund was extremely light on her feet and was now fast asleep.

Kasper removed Hermann's portrait and propped it against the cutting table. He then unlocked the wall safe and reached inside. His hand sensed the unnatural heat pulsating from the very back. He didn't need to reach that far, however. Not that day. He fetched the indigo-dyed portfolio, shut the safe, and rehung the portrait. He flipped on the roll-top desk's gooseneck lamp. Then, with the gentility and reverence of a high priest, he slid Lorenz Mützenmacher's centuries-old letter from its protective silk case.

Kasper imagined Hermann's ghost hovering over his right shoulder, admonishing against mishandling the pages and quizzing him on the curse's minutiae. Hermann's moist, gin-soaked breath had buffeted Kasper's neck so many times as a child that, by age sixteen, he'd developed a permanent muscle knot in his right shoulder. Kasper forgave Hermann, who'd probably endured the same thing from Kasper's grandfather, who'd probably endured the same thing from Kasper's great-grandfather. He pictured a row of shoulders and faces, alternating like dominos, stretching back three hundred fifty years. *Christ,* thought Kasper, *that's a helluva lot of bad breath and shoulder tension.* Yet those unpleasantries were small sacrifices for the paternal continuity that gave the family purpose. For better or worse, the Mützenmachers mattered in Fate's grand scheme. As with any animal, a man's muscle could be massaged and his mouth rinsed clean. Mattering, however, was divine.

Kasper re-read the letter, focusing on those portions that might help him figure out whether Rosamund descended from a water nymph.

Dearest Son:

Thou hast asked me to put to paper the fantastical story of the curse we long have endured, so generations to come can fathom the depth of our ancient wrong. 'Til now, this knowledge hath been conveyed from mouth to ear, subject to the vagaries of human misunderstanding, forgetfulness, and embellishment. 'Tis my hope these words, inked indelibly on parchment, provide form and fixity to our traditions, and lend them an imprimatur of dignity and truth no less legitimate than the scrolls and texts of the great religions.

For a space of some twelve centuries, the men of the Petasos (now Mützenmacher) bloodline have known no other occupation than millinery. Fate doth not permit it. Petasos daughters be not so accursed...

* * *

The mountain nymph Maia came upon a dying gryphon in Olympus. She unsheathed her knife, sliced open the beast's throat, and excised a flag-sized swatch of flesh near'st its vocal chords; through this organ the animal had produced its unique call. Maia cleansed the leathery membrane in her urine and then dried it in the sun, whereafter she fashioned the scaly leather into a broad-brimmed hat and placed it on the head of her sleeping son, Hermes, son of Zeus. Too large at first, the hat soon constricted to the shape of the infant god's skull. Such is the nature of gryphon leather; it lives on, though its original owner doth not...

* * *

In the Year of Our Lord 390, our ancestor, Aesop Petasos, did administer a hat shoppe, a granite and stucco structure on the road to Delfi. A foul, unclean man was he, with little care for his art... Aesop betook himself to Kirra to wager his dwindling fortune on a three-day wrestling competition, leaving his nephew Faustus, a mere boy, to mind the shoppe.

'Twas a decision most regretful...

* * *

At Apollo's Temple in Delfi, Hermes, now grown to maturity and assigned the epithet "messenger god," conferred with a Pythian priestess. She handed him a scroll for delivery to Apollo. 'Twas inscribed with these solemn words: "Thy followers have dwindled; they no longer believe. Show thyself now; else the Temple closes this eve." The rising winds had deposited a thick layer of dust on Hermes' wishing hat, which prevented his travel to Olympus, where his brother Apollo then resided. On the Pythian priestess's recommendation, Hermes walked the Delfic road to the Petasos hat shoppe. He entered and set a large gold coin on the counter and demanded a prompt hat cleaning. The boy Faustus was ignorant of this traveler's divine identity, in spite of peculiarities revealing him to be extraordinary in stature, voice, and guise. Faustus nodded. With wishing hat in hand, he passed through the curtain separating the public area from the workroom...

* * *

Meanwhile in the Olympian woods, Apollo bickered with Eros... Thereupon, the cherubic love god shot Apollo with a golden arrow, and when the heart-stricken god spied the water nymph Dafne, he fell instantly, profoundly, and madly lovesick. Eros then reloaded his bow with a leaden arrow and let it fly into Dafne's bosom. The opposite effect this arrow had on the unsuspecting nymph. The moment she spied Apollo's face, the repulsed Dafne took flight.

Back in Delfi, Faustus donned the wishing hat and beheld his reflection in a polished bronze plate. The hat was preposterously large, but, as he gazed upon his visage, it settled into a perfect fit. He fancied himself a sailor on Odysseus's ship, the hat's wide brim shielding him from the harsh Aegean sun. He wished he could go to the Sirenum scopuli, the Sirens' realm. With that thought, an invisible force squeezed young Faustus from all sides. A tunnel opened before him and pulled him inside. He was stretched long and thin like a hemp rope and then spat out on his face. At once, the most horrible pangs racked his innards, and he was stricken with a profound sickness. Spasm upon spasm expelled his stomach's contents...

* * *

The nymph Dafne ran toward the Olympian river from which she had sprung. Apollo gave chase and backed her to the muddy shore. "Grant me a form that thwarts Apollo's lust," she beseeched her father, the god of the river. At once, Dafne's feet sunk into the muck and spread wide along the bank. No longer were they flesh and sinew but root and hair. Her legs and torso also relinquished their animal essence, becoming heartwood and bark. Her arms and head swelled into graceful, sweeping branches and a thick, full crown of green. Apollo was powerless to prevent the metamorphosis…

* * *

Hours stretched into days as Faustus wished himself from Alpine forests to the hot, dry Persian lands to the Ganges' cooling waters. He did not tarry long at any one place. Each journey's exhilaration inspired him to crave the next wish, such is the bewitching lure of travel by wishing hat. After three days of compression and expansion and elongation, the hum in his head had grown deafening and he weak from the absence of rest and nourishment. He longed for home. And that was where the hat took him. But Faustus arrived not at the home he had left. O, 'twas Delfi, but its blue sky was gone, as was the blazing sun. A gray-purple cloud hailed iridescent droplets that hissed with music as they streaked through the atmosphere…

* * *

Uncle Aesop revealed the grave news to his nephew. Due to Faustus's theft, Hermes could not deliver the Pythian's plea for Apollo to appear at his temple and restore the people's faith. Instead, Apollo remained in Olympus and absorbed the love-god's golden arrow, which infected him with an insatiable lust for the nymph Dafne. Without the people's faith to sustain the immortal realm, the levees of Oceanus crumbled, and the great river washed the gods to Oblivion.

Disgusted, Aesop cast Faustus from his presence. Faustus could not return to his former life. He tried to resume his studies, but the academy he previously had attended burned down, as did the next two in which he enrolled. He had to take up a trade. He tried his hand at smithing but chopped off his pinky finger. He attempted wine-making, but his feet contracted an aggressive fungus. He abandoned his position modeling for art students after developing an oozing rash on his chest. He consulted three different Arcadian priests, who all rendered the identical pronouncement: He and his progeny were cursed to remain in the hat business, on pain of disease, dismemberment, or disaster. With no gainful employment, Faustus returned to his uncle's hat shoppe. Aesop took pity and reemployed his nephew, extending his involuntary servitude in perpetuity…

* * *

In 1603, when I carried the appellation Andolosia Petasos, Fate crossed my path with Carlotta Lux's. The flaxen-haired Sicilian possessed the most exquisite singing voice. Melodious, aye, but also invested with peculiar syncopations that made me simultaneously merry and doleful. When the afternoon sun caught her eyes just so, two indigo points flashed inside each green iris, beacons for my lonely heart. Most striking was Carlotta's claimed blood-link to the water nymph Dafne. She sayeth Apollo hath devised a means to leave Oblivion for short spells by possessing a mortal vessel on Earth. Through these unwitting human hosts, Apollo pursues Lux women to complete the rape that Dafne thwarted in Olympus. Carlotta called it the Dafne Curse, an intergenerational plague stemming from Faustus's theft of Hermes' hat.

Carlotta and I traveled to Delfi, where a woman knowledgeable in the Pythian traditions revealed how to lift the burdens that intertwine our two families. The priestess prophesied these words:

* * *

> Thus is the curse on the kin of Petasos:
> Keep the status quo at the time of the theft.
> Sell hats through the ages or end up bereft.
> Freedom they'll know when Hermes comes back
> for the hat that his head doth now sorely lack.
>
> Thus is the curse on the nymph Dafne's kin:
> Fate assigns mortals for Apollo to possess,
> so the god may awake from Oblivion's rest.
> Apollo's rebirth will cause great trepidation
> for the Luxes, with whom he seeks consummation.
> These nymph-kin may run or put up a fight,
> but killing the host won't end the Lux plight,
> only pause the pursuit for the briefest duration.
> The god will return for the next generation.
> Apollo abstains when a Lux is a mother.
> Pre- or post-birth, the nymph is not bothered.
>
> Heed these directions, which Fate doth decree,
> and the intertwined scourges will no longer be:
>
> Find sisters of Dafne who are twins by mistake.

The soul that they share only one person makes.
After Apollo doth surface, Hermes will arrive,
for these sons of Zeus live intertwined lives.
Both clever and strong, and dripping with guile,
sharing high cheekbones and wily, broad smiles.
Their eyes emit love when beholding each other,
but also the envy of two jealous brothers.

Give Hermes the hat that doth answer to wishes,
to aid sick Apollo through means expeditious.
Travel they must to Wisdom's great tower,
where the arrows of Eros carry no power.
Among Plato's Forms, Apollo's heart shall be freed,
and his capture of Dafne no longer a need.
The threat from the Twelve at last shall abate,
as Dafne and sisters incorporate,
And transmit the note inside all the people—
an inaudible song from the indigo steeple.

* * *

...After delivering Carlotta's corpse to Taormina, I could no longer bear to live as a Petasos. Hence, I rechristened myself Lorenz Mützenmacher of Berlin.

My dearest Lambert, it befalls thee and thy male progeny to abide the curse that poisons our blood. Take care with the wishing hat. In my adventures with Carlotta, I used it much, and, like Faustus, found hat travel more seductive than opium. 'Twas only Carlotta's unexpected passing that quelled the cravings. I know not what became of her descendants, for I made no subsequent effort to visit or correspond with them. Forgive me, but my conscience was so cracked with woe I could not bear even the thought of the Lux name. 'Twas a foolish, selfish oversight. Teach thy son vigilance for the twin sisters named Lux with golden hair and eyes like the evergreen laurel 'neath brows arched like an eagle's wings. They carry the blood of the water nymph Dafne. Only their liberation shall purify our blood of the wishing hat's ancient curse.

Most affectionately,
/s/
Lorenz Mützenmacher, né Andolosia Petasos

Schwarz Boden, 21 November 1661

Did Daphne's blood course through Rosamund Lux's veins? Kasper wasn't sure. Rosamund fit the description: blonde, green eyes, arched eyebrows. But, then, so did many other women. Moreover, the surname Lux wasn't unusual in Germany. In 1930, Kasper had sold a homburg and two belts to a Wolfgang Lux. In the early twenties, he'd rooted for Hermann Lux, the star soccer player for SC Union Obserchöneweide. Anyway, names were tenuous and fickle. Kasper's ancestors had been Petasoses for two millennia before Andolosia Petasos snapped his fingers and became Lorenz Mützenmacher. Rosamund's ancestors could've adopted ten different names before settling on Lux.

The clearest way to settle the issue would have been to flat out ask her, only there was no way in hell Kasper was going to do that, not yet. He didn't want to scare her off. This called for subtlety and patience. He'd have to appear to uncover her nymphly origins innocently, seemingly by accident, or not at all. Kasper therefore decided to begin his detective work with a ruse. Just prior to the shop's opening, he spread Rosamund's employment verification forms on the writing desk in the cutting room, and waited for her to descend.

"Oh," said a surprised Rosamund. "You're up early."

Kasper swiveled around. "Morning! Just catching up on paperwork. You probably should fetch your identity documents before starting work."

"About that. I should have been clearer. I lost my papers a few weeks back. I've applied to the police and Labor Office for new papers. It may be a while yet. I'm sorry I misled you, but I was embarrassed."

"The Labor Office didn't give you temporary cards?"

"No."

"Strange."

"Should I go back and ask for them?"

"No. Don't bother."

"I suppose, then, I'll have to stop working."

"Absolutely not. The papers can wait a few weeks."

"I'm glad. I really like working here."

Kasper blushed. "And I like you working under me—*for* me, rather."

"If that is all, I'll head to the sales floor."

"Actually, I was hoping to get more information about you for my own employment files."

"Such as?"

"Such as... are there any next of kin I should know about... in case of emergency?"

"No one in Germany, so far as I know. My mother mentioned a sister in America. In Detroit."

"Your sister or hers?"

"Hers."

"So you don't have a sister?" asked Kasper, disappointed.

"Not as far as I know."

"That's too bad."

"It is? Why?"

"Oh, well, I was an only child myself. So much attention focused on me all the time. I often wished I had a brother exactly my age."

"Like a twin?"

"Exactly. You ever wish that?"

"No."

There was a long pause.

"Anything else?" asked Rosamund.

"Did your mother tell you how the Luxes settled in Germany?"

"Is that important for your employment files?"

"Just curious. The name Lux isn't German. It's Latin for light, I believe. Did your mother have roots in Italy... *or Sicily*?"

Rosamund bit her lower lip. "I was ten when she passed. I don't remember much." She added impatiently, "Are we opening on time today?"

"Yes. Yes, go ahead."

Kasper's detective work wasn't going to be easy. Still, Rosamund's reticence was understandable. She hadn't known Kasper long enough to reveal her connection with the nymph Daphne, if one existed. If it did, she probably feared that even hinting at that fantastical fact would trigger her termination and a quick call to the Krankenhause for the men in white jackets. He would set the matter aside for the time being.

Nymph or not, Rosamund quickly proved herself invaluable in the hat shop. Customers fully embraced her "less is more" concept. They asked if Kasper had remodeled the shop or created new designs. The answer was no. He simply was presenting what was already there in a different light. Customers made their purchases more quickly, too, perhaps because their choices were starker. Most impressively, Rosamund sold certain customers hats Kasper never could've imagined on their heads.

A case in point: Frau Edith Stein. Approaching seventy, Frau Stein had been purchasing the same hat every year for the past ten years, a mushroom-shaped cloche covered in taffeta and crepe chiffon, rosettes of wheat, and two chiffon streamers off the back, a solidly French design. From year to year, Frau Stein altered only the fabrics' colors, although they always had to be pastels. This time, Rosamund suggested she consider a simpler design.

"Where is Kasper?" Frau Stein asked impatiently, scanning the shop floor. "He knows what I want."

Kasper was helping Fraulein Blucher. He'd heard Frau Stein's belligerent tone and considered intervening but was curious to see whether Rosamund could sway the old woman.

"I'm afraid you are stuck with me. Rest assured, Frau Stein, you shall leave here today with the hat of your dreams. Indulge me. If you are not one hundred percent satisfied, I will take your standard order, and there will be no charge."

Kasper shot a "what-the-hell" gaze at Rosamund, who returned unflinching, steely eyes.

"Well," said the rarely pleased Frau Stein, "when you put it that way..."

Rosamund brought out a hand mirror and instructed Frau Stein to study her face, to which the old woman responded, "Oh Heavens, why would I want to look at that beaten up old satchel?" Rosamund complemented Frau Stein's elegant cheekbones and velveteen skin. Frau Stein remarked that Rosamund was teasing but was intrigued enough to judge for herself.

Rosamund removed the old woman's hat and the pins binding her hair. She raked her fingers along Frau Stein's scalp, triggering a shiver of delight. Silvery white hair descended to her shoulders and framed her face like a proscenium arch. Rosamund dropped her voice an octave, and she slowed her speech to a soft, deliberate cadence that evoked the hypnotic, snare drum patter of a steady rainstorm. She told Frau Stein that the frilly French hats were upstaging her beautiful face. She needed a hat that didn't overshadow her sturdy good looks. Rosamund fitted her with a small—too small, it seemed—black felt hat with a subtle crown and a wide brim. It looked like a parson's hat. Correction: It looked like a *midget* parson's hat.

Frau Stein cocked her head, confused. Rosamund shifted the hat's axis and then grasped Frau Stein's neck with her thumb and forefinger and oriented her head back to vertical. Frau Stein's eyes rolled into her skull. An instant later, her gaze fixed forward. She looked at her reflection as though bewitched, as though another woman was staring back at her. The muscles around her eyes relaxed, smoothing the crow's feet. Her lips, usually coiled and cinched like a fat earthworm, unpuckered and expanded into a graceful oval. Color flooded her cheeks. Rosamund had performed a brilliant act of millinery sorcery, transforming Frau Stein from a washed-up Vaudeville act into the paragon of aged beauty.

"I am one hundred percent satisfied," beamed Frau Stein.

Then, seemingly as a reward for submitting to her will, Rosamund promised that Kasper would decorate the crown with a strip of orchid-colored silk, clarifying that the strip would be thin and understated. The hat would remain a clean, elegant, German hat, because Frau Stein was a clean, elegant, German woman.

This scene repeated itself with Fraulein Schwartz, Herr Doctor Goldberg, and Herr Professor Bieber. With a touch of the neck, a drop in her tone, and a tilt of the head, Rosamund converted them from, respectively, a chenille turban, a mohair slouch hat, and a shiny lamé deerstalker to a cloche hat, a homburg, and a fedora—all simple, clean, and black. And conversions they were, because they all left Kasper's shop with beatific smiles and the confidence to showcase their faces, not their hats.

To keep up with increased demand, Kasper involved Rosamund in the production process. He taught her to make wire frames for the crowns and brims, freeing him to focus on the coverings and finish work. The shared labor gave him time to create new designs, and Rosamund's presence gave him the energy to implement them. As they worked in close quarters, frequently brushing shoulders, Rosamund would sing tunes from the twenties, like *Mandy* and *There's More to the Kiss than the Sound*. Her voice was pure and strong, as good as any he'd heard in the clubs or on the stage. He was deeply smitten and had to make a concerted effort to tamp down his sexual giddiness.

"How do you know so many songs?" he asked one evening.

"I sang all the time on the farm."

"Despite your father, you had some happy times?"

"Yes. My best friend—my only friend, really—lived on the neighboring property. We used to ride our horses to the water."

Rosamund seemed far away, as though in a pleasant dream. But then her smile collapsed. Her eyes flashed through a range of emotions—shock, sadness, rage—before melting into resignation and last, stillness.

"It was so long ago she hardly seems real," she continued. "Maybe I dreamed her. Maybe I made her up in the concentration camp to keep from going insane. We made up many tales there."

"Often tales are based on a kernel of truth. And, sometimes, the truth doesn't even seem possible, yet it is."

"Such as?"

Such as people descending from nymphs, thought Kasper.

"Oh, I don't know. Such as people who live impossibly long lives."

"Like to one hundred?"

"Much longer than that. Practically forever."

"Like gods?"

"Such as."

"I know precisely what you're saying."

Kasper's heart skipped a beat. "You do?"

"I have a confession... No. Never mind. It will sound crazy. It *is* crazy."

"Tell me, Rosamund. I won't judge."

"Someone is after me."

Apollo?

"Who is after you?"

She shrugged.

"You know his name."

"I do?"

Yes, I do. Apollo. But I want you to say it.

Kasper trembled with anticipation. She'd reveal her nymph ancestry, and he would tell her about the wishing hat. They would finally breathe easy, the weight of their mutual secrets lifted.

"His name is... Klaus," she said, followed by a sigh.

"Klaus?" Kasper echoed like a confused idiot. "Of course... Klaus. You were his prisoner. He tortured you."

"What's wrong, Kasper? You look deflated."

"No, I... I was only going to add it's not crazy at all. It's natural for you to think Klaus is still after you, but he's not. And even if he is, he can't hurt you. Not as long as I'm around."

Rosamund gripped her forehead. "Oh," she muttered. "My head."

"Another headache?"

She nodded.

"Jesus, Rosamund. This is becoming a regular thing. You're going to the doctor."

"No doctors. Just take me upstairs."

"All right, but then I'm calling—"

"Will you lie with me?"

Her request so flustered Kasper, he forgot about the doctor. Later, he couldn't even recall climbing the stairs to Rosamund's room. He'd made it there somehow, because he had a distinct memory of lying on her bed for an hour, his left shoulder and hip touching hers the entire time. But the way he'd felt, impossibly light and tingling with exhilaration, he wondered if he hadn't floated up the stairs.

CHAPTER ELEVEN

1935

Materials became increasingly scarce as Hitler rearmed the nation. Kasper considered using the wishing hat to travel to the nether reaches of Germany and beyond. He could've gone to Plauen for lace, the Black Forest for amber, and Leghorn for straw. He had family in County Antrim, Ireland, who could supply him with fine Irish linen. But he didn't. He'd use the hat only for a true emergency. He wouldn't risk a relapse into addiction. Instead, he used his creativity to make do with materials at hand. When a shortage of key chemicals made it difficult for women to get permanent waves, Kasper created a ruffled silk hat that simulated the look of curly hair. The hats were a huge success, and most fashionable women in Schwarz Boden were wearing one by year's end.

The competition did not welcome Kasper's success. One slow afternoon, Kasper spotted Dieter Daimler loitering outside the shop. Dieter was scrutinizing the window displays and jotting notes on a clipboard.

Kasper hadn't spoken to Dieter since Isana's run-in with Klaus in 1923. He'd always felt a bit sorry for stripping the little fool of his SA uniform just so Isana could carry out the greatest prank ever played on the Nazis. Then, after Klaus took Isana, Kasper had to lean on Dieter until he gave up all the possible locations where Klaus might have been holding her. As far as Kasper knew, Dieter hadn't suffered any serious trauma. Dieter later took over his father's gigantic clothing store, Daimler's, which sold off-the-rack men's suits, shirts, and hats. Daimler's was a massive operation for the masses, in contrast to Mützenmacher's, which focused on design and craftsmanship for the individual.

Dieter finished his notes and moved toward the shop's entrance. He navigated around a cordoned area, where city services workers were mounting another attack on a stubborn tree root that was buckling the sidewalk. They'd previously employed shovels, pick axes, and a manual soil auger to remove the root, all to no avail. Now they'd set up a diesel-powered auger, which they flipped on before Dieter could enter the shop. A sooty, black cloud enveloped his head, triggering a violent coughing fit. He staggered toward fresh air, as the auger's helical drill bit kicked copious dirt onto his pant leg.

Dieter scolded the men, ordering them to switch off the machine, which they did. He demanded their names, as he would be reporting them to the *Blockleiter*. The unperturbed workers stared at Dieter, stone-faced, and then restarted the auger. Exasperated, Dieter turned away, removed a kerchief from his breast pocket, and fastidiously swiped at his pants, as though chiding the material for communing with such filth.

Dieter entered the shop, sporting a Nazi lapel pin on his black suit. Kasper was disappointed Dieter hadn't forsaken his affiliation with the Brownshirts. Dieter pulled a thin leather booklet from his breast pocket and flashed credentials for the Working Association of German-Aryan Manufacturers of the Clothing Industry, abbreviated to "ADEFA" in German. ADEFA's goal was to break the clothing industry's "Jewish monopoly." Its official motto was "We can do it better!" which really meant "We can do it better [than the Jews]!" ADEFA encouraged consumers, wholesale buyers, and retailers to demand ADEFA-guaranteed Aryan products.

"Dieter Daimler," said Kasper congenially. "How have you been all these years?"

"This is not a social visit, Kasper."

"What is it, then?"

"An inspection. If your store passes, I will issue a decal."

"Decal?"

"A sign assuring your customers that Jewish hands haven't touched your fabrics."

"What about Jewish feet? Do you have a separate decal for that? Last thing I want is my customers catching a foot fungus from my fedoras, especially a Jewish foot fungus. Makes them itch in Yiddish."

Dieter returned the credentials to his pocket and removed a pen, which he used to mark the form on the clipboard.

"Who manufacturers these hats?"

"I do, personally."

"And the materials?" asked Dieter, gesturing to a row of black wool fedoras.

"I have to give credit to the sheep."

"I meant where do you acquire the wool."

"The typical place. Biddleman's."

"Wool is one thing, but you also use materials very hard to come by. Linen, chenille, chiffon, lace. Who is your supplier?"

Kasper had paperwork for some fabrics. For others, he'd paid cash to Jews, who didn't want a paper trail.

"I have the paperwork if you'd like to see," Kasper bluffed.

"Later. For now, tell me where you acquired the exotics—the amber, the Chinese silk, and the Leghorn straw. You realize black markets are illegal?"

Kasper knew full well that mere possession of these materials, without more, proved criminal activity. He therefore shifted tack to intimidation. He stepped close to Dieter and offered his wrists. "I guess you'll have to arrest me, Dieter. Take me away."

Dieter cleared his throat. He turned to the display card next to the hats, which described the style, fabric, and available colors. Dieter shook his head disapprovingly. He crossed out words on several cards.

"The Propaganda Ministry's latest circular clearly states that the colors 'medium blue' and 'beige' no longer exist."

"How can they not exist? I see them with my own eyes."

"The *names* no longer exist. They are un-German. The accepted terms are 'national blue' and 'breadcrumb.'"

"Ahh, yes. Nothing evokes the Fatherland better than stale bread. Makes perfect sense. The Kaiser has his roll. Now the Führer has his crumb."

Dieter gestured to the window's banner advertisement, which read, "Berlin's Exclusive Source for the Chic Permanent Wave Hat!"

"Where is your license for this?"

Kasper had no license, a fact Dieter duly noted on the form because all advertisements required a license from the Propaganda Ministry. Kasper also had committed a secondary violation by using the word "Chic" instead of the authorized German spelling (Schick).

Dieter cocked his head. Something in the air displeased him—the jazz music streaming from the back room. Radio Luxembourg was playing, which was a grave violation, for only a month earlier the government had banned jazz on the radio, sweeping away the last remnants of the "culture-destroying activities of the Bolshevistic Jew." Dieter parted the curtain to the cutting room and tuned the dial to Radio Schwarz Boden.

"That's better," said Dieter. "Heidi Geissmütter will be on soon. She's a true German."

"And jazz is true German music."

"Don't take me for a fool."

"Oh, I do. Regardless, jazz is as German as Heidi Geissmütter. Beethoven invented it."

"He most certainly did not."

"Listen to the scherzo in his B flat Quartet. Swap a saxophone for the first violin, add some more drums, and you've got yourself Duke Ellington!"

"We are through."

"I've been meaning to ask, Dieter. You never returned my overcoat from the night we borrowed your SA uniform. Did you leave it at the dry cleaners?"

Dieter cinched his lips. "Tell you what. Come by my shop. Pick any coat you like. On the house."

Dieter scrawled a signature on the form, tore off the top sheet, and handed it to Kasper.

Kasper shook his head. "I'm really disappointed, Dieter."

"Your violations are quite fixable."

"Not about this ADEFA bullshit. About you. Remember what Nietzsche said: 'He who fights with monsters might take care lest he thereby become a monster.'"

"'And if you gaze for long into an abyss, the abyss gazes also into you.' Yes, I remember."

"So where are you gazing now, Dieter?"

Dieter's chin quivered. "You don't know me, Kasper. You never even tried. It was always brute force with you."

———o╂o-◇◇━◇━o╂o———

Kasper felt a pang of guilt as he recalled his boiler room confrontation with Dieter during sophomore year. He'd backed Dieter to the wooden chair favored by Hans Wörgl, a big-boned Tyrolean with a penchant for vigorous rocking during Kasper's secret cornet recitals. When Dieter sat, the fatigued chair legs swayed, startling him. He gripped the arms to steady himself. Kasper placed his hands on top of Dieter's, leaned in close, his fat nose mere inches from Dieter's, and demanded he the real reason for his opposition to sword fighting.

Dieter proffered the same explanation he'd uttered in class and at school assemblies countless times before: Though, on the surface, sword fighting epitomized manliness, in truth, participants "feminized" themselves by drawing blood, by reducing themselves to "the red flow," a flow that, if left unchecked, would deluge the entire school.

Kasper excoriated Dieter for his ill-informed—nay, warped—theories of gender identity. But Dieter refused to discuss it further. What was the point? He was clearly in the minority, a minority of one. No one listened to him. He was a ghost. Less than a ghost. At least people saw ghosts from time to time. Dieter was perpetually invisible. He told Kasper to get it over with. Smack him around. Break his arms. Slit his throat, even. It didn't matter. His blood didn't matter.

How small and helpless Dieter had looked in that chair. With his round, wide-set eyes and stubby nose, with his compact, downturned lips and tiny ears, with his down of matted, gray-brown hair and nascent whiskers at the corners of his mouth, he was more a bedraggled river otter than a man. Kasper was overcome with a desire to pick up this creature, cradle him, carry him to the water, and tell him everything was going to be all right.

Dieter seemingly sensed Kasper's mood change, because suddenly his face projected an openness, a naked vulnerability, that Kasper had never seen in Dieter or any other man. Dieter bowed his forehead into Kasper's, not aggressively but intimately. He was going to say something, bare something, confess something. Kasper lost his nerve. He was terrified by what might spring from Dieter's mouth. It seemed like he was about to slice out his own heart and hand it to Kasper. Kasper had to end it before that happened. He ordered Dieter to get the hell out of his sight.

Although Dieter left, his unspoken words gnawed at Kasper for the next year. As he'd lay in his dormitory bed, he'd try to guess what Dieter might have been thinking. These contemplations spilled into his subconscious, triggering the same dream every time—at least he assumed it was the same dream. He couldn't be sure. As hard as he tried, Kasper never could recall the dream's specifics, only the peculiar sensations that haunted him upon awakening: the scent of blood and an unsettling twinge in his anus. The dream and the ensuing sensations declined in frequency as Kasper spent more and more time at the whorehouse. By senior year, when neither he nor the ten women he'd bedded harbored any doubts about his unfettered heterosexuality, the dream had stopped altogether.

Kasper dropped his tough pretense and asked Dieter, "That day in the boiler room, sophomore year. What were you going to say?"

"I don't remember."

"Sure you do. Right before I told you to get the hell out."

Dieter paused. "Oh, well, it doesn't matter now."

"I think it does."

"It's too late... You're not..."

"I'm not what."

Dieter shook his head.

"Please, Dieter. I'm sorry for how I treated you."

Dieter gathered himself, tightening his face and puffing out his chest. "Don't be sorry. That Dieter was a degenerate relic. He's buried and forgotten, as he should be. Goodbye, Kasper. Fix those violations or else there will be consequences."

On the way out, Dieter slapped a sticker on the display window reading, "This shop is not ADEFA compliant. Support Germany. We can do it better! D. Daimler, ADEFA Block Captain."

Seconds later, Heidi Geissmütter began her broadcast.

Greetings, girls of Schwarz Boden. I have a story to share with you about my Uncle Bernd. He's a hard-working, honest man. He's not rich. He's a farmer. To bolster wheat production on his twenty-one acres, Uncle Bernd purchased a bigger tractor, which meant he needed a bank loan. As you know, I don't like to name names, so let's just say he sought a loan from a fellow named Greenbaum. I went with my Uncle Bernd to the bank. I shook Greenbaum's pudgy hands, rough and dirty from all the Reichsmarks he handles. Greenbaum pretended to listen. He feigned interest in Uncle Bernd's farm. He said he understood the importance of expanding crop production to feed the Volk. But at the end of all that, Greenbaum said no. No money. Do you know why? Because Uncle Bernd had insufficient collateral. The bank already had a lien on the farm. All Uncle Bernd could offer was his hard work and a promise to pay. In his eleven years dealing with the bank, not once had he missed a payment. But that was insufficient for Greenbaum. No matter that the Volk is hungry and will grow hungrier. Greenbaum is an unnatural creature. He feeds off money, whereas the people live off Earth's bounty.

But don't fret, girls. This story has a happy ending. Uncle Bernd went to another bank, this one run by a man named Weiss. Such a handsome man, this Weiss. Blond. Blue eyes. A paragon of German beauty. He lent Uncle Bernd the money. An honest man's promise to work hard and pay his obligation was more than enough collateral. Weiss understood the German way because he is one of the Volk.

After all this, Uncle Bernd harbors no malice toward Greenbaum. To the contrary. He pities him, because his bank will not last long making such poor investment decisions. Greenbaum lives for himself, not the Volk. He will end up destitute and alone.

This is—

Kasper rotated the dial to Radio Luxembourg. The shop door opened. Rosamund was back from the doctor.

"Who was that man coming out of the store?" she asked, haggard and weary.

"What man?"

"The slight fellow in the dark suit. He looked very official with his clipboard."

"Oh, just an ADEFA agent. He didn't like our display cards and the window banner."

"I could kick myself. I knew about those requirements, but I forgot. I'll make the changes at once."

Rosamund gripped her throbbing head and then swayed, seemingly about to faint. Kasper put his arm around her to steady her.

"The signs can wait. You need rest."

Rosamund didn't resist as Kasper escorted her upstairs.

"What did the doctor say?"

Rosamund shook her head. "Nothing new. I have migraines. He prescribed aspirin and coffee. It's hopeless."

Kasper stopped Rosamund at the base of the stairs.

"We'll find another doctor. A specialist."

"There's no cure for the tortures I endured at the camp. Klaus put something awful inside my head. It's alive, and it's growing. It's killing me."

"Don't talk like that." Kasper guided her upstairs. "You've been working too hard, that's all. You have a cruel boss. I'll have a talk with him."

Rosamund allowed herself a tiny smile. She then lay on the bed, and Kasper drew a blanket over her. He laid a palm on her forehead.

"You rest, my dear. Then, you will come home with me. Mama Elsie is preparing a feast, and Duke and Bessie are expecting their Tante Rosamund."

"Tante? They call me that?"

"Sure do."

They didn't call her that, but Kasper would make sure they started that night. Rosamund had been over only twice. Kasper wished she'd come over more often, but she usually behaved like a wounded animal, reluctant to leave her den. He remained at her side, pressing his warm palm into her forehead, humming *Mood Indigo* until the muscles around her eyes relaxed, and she drifted into sleep.

Rosamund awoke refreshed and headache-free. The bags under her eyes had shrunk and faded. Her face was filled with color. Feeling liberated, she unbound her hair and let it drape onto her shoulders. She wore a small high-crowned hat tilted at a sharp angle. Kasper's humming must have filtered into her subconscious because she'd wrapped the hat with a silk indigo bow. As Kasper adjusted her hat, he noticed her eyes weren't pure green. The late afternoon sun streaming through the window had illuminated an indigo speck in each iris. When Rosamund caught him staring so deeply at her, Kasper flushed hot and quickly looked away.

The dinner was a festive affair. Rosamund told a story about growing up with a cow named Bessie, which Bessie, the girl, found hilarious. Rosamund had taught herself to milk Bessie out of necessity because the desperate cow's utters were swollen. Streams of milk blasted her face several times before she figured out how to direct the teats toward the bucket. She also gathered eggs from the hens in the coop. She fed oats to Chess, her horse, and then rode him around the property for hours.

"Did you have friends, Tante Rosamund?" asked Duke.

Rosamund mulled the question before answering, "I'm more interested in your friends."

Kasper interjected. "Duke gets bullied a lot, but we're fixing that."

"Who is 'we'?" asked Rosamund.

"Herr Charles Atlas and I," Kasper answered.

Rosamund squeezed Duke's emaciated biceps and said encouragingly, "Ooh. Yes. I feel the bulging muscle."

"You do?" asked Kasper. "Because we've been at it four months and the only muscles that've grown are mine."

Duke looked down, embarrassed.

"I know a thing or two about muscles," said Rosamund. "See, Kasper, you have the showy kind of muscle. They look good on the beach, but the fibers are all stretched out, like a balloon that gets thinner and thinner the bigger it gets. Duke's muscles are dense and powerful."

"You're just trying to make the boy feel better."

"I'll prove it."

Rosamund surveyed the apartment for an object with sufficient mass. She tested an end table, a wingback chair, and the grandfather clock, until settling on the hat rack.

"This should work perfectly. Duke, Kasper, come here."

"That is your test?" Kasper asked dismissively. "The hat rack? I could lift ten hat racks."

Rosamund dropped her voice and spoke in a monotonous cadence. "Then this should be no trouble at all." She gestured for Kasper to stand before the hat rack. "Please."

"Why are you talking like that?"

"Are you going to criticize my voice or prove your physical prowess?"

Kasper gripped the hat rack.

"Have you limbered your muscles?"

"To lift this flimsy thing? No. For God's sake, stop talking like that."

"Like what?" she asked in a dead monotone.

Kasper felt like he was trapped in a downpour, only this rain was falling inside his mind, washing his will to Oblivion. He shook his head to clear it. "Never mind."

"A man of your age should be careful. One false move can throw off the entire musculoskeletal system. At the camp, there was a guard—a gargantuan—who crumpled like a wet matchbook after bending over to pick up a cigarette butt. You know why? He hadn't limbered up."

Kasper backed away from the hat rack and then swung his arms and touched his toes. "Fine. I'm limbering up. You happy?"

"Be sure to loosen your neck, especially. There was another fellow who popped a vertebra combing his hair. You could see the bulging bone under the skin."

Kasper looked disturbed. He rolled his neck a few times, clockwise and counter-clockwise.

"Here. Let me make sure your neck muscles are loose."

Rosamund rubbed the back of his neck. Initially pleasurable, the massage quickly grew invasive. Kasper envisioned her fingertips fusing with the nerve fibers running along his spinal cord and out to every muscle. He seemed to have lost control of his faculties. She'd molded him into a sentient marionette, utterly vulnerable and manipulable. He tried opening his mouth to speak, but he couldn't, or Rosamund wouldn't let him. After a brief panic, he turned sleepy and light. He thought he might float away.

"How's that, Kasper?"

Kasper felt such ennui, he could manage only a slurring sound, like a stroke victim.

"I didn't quite catch that," said Rosamund, relaxing her hand.

The moment she released her grip, Kasper felt alert and in control. He wiped the drool from the corner of his mouth and asked, "What did you do to me?"

"Just a little massage. How do you feel?"

"Good. No. Great."

"Relaxed?"

"Yes."

"Strong and powerful?"

"Yes."

"Then enough dilly-dallying," she said while gesturing to the hat rack. "Lift it... if you can."

Kasper gripped the rack but couldn't budge it. He re-gripped it, bent his knees, and made another attempt. Again, he couldn't move it. He wondered if Rosamund was standing on one of the feet or if she'd jammed a foot under the radiator. She hadn't. Kasper made one more attempt with the same result. He felt his muscles. They were big and tight but useless against this formidable hat rack. He plopped in his chair at the dinner table, defeated. Meanwhile, Mama Elsie regarded Rosamund with astonishment.

"Your turn, Duke. Give it a shot. Being so young, and having such thin, dense muscles, you shouldn't need to limber up. Go ahead. Put the rack back in the corner."

Duke looked at Rosamund skeptically.

"Come on, young man. We don't have all night. Mama Elsie has prepared an excellent strudel."

Duke faced the hat rack and gripped it. He looked over his shoulder at his visibly shaken father, this hulk of a man vanquished by a few sticks of wood. The boy closed his eyes, bent his knees, and lifted. The hat rack rose easily. He set it down in the corner.

Kasper was upset. "What is this sorcery, Rosamund?"

Rosamund had an accusatory expression. "Something I picked up from Klaus. As you know, he was very hands-on with me."

"Oh, well, then it was all a mind game."

"But where do you think true power comes from? Not rippling muscles. You remember that, Duke. You'll always be stronger than any bully because you have the stronger mind. Repeat it back to me. I have the stronger mind."

"I have the stronger mind."

"Good. Now, the strudel. You've earned an extra-large piece. What size piece should your father get, or should he get a piece at all? Should we give him a piece for his effort?"

Duke nodded.

"You're a good sport. Mama Elsie, strudel for everyone. Make your son's a tad smaller."

Kasper shot Rosamund a "what the hell?" look. She dropped her serious demeanor and smiled. He smiled back tentatively and then completely abandoned his frustration upon spotting the joy on Duke's face. Mama Elsie set a dessert plate before Kasper and handed him a fork. He then dug in and savored every last morsel of his smaller than average strudel slice.

After dinner, Rosamund and Bessie played with dolls in her bedroom. Duke asked to be excused so he could read the latest *Amazing Stories* issue. Kasper and Mama Elsie stayed at the table.

"She's quite the woman, isn't she?" Kasper remarked with pride.

"She's quite the something," Mama Elsie answered with trepidation.

"What's that mean?"

"Nothing."

"No, Mama. I know that tone. Tell me."

"Don't get me wrong. I like Rosamund. She's a strong woman, very beautiful. A good role model for Bessie. She clearly likes the children. And yet…"

"And yet what?"

"Something's off with her."

"What are you talking about?"

"You don't see it because you're smitten."

"That is outrageous. Rosamund is my associate, a valuable employee, that is all."

"Please. You're talking to your mother, not the Labor Office."

"So what if something's off with her? She was a prisoner for two years, for godsakes."

"I know."

"And you know what Klaus did to her," Kasper pressed.

"I know what she's told us."

"You think she's holding back?"

"I don't know. Maybe."

"She doesn't need to tell us anything about that time. It was traumatic. It's best she forgets it entirely."

"I don't disagree, but didn't you find her mind control a bit disconcerting?"

"It's boosted business significantly. You should've seen how she handled Frau Stein. Turned her into putty."

"She did that in only a few minutes. Klaus held Rosamund captive for two whole years. What do you think he turned her into?"

Kasper was at a loss for words.

Mama Elsie went on. "Plus, she's a Lux."

"So?"

"So, if she's one of those Luxes—the *nymph* Luxes—she may have bigger problems. It's the laurel in their blood. Tree and human genetics don't mix so well. Your papa said—"

"I know. I know. They're born touched in the head or with no legs or too few fingers or too many nipples."

"Right. They're not normal."

"Normal's boring."

"If the only surprise she has in store is a third nipple, I wouldn't say anything."

"You're getting yourself worked up for nothing, Mama. We don't even know Rosamund is a nymph."

"No, we don't."

"Which means she may be a typical human lunatic."

"That's reassuring."

"What would you have me do, Mama? Fire her? Throw her on the street?"

"Until you know who Rosamund really is, you need to be careful."

"I can protect myself."

"I was thinking of the children."

Kasper's head trembled. "Listen. I don't care if Rosamund sprouts leaves from her armpits or a tap root from her ass, you hear?" He banged his hand on the table. "Rosamund is the most wonderful, beautiful woman I've ever known!"

Mama Elsie recoiled. Her eyes darted to the copper vase, which she kept turned toward the wall to hide the dent. She stood, cleared the plates, and left for the kitchen.

"Sorry, Mama," said Kasper after the door shut behind her. *Okay*, he thought. *Maybe I am a tad bit smitten.*

In Bessie's room, Bessie sat Rosamund at the toy table. When Bessie spoke for the Gretchen doll, Rosamund interrupted with a voice of her own, playing right along, much to Bessie's delight.

"Hello, Gretchen," said Bessie. "Your voice sounds different."

"That's because I've been away for so long," said Rosamund. "I'm older."

"Where were you?"

"Don't you remember? Did you get my letters?"

"I got them. You were in Holland, on your uncle's farm."

"Why didn't you visit me?"

"I couldn't."

"Why not?"

"I'm a *Mischling*."

"What's that?"

"A quarter Jew."

"Quarter Jews can still visit Holland, can't they?"

"The mean boys took my passport and ripped it up. I wrote about it in the letter, remember?"

"I do. I'm so sorry. But we're together now."

"Promise you won't go away again."

"I promise."

Bessie hugged the Gretchen doll.

"Let's play dress-up now. I have my mother's old makeup."

Bessie opened the vanity's drawers and pulled out a rouge and several lipstick cylinders.

"Make me look like you, Tante Rosamund."

"But why? Your face is far more beautiful than mine. Come to the mirror and look."

Bessie sat on the chair in front of the vanity. Rosamund teased the girl's dark ringlets.

"See?"

"It's an ugly Jew face."

"Why would you say that?"

"That's what everybody says."

"Who's 'everybody'?"

"Heidi. Wolfgang. Otto."

"I think Heidi, Wolfgang, and Otto are ugly."

"No, Heidi is pretty, like you. Start with the lipstick."

"Which color? We have fruity plum, earthy brown, tulip orange, and orchid red."

"Red, like yours."

Bessie puckered her lips, and Rosamund carefully anointed them.

"There. Let's take a look."

Rosamund squatted next to Bessie to admire the girl's face. She then kissed her cheek. Bessie turned and kissed Rosamund's cheek and hugged her tightly.

"Promise you won't go away."

"I promise."

Kasper peeked into the room and caught Rosamund and Bessie giggling as Bessie puckered her lips in Rosamund's face. He was falling in love.

Bessie turned and puckered her lips in the mirror. "Look, Tante Rosamund. Look at how funny it looks on your own face."

Rosamund looked, apparently forgetting she wouldn't see anything but a void. Her eyes darted about the mirror, confused. Then her face crumpled in horror.

Rosamund stood and stepped backward. "No. Not you."

"Not who?" asked Bessie.

"I'm sorry. I have to go."

Rosamund raced toward the door, oblivious to Kasper's presence until she collided with his thick torso.

"What's wrong?" asked Kasper.

"My head... Take me home... Please."

Kasper sipped Bushmills while stitching together Leghorn straw braids. The work kept his hands busy, and the whiskey took the edge off Rosamund's post-dinner breakdown. She was moaning incomprehensibly in her sleep. After she screamed "Klaus" for the third time, Kasper grabbed the whiskey and a glass and headed upstairs.

Kasper flipped on the light. Rosamund was sitting up in bed. Her nightshirt was soaked, and sweat matted thick strands of hair against her forehead. He poured her three fingers' worth and handed her the glass, which she refused.

"If you don't mind then..." Kasper said sheepishly.

Rosamund nodded. He swigged down the booze and sat on the bed.

"That little trick with my neck. You did the same thing to Frau Stein and the others. That's what Klaus did to you?"

"Repeatedly... and other things, too."

"Like what?"

"I'd rather not talk about it."

"Klaus will keep haunting you, unless you get it out in the open."

"I know."

"So you agree you should talk about it?"

There was a pause as Kasper waited for Rosamund to say something.

"Do I need to pull rank, and order you, as my employee, to speak?"

"No."

"Then speak." Kasper set the glass on the nightstand and clasped his hands behind his head. "I've got all night."

She began haltingly, but then her words flowed in a torrent. Over the next hour, Rosamund recounted the unrelenting cold, the long marches to nowhere, the thin potato water passed off as stew, the lice. And, of course, the interrogations. Ironically, the only time she was warm and well-fed was during her private sessions with Klaus. A plate of meat and potatoes would arrive at 5:15. She would eat it with gusto, her empty stomach protesting against the influx of so much solid food.

Klaus would ask a few questions and grasp her neck in that overly familiar way. His touch was soft as silk, his fingertips like the probing tips of a spider's legs. She'd envision Klaus behind her, spinning his tar-black silk directly into her brain stem like hair-thin daggers. He didn't inflict pain. Just the opposite. He imparted pleasure so intense and overwhelming, she'd give herself over to him, ceding him dominion over body and mind. Then, he'd let go, and she'd have control over her faculties again... at least it seemed that way until another plate of meat and potatoes would arrive minutes later. But it wouldn't be minutes later, for the wall clock would read 1:15, as though it were lunchtime the next day. Or would she be dreaming about the previous day's lunch? She couldn't be sure because Klaus's razor-sharp web trapped time and slashed it to bits. Yet, time had to be passing, because that blank spot on her face would be a little bigger, until the final day of her incarceration, when her face was wiped clean because Klaus had completed his psychosomatic swindle.

Before Klaus released Rosamund from the camp, he gave her fresh clothes, a book, and a radio. The radio, now sitting on Rosamund's dresser, was smaller than the popular Volksempfänger ("People's Receiver"), the cheap Bakelite box the Nazis had been promoting to the masses. According to Rosamund, its range wasn't much better than two paper cups connected with string. It pulled in only one station, Radio Schwarz Boden. The book was *Face of the Fatherland* by Friederich von Tannenberg, Retired.

Kasper lightly wrapped the book with his knuckles. "At least the radio has some practical use, but why hold on to von Tannenberg's missive?"

"*Face of the Fatherland* foretold of Klaus, named him as the 'Führer's prophet' years before he stole a single face."

"So?"

"So, the general may have known Klaus, conspired with him, created him, for all we know. If his book explains how Klaus stole my face, then maybe there's a clue about how to get it back."

"And is there?"

"If there is, I sure can't find it." Rosamund glanced at the floor. "Frankly, I can't bring myself to read the damn thing again."

"Then don't. It's not good for you."

"Sometimes when I think about Klaus, I see *myself* in the interrogation chair. Like I'm looking at myself through Klaus's eyes. It's crazy."

"It's basic psychology. Identifying with your aggressor gives you a sense of control. But you're free now. Klaus hasn't stolen a face in a year. He probably retired, like the general."

Rosamund's face reddened.

"*Retired*? Jesus Christ, Kasper. Psychopathic face-stealers don't just hang up the veil. You think Klaus is living it up in an Alpine chalet, sporting lederhosen and a Tyrolean hat? Maybe taking lessons on the alpenhorn?"

"Well, no, I don't—"

"Do you see him sitting around a hearth, blanket over his lap, eating fondue? Maybe reminiscing with his face-stealing brethren about the good old days—like a boastful fisherman, spinning tall tales about the most faces snagged in a single day or lamenting 'the one that got away'? Is that what you envision, based on your expertise about sadistic interrogators?"

"No. No, I don't."

"You're damn right you don't. Men who wear veils and steal faces don't go quietly into the night. They change tactics. They scheme. They lie low until it's time to smash everything to bits."

"All right. Calm down. I take your point. But he could be dead. Ever consider that? High-ranking Nazis don't exactly have job security. He might've crossed someone, maybe Hitler himself. You remember what happened to Röhm?"

"Even if Klaus is dead, a piece of him lives inside his victims. Inside me."

"That's impossible."

"Then explain why I saw him staring back at me from Bessie's mirror. A jagged circle for a mouth. Five fangs poking at odd angles. Exposed bone around his eye sockets. A wrinkled flap of skin for a nose. And you know what else? He spoke to me. He called me his soldier. He's planned something big, something awful for Schwarz Boden."

"You need to keep reminding yourself of the facts. Klaus hasn't kidnapped anyone in years. He's only a face on a poster. You're not his soldier. He doesn't control you."

"How do you know?"

"Because Isana was a victim. He took her face too. But she filled that blank with Duke's face. *She* decided what to see in the mirror, not Klaus."

"I wish I had her strength. He's coming for me, and I don't think I'll get away."

Kasper wondered how many times a Lux woman had uttered those words over the past sixteen centuries. The question was, was it Klaus whom Rosamund feared or Apollo? Was she manifesting the residual terror that former captives suffer, or was she demonstrating a pathology rooted in an Olympian bloodline and triggered by a marauding god? Kasper couldn't stand it any longer. He had to know the answer, even if the question ultimately made him look like a crackpot.

"Rosamund, I have to ask something. If it sounds bizarre to you, then don't answer. Forget I even mentioned it. Dismiss it as the ramblings of a brain fogged with worry and whiskey."

"What kind of question?"

"A ridiculous question. An impossible question. The second I ask, you'll either immediately know the answer or realize your employer is a sad, crazy man."

Rosamund blushed. "For God's sake, Kasper. You sound like you're proposing marriage."

Kasper blushed, and his eyes expanded into two wide circles. "What? No. That wasn't... I mean, not that I wouldn't... We haven't known each other very... But suppose I were... hypothetically... for the sake of argument... would you see that as an impossible, ridiculous question? Forget it. Don't answer that. Never mind. I should get home to the children."

But Rosamund wouldn't let him leave. "Hold on." She took his hand. "I'm sorry for throwing you off track. Obviously, this is weighing on you. Just spit it out."

Kasper sighed and then steeled himself. "Have you ever heard of a water nymph? Daphne?"

"The one who turned into a laurel tree to escape Apollo. Yes, I know the story."

"Is that all it is to you? A story?"

"What do you mean?"

"I mean, are you...?"

"Am I what?"

"Related to Daphne in some way?"

Rosamund gave Kasper a long, blank stare. She rose from the bed and strode to the opposite nightstand. She poured a splash of Bushmills into the empty glass. She set the bottle down, evidently changed her mind, and then added another splash. She picked up the glass, contemplated its golden contents in the overhead incandescent light, and then swallowed the liquid in one gigantic gulp. She winced and set the glass down. She returned to her side of the bed and lay back down. She still hadn't said anything. Kasper didn't know how to interpret her reaction. She hadn't run screaming, nor had she brained him with the whiskey bottle. It could've been much worse.

"You were right," Rosamund said. "It is a ridiculous question, an impossible question."

Kasper's heart sunk. "Like I said. Too much booze. I'll go."

He stood and made for the door.

"My mother called me her little nymph."

Kasper stopped with his hand on the doorknob.

"She said we have nymph blood in our veins, which makes us strong and fast. But it's also a bad thing because Apollo might surface in a strange man and come after us... in a sexual way. She promised to train me in self-defense and survival tactics when I got older. But after she died, her wild stories didn't matter anymore."

"They matter to me."

"Why?"

"Three hundred years ago, my family name was Petasos."

Rosamund got off the bed and went to Kasper.

"Your ancestor stole the wishing hat from Hermes?"

"Yes."

"Do you have it?"

"The hat? Yes."

"So it's real? It works?"

"Absolutely."

"Have you used it?"

"Not in a long while. Not since I rescued Isana from Klaus."

"Then Klaus knows about the hat."

"We vanished before he walked in."

"Are you sure?"

"It all happened so fast, but yes."

"So you're not absolutely sure. Klaus might have seen you."

"He didn't."

"He could have."

"Then why didn't he come after Isana or me afterward?"

"I don't know."

"I'll tell you why. Because he doesn't have a clue about the hat."

"I hope you're right. In any case, you must be very careful. Should the hat fall into the Nazis' hands—"

"It's locked in the wall safe."

"Good."

"Do you think Apollo surfaced in Klaus to get to you?"

"Klaus didn't show the signs of divine possession. No excessive perspiration, at least from what little of his forehead I could see. He was always cool as a cucumber, always speaking in the same flat tone. Frigid and detached. He never called me a nymph, never called himself Apollo."

"You said Klaus hypnotized you, bent you to his will. Maybe you just don't remember. Maybe Apollo did surface in him, and… forgive me for suggesting this… maybe he raped you in that camp."

"It didn't happen."

"But you can't be sure."

"He's not Apollo. He's a twisted, evil man, but he didn't rape me."

"All right. Good. Well, not 'good.' It's still horrible. I meant only—"

"I know what you meant. At least Klaus is not Apollo. Not much of a consolation."

"But it is. It means Klaus is just a man. He can't pop in and out of mortal vessels. He has to enter through a door or climb through a window like any other flesh and blood person. And if he does, I'll whisk you away instantly."

Rosamund brightened. "Because you have the wishing hat."

"Precisely."

"We can leave Germany whenever we want."

"And there's not a thing Klaus can do about it."

"What if Klaus takes me when you're not around?"

"Then I will find you and wish you away. He's utterly powerless against the hat."

"He is, isn't he?"

"Now, do you feel better?"

Rosamund held Kasper's face and kissed his nose. "I do."

Kasper's cheeks got hot again, as though he'd just stepped into the summer sun. He tried to subtly extricate his face, but Rosamund didn't take the cue to release him.

"Please don't mention the wishing hat to the children. It's a long story, but, as far as Duke knows, I destroyed the hat, and Bessie is too young, and terrible at keeping secrets."

"As you wish."

Kasper shifted his weight to his heels, but Rosamund held fast to his face. She leaned in and kissed him hard. His body quaked with exhilaration.

"What was that for?" he asked in a croaky voice.

"For being the best boss in the world."

Rosamund kissed him again. His breathing quickened. He was losing control. If he didn't leave that moment, he'd rip off her nightgown. But the threat of bodice-ripping abated when Rosamund unfastened her cotton gown and it fell to the floor.

"Something's fallen," Kasper observed innocently, still kissing Rosamund's lips.

She unfastened Kasper's belt buckle and reached down the front of his trousers. It had been so many years since Kasper had felt a woman's touch there.

"Something's risen," she retorted.

Kasper undid the clasp on his pants, and Rosamund slid them to the floor. She then lay on the bed and pulled Kasper's thick body on top of her. As the bedsprings creaked and groaned, a breeze kicked up on Mauer Street. It peeled one of the ubiquitous Klaus fliers from a kiosk and plastered it against Rosamund's window. The veiled interrogator's dead eyes gazed down at the two lovers, until the violent wind ebbed, causing the flier to see-saw away. A storm was coming.

CHAPTER TWELVE

1936

Good afternoon, girls. It's your friend, Heidi Geissmütter. I want to share the results of a little experiment I've been conducting for the past three weeks. Did you know orchids grow on every continent except Antarctica? I prefer the variety grown right here in the Fatherland. Orchids require special care. You mustn't overwater them, nor give them direct sunlight. They flourish only in a narrow window of temperatures.

I've read a lot about orchids, but I've never read a thing about what type of music these delicate beauties need. You heard me right. Music. When I'm at home, working in the kitchen or cleaning the house, I listen to Wagner or Bach or Beethoven. You can't go wrong with the great German composers. They always put an extra spring in my step. I feel more alive because they remind me of my powerful German roots.

I had a thought. If German music is good for me, how about for my orchids? Would they grow stronger and straighter, would they bloom bigger and brighter, with German music, compared to foreign music? I did a test. I took two young orchids of the same variety and placed them side by side. I gave them the same amount of sunlight, water, and fertilizer. The only difference was the music I played for eleven minutes each evening. Plant A listened to Wagner, Brahms, and Schumann, while I stored Plant B out of earshot… or leafshot, I suppose. Then, I moved Plant B back, and put Plant A in storage. Good thing for Plant A, too, because Plant B had to listen to the most profane music known to mankind—jazz, that abomination spawned by niggers like Jelly Roll Morton and Louis Armstrong and popularized by kikes like Benny Goodman and Artie Shaw. Well, twenty-one days later, the results of my experiment were in. Plant A, which had listened to some of the greatest German music ever produced, had thick green leaves and rich red flowers. Plant B was not so fortunate. Its leaves were pale, wrinkled, and drooping, its flowers barely half the size of Plant A's.

So you see, girls, if jazz for a mere eleven minutes a day can stunt an orchid's growth, imagine what it does to the German soul? How much jazz do you listen to each day? I'm not judging you. You probably had no idea. All I'm saying is you'd never purposefully poison your plants. Now that you know the danger, shouldn't you be taking better care of your soul?

The cigarette smoke preceded Frau Magda's flamboyant entrance into the hat shop. She sashayed through the door, shaded by an oversized blue slouch hat wrapped with a brilliant red silk bow. Her blue gabardine suit coat was trimmed with piping of the same red silk. Her deeply-pancaked skin set off her white-blonde hair and icy blue eyes. Despite being the Minister of Propaganda's wife, Frau Magda Goebbels was the antithesis of the scrubbed-cheeked, tight-braided "Gretchen" girl idealized by the Nazis. Her prune-faced husband, Joseph, followed her into the shop.

Kasper lamented he hadn't taken Dieter's ADEFA inspection more seriously. Though Rosamund had rewritten the display cards Dieter had defaced with the "correct" Germanized color names, she hadn't yet changed "chic" to "schick" on the window's banner. Kasper had used double-sided carpet tape to mount the banner, and Rosamund would need to devote an entire day to scraping it off. Worse, Bennie Goodman's version of *Carry Me Back to Old Virginny* was streaming from the back room. Still, why would someone of Goebbels's stature be wasting his time enforcing the ADEFA code? Was the master of propaganda trying to set an example? Perhaps Goebbels intended to deliver a very harsh, very public punishment against Kasper's innocuous violations to deter far more serious attacks on public order.

Goebbels stepped in front of Frau Magda and began the interrogation.

"Your sign says you sell the chic permanent wave hats, does it not?"

Kasper swallowed hard. "It does, Herr Reich Minister."

"My sources tell me you originated this idea?"

"Yes, Mein Herr."

"There has never been such a hat in the Fatherland."

"Not that I know of."

"You are pure German, yet your children are Mischlinge. Did they have a hand in these hats?"

Kasper turned his back to the stack of bonnets. Duke had cut numerous circular silk swatches to line the crowns, and Bessie had sewn them in place. To spare himself the aggravation, Kasper had excused Duke from the stitching.

"No, Mein Herr. I made them all myself."

"This is good. It would be a shame to soil such fine work with Jewish fingers. No offense."

"None taken, Mein Herr."

Goebbels studied Kasper's face, perhaps searching for weakness or deception. With overwhelming force at his command, Goebbels could have had Kasper arrested and tossed in a camp, even though he was a "pure German" with full citizenship rights. By the time any legal wrongs were righted, Kasper would be dead and his children shipped to an orphanage.

Kasper stayed strong, knowing he had absolute dominion over the most important thing—how he responded at that moment. Goebbels was a bully, fundamentally weak at his core. Kasper turned his face, brandishing the scar shaped like the Runic mark of Thor. It never failed to instill respect and fear in those who invested such shapes with significance. Goebbels was just such a man. He had no more questions.

Frau Magda interjected. "Enough, Joseph. I'm here for a hat, that's all. Mine must be custom made of royal blue silk and brocaded with golden thread."

Goebbels reacted angrily. "Such ostentatiousness! It is not becoming of the modern German woman. You're as bad as Goring."

"Would you have me braid my hair and wear burlap dresses?"

"Yes, for the Fatherland."

"The Fatherland doesn't attend state dinners or the opera, or waltz around the dance floor. So, until you make me a country, I'm going to dress like a woman." Frau Magda turned back to Kasper. "How long will it take?"

"The material may be difficult to obtain in the current state... Two weeks?"

Frau Magda nodded and then turned abruptly toward the door. The tip of her hat's red ribbon caught her husband's nose. He flinched, causing his peaked military cap to tip to a jaunty angle. Goebbels adjusted his hat and turned to Kasper.

"This music... it's jazz, is it not?"

Shit.

"It is."

Goebbels grunted. After he listened to a few bars, a smile struggled to bloom on his dour asshole of a face.

"The Golden Seven does Goodman's swing better than the Jew himself, don't you think?"

"Oh, most definitely, Mein Herr.

"Let's go, Joseph! Schnell!" ordered Frau Magda through the plate glass.

Goodman's orchestra punctuated the Nazi's ignominious exit with a trumpet blast and a rim shot.

After locking the shop and turning left, Kasper stubbed his toe on a displaced brick. That intrepid tree root was resurfacing through the sidewalk. He ran a thumb over the scuff in the leather, irritated he'd now have to spend the ten minutes before dinner polishing out the abrasion instead of retreating to his study with the latest issue of *Metronome* magazine.

Everything came at a cost, Kasper supposed, including love, and Rosamund's inevitable fixation on his chafed wingtip—she didn't limit her fastidiousness to the hat shop—wouldn't be worth the enjoyment he'd derive from the article about Bennie Goodman or the advertisement for the double neck electric Hawaiian guitar. Perhaps he could avoid Rosamund's scrutiny by surreptitiously slipping on other shoes when he got home and then stop for a shoeshine in the morning (during which he could read another article) before opening the shop. But what shoes would those be? He owned only two other pairs: the dilapidated Chuck Taylor's from his university days and the hideous purple house slippers from Kimball's that Bessie had given him for his birthday.

Maybe he'd go shoeless this evening. Just socks. "My feet are so tired and hot," he might announce. No, that wouldn't work either. Kasper always wore his wingtips in the apartment. Any deviation from habit surely would arouse Rosamund's suspicion, spurring an interrogation about his "aberrant footwear." Was his blood pressure elevated? Was he suffering from gout? Kasper would ask why a man couldn't simply have tired, hot feet without an underlying medical condition, but then Rosamund would pivot to deficiencies in his diet (too little red meat, too much red wine) and his activity level (too sedentary). She'd retreat to the study and type up a regimen for his tired, hot feet.

"You agree you must begin at once, Kasper, do you not?" she'd then ask. "Of course you do," she'd immediately answer for him. The regimen, which Rosamund would enforce through a confounding combination of cold stares and sexual enticements, would consume Kasper's every waking moment plus intrude on moments he'd already rationed for sleep and bathroom activities, while his magazine stash grew taller, more precarious, and dustier.

Fine. He'd polish the damn shoe the instant he got home but then reward himself with the Parisian magazine, *Sex Appeal*, he'd had his eye on. It didn't matter whether he'd get the chance to crack its cover. The hope, slim as it was, would sustain him.

As he did most Fridays, Kasper took a detour before heading home. He crossed Mauer Street and entered Schwarz Boden Platz. He couldn't access the memorial, however, because a stonemason was chiseling names from the limestone. According to the mason, Goebbels had issued a decree forbidding Jewish soldiers to be named among the dead in World War memorials. Kasper's timing had been impeccable because the next name on the mason's list was Hermann Mützenmacher.

Kasper insisted the mason was mistaken because Hermann had had only one Jewish grandparent. The mason examined his paperwork, which identified Hermann's grandparents. Kasper's paternal grandmother, Edda, had been a full-blood German, and his paternal grandfather a Jew. Kasper had known about that, but one Jewish grandparent didn't make Hermann a Jew. The mason then pointed to Hermann's maternal grandparents, Manfred and Gerda Schlein, whom the papers identified as Jews. Kasper argued that was impossible, given the Schleins' daughter, Sara, had been a Protestant. The mason nodded knowingly and then explained that more than half the other soldiers whose names he'd chiseled away had had a Jewish relation or two who'd converted to Protestantism or Catholicism. It didn't matter that Hermann had never celebrated a Jewish holiday, drunken wine, broken bread on the Sabbath, or touched a Torah. Goebbels didn't care about conversions. He cared about blood.

The mason jammed his chisel into the "H," struck it with his hammer, and sent a limestone shard ricocheting through the void at the sculpture's center. The Fatherland no longer had use for Hermann Mützenmacher. He wasn't even worth being remembered. And that meant Kasper was no longer a true German either. The Reich had reclassified him to a Mischling First Class, which meant Duke and Bessie were now full-blood Jews.

Duke greeted his father at the door, wearing a Jewish skullcap. Kasper was flabbergasted. How could the Nazis have transformed his son into a full-blood Jew so quickly? Had a "Jew Fairy" descended on Duke right after the mason blasted the final letters of the Mützenmacher name from the memorial? Duke placed a spare skullcap on Kasper's head and draped a fringed prayer shawl over his shoulders. Klezmer music and pungent incense permeated the apartment.

Rosamund remarked on Kasper's scuffed shoe and announced it must be buffed and polished right away to prevent the damage from becoming permanent. Duke raised a hand and declared that the shoe repair must wait until Saturday evening, as Jewish law forbade work on the Sabbath. Duke then escorted his befuddled father to the dining room table, where tall white candles illuminated a deformed challah bread and a carafe of red wine. Duke explained that this night was special because it was both the Sabbath and Rosh Chodesh, the first day of the month on the Hebrew calendar. The trombone-heavy Klezmer music and incense honored the Biblical command to sound trumpets and make burnt offerings to the crescent moon.

Kasper looked to Rosamund and Mama Elsie for clarification. They shrugged. Duke then revealed he'd been studying at a yeshiva for the past two months.

"... I made the challah myself," he said with pride.

"What's this all about?"

"I'm a Jew."

"How did you find out so quickly?"

"I've known for a while. Rabbi Kimball says Mama was a Jew, so that makes me a Jew under Jewish law."

"Rabbi Kimball? As in Kimball's toy shop? He's a Jew?"

"Yes. He has a separate room where some of us boys study after school."

"You study Jewish toys?"

"The Torah. For our Bar Mitzvahs."

"Bar Mitz—Jesus Christ!"

Kasper ripped the skullcaps off his and Duke's heads.

"Calm down, Kasper," said Mama Elsie. "He's simply exploring his heritage."

"I'll teach him about heritage. His mother was more a Communist than a Jew." He turned to Duke. "Why don't you read *Das Kapital*? Or go back to the moon stuff. Build a rocket. I'll even help. But damn it, don't parade around Berlin with a Torah."

"I'm not parading, Pops. I'm only spending a few hours in the toy shop with my Jewish friends. I feel safe there."

"But not here?"

"No, that's not—"

"Don't you think I can protect you?"

"You're not around all the time. And let's face it. I'm no Charles Atlas. I never will be. Maybe God can make me a little stronger."

"A fantasy won't make you stronger."

"God is real."

"How do you know?"

"The same way you know Hermes is real."

"Hermes is as far from the Almighty God as that hat rack is from Duke Ellington."

"What's the harm of letting Duke study?" asked Mama Elsie.

"Do you know why I was late? I stopped at Papa's memorial to touch his name, only someone was chiseling it away. He's a blank now. An empty space. A nothing, because it turns out his Protestant mother was born a Jew."

"No." Mama Elsie left the stove and sank into a chair. "God damn those Nazis."

"Is that what you want, Duke?" asked Kasper. "To be erased like your grandfather?"

"Jews have been around for three thousand years. They haven't been erased."

"You're right. They've been beaten and murdered but not erased. More like smudged. But smudges get wiped away, too. Look at their history. Egypt. Russia. Germany is next, unless they start behaving like Germans."

"The Jews' safety doesn't have anything to do with their behavior," said Rosamund. "It's everyone else who are the problem."

"The German people are fundamentally good," Kasper protested. "The Jewish question will get sorted."

"The 'Jewish question'?" Rosamund repeated back. "How *Mein Kampf*-ish of you."

"You know what I meant."

"Do I? Do you? Are any of us in his right mind? Think how many German women Klaus kidnapped over the years. Hundreds. Thousands."

"Klaus hasn't stolen a face in two years. He's out of that business. He's a relic, if not dead."

"He's very much alive, at least his legacy is. The few lucky ones like me have headaches and can't see their faces in the mirror. I'd bet all the others see the Führer."

"All right. All right," Kasper interjected. "Let's get off this topic. Where's Bessie?"

"Lying down in her room," said Mama Elsie. "She has a tummy ache."

"Since when?"

"This afternoon."

"I should go see her."

Mama Elsie shot to her feet. "No!"

Kasper was alarmed by his mother's dramatic reaction.

"No," Mama Elsie repeated more calmly. "She really needs to rest. You shouldn't disturb her."

"I'm just going to peek in."

"No!" Mama Elsie shouted again.

"What is it with you, Mama?"

"I... I'm just thinking of the child. Even the slightest crack of light could make her headache worse."

"You said it was a stomachache."

"Yes. Both. An ache in her stomach *and* her head."

"This sounds serious. I'm going in."

Mama Elsie stood between Kasper and Bessie's bedroom.

"Mama, get out of my way."

"Listen to me, Kasper. I don't want you overreacting when you see Bessie."

"Why would I overreact? You're scaring me."

"The damage is purely cosmetic. It'll grow back."

"What'll grow back?"

Bessie's bedroom door flung open. She stepped out in a red, French Renaissance-style wig. Her face was beaming.

"What do you think of my new hair, Pops?"

Kasper's trachea constricted. He produced an unintelligible squeak, cleared his throat, and asked, "What... what happened to your old hair?"

"I like this hair better."

"Take off the wig."

Bessie froze. After a pause, she said, "But I like this hair."

Kasper turned his scarred cheek toward Bessie. She reluctantly removed the wig, revealing a shorn head. The haircut was uneven and close to her scalp, as though she'd stumbled head-first into a combine harvester.

Kasper moaned.

"Take a deep breath, Kasper," advised Mama Elsie. "Promise you won't scold her."

Kasper inhaled deeply and held his breath, temporarily forgetting the second step in the respiration process.

"You should breathe out now."

He did.

"Are you calmer?"

Kasper nodded.

"And you're not going to yell at Bessie?"

He shook his head.

"Good."

Instead, Kasper turned his fury onto his son. "What the hell have you done?"

"Nothing, Pops. Honest."

"You think shaving your sister's head is nothing?"

"But I didn't do it. Frau Kimball wears a big red wig because she's an observant Jew. She told Bessie all the Jewish women get wigs when they shave their heads. Bessie cut her own hair off, so she could get one. I would've stopped her, but I didn't know until too late. Tell him, Bessie."

Kasper looked at Bessie searchingly, teetering on the precipice of incurable disappointment. Bessie's terrified eyes darted from her father to her brother, until her face crumpled.

"Duke... held me down... and cut and cut... He was too strong..."

"She's lying, Pops!"

"Shut up, Duke. Just shut up."

Mama Elsie interjected, "Kasper, I believe Duke. Bessie did this to herself."

"Even if he is telling the truth, he shouldn't have dragged her to that synagogue disguised as a toy store. And you, Mama. How could you let this happen? You have one responsibility these days."

"Don't turn this on me. I can't watch them every second of the day."

"Obviously not."

"You're just as pig-headed as your father."

Kasper went to the study and slammed the door behind him. The gramophone needle scratched across the Klezmer record. A moment later, the vinyl disk shattered against the wall. Kasper burst back through the office door, grabbed his coat, and announced he was heading early to Mooch's Minions.

The Sabbath celebration was over.

"Why, Bessie? Why would you lie?" Duke demanded.

Bessie remained silent.

"Next time, you're dead. I'll kill you! I mean it!"

Mama Elsie ushered Duke to his bedroom, leaving Bessie and Rosamund alone.

Rosamund lit a cigarette, took a long drag and blew a jet of smoke from the side of her mouth. "I'll say this, kid. That's one helluva wig."

———⚬┼⚬─◇─⬬─◇─⚬┼⚬———

Girls, we've known each other a while now. One year, eleven months, and twenty-one days, to be precise. I consider you all friends. I'd hope you consider me the same. Unfortunately, at least one person out there, perhaps more, considers me an enemy. Yesterday, I received a most hateful piece of mail. The letter called me an idiot and a racist. It said I stoke hatred against non-Aryans. The letter concluded with this statement: "You'd better watch your words. Someday, you may be silenced." Well, I don't know about you, girls, but I take that as a threat. It's a coward's threat, too, because the letter is unsigned. Whoever you are, at least have the courage to acknowledge your threat. Better yet, make it to my face. Look me straight in the eye.

Now, girls, I don't want you worrying about me. I'll be fine. True, I don't know the coward's identity, but I have my suspicions. The handwriting is curious. The letters are inconsistently drawn, as though German is not his native tongue. And the cursive flows awkwardly, as though he wrote in an unfamiliar direction—left to right, instead of right to left. That's right. The letter appears to have been written by a Jewish hand.

This Jewish coward doesn't speak for all Jews in Schwarz Boden. At least, I hope he doesn't. I am not afraid because I know all the true citizens of Schwarz Boden stand with me. Any of you would put yourself between me and that Jewish coward's knife, and I'd do the same for you. Buck up, fellow citizens. The coward who writes in a Jewish hand has made a serious miscalculation. He's only deepened our resolve, should the day come when we have to act—

Kasper switched off Rosamund's radio.

"Turn it back on!" Rosamund yelled from the bed.

"That woman is hateful."

"Have you noticed how she always mentions the numbers eleven and twenty-one in her broadcasts?"

"I try not to listen."

"She does. Every single time."

"I doubt that."

"You think I'm lying?"

"No. It's just that—well, so what if she mentions eleven and twenty-one? It doesn't mean anything. It's a coincidence."

"There are no coincidences with Klaus. He's gotten to Heidi Geissmütter. She's a soldier, too."

"That's crazy."

"But it all fits. That's why he gave radios to his victims. So he can activate his soldiers through the airwaves."

"*Activate his...?* Jesus, Rosamund. Listen to yourself."

"We should wish ourselves out of Germany while we still have Hermes' hat."

"What do you mean while we still have it? No one's going to take it."

"I meant while we're all still together and alive."

"We're safe, Rosamund."

"Some of us won't survive. Maybe all of us."

"I've had enough of this Klaus shit!"

Kasper slammed his fist on the radio, shattering the Bakelite and strewing parts across the floor.

"What the hell, Kasper?"

"Now there's no way Klaus can activate you. Happy?"

"No."

"Get dressed. We're going to the Asylum."

Rosamund clenched her fists, seemingly ready to fight Kasper. Instead, she brushed past him and slugged the full-length mirror. The punch sliced the reflection of her lips into two scalene triangles and opened a gash across her flesh-and-blood knuckles.

CHAPTER THIRTEEN

1937

Duke was feverishly studying his Torah portion while trying to figure out what it meant to be Jewish. The so-called "special covenants" confused him. God first had promised Abraham to make the Jews a "great nation" in exchange for circumcision, and later promised Moses to make the Israelites the "most treasured people" on the condition they observe the Ten Commandments. To Duke, God had duped Moses by promising something he'd already promised Abraham. What the heck was the difference between a "great nation" and the "most treasured people"? Nothing. Yet, after Moses, the Jews suddenly were bound to a whole set of laws. Perhaps after forty days on Mt. Sinai without food, water, or sleep, Moses had caved.

Duke's first thought was that his father would never enter such a bad deal; Kasper was too shrewd a businessman. His second thought was, "Jesus Christ! They're gonna slice a hunk of my skin from *where* exactly?"

Duke read up on the procedure, the bris, and then immediately regretted his curiosity. If done according to tradition, an expert circumciser called a mohel would rub his penis to make it erect. He'd then peel the foreskin over the head, gather a flap between pincers, and tear away the flesh. Next, the mohel would alternate between sucking on Duke's wound and drinking mouthfuls of wine until the bleeding stopped.

Duke swooned. He wanted to run, but he was too weak to rise from his seat. He pinched his thighs to make sure his legs weren't paralyzed. He'd had no idea a bris involved so much intimate contact—an abbreviated hand job, followed by a sadistic slice of the knife, and concluded with an act of fellatio, which the law would deem pedophilia were it not shrouded in ceremony. There was no way he could fulfill the covenant. Even if he wanted to, if his father were to find out, he'd murder the mohel and Rabbi Kimball and then disown him.

Rabbi Kimball tried to reassure Duke, explaining that the bris had evolved over the centuries. Because Duke wasn't an infant, the mohel would fit a metal plate with a round opening over Duke's flaccid penis, gather a little foreskin, and rapidly slide a sharp knife along the plate. It wouldn't be painless, but it would be quick. And, the mohel wouldn't place his mouth on Duke's private area. He'd suction the excess blood through a glass straw.

So much for reassurance.

Duke spent restless nights contemplating the pain before descending into nightmares. In one dream, Rabbi Kimball was a robot, and Duke lay on a gurney. The rabbi's skullcap and overcoat were white, like a doctor's hospital scrubs. An elderly mohel stood in a cage, sporting a full white beard and a broad-brimmed black hat, typical of the Orthodox Jew. He held a carving knife in one hand and a lipstick container in the other. Below the waist, he wore panties and heels at the end of shapely, slender dancer's legs. Rabbi Kimball pulled a drape over the mohel's cage and then signaled to four wind-up Nazi soldiers, also in white scrubs, to wheel over Duke's gurney. Rabbi Kimball picked up a scalpel and a metal plate from a tray and examined the shiny instruments in the light. He didn't like what he saw, so he set them down and beckoned for something else. A giant tortoise-man entered the operating theater with a clumsy wooden replica of a guillotine. The rabbi slid Duke into the contraption and said, "Welcome to the tribe," before releasing the guillotine blade and severing his body's lower half.

That was one of the milder nightmares.

Aside from the short-term trauma, Duke feared the finished product—the fully healed, circumcised penis—would look odd. The sketch in a medical text he'd found in the library depicted the dorsal side of the penis head with two carved swags, like the banners hung from railings during official parades, or crescent moons balanced on their sides. Did he really want a parade/moon penis for the rest of his life?

Duke considered asking the rabbi if he could skip the bris. After all, one of the most important Jews ever—Moses—never got clipped. On the downside, God didn't let Moses enter the Holy Land. Evidently, customs agents had been checking foreskin at the border. Hemophiliacs also could avoid the procedure, but Duke figured God would know if he were to lie about a genetic blood condition. And the Biblical God was wrathful. He'd concoct a curse for Duke far worse than being turned away at the Holy Land's border—like his penis shriveling up during his Torah portion.

It would've been so much easier had Duke been born female. Jewish women were physically incapable of entering into Abraham's covenant. They belonged to the Jewish tribe as non-voting members because the powers-that-be had denied the franchise to the "non-membered."

Duke wondered what his deceased mother would've wanted him to do. As he often did, he pictured Isana on the moon's dark side, wearing an iridescent flapper dress and seated on a pearl-encrusted throne, sentient turtle people and man-sized worms at her feet. But he had no way to get to the moon and ask her, if that was where she even resided in death. She must not have thought circumcision important; otherwise, she would've gotten Duke clipped as an infant. But perhaps this omission had been more than indifference to Jewish tradition. Perhaps she'd vehemently opposed the practice. Kasper might've known the answer, but Duke refused to draw his father into a lengthy discussion about mutilated genitalia. Kasper had turned apoplectic when Duke had tried to alter his nose with that ridiculous mail-order harness. Penile disfigurement would've caused his head to explode.

Duke felt like a coward. Abraham, the proud owner of the very first penis to roll off the circumcision assembly line, was a hundred years old at the time of his procedure. It rejuvenated him, imbuing him a teenager's sexual vitality. He went on to father many more children and picked up a substantially younger wife in the process. But Duke was no Abraham. He didn't have a special relationship with God. He had nothing in writing saying that circumcision would make him a great lover, and with God, you had to have it in writing, because He was a sly One. So what was the point?

Maybe circumcision was a test, a way to prove he could not only face the pain but endure it of his own free will, unlike infant Jews, who had no choice or awareness in the matter. Babies weren't brave. They were clueless sacks of helplessness. That, Duke realized, was why having the flesh sliced off his penis mattered. The procedure would excise his cowardice and make him a man.

It was settled. He'd go through with it. He sighed, closed his eyes, and enjoyed his first dreamless slumber in weeks. He awoke refreshed and famished. At breakfast, he unconsciously opted for the strudel over the sliced Schnitzengruben.

Duke's resolve about the circumcision emboldened him at school. He walked more confidently. He looked his tormenters in the eye. When they tore up his homework, he shrugged. When they verbally abused him, he smiled. When they threw him against the wall or punched him in the kidneys, he laughed. The abuse was like a tickle compared to circumcision. Duke's benign reactions unsettled his enemies. They deemed him a freak. They didn't want to touch him or even breathe the same air, lest they degenerate too. Within a week, the bullying had stopped completely. The impending bris had liberated him.

Kasper noticed Duke was happier, more self-assured. He would've preferred his son place his faith in Charles Atlas, a man who promised stronger muscles in seven days, not an intangible deity that supposedly created the entire world in the same amount of time. But Kasper had lost that argument, and he was savvy enough to know that forcing his son to abandon Judaism would only make it more desirable. He'd permit Duke to study Torah, but on condition he be discreet, given the growing anti-Semitic climate, and continue to work at least an hour a day in the hat shop.

Even Kasper was taking precautions because jazzists weren't safe either. Goebbels was pressuring retailers not to sell records by non-Aryan artists, and pending legislation eventually would outlaw the practice for good. Since people of color usually produced the best jazz, this policy was a death sentence for Kasper's primary source of artistic pleasure. Plainclothes policemen took notes outside his favorite record store, Alberti's on Rankenstrasse, peering in bags and jotting down customers' names and their purchases. It got so bad that Alberti's began stickering the records by *verboten* foreigners with labels of German artists. As extra precautions, Kasper picked up records on different days of the week, wore different hats, and varied his routes to and from the store.

Kasper implemented similar "cloak and dagger" precautions for his Friday night get-togethers with Mooch's Minions. He trusted his nine fellow Minions implicitly, but all it would take was a nosy neighbor or an ambitious member of the Hitler Youth to report the raucous, jazz-loving bunch as treasonous conspirators. Several Minions were politically active and had been followed. Jaime Fellender had been arrested earlier in the year for "suspected homosexual activity." Ironically, he'd been arrested at a gay bar popular with certain high-placed Nazi officials. His interrogators warned they'd be watching him and his gay friends. Jaime was confused about what he'd done wrong, since the Nazi officer at the bar had given his blowjob high praise. He didn't volunteer this fact, figuring it unlikely to move his interrogators. Though they literally had Jaime on his knees, he was better off keeping his mouth shut in front of these particular Nazis.

Duke assured his father he was being careful. Rabbi Kimball's Torah study room had a separate entrance from the toy shop, located in the alley and obscured from the main street by stacks of wooden crates. Although one internal door led from the study room to the back of the toy shop, Rabbi Kimball kept it under lock and key. Duke neither brought Torah study materials to the shop nor left with them. Also, the boys staggered their arrivals and departures by five minutes, so as not to create a crowd that might draw attention.

But even extreme prudence couldn't immunize Duke from Matthias Belk, who led a Jungvolk (Hitler Youth) contingent at school. Though a year older than Duke, Matthias was in the same grade because he'd repeated the sixth grade, allegedly due to illness. No one knew what illness had afflicted him, as he hadn't missed a day of school that year. In all likelihood, he suffered from a chronic bout of stupidity. Despite his academic shortcomings, Matthias was a natural leader outside the classroom, commanding his followers with a quiet intensity. He rarely yelled, nor had Duke seen him personally beat a Jew or a Roma. He didn't get his hands dirty. He let the others scuff their knuckles, make a scene, and ultimately take the blame when it ostensibly still violated school rules to pummel a non-Aryan classmate. A moron in all things intellectual, Matthias was a budding genius from the perspective of an aspiring SS officer.

Rabbi Kimball had given Duke a jersey of the undefeated German national soccer team, in advance of his impending circumcision. There was nothing ostentatious about the jersey. It was a long-sleeved V-necked shirt, mostly white, except for the black collar and cuffs and the red, white, and black team crest over the left breast. The Nuremberg Laws prohibited Jews from displaying the national colors, so Duke wore the jersey under another shirt and then secretly showed it to three friends during outdoor exercise. They broke away from the masses and retreated behind an old storage shed, where Duke removed his top shirt. After enjoying his buddies' admiration, Duke recovered the jersey and exited from behind the shed.

Matthias Belk was waiting for him, along with three Jungvolk cohorts, who surrounded Duke and his friends. Matthias asked what "the Jewish pigs" were plotting. When the boys denied any wrongdoing, Matthias asked why they would meet behind the shed if they weren't plotting something. Or perhaps they were showing off their circumcised penises—seeing which one was the least deformed. Matthias suggested they all go behind the shed and compare penises. He moved in close to Duke, trying to direct him backward. Fortunately, the outdoor monitor saw what was going on and ordered the boys to break it up. Matthias had lost that battle but warned Duke he was onto him.

Matthias followed Duke and Bessie after school, forcing them into a circuitous route to the toy shop. Bessie complained they weren't going the right way, even though Duke kept reminding her that Matthias was behind them. What was usually a ten-minute walk to Kimball's stretched to an hour, with Duke and Bessie weaving through parks, cutting through alleys, and resting under bridges. With Bessie dragging, and Duke already thirty minutes late for Torah study, he decided to seek refuge at the hat shop. Rosamund greeted them warmly and then, upon noticing Bessie's disheveled appearance, ordered her to clean herself upstairs.

"What have you two been doing? Running a marathon? Why aren't you at Torah study?"

Duke was sweating heavily. He pulled off his top shirt and wiped his brow. Matthias entered.

"I knew you were hiding something, Jew-boy. Take it off! You can't display those colors!"

Duke circled behind the stand of straw hats.

"Technically, I'm not displaying anything. I'm inside my father's store."

Matthias moved around the stand, but Duke moved correspondingly, maintaining a safe distance.

"Anyone from the public can come in here, Mützenmacher. That makes this place public."

Duke had to give Matthias credit for that one; not bad for a moron.

"What's going on here? Who are you?" Rosamund asked.

"Matthias Belk, Jungvolk Section Leader. This Jew here is breaking the law."

"That's a very serious charge. I should summon the Schutzpolizei at once. What has he done? Theft? Murder?"

"He's wearing that."

Rosamund tilted her head, confused.

"I'll admit that darker trousers would better complement the football jersey, but so far as I know, poor fashion sense is not yet unlawful."

"Jews cannot display the national colors."

"This is true," Rosamund conceded. "But given we're among friends, why don't we let this infraction slide."

Matthias pulled out a paratrooper knife. He flipped a thin lever and flicked his wrist, causing the blade to snap from the walnut hilt.

"We are not friends."

"Handsome knife," commented Rosamund.

"It was my papa's. He was in the Luftwaffe. He taught me to use it."

"I'm sure he did."

"Take it off," he ordered Duke.

Duke started to remove the jersey, but Rosamund gestured for him to stop.

"You need your mommy to protect you?" Matthias taunted.

"I am not his mother... not officially."

Rosamund's response struck Duke as odd, for she seemed to imply she was his "unofficial" mother, as though she simply needed to file a form in triplicate to make it official. Duke hadn't considered Rosamund a mother, but perhaps he should have. She certainly behaved like one, planting kisses on his and Bessie's cheeks with each greeting and farewell, talking to them about school and their friends, playing "tea party" with Bessie, discussing science fiction with Duke, helping them with their lessons, and making them strudels and chocolate cakes. The more Duke thought about it, Rosamund was very much like a mother, and a pretty good one, to boot.

"Please leave, Matthias," Rosamund continued. "I have a business to run."

"Protecting the Fatherland is my business."

Rosamund moved close to Matthias and stared into his pale blue eyes. He tried to look away but couldn't extricate himself, let alone turn his head. Rosamund broke off her gaze and then smiled cruelly.

"What are you smiling about?" Matthias asked nervously.

"Your soul. It's a rather puny thing. What else is puny about you?"

Rosamund's eyes glanced toward Matthias's crotch.

"It's not puny! It's a strong German soul."

"Strong, perhaps... German, perhaps... puny, definitely."

Rosamund had changed her voice, speaking lower and slower.

"Shut up, bitch!"

"Manners, boy. Manners."

Rosamund circled Matthias slowly, her stare burning into his pink, brush-cut scalp. Her black pearl necklace glinted in the light like a winking eye.

"The Luftwaffe, you say? Your father's last name?"

"Belk."

"Belk... Belk... yes. The resemblance is uncanny. Hans Belk of the Luftwaffe. He was your father, yes?"

"Yes."

"Hans Belk, personal attaché to Commander Göring?"

"You knew him?"

"I knew of him. You say he taught you to wield the blade. Did he also teach you the Horst Wessel song?"

"Of course."

Rosamund sang in a colorless voice. She hit all the right notes, but they were lifeless—an automaton's serenade. "Clear the streets for the brown battalions... Clear the streets for the stormtrooper... Millions are inspired when they see the swastika." She stopped. "Go ahead, Matthias. Sing the next line."

"The day of freedom and of bread dawns!"

"Excellent. Your father taught you well. But there is one thing I don't see, which I should see, if indeed you are the son of Hans Belk."

"What's that?"

She inspected his face and fingers. "Not a hint of rouge on the cheeks or a spot of polish on the fingernails. Oh, don't look so surprised. We all know about Commander Göring's penchant for such niceties. Your father was his makeup man, was he not?"

"Certainly not. He headed his security detail. He was the Adjutant for Personal Welfare."

Rosamund nodded. "I can see how a child might misinterpret that lofty title. Perhaps your father aided the deception. In truth, the State Police handled the Commander's security. Your father handled his personal comfort, which meant oversight of his wardrobe."

"You lie!"

"It's nothing to be ashamed of. The Commander has an extensive wardrobe. Prior to working here, I personally sold him several cream-colored silk shirts, because he found the typical brown shirt too pedestrian. This very store sold him a suede hat to match his sleeveless leather jacket and buckskin boots. Your father's job, the all-important Adjutant for Personal Welfare, was ensuring this clothing met the Commander's exacting specifications. Just as the Commander was very particular about his brand and color of nail polish and rouge, so, too, was he particular about the cut of the silk dresses he wears in private. Göring obviously appointed your father to this position because of his keen eye for fashion. It's good to see a Nazi so in touch with his feminine side. Perhaps someday you will be the Adjutant for Personal Welfare."

"Shut up! Just shut up!"

Matthias's face turned a hotter hue of red. The knife blade quivered against his thigh. Duke backed toward the cash register.

"Yes. I definitely see that title in your future," said Rosamund. "Tell me, Matthias. Your lipstick. Max Factor, is it?"

"You're crazy!"

"Am I?"

Rosamund retrieved a hand mirror from next to the register.

"See for yourself."

She handed Matthias the mirror and then crossed behind him. As he stared, Rosamund subtly placed a thumb and forefinger on the back of his neck. He was too agitated to notice.

"You've applied your lipstick brilliantly. Such a beautiful specimen. Congratulations. You have exceeded your father's fashion talent."

Matthias looked horrified. Rosamund released her grip on his neck and came around to face the quaking Hitler Youth.

"What did you do to me?"

"Why, I've only paid you a compliment, Matthias. I believe the appropriate response is thank you."

Matthias wiped his lips, but the color remained in his reflection, at least his view of his reflection. He wiped them again and again, to the same effect.

"You Jewish witch cast a spell on me! Undo it! Undo it!"

"I'm sorry, Matthias. The mirror merely reflects the truth. You must accept it."

"No!" Matthias screamed.

He plunged the knife into Rosamund's abdomen. She crumpled to the floor. Shocked by his violence, Matthias dropped the blade and fled the store. Blood seeped through Rosamund's fingers where she pressed on the wound.

As Rosamund lay in the hospital bed recovering from surgery, Kasper held her hand and kissed her forehead. The display dismayed Duke. Although still scarred with the sign of Thor, his father's face was no longer that dauntless, sphinx-like fixture of confidence and strength. It was reddening and caving in on itself like a melting zeppelin. Duke envisioned the skin and muscle sloughing from his skull, leaving behind only bone and brain.

Guilt overwhelmed Duke. What had he been doing, jeopardizing his family's safety by studying Judaism? And he didn't want an old man slicing his penis, even if he'd suck the blood with a glass tube instead of his mouth. Although a cut foreskin would set him apart from non-Jews, it also would place him above the women of his community. Why shouldn't women have their own distinctive scar, maybe one like his dead mother's? They were just as strong as men. Stronger even. Rosamund clearly proved that when she took that knife in the gut—a knife Matthias had intended for him. Three thousand years of tradition hadn't given Rosamund that courage. She didn't need to have faith that a god stood between the glint of Matthias's blade and her pearly flesh.

Rosamund would recover. Duke's budding Judaism would not. He stopped visiting Rabbi Kimball. He didn't go through with the circumcision. His colleagues were bar mitzvahed. He was not, and he didn't care. Yet, the stabbing incident hadn't been a total loss. It inspired his father to openly declare his love for Rosamund. Soon, he was spending nights at the hat shop, no doubt in Rosamund's bed. That was okay with Duke, because that was what fathers and mothers did. He loved both equally and deeply. He utterly despised himself.

CHAPTER FOURTEEN

1938

Isn't it just a lovely morning, girls? I was worried yesterday, when the first day of spring rolled around and the sky was gray and the wind was cold. But today, the 21st of March, is glorious, is it not? A perfect day for a stroll down Mauer Street. What wonderful shops we have in Schwarz Boden. Schmidt's Cleaning and Dyeing, Daimler's Clothiers, Hess's Hardware, Zeiss's Bakery. They are clean. They sell unadulterated goods touched only by Aryan hands. These shops are Schwarz Boden's backbone. No, they are more than that. They are the heart and the flesh, too. They teem with the life and blood of the Volk. Our town, our body, could not survive without them.

Like a body, our town is susceptible to disease. We have done the utmost to purify our body of toxins and parasites. Like white blood cells, Aryanization has mostly eradicated the Jewish plague. But they won't go without a fight. These cancer cells are stubborn and slippery. They evade. Pockets of disease remain, tumors to be excised.

By my count, eleven stores remain infected with Jewish blood, including a fabric store and a certain toy store that lures in our innocent children. You know of what I speak. You can't miss them, because the smell of rot, like giant corpse flowers, punctuates the otherwise sweet smell of the blooming apple and chestnut trees. Perhaps the air will be clearer by the fall, when the last thistle has withered in our window boxes.

By the way, I received another threatening letter, written in the same Jewish hand as before. Please know I am not afraid, because I have received hundreds of your supportive letters. It moves me to know that I speak for the people and you will fight for me. That together we are the body Schwarz Boden. I am the voice. You are my hands. If the time comes, you will be my fists. I love you all.

Kasper bought Max Braunfeld's fabric store in April. Max Braunfeld had been in business for forty years, selling the finest linens and silks in Berlin. He'd been Kasper's top fabric supplier. Braunfeld's business, however, had dried up. Suppliers refused to fulfill his orders, and many customers stopped buying from him. He tried expanding his customer base, but magazines refused to run his advertisements. Max Braunfeld hadn't suddenly forgotten how to run a fabric business. He hadn't raised his prices or lowered his quality. Everything was the same. That was the problem. He'd been a Jew forty years ago, when it didn't matter. Now, it did. He was an Aryanization victim.

At first, Kasper flatly refused Braunfeld's offer. Oh, Kasper could afford it. His business was booming. One of Kasper's hats had even made it into *Marie Claire* magazine, thanks to Magda Goebbels showing off her "permanent wave" hat in Paris. He had more than enough capital to pay a fair price. Plus, owning his own fabric store would expand his access to key materials. Kasper simply didn't feel comfortable profiting from Braunfeld's misfortune. But Braunfeld had made a persuasive case. If he didn't sell to Kasper, he'd have to sell to Dieter Daimler, and he preferred to see his legacy in Kasper's hands. Also, the rumor was that Daimler had bought out Franz Goodman and Sam Greenbaum for a tenth of what their businesses were worth. Given Braunfeld's desperation, Kasper could've paid substantially below market price. Instead, he paid a fair price—that is, a price that assumed Braunfeld wasn't a Jew. Braunfeld called Kasper a mensch and later hid the sale proceeds inside bolts of fabric, which he shipped to New York. Braunfeld and his family then left on the next boat.

Aryanization also had indirectly put Kasper in the jewelry business. Years before, Sy Silverman had sold him Isana's engagement ring and wedding band at near wholesale prices. Sy also had been his father's good friend, having fought side by side with him in Africa. Sy sold Kasper the jewelry business (except for the remaining diamond and gold inventory) for a single Reichsmark because the Customs Investigations Centre would end up confiscating any cash from the sale as a Reich Flight Tax. Sy would take his chances concealing the jewelry in his suitcases' false bottoms, jacket linings, and, if necessary, a bodily orifice or two.

Kasper felt unclean. His personal wealth had grown at the Jews' expense. He now owned or controlled nearly half of Schwarz Boden's clothing economy, including lucrative military contracts to supply fabric for uniforms, bedding, tents, and parachutes. Dieter Daimler controlled the other half of the market. But that didn't make them equals, because Dieter also belonged to the Nazi hierarchy. Aside from his roles with ADEFA and the Advertising Council, Dieter was the Blockleiter for the households surrounding the commercial district. As Blockleiter, Dieter was the local conduit for Nazi propaganda and denunciations to the Gestapo about activities against the Reich. Neighbors turned to him with their petty disputes, denouncing fellow citizens for playing their music too loud or leaving empty trash bins on the sidewalk overnight.

Within two weeks of buying Braunfeld's, Kasper got in trouble for a newspaper ad claiming that Braunfeld's had been "proudly serving the German people for 40 years." The Advertising Council issued a fine and a cease and desist order because a formerly Jewish shop could advertise its number of years in business starting only from the day it had become Jew-free. Kasper suspected that Dieter, an advisor to the Council, had been behind it. Dieter already had acquired Rosenberg's and Grünfeld's, and no doubt was angry about losing out on Braunfeld's, which would've given him a fabric monopoly in Schwarz Boden.

Kasper suspected that Dieter also was wielding his influence with ADEFA. Mützenmacher's weathered several small-scale boycotts of non-ADEFA shops. Brownshirts holding anti-Semitic placards planted themselves in front of Kasper's store and painted Stars of David on the windows. They harassed his customers on the way into the store and, upon their exit, slapped stickers on their backs proclaiming, "I am a traitor of the people. I shopped at a Jewish store." Most merchants found it easier just to stick the sign in the window, so Kasper reluctantly joined ADEFA. But that innocuous action committed Kasper to repeated inspections. He also had to sew a special label into each hat's lining signifying that every stage of production was accomplished by Aryans. In a triumph of passive aggression, Kasper paid his Jewish son to perform that task.

Speaking of Duke, he was looking less and less like the stereotypical Jewish boy. He'd dyed his hair blond, shot up to five foot eight, and packed on twenty-five pounds of muscle from a combination of Schnitzengruben (sausage), Spatzen (dumplings), and Charles Atlas (fitness maven). Each day, Duke stuffed his rucksack with exercise clothes and then disappeared for the day, hiking or weightlifting with friends on the other side of Schwarz Boden. Kasper was so impressed with Duke's physical transformation he didn't ask about his son's new cross-town friends and forgave Duke's failure to put in his time at the hat shop.

Curiosity got the better of Rosamund, and she inspected Duke's rucksack when he wasn't around. She discovered long brown shorts, a brown shirt, a necktie, and an armband and belt buckle with the lightning bolt-shaped symbol of the sig rune. These were not exercise clothes but a Hitler Youth uniform. The shock triggered a vicious headache. Rosamund retired upstairs and lay down in the dark, until Kasper came to check on her.

"They're closing in, Kasper," Rosamund moaned. "They just Aryanized Kimball's. We should leave Germany before war breaks out."

"This is our home, the children's home. Duke will be safe now that he's given up Torah study. And have you seen how big he's gotten? I think he could take me."

"How can you be so clueless? He's turning into a Nazi."

"So he dyed his hair. Big deal. That doesn't make him Hitler Youth."

"Right. That's what his Hitler Youth uniform is for."

"Ha. Ha."

"I'm serious, Kasper. I saw it myself. The shirt, the shorts, the armband."

"Not possible."

"Search his rucksack if you don't believe me."

Kasper went downstairs. Thirty seconds later, he raced back upstairs, horrified.

"Jesus," he said breathlessly. "What the hell's the matter with that kid?"

"He's trying to blend in, which is what you wanted all along, right? Keep our heads down. Don't cause trouble."

"Not by becoming a Nazi."

"What other choices does he have here?"

"Plenty. To be my son, for one. To run the hat business when I'm gone."

"The Nazis won't let him run anything. He's a full-blooded Jew."

"Look, I'll talk to Duke. He's in a phase. He'll tire of it."

"Assuming his friends don't discover his lie first. Please, Kasper. Sell everything to Dieter, and let's go to America."

"If Germany's going to survive the Nazis, the country needs people like us to stick it out. We can't let Dieter win."

"Is this about the Nazis or Dieter?"

"The Nazis... and Dieter. Both, I guess."

"Ugh. Ego."

"There's nothing wrong with a little ego in aid of a just cause. And remember, we're talking about Dieter Daimler. One hard stare and the man craps in his boots. I won't bow to that flimsy man-turd."

"The problem is, there's an army of Nazi man-turds right behind him. We need to get the hell out. Open your eyes."

"I'm not blind to what's going on, but we can't just abandon everything. I've amassed a mini empire here."

"You're worried about your empire?"

"I control a lion's share of the fabric supply. You know how much cotton the military uses? Silk? The Nazis need me."

"Until they don't. They can take it all away with a stroke of the pen."

Rosamund was trembling. Kasper worried she might be teetering on a breakdown. He rested his meaty hands on her shoulders to settle her.

"I promise you, at the first sign of danger—true danger—we'll apply for visas and leave for America."

"It'll be too late by then. They won't let us go."

"We don't need permission. Even if they don't give us visas, we have the wishing hat, remember? No one can stop us. We've got the ultimate immigration trump card. As long as we stick together, we're totally safe."

"I guess you're right."

"I'm absolutely right."

Rosamund smiled. He kissed her lips.

"Forgive me."

"You're flush." Kasper felt her forehead. "And warm. Are you ill?"

"If you consider pregnancy an illness."

Kasper burst out in laughter. Rosamund's feeble smile quickly quashed any notion she was joking. Still, it didn't stop Kasper from claiming otherwise.

"You're joking."

Rosamund's forced smile dissolved into turned-down lips. Her eyes welled with tears. "I knew you'd be horrified."

"I'm just surprised. It didn't even occur to me that... the thing you just said was a possibility."

Rosamund scrunched her eyebrows, irritated. "What do you think happens when a man puts his—?"

"I understand the mechanics of it all. I didn't think it would happen for us. We were so careful."

"Rumor has it the condom factories are poking holes in the rubbers. Himmler's way of guaranteeing the next generation of Hitler Youth."

"And you planned on telling me about your... situation when exactly?"

"I only just found out about *our* situation." She threw up her hands. "Oh what's it matter when I told you? You don't want a child. I'll get rid of it. It won't be easy now that abortion's illegal, but I suppose for enough Reichsmarks..."

A baby complicated an already tenuous situation. Should they need to make a hasty exit with the wishing hat, would a pregnant Rosamund be strong enough to survive the journey? Would the baby?

On the other hand, this life-in-being—this shared flesh—would bind Rosamund to Kasper like no marriage certificate ever could. Of course, they'd have to marry soon to avoid scandal. But the biological facts obviated any handwringing on Kasper's part. He didn't have to worry about Rosamund rejecting a proposal. Her womb already had given its unconditional assent. Also, shifting Rosamund's focus to their child might make her feel less desperate to flee Germany.

Finally, there was the Daphne Curse. According to the prophecy, motherhood would immunize her from Apollo's fixation on raping Lux women. One less thing to worry about.

"You'll do no such thing."

"What?"

"You heard me. We're having this baby."

"Really?"

"I couldn't be happier."

Kasper hugged Rosamund tightly while contemplating what the hell he was going to do about his Nazified son.

Duke freely admitted he'd joined the Hitler Youth. A graphic artist had forged false identity documents with the name Duke Leghorn and the racial classification of a pure-bred Aryan. With his membership in the Hitler Youth in the open, Duke made it clear he was immersing himself in Nazi dogma just as intensely as he'd learned Jewish law for his inchoate bar mitzvah. He wouldn't break from his Hitler Youth character, even amongst family. He claimed he had to remain vigilant, lest he get complacent and give himself away.

Duke corrected Kasper and Rosamund's "misinformed" views of National Socialism. When Kasper bemoaned Hitler's return from Munich after securing the Sudetenland, Duke admonished that "Dear Führer" was the appropriate reference for their leader. He also lectured him on Hitler's great accomplishments—the elimination of unemployment, the autobahn, and Aryanization—which all benefited Kasper's commercial interests. Kasper stayed quiet until Rosamund brought up her ordeal as a camp prisoner. Duke referred to concentration camps as "modern rehabilitation facilities for the Reich's enemies." Had Kasper not been spooning Spatzen in his mouth, he might've bitten his tongue clean in half.

"It would be much better were you arrested today," Duke concluded.

Kasper clanked his spoon on the plate and choked on several false starts.

"What... Did he... I can't... Scheiße..."

Rosamund handed Kasper his wine glass, and he gulped it down.

"Duke, where do you get your information?" asked Rosamund.

"From the Jungvolk."

"Your new friends are lying to you," said Elsie.

"Mama Elsie's right," said Rosamund. "You're spouting the Nazi party line."

"There is no 'party line.' Only true and false."

"As you know, I was imprisoned in a camp only a few short years ago. They haven't magically transformed into rehabilitation centers. If anything, the interrogations and torture have gotten more brutal."

"That's good. Klaus was too soft on his prisoners."

Rosamund's face flushed with fury.

"How can you say that?" asked Mama Elsie. "You know that Klaus stole Tante Rosamund's face."

"And he did the same goddamn thing to your first mother!" added Kasper, who'd rediscovered his voice.

"That was... unfortunate," Duke conceded, "but that's the price of security. Sometimes good people get caught in the filter."

"Filter?" asked Kasper. "We're talking about people, not pubic hairs. And not just any people. Your mothers."

"Rosamund is not my mother, Pops. Not officially. Certainly not biologically."

Kasper rose. His thigh crashed into his plate, causing the tablecloth to slide, and the wine glasses to topple. Two crimson circles expanded from their respective place-settings. Rosamund squeezed Kasper's hand to help contain his rage.

"You sound like an idiot," said Bessie.

"Shut up! You're too young to understand," said Duke.

"I'm old enough to know an idiot when I hear one."

Duke ignored his sister's remark and turned his attention to the others. "They explained it on Radio Schwarz Boden. People are like cells in the body. The Reich cannot exist without them. But some cells are cancerous. If not exterminated, they'll multiply and kill the body. Just as there's no precise way to target cancerous cells without killing some good ones, there's no surefire method to root out those working against the Volk's health. Some must be sacrificed for the greater good, even if one happens to be my own mother."

"What if she happens to be your sister?" asked Bessie. "Are you and your friends gonna kill me?"

"No, Bessie. Why would you ask such a thing?"

"The teachers say the stinking Jews are a cancer. I'm a Jew."

"Well, the Jungvolk doesn't know that."

Bessie broke into tears. "But if they find out, they'll kill me."

"They don't even know you exist."

"You'll tell them."

"Why would I do that?"

"You said you'd kill me for saying you shaved my head."

"That was like two years ago, and I wasn't serious."

Bessie got up from the table and fled to her bedroom.

Duke called after her. "No one's going to kill you, Bessie. I won't let them."

"I can't stand it any longer!" Kasper declared. "You're done with the Hitler Youth. We're leaving Germany."

"I'm not going anywhere," Duke protested.

Kasper rounded the table, grabbed Duke's collar, and yanked him to his feet.

"Calm down, Kasper," said Elsie. "You're making it worse."

"You're still a child, Duke. My child. That gives me the right to tell you what to do."

"I am the Führer's child."

"Stop playing Nazi, goddamn it! You're with your family."

"I have a new family."

When Kasper tried to pull Duke close, he pushed back with a strength that surprised Kasper, who crashed into the table. Duke clenched his fists, ready for blows. Kasper wasn't sure if he could subdue him. Although Duke was shorter and lighter, he was leaner and quicker. Kasper eyed Rosamund and Mama Elsie's mortified expressions. He had to defuse his anger. He lowered his fists and changed tack.

"Please, son. I love you. We all do."

"The Führer loves me. My brothers love me, and there are way more of them."

"You heard Bessie. She's a 'stinking Jew' to them. So are you."

"They don't know that."

"Shall I tell them? Don't force my hand, because I will."

Duke strained to maintain composure. "You'd do that to me?"

"For your own good, yes."

Duke turned, embarrassed at the tears rolling down his face. Mama Elsie reached for his hand to comfort him, but he pulled away. A few seconds later, Duke took a deep breath, raised his shoulders, and stood erect. Although his eyes were red and watery, he held his chin strong and high.

"Okay, Pops. You're right. You are my family. I will resign from the Jungvolk this evening. They don't love me—not the real me, not like you all do. Just let me say goodbye to them."

It took Kasper a moment to absorb his son's conciliatory words.

"Good. And tomorrow, you will find new friends… in America."

Rosamund's eyes lit up.

"Tomorrow?" asked Duke. "How can we leave so soon? We need visas. You have to buy passage."

Kasper looked deep into his son's eyes until the boy deduced his father's divine secret.

"Oh my God," said Duke. "You have the wishing hat. How? You said you destroyed it."

"I lied."

"Why? Didn't you trust me?"

No, he did not.

"That wasn't it."

"Did you think I'd wish myself to the moon?"

Yes, he did.

"It was safer you not know about the hat, in case you fell in with the wrong crowd, which, as recent events show… Please don't be offended. My own father didn't even let me touch the hat until I was sixteen because I was such a screw-up. Not that you're a screw-up, it's just—"

"I get it, Pops. Where is it?"

"I'll show you tomorrow, when we leave."

"Why not now?"

"Because we have to plan our journey."

"You still don't trust me."

"That's not it. You'll see it tomorrow. I promise."

Duke shook his head in disbelief and headed for the door.

"What time will you be back?" asked Kasper.

"Late."

Duke slammed the door behind him.

Kasper lay awake, mulling the logistics of leaving for America the next day. They would arrive in a new country as undocumented aliens. It would be near impossible to rent an apartment, restart the hat business, or enroll the children in school. They'd have to find a document forger and likely pay him a handsome fee, which raised the issue of money. A day's notice wouldn't be sufficient time for Kasper to sell his holdings. They'd have to survive on savings, which were small because he'd been reinvesting his profits into buying out Aryanized businesses. Also, they'd be illegal aliens. If caught, they'd be thrown in jail and then deported back to Germany. They'd have to wish themselves to another country and try again.

There were health risks, too. Mama Elsie was battling high blood pressure. She might not survive the toll hat travel inflicted on the human body. Kasper also couldn't be sure about the effect on Rosamund's fetus. Even if Rosamund arrived intact, would the strain of extreme compression and expansion tear the delicate embryo apart?

Kasper rolled to his side and pounded the pillow. Damn it. He'd gotten caught up in the heat of the moment with Duke. He shouldn't have even mentioned the wishing hat. The hat had to be the absolute last resort. They didn't need to leave the very next day. They had more time. After breakfast, Kasper decided, he'd apply for exit visas and book steamship passage to New York. They'd become American citizens the conventional way. He sighed deeply and closed his eyes.

A moment later, his eyes popped open.

Where would they settle in America? Kasper considered New York, Chicago, and New Orleans, because of their jazz scenes. He dismissed New Orleans because of the humidity, and Chicago because of the bone-shattering wind. That left New York, which seemed too big. There were hundreds of milliners there. It might be difficult to get established. Also, the metro area was crawling with fascists from the German American Bund.

Kasper wanted a place like Schwarz Boden—a small enclave in a big city on the river, surrounded by a thriving population thirsting for hats, just without all the Nazis. Of course! Schwarz Boden translated to Black Bottom, and there was a Black Bottom in the heart of Detroit. Kasper could mine the millinery gold rush fueled by the booming automobile industry. Also, Rosamund had family in Detroit. It would be good for her to be near her Lux kin.

Too wired to sleep, Kasper crawled from Rosamund's bed, careful not to disturb her fitful rest. He went downstairs to survey the shop and decide what he'd bring to America. Not much. Thimbles, scissors, pins, pencils, pliers, and cutters were replaceable. Hermann Mützenmacher seemed to agree from his perch above the small worktable. At least that was what Kasper read into his father's eyes, big nose, and you-know-what-must-be-done expression. He stroked his father's shadowed cheek, remembering back to his childhood, when he couldn't understand how skin so dark could feel so smooth. His nostrils puckered, reflexively anticipating his father's witch hazel after-shave. The odor had comforted Kasper as a young boy, and the memory calmed his mind.

Then came the scream. Rosamund was in trouble. Kasper grabbed the cutters and raced upstairs. She was alone. Of course, she was alone. No one could've gotten into the shop and snuck upstairs without Kasper noticing. Rosamund was holding the brass table lamp in a defensive posture.

"He was here."

"Who?"

"Klaus."

"He couldn't have been. I would've seen him."

"He was on top of me."

"It was a nightmare."

"It was not a fucking nightmare!"

"Okay. He's gone now. Lie back down."

"He knows we're going to have a girl."

"How would he know that? We don't even know."

"He's going to take her, make her his prisoner."

"He can't touch her, not in America."

"I'm not going to America."

"Why would you say that?"

"Klaus won't let me go. He won't let any of us go."

"Rosamund, please. We're going to be so happy."

She fell silent. Her breathing was steady and deep, and her eyes half shut. Kasper pried the lamp from her hands and set it on the bedside table. He guided her into bed and pulled the sheets to her chin. As he was about to switch off the overhead light, he glimpsed the dresser, which held Rosamund's copy of *Face of the Fatherland*, and next to that, a small, Bakelite-finished radio.

What the hell? I crushed that radio two years ago.

Rosamund was already fast asleep, so the mystery of the replacement radio would have to wait until morning. Kasper sat on the bed's edge. Restless, he grabbed the book and began to read.

The tome's first half recounted Friedrich von Tannenberg's meteoric rise from musketeer to general in only a decade. The general's "brilliance" as a military tactician was allegedly foreshadowed during his childhood, as evidenced by the numerous apocryphal anecdotes that peppered the text. For example, at age three, Friedrich supposedly thwarted a home invasion by arranging twenty-five prams into an impenetrable wall extending from the front door to the barn. (The book didn't explain how a three-year-old had acquired twenty-five prams, which struck Kasper as a far more impressive feat.) At age twelve, Friedrich darkened his skin with a caustic mixture of tree bark and dog urine, dressed as a woman in a blouse and ankle-length skirt, infiltrated a band of fifty Roma, and exposed their plot to poison the beer barrels at Oktoberfest. In both instances, an angel had guided Friedrich's actions. "I cannot take credit for my precocious demonstrations of superhuman courage and guile," Friedrich recounted. "I owe everything to the Lord and his angel, who carried out their greatness through me."

A most humble fellow, that Friedrich.

As an adult, Friedrich fought in numerous skirmishes in far-flung African villages bearing obscure names that "most expert geographers could not locate on a map." Kasper wondered whether these villages even existed, let alone served as backdrops for Friedrich's alleged heroics. According to the book, the natives proved formidable foes due to their guerilla tactics and poison darts, which enabled them to strike with stealth from a distance. Friedrich's commanders, schooled in conventional tactics, didn't know how to fight these irregular combatants. As a result, the army was hemorrhaging soldiers and bleeding confidence. But then Friedrich, a lowly musketeer, asserted himself. For the sake of his demoralized comrades, and at the urging of his childhood angel, he defied protocol, marched into his commander's tent, and forcefully recommended they implement shock tactics to exert both physical and psychological pressure on the enemy. The desperate commander gave the brash young soldier a chance.

Soon, German soldiers were setting fires to hectares of lush savannah to flush out tribesmen and pick them off with firearms. They were surrounding isolated pockets of hostile natives and unleashing volleys of cannon and musket fire, leaving only a traumatized survivor or two to tell the tale to "their savage brethren in the next village." They were raping tribal women, not only to demoralize their husbands, fathers, and brothers but ultimately to dilute their blackness and, hence, the trait that unified them. Friedrich was promoted and promoted again. Before long, he was planning and executing his very own micro-genocides.

The book devoted only one short paragraph to the Battle for Perdeau Valley, which had claimed the lives of hundreds of the general's men, including Kasper's father. The general quoted two lines from Sun Tzü's *The Art of War*: 1) "Military tactics are like unto water; for water in its natural course runs away from high places and hastens downward," and 2) "In war, then, let your great object be victory, not lengthy campaigns." About his decision to blow the dam and drown all the combatants, the general wrote only this: "The deluge instantly ended the campaign." He kept mum on how drowning his men manifested the victory aspect of Sun Tzü's aphorism.

Nauseated, Kasper flipped to the general's post-military endeavors.

In 1908, the angel informed Friedrich that God Almighty had anointed him the official scribe for a divine prophecy. For three days, the angel dictated the heavenly words, which became *Face of the Fatherland*'s latter half. In this section, the general warned of a looming threat from the backstabbing Marxists and profit-mongering Jews and claimed the world's only hope was a powerful dictator to unify all pure Germans into a cohesive body politic. This future *Führer* (emphasis on the capital F) would inevitably resolve in the national consciousness, like a distant star coming into focus on a telescopic mirror. Germans would come to see this face in shop windows, in lakes, ponds, and puddles, in their finest silver plates, and on their spit-shined shoes. Eventually, every reflective surface would project the Führer's face, and only his face. Every German would bear the face of the Fatherland.

The Führer would not rise without help, warned the ex-general. He would need a powerful prophet to set the stage for his ascension, someone to compel the Volk to willingly relinquish their individualism. The book concluded with this prediction: "This prophet's name will be Klaus," thereby driving home what had been obvious from the opening page: General Friedrich von Tannenberg lived and died a hopelessly insane man.

Kasper snapped the book shut. Rosamund clearly needed better reading material. Tomorrow, he'd renew his *Vogue* subscription and instruct her to read *Marie Claire* cover to cover, so they could start hashing out designs for the upcoming season. He doubted the ability of beautiful faces in the magazines' color pages to reinvigorate a soul that was turning monochromatic and faceless. But for Rosamund's sake, he had to have faith.

CHAPTER FIFTEEN

Before sunrise, the Gestapo arrested Kasper on "suspicion of activities inimical toward the State," in his case, false advertising. An anonymous informant had denounced him as a secret Jew, who'd illegally been using the ADEFA label to pass off his goods as Aryan-made. The Gestapo remanded Kasper to a prison camp for "protective detention," pending a more thorough investigation into his racial status and eventually a trial in a race court. They stripped him, gave him a striped prison uniform, and shaved his head. They denied him contact with an attorney or his family. In the morning, they assigned him to a work crew clearing rubble and dirt for the autobahn.

Kasper worked twelve-hour days, consumed thin broth and stale bread at mealtime, and then slept in a drafty bunk. As days stretched into weeks, he worried the camp might become his permanent home. He figured starvation and fatigue would kill him in a year, maybe two. One day, he'd collapse in the autobahn's wet cement, and the work crew would pave right over his corpse. Despair set in when his incarceration hit the one-month mark without any word from his family or on the status of the investigation. If only he could get word to Duke and Mama Elsie, they could rescue him with the wishing hat and wish the whole family to America. But Kasper was completely cut off.

Kasper's spirits briefly lifted when he was unexpectedly reunited with his Uncle Axel. Axel had a pink triangle affixed to his coat because the Nazis had convicted him of sexual deviance. Kasper was quietly ashamed for feeling so happy that his favorite uncle was a fellow inmate. At a lunch break, they reminisced about the Kabarett de Karneval and Moses Muznick. Then, at dinner, Uncle Axel brought raucous laughter to the weary inmates with his spot-on impersonation of Louis Armstrong singing *Ain't Misbehavin'*. Kasper went to sleep thinking he could survive five years in the camp, maybe even ten, with Uncle Axel around. The next morning, however, Uncle Axel was gone. To spare Kasper the worry, Axel hadn't mentioned he and the other pink-triangle-branded inmates were only passing through on their way to Dachau.

That afternoon, two guards pulled Kasper from the work crew. To his astonishment, they were releasing him. No, the matter of his race hadn't been settled. Rather, Goebbels had granted him a temporary furlough. Kasper would later learn that Fräu Magda had visited the hat shop, wanting Kasper to reproduce a velvet conical cap pictured in *Marie Claire*. Told that the shop was closed during Kasper's detention, Frau Magda flew into a rage. She prodded her husband to release Kasper at least long enough for him to make the hat.

The guards dropped Kasper outside the hat shop. In his absence, the tree root had not only pierced the brick sidewalk again but had grown at a prodigious rate. It was a laurel tree. Of course it was a laurel. What other tree could be that resilient? What other tree could endure shovels and pick axes and augers, and not only survive but flourish? Kasper felt exhilarated. Rosamund's nymph blood was fortified with that same strength. It followed that she, too, was resilient. She, too, was flourishing. He couldn't wait to enter the shop, embrace Rosamund's warm pregnant body, and kiss her skin, which exuded tinges of nutmeg, milk, and cloves.

Rosamund wasn't inside. Instead, Kasper was greeted by Dieter Daimler's thin, pasty face. Kasper had no desire to embrace that willowy frame, which he imagined reeked of sauerkraut, dry-cleaning fluid, and cowardice.

"What are you doing here, Dieter?"

"Minding the shop. You have quite a backlog of orders."

"You've no right to be in here."

"I was invited."

"By whom?"

"Rosamund."

"She'd never invite a Nazi in here. Where is she?"

"Resting at my apartment."

"*Your* apartment?"

"The stress of your arrest was hard on her. The doctor put her on bed rest. And your mother... well, I'm afraid she's had a mild stroke. She's also at my apartment, along with Bessie."

"What the hell!"

Kasper brushed past Dieter and ran upstairs. Rosamund wasn't there. He hurried back down and phoned his apartment. There was no answer.

"Call my apartment," offered Dieter. "The number's Berlin 1121."

Kasper made the call, and Mama Elsie answered. He was relieved she sounded okay. She reported that Dieter had been very kind to them. The day of Kasper's arrest, Rosamund began having pre-term contractions. Then Mama Elsie suffered a stroke while guiding Rosamund down the stairs. Dieter took them both to the hospital. Mama Elsie was fine, except for weakness in her left arm. Rosamund's contractions were under control, but she was suffering nightmares.

"When are you coming home?" Elsie asked.

Since when is Dieter Daimler's apartment "home"?

Kasper was non-committal. "Soon... What's that, Mama?" Kasper frowned and then turned to Dieter and handed him the telephone. "Bessie is asking for her Onkel Dieter."

Dieter took the phone, his face expanding into a huge smile. "Zaubermaus?... Yes, Bessie. I will be home soon. I have a surprise for you... No, not lipsticks. Your papa... That's right! He's coming home... No, I don't think he has any lipsticks with him... Okay, I love you too, my little mouse. Goodbye."

Kasper crossed his arms and leered at Dieter. "What the hell are you up to?"

"Just being a good friend."

"We've never been friends."

"Maybe now we can be. You have a beautiful family."

"Right. I have a beautiful family, not you."

"Perhaps you could give me a chance. Get to know me."

"I can't be friends with a Nazi."

"I am not a Nazi."

Kasper laughed.

"I admit I'm a Nazi party member," Dieter continued. "I wear the Nazi pin. I have a Nazi title. By all appearances, I am a Nazi. But I'd hope you'd measure a man by his deeds, not pins and titles."

"What are you saying? You're in the resistance?"

"Not formally. I don't have co-conspirators, if that's what you mean. I work alone."

"Really," said Kasper skeptically. "And exactly how does buying Jewish businesses at distressed prices constitute resistance?"

"The low offers were necessary. I needed a reputation for ruthless negotiating skills. For those businesses I actually purchased, I paid fair market value. Why do you think Gelzer's never approached you? Or Goodman's? Or Greenbaum's?"

"You lie. Word on the street was—"

"Just words. False rumors I encouraged to maintain my guise. You've known only the weak Dieter, the pitiful Dieter, the Dieter who'd do anything just to fit in. I've changed, Kasper. I owe that in part to you. That night of the attempted putsch, when Isana took my clothes, I felt demeaned, humiliated. As I shivered, I plotted all the ways I might get my revenge. But then you gave me your coat. You wrapped it around my body and told me to go home, that I could do better. I know, it probably seems like nothing to you, but your simple kindness started me on a different path."

"That's touching, Dieter," said Kasper, unimpressed. "Then again, if you've really changed, you'd have proof."

"What proof? You want me to rip my heart out and show it to you?"

"Let's start with the sales contracts for Gelzer's, Goodman's, and Greenbaum's. How much did you really pay them?"

"You take me for an idiot? Those contracts don't show the true prices."

"How convenient for you."

"And for them. I wired the money to England or America, so they could avoid the Flight Tax. I set up shell companies to make the transfers untraceable. That's my hope, anyway. There was no small risk on my part. If the Reich finds out, I'll be labeled an economic saboteur and sent to prison. You don't believe me. Fair enough. Why should you? Naturally, you're skeptical, given our history. You're especially cautious, given your stint in the camp."

"You're goddamn right I'm cautious! Had Frau Goebbels not wanted a new hat, my carcass would've been steamrolled into the autobahn. This is all bullshit. You were the one who put me in that prison."

"I didn't denounce you. In fact, I've been charged with getting to the bottom of this."

"You? *You're* investigating me?"

"It made the most sense. You're charged with fraudulently using the ADEFA label. I'm an expert in that area."

"But you're not an expert in determining whether I'm a Jew. I need a lawyer. Plus, you have a clear conflict of interest."

"Once again, I did not denounce you."

"Who then?"

"It doesn't matter. The point is, the denunciation has been made, and the process is in motion."

"I should have the right to confront my accuser."

"To what end?"

"Presumably, this person claims some special knowledge. I'll get to talk to him when this ends up in race court, so why not let me do it now?"

Dieter sighed. "You're going to be very angry when I tell you."

"I'm already very angry. I'm still certain it was you, so any name you blurt out won't change my mood one whit."

"Very well. It was your son."

"Oh, for God's sake. Seriously."

"I am serious. Duke came to me with his allegation. He was very hurt because you were making him abandon his friends. I told him this was not the solution and I would not forward his complaint. He left, and I thought that was the last of it, but he went over my head, to the Zellenleiter."

"I don't believe it. I just don't. He'd never do that to me."

Dieter handed Kasper a dossier labeled, "Investigative File: *In re* Kasper Mützenmacher." A carbon copy of an intake form affixed to the inside cover identified the complainant as Duke Leghorn, Hitler Youth.

"My own son turned me in? Impossible."

Kasper searched Dieter's face for some sign this was some horrible Nazi joke. He didn't find one.

"Son of a bitch! He looked me in the eye and said he was breaking from the Hitler Youth."

"I'd say he changed his mind, or he lied to your face."

"Where the hell is he?"

"He disappeared the day of your arrest."

"He's with the Hitler Youth, then. Across town."

"I made inquiries with the Blockleiter over there. Duke hasn't been seen for weeks. He told no one where he was going. I'm sorry."

Kasper felt as though the floor had given way. He'd ignored the precariousness of the family's situation for months, and then, while he was in prison, the ground beneath them had caved in. He pictured Duke trapped in an ever-deepening hole as a flood of dirt inundated him. He wanted to transport himself into that crevasse and wish his son to the light. But it wasn't possible. Hermes' hat could take him only to places, not people.

Kasper was crying. An hour earlier, he would've sooner soiled himself than displayed such vulnerability in front of Dieter. Now, he was burying his face in Dieter's shoulder and welcoming the pseudo-Nazi's embrace. Dieter might've been a fraud, but he was there and he was warm, and for that Kasper was grateful.

Based on his investigation, Dieter concluded that, on balance, the evidence showed Kasper wasn't Jewish under the Nuremberg Laws. Although the Reich had reclassified Hermann Mützenmacher to a Jew, that made Kasper only a Mischling First Class. True, Kasper had once married a Jew, but Isana was long dead, and neither Kasper nor his children practiced Judaism. Kasper was relieved when Dieter didn't mention Duke's brief dalliance with Torah study. He silently thanked Herr Kimball for the secrecy and discretion with which he conducted his rabbinical activities.

Kasper mentioned an additional fact he thought worked in his favor: Rosamund, a pure-blood Aryan, was carrying his child. At this point, Dieter began shaking his head so vigorously, Kasper thought it might dislodge from his little torso. Dieter advised Kasper to keep Rosamund out of the matter at all costs. Why? She had no passport or other identity documents, not even her prison discharge papers. And because Kasper had failed to submit her information to the Labor Office, she also lacked an employment record book (an Arbeitsbücher).

Kasper buried his face in his palms. How could he have been so stupid, allowing Rosamund to work illegally all those years? He'd requested her identity papers at least twice, and both times she'd rebuffed him with innocuous excuses. Months passed, and then years. Then he'd fallen in love and forgotten all about it. Dieter added that the labor violations would be the least of Kasper's problems. Should the race court declare Kasper a Jew, he'd be found guilty of "racially defiling" Rosamund under the Law for the Protection of German Blood and German Honor. Kasper could spend decades in prison.

As Kasper recovered from an apoplectic coughing fit, Dieter emphasized it was extremely unlikely that Rosamund's employment or racial status would come into play. Indeed, Kasper's case wouldn't even reach the evidentiary stage because Dieter already had asked the Assistant State's Attorney (ASA) to consent to a dismissal. Why would the ASA agree to that? Because he was Dieter's regular customer, a frequent purchaser of lace brassieres, striped bustiers, and silk underwear (for his wife, presumably). And what had the ASA said? Although he lacked the authority to unilaterally drop the matter, he had agreed to recommend a dismissal to the judge. Therefore, Dieter added, Kasper's court appearance would be a "mere formality," especially because Josef Seitz, the presiding State Court judge, also was his good customer.

"I still think I need a lawyer," said Kasper.

"Like I said before, the proceeding is a formality. Don't waste your money."

"But if problems arise—"

"They won't. I assure you. Anyway, this is just your initial appearance. You can hire a lawyer later, if it comes to that, which, as I've said, it won't."

Unfortunately, it would. Judge Seitz was not presiding on the day Kasper appeared in race court. He had injured his back after slipping on a sausage that his invalid mother-in-law had flung to the kitchen floor. Judge Otto Rothaug was filling in.

Judge Rothaug was a former military judge who'd carried his reputation for harsh justice to the civilian bench. He prided himself on zeroing in on evidence that well-schooled attorneys often missed. These "discoveries," however, usually were complete misunderstandings, stemming from his cursory review of the record and profound myopia (both ophthalmic and intellectual). He was the antithesis of the unbiased truth-seeker, not because of what he didn't know but because he didn't know what he didn't know, and didn't care. Worse, he despised anything he considered "superfluous," his top three being fashion, music, and religion. Kasper already was a hatmaker and a jazz-lover. It would be no great leap for Judge Rothaug to complete the trifecta and deem Kasper a Jew.

Dieter asked the ASA to request a continuance until Judge Seitz's return. Dieter's voice had carried to the bench. Before the ASA answered, Judge Rothaug banged his gavel and declared there would be no continuance.

The judge flipped through Kasper's file for a good sixty seconds, twice as long as he spent on the typical case. When the ASA rose to request a dismissal, the judge cut him off and began opining about Mooch's Minions. He didn't buy Kasper's explanation that the Minions was merely ten jazz lovers who gathered for a few hours on Friday nights. Friday night, the judge noted, was the holiest night for the Jews, and the fact there were ten Minions—not nine, not eleven—was significant, because Jews need ten men—a "minyan" in the Hebrew tongue—to conduct a prayer service. The similarities to a synagogue were beyond coincidence. That Kasper had married a Jewess who'd produced two Jewish offspring buttressed the conclusion he had an undeniable affinity for Judaism.

Judge Rothaug declared he was ready to rule. Dieter reminded the judge that the trial hadn't even been scheduled. Indeed, the ASA had agreed that the matter should be dismissed. If there was to be a trial, Kasper should at least have the benefit of an attorney.

The judge was unmoved, deeming lawyers superfluous. (Evidently, attorneys occupied the fourth spot on the judge's list of superfluous things.) The key ingredient for fair and efficient justice was a "healthy Volk sentiment," which, the judge claimed, he had in ample supply. He declared Kasper a Jew, which meant he was guilty of false advertising. The judge would leave sentencing to Judge Seitz. Although Kasper could remain free in the interim, Judge Rothaug would be sure to recommend a lengthy detention. Matter adjourned.

"What just happened, Dieter?"

Dieter had gone pale. "I'm not quite sure."

"So, that's it? I'll spend the rest of my life in detention?"

"No. No, you'll appeal. We'll also make a formal request for racial reclassification."

"What are my chances?"

"As far as the appeal, the German Supreme Court hasn't reversed a single lower court finding a defendant Jewish."

"That's hopeless. What about reclassification?"

"Hitler personally reviews all reclassification requests."

"Beyond hopeless."

"I will do everything in my power to help you."

"How much power do you have?"

"Unfortunately, very little. I still control ADEFA, which reminds me, I'll need to confiscate your membership card."

"You're serious."

"My hands are tied. You're a Jew, at least for now."

"This is ridiculous."

"You'll also have to remove ADEFA signage from the store and ADEFA labels from the hats."

"Anything else? How about my trousers and my underwear? Do you want those now, or should I have them starched and pressed first?"

"No, that's not..." Dieter lost himself in thought until his face suddenly brightened. "I have an idea. I want you to hear me out because it may sound outrageous at first. There's a way you can keep your ADEFA affiliation."

"How?"

"Sell me your stores." Dieter raised his hand. "I know what you're thinking.

'Dieter's using my unfortunate circumstances to steal my livelihood.' But I assure you, Kasper, the sale would be a mere formality. You'd still control day to day operations and keep the profits. Meanwhile, my role as Blockleiter and close friendship with the Gauleiter will be the perfect camouflage. What do you think?"

Kasper didn't detect a whiff of insincerity, which made him only more suspicious. He wondered whether everything was transpiring according to Dieter's master plan to feign concern and then offer help, when his endgame was complete dominion over Kasper's assets. Although Dieter had conveyed distress at the sight of Judge Rothaug, it could've been an act. He'd actively discouraged Kasper from hiring a lawyer. For all Kasper knew, Dieter and the ASA had a tacit agreement under which Dieter would make a futile motion to dismiss the matter in exchange for garter belts or silk stockings for the ASA's wife (if the ASA even had a wife).

Indeed, Dieter may have set this whole thing in motion. True, it was Duke's signature on the denunciation form, but Dieter easily could have forged it. And, although the denunciation contained personal details about Kasper that Dieter shouldn't have known, Dieter could've learned them surreptitiously, perhaps with the Gestapo's help. Rosamund's apartment might have been infested with listening devices inside the light fixtures or in the dresser knobs or—

The radio!

Kasper had smashed the radio to bits, but then it reappeared. Who's to say the radio wasn't transmitting conversations and other sounds to a Gestapo agent's keen ears? Rosamund had gotten the radio upon leaving the prison camp. Perhaps Klaus used these radios to keep tabs on his victims. Kasper had dismissed Rosamund's nightmares and delusions about Klaus, but maybe he shouldn't have. Maybe Klaus had actually visited her.

Kasper recalled the night Klaus, a short, slight man, had emerged from the car and arrested Isana. He had the same build as Dieter. Later, Kasper left Dieter in the alley and told him to go home. Dieter would've had plenty of time to change into the black uniform and slip on Klaus's signature veil. Dieter came off as weak, as a bumbler. No one took him seriously. What better guise for a shrewd, ruthless interrogator like Klaus? And the numbers—eleven and twenty-one in the Radio Schwarz Boden broadcasts were identical to Dieter's telephone number—Berlin 1121.

It all fit. Dieter was Klaus.

Kasper threw Dieter against the marble wall and spat his accusations while compressing Dieter's windpipe. Dieter feebly pried at Kasper's hands.

"Please... please... mistaken... not Klaus..." Dieter pleaded, as a spot of urine welled on his trousers.

Dieter wasn't putting up much of a fight. Surely, Klaus would have had a unique move or two to extricate himself from the grip of a stronger man, or a needle laced with a neurotoxin or a sleep agent he could jam into his assailant upon triggering a spring embedded in his shirt cuff. Dieter, however, just floundered. His nail-bitten fingertips barely made a dent in Kasper's skin. He had thoroughly pissed himself, and his face had turned from red to purple. His breathing slowed. He had another thirty seconds of life, at most.

Something fell from Dieter's pocket and clanked on the marble floor—a lipstick canister, presumably for Bessie. No, Kasper realized, Dieter couldn't be Klaus. The real Klaus wouldn't die so pitifully. Kasper envisioned Bessie's innocent face exploding into tears upon learning her father had strangled "Onkel" Dieter. Kasper released Dieter, who slid down the wall like a gob of warm gelatin. Kasper caught him and propped him up.

"Forgive me. I let the stress get the better of me."

"I... I understand. I haven't... haven't yet earned your trust."

The urine stain had overtaken the entire front of Dieter's trousers. Kasper removed his coat and handed it to Dieter.

"What's this for?" Dieter followed Kasper's glance downward and then added an embarrassed "Oh."

"Fold it over your arm and hold it in front. It'll hide the stain until you can change."

"Your coat-giving is becoming a habit. At least this time, I get to keep my pants on. I guess that's progress. In fifty years, you might let me shake your hand."

Kasper cracked a smile. He still wasn't sure whether Dieter was an ally or an enemy, but at least he wasn't Klaus. That would have to do for now because he had no option but to trust Dieter. In days, perhaps hours, soldiers would daub the hat shop's windows with a Star of David and the word Juden. Then, if they didn't blockade the entrance, they'd take down customers' names and slap stickers on their backs, shouting that they'd betrayed the Volk. The Nazis would force Kasper to sell the shop, if not to Dieter, then some other random Aryan who wouldn't give him as favorable terms.

There was also the matter of getting the hell out of Germany. Theoretically, Kasper could wish himself and his family anywhere he wanted. But he wouldn't leave Germany without Duke. Though he could've brought

Bessie and Elsie to America while he searched for Duke, Rosamund was in no condition to travel via wishing hat. She was far along in her pregnancy and on bedrest. Plus, there was the risk of five Germans arriving in America without documentation. Kasper would constantly be looking over his shoulder, wondering not if but when, the authorities would discover their illegal status. Legal emigration remained the most prudent course.

According to Dieter, America was not a realistic, legal destination for Jews. The choice was between Bolivia and Shanghai. Dieter joked that Kasper would be a giant in either place but especially Bolivia, where the average height was five foot three. Kasper opted for Bolivia, figuring it would be easier to integrate into South American culture and get by on broken Spanish until he could devise a legal means to get to America. He was disappointed, but a temporary layover in South America was far preferable to a German concentration camp.

"I will get your papers in order," promised Dieter.

CHAPTER SIXTEEN

Due to the judicial backlog, Kasper's sentencing wouldn't take place for at least a month, which was good, because it took Dieter several weeks to secure the visas from the Bolivian consulate, as well as new passports for Kasper and the children. Each passport was stamped with a large red "J" for Juden, and per German law, Kasper and Duke now had the middle name "Israel," and Bessie had "Sarah."

Obtaining identity documents for Rosamund through legitimate channels would've taken too much time and required her to appear before the Schutzpolizei, which she couldn't do on bedrest. Also, Kasper wanted to stay as far away from the police as possible. Dieter therefore recommended a forger on Krumm Street. Yet another crime to add to Kasper's expanding rap sheet. He told Dieter to get it done, hung up the phone, and then poured himself a well-deserved whiskey shot. He drank four more, well-deserved or not, and climbed into bed next to his extremely pregnant fiancée. After Kasper's stint in the camp, they abandoned all pretense of a sexless relationship, and Rosamund was now living in the family's apartment.

Kasper closed his eyes, but his slumber lasted all of fifteen seconds. After he released a soft snore, Rosamund violently threw off the covers, clambered out of bed, and began pacing with heavy, shuffling footsteps. She was trying to induce contractions so she'd give birth before the expected due date of November 21. She was determined that their baby not be born on 11-21, because "those were Klaus's numbers." Rosamund eventually tired and returned to bed.

Kasper remained wide awake with worry about Rosamund, the baby, Elsie, Bessie, and Duke... especially Duke. He staggered from the bedroom and groped for the Bushmills, figuring a few more shots would knock him out for the night. After flipping on the dining room light, he noticed an envelope on the table. It was addressed to him. He grabbed a letter opener from the foyer table and tore it open.

Dear Pops:

I don't expect you to forgive me. What I did is unforgivable. I was angry, and I wanted to hurt you. I'm so stupid. I don't know what I was thinking going to the Gestapo. Just know I won't be around to do any more stupid things. I have found a new family. It's not the Hitler Youth. We don't sing about stormtroopers or swastikas or Hitler's banners. We don't celebrate Jewish "blood spurting from the knife." We are the Pirates of the Crescent Moon. Our sole purpose is to destroy the Hitler Youth. We move in the dark, when they're asleep in their camps, when they're not expecting us. One time, we replaced the stuffed Jew hanging in effigy with a stuffed Führer and set him aflame. We sang about the "shit spurting from their pants," as they skittered from their tents, tripping over each other and squealing like frightened mice. I wish you could've seen it.

We are nomads, carrying only our rucksacks and sheath knives, stalking our prey, lulling them into complacence. Right now, we're kids playing pranks. We're hungry sometimes, and cold, too. When we're a little older, we'll form a real resistance against real soldiers. We'll slit their throats. We'll set fire to their tents. I can't wait.

Boy, it'd be something if we had the wishing hat. Think what mischief we could cause, popping in and out of the Nazis' barracks, taking their uniforms and their weapons, drawing a big handlebar mustache on Der Führer. We'd have so much fun.

I'm still doing Charles Atlas. My chest has grown another inch! Are you keeping up with the exercises? How's Bessie? How's Mama Elsie? I don't know why I'm asking questions. You have no way to write back, and I wouldn't expect you to, even if you did. Anyway, I miss them, but I'll get used to it, I guess.

Okay, so I have to go now. We're on the move. We're tracking a troop not too far from Schwarz Boden. I may even get close enough to see a light in your apartment window. Don't worry. I won't show my face.

Love,
Duke

The envelope had no return address or postmark. It had been hand-delivered, and it hadn't been on the dining table before Kasper had gone to bed. Kasper looked out the window, hoping to see his son on the street below, looking up at him. There was no one. He backed from the window and turned. A man with a broad chest, square chin, and rucksack stood before him. Kasper's heart thumped with pride.

"Duke!"

When had he become a man? Certainly not in their months apart. It had been happening all along. But Kasper had been too preoccupied with telling his son what not to be—an astronaut, a weakling, a Jew, a Nazi. Duke had become a man in spite of Kasper, by defying his father's push to make him strong and independent. Kasper was the anti-father, or Duke, the anti-son. Each action had produced an equal and opposite reaction. Father had pushed son away, son had sent father to prison, yet now they were together.

"I won't stay long, Pops. I just wanted to see you once more. I had to see your face, tell you I'm sorry like a man. So, sorry. I'll go."

"You're not going anywhere."

Kasper hugged Duke tightly. He wouldn't let go, fearing his son might slip away again.

Duke cried into his father's shoulder. "I'm so sorry, Pops. I—"

"No. No apologies. Forget about everything that came before. All that matters is you are home where you belong, where I need you to be."

"You need me?"

Kasper squeezed his son's bulging biceps. "You're the strongest man in the house. I can't carry everyone out of Germany by myself."

Duke smiled. "I can come with you?"

"We were never going without you. We go as a family or not at all."

"When?"

"We're waiting to hear from Dieter. He's arranging passage."

"Before the baby comes?"

"Oh long before that. The due date's not for two weeks. Could you imagine making the journey with a newborn? What a nightmare."

"Kasper!" yelled Rosamund from the bedroom. "The baby's coming!"

Rosamund was in the throes of a precipitous labor. She couldn't slow the contractions, and the baby was crowning before the doctor arrived. Kasper tried to stay positive, saying idiotic platitudes like, "Don't worry, Rosamund. She just wants to show her face to the world"—an unfortunate turn of phrase, in retrospect. Although the sex organs made the child female, her purple color and featureless face made her an abomination. Her eye sockets and mouth were shrouded in skin. Her nose was a barely discernible mound. She flailed her arms as though desperately swimming toward a pool's surface.

After cutting the umbilical cord, the doctor determined that the mask of skin over the infant's face was not a birth membrane. He couldn't simply cut it away and liberate the child's facial features. There were no underlying features. There was nothing he could do. The child was doomed.

Kasper took the squirming lump from the apologetic doctor and cradled her. He wiped his thumbs over the face that wasn't to be. Her heartbeat grew fainter and fainter until fading into utter stillness.

Rosamund was silent and emotionless as Mama Elsie patted her forehead with a damp cloth. She gestured for her daughter. After receiving the infant, she peeled back the blanket and inspected the corpse like an engineer might evaluate a defective part pulled from the production line. She touched the perfect toes and fingers. She gently squeezed the soft flesh on the midsection and shoulders. She grazed her index finger over the facial area, mentally sketching on the blank flesh canvas where the eyes, nose, and mouth should have been. She then nodded, handed her back to Kasper, and resumed her unfocused stare. Kasper assumed she was in shock. He covered the child's head with the blanket and handed the bundle to Mama Elsie.

"Don't let the children see. Put her in the study for now."

Kasper wiped his eyes, which had blurred with tears. Their daughter had represented his future with Rosamund. Now, like that horrific face, that future was undefined and amorphous.

Rosamund spoke in a flat, colorless voice. "Don't grieve, Kasper. She wasn't even yours."

"What?"

"You weren't her father. Klaus was."

Kasper contained his rage, reminding himself that the trauma was speaking, not Rosamund.

"Rest, Rosamund."

"Don't change the subject."

"Sometimes, when bad things happen, we seek a reason, we seek someone to blame. But most often, bad things just happen. No one's to blame but Fate."

"Who else could've fathered a faceless child other than a faceless father and mother?"

Kasper understood that Lux women were prone to have children with birth defects. The child was an accident of genetics, not evidence of illicit intercourse.

"How could Klaus be the father? The timing doesn't even work. You haven't been in prison for years."

"You fool! Klaus has been visiting me… here… in this very room… night after night."

"Dr. Friedlich explained that. Klaus is all in your mind."

"He fucked me, Kasper! Klaus fucked me!"

"Keep your voice down, goddamnit!"

Even though Rosamund wasn't in her right mind, her words stung. Kasper took a breath to remind himself, yet again, this wasn't the true Rosamund but the reduced, mentally ill version. Further engagement was pointless.

Kasper rose from the bed. "I think I hear the doctor asking for me."

"I warned you, Kasper. Klaus never was going to let us have a child."

"I'll have Mama Elsie bring some towels and clean up." He forced a smile and added, "Things will get better, my love. We leave Germany soon. I'm just waiting to hear from Dieter."

"We waited too long."

"We have plenty of time."

"Klaus is going to call for me any minute."

The phone rang in the foyer. Nervous electricity shot through Kasper, as he envisioned the veiled interrogator on the other end of the line. He was relieved to hear Dieter's voice. Dieter apologized for calling so late. He said he'd reserved seats for the family on the "Flying Hamburger" in two days' time. That train would take them to the Hamburg port, where they'd pick up a South American steamer.

"That's… that's good news, Dieter. Thank you," said Kasper despondently. "No, I'm fine. Just tired… Everything is all right… Let's talk further in the morning."

Kasper couldn't discuss his child's death and his lover's madness, not then. He was too sick with dread. Logic told him that Rosamund's fixation on numbers, dates, and secret messages through the radio was the product of a sick mind. Yet he couldn't shake the feeling that something—or someone—awful would be calling very soon.

CHAPTER SEVENTEEN

The image of the faceless, suffocating infant haunted Kasper until morning. He played Jelly Roll Morton's *The Pearls* on a continuous loop inside his head, imagining the cornet washing away the tiny purple corpse. When that stopped working, he drank. He alternated between *The Pearls* and whiskey shots through the night. Because his grief was deep, and his black mood had many crevices and nooks, he was still drunk at sunrise.

Although Dieter had gotten the tickets and visas, their travel plans were not guaranteed. The "J" on Kasper's and the children's passports might single them out for "special treatment"—i.e., a bribe demand, a beating, or worse. A guard at the train station or the port might challenge their paperwork and not let them board. The station agent or the purser might advise the "Juden" that the train or the steamship was overbooked, and they'd have to wait days or weeks to leave. There were too many contingencies that could work against them as long as human beings stood between Germany and freedom. The only means of travel in which Kasper could have absolute faith was the wishing hat. The hat was their insurance policy. Hopefully, they wouldn't need to make a claim.

Rosamund arose at ten. Had it not been for some post-partum blood in the sheets and the tightly wrapped bundle in the office, there was little evidence she'd given birth during the night. She didn't seem fatigued. She hadn't torn during delivery. If she was suffering afterpains or sore breasts, she didn't betray her discomfort with a wince or a moan. She was stoic. Indeed, she was a stone. She projected no emotion at all.

Kasper embraced Rosamund. Her body was stiff, her cheek cool and dry against his. Her respiration was so shallow, Kasper couldn't detect breath from her lips or any expansion and contraction in her chest. He may as well have been hugging a mannequin. She was in denial. She'd detached herself from the prior night's horror, which was understandable. Kasper didn't know if the manifestation of her denial was typical or healthy. He worried she was giving up, allowing her bodily systems to peter out and wind down like a neglected watch. She needed to feel some sadness, some sense of loss, so she could appreciate life and find the will to press on.

"You're cold," said Kasper.

"Am I?" she asked flatly.

"It sounds ridiculous to ask this question given all you've gone through, but are you all right?"

"Yes."

"You seem... vacant... empty. I think we should see the doctor."

"You'd be happier if I were crying my eyes out and tearing my clothes?"

"It's not healthy to keep all that grief bottled up."

"A bottle. That's a good analogy. Mine is a champagne bottle, I think. It's corked tight. If opened, my grief will shoot out in a fountain. I can't shed just one tear without spilling all the contents. I'm afraid what'll be left once my bottle is empty. I will have to find out someday. But right now, the hope of leaving Germany is the only thing keeping that bottle corked. For the sake of the entire family, it must stay in. Not a single tear."

"All right. I'll let it go... for now. In the meantime, let's focus on our new life. Once we get settled in Bolivia, we'll figure out the quickest way to America."

"If war breaks out, it could take years."

"What other choice do we have?"

"The one sitting in your wall safe."

"We've been over this. The hat is an absolute last resort. We don't have visas for the U.S. Even if we get forged documents, the Americans will find us out. It might be in a week, or a month, or ten years from now, but either way, we'll be uprooted and shipped back here. I can't live like that. And don't forget, hat travel is dangerous for Mama Elsie. She's getting more frail by the day."

"With all the SA hovering around the 'Juden' shops, is it smart to leave the wishing hat at the shop? The Nazis roughed up Hans Spelk quite badly. Wouldn't even let him go inside."

"You're right. I'll go fetch it."

Kasper kissed Rosamund's lips, which were colder than her skin. He kept his lips pressed to hers, trying to transfer his heat and hope into her flesh. The embrace was too brief to make a difference, as Rosamund pushed him away after only a few seconds.

"We must bury Gretel," she announced.

"*Gretel?*"

"Our daughter. Do you object to the name?"

Kasper didn't care about the name. Any name would do. Rosamund's naming her grief had to be a positive sign. A name would define the outlines of her sadness. It would allow her to categorize it, compartmentalize it. That seemed healthy.

"Gretel is a beautiful choice. We can bury her whenever you're ready."

"I'm ready now."

"I'll make the preparations."

The brittle leaves crunched under Kasper's feet as he approached the hat shop's entrance. His heart sunk when he realized they were laurel leaves. While the tree canopy's left side remained evergreen and healthy, the foliage on its right side had curled, dried, and fallen. Had city workers abandoned their brute force eradication techniques and opted for the insidiousness of pesticide? If so, why had the poison affected only one side? Unless poison wasn't the culprit. Maybe certain trees could sense the horror that darkened the skies of their environment. Maybe this laurel tree was of two minds: one side ready to abandon the fight, the other ready to dig in for battle. Which would ultimately prevail?

Kasper unlocked the hat shop, set the blanketed bundle on the cutting room table, and got to work. He emptied a wooden box of its bobbins, thread, and random fabric swatches. It was small by coffin standards but large enough for the tiny corpse. Though Gretel was an empty shell with no wants or demands, Kasper treated her with the dignity he'd afford a customer. He applied linseed oil to the box to bring out the grain and the shine. For the cushion, he chose a yard-and-a-half of indigo silk. He assumed that Gretel would've liked the color, which matched the flecks in her mother's eyes. He sewed the fabric into a three-sided rectangle, stuffed it with wool, and then sewed the fourth end shut before setting it in the box and laying Gretel to rest. She barely dented the cushion. He closed the lid and pounded it shut with three finish nails. Kasper then retrieved the wishing hat from the safe on his way out. The supple leather easily compressed into the breast pocket of his giant overcoat.

They buried Gretel in the plot that Hermann Mützenmacher's remains would've occupied had there been any. Mama Elsie and Bessie held hands, while Kasper and Duke flanked Rosamund. No priest or rabbi presided. No prayers were uttered, only simple goodbyes. That was all fine with Kasper. He had no doubt divine beings existed; the proof had been in his wall safe for decades. He simply doubted there was a supreme god who listened to, let alone answered prayers. If there was such a being, it was a "watchmaker God." It had created the world, set it in motion, and moved on to the next timepiece. This indifferent God wasn't interested in prayers any more than the corner jeweler was interested in customer complaints. He sold goods on a strict "as is" basis. No warranties. No customer service. There was only Fate, the great *Über*-soul permeating the universe's fabric. You could beseech Her, question Her, ask Her for forgiveness, but these were futile gestures. Fate had Her own agenda, and she didn't care about your faith any more than a storm cloud cared that you believe in rain.

Mama Elsie and Bessie took turns shoveling dirt over Gretel's coffin. Kasper finished the job, while Duke gazed longingly at the gibbous moon. Rosamund then laid a crimson orchid near the headstone. That was that. She embraced Kasper and then patted the bulge in his overcoat's breast pocket.

Back at the apartment, Rosamund filled two suitcases with dresses and hats. She then prepared and baked an apple strudel. She was moving differently, better than she'd moved in a long time. She wasted no energy, her sinews and muscles perfectly coordinated. Her footsteps made no sound on the oak floor, not even a creak from the loose planks. She glided. But her newfound fluidity was intermittent. She repeatedly stopped and glanced at the dining room or bathroom mirror, closing one eye and then the other, like a hypochondriac trying to convince herself she wasn't going blind. Kasper didn't ask her about it. He was just heartened that she seemed physically and mentally strong enough to cope with the journey. She was looking forward, and that was the only direction that mattered.

Mama Elsie set out all the remaining food for dinner. After they sat down, Kasper revealed a surprise. He'd fashioned traditional Bolivian bowler hats for Mama Elsie, Bessie, and Rosamund, and chullo hats for himself and Duke. The bowlers were black felt wrapped with an indigo grosgrain ribbon. The chullos were black alpaca; a line of indigo yarn spiraled around the skull and terminated in a small indigo tassel.

The family stuffed themselves with sausages, cheese, bread, pickled herring, smoked ham, and fresh apple strudel. Rosamund ate nothing. Kasper drained three bottles of the Hacker-Pschorr wheat beer he'd bought in bulk "at an unbelievable price." He was sorry to abandon so many bottles of such a fine brew. Whatever they didn't drink he'd give to Dieter, though he doubted Dieter was an imbiber. Kasper offered bottles to Mama Elsie and Duke. Elsie declined, but Duke happily accepted. Kasper figured his son would take one humoring sip and then put down the bottle, disgusted. Instead, the boy swigged and swigged, until half the bottle was gone.

"Duke's gonna get drunk," Bessie announced.

"I suspect this isn't your first beer," Kasper commented. "What other vices did these Pirates of the Crescent Moon teach you?"

Kasper felt strangely good, and not just from the booze. Was it wrong to express happiness so soon after burying a child? How much time needed to pass before it was appropriate to experience even a hint of joy? A week? A month? Any amount of time was arbitrary. He needed hope right then, even if just a smidgen. They were on the precipice of a new life. He and Rosamund would try again, and next time they'd have a healthy child. He was sure of it. Best of all, there was no such thing as a Mischling in Bolivia.

"I think we should bid farewell to our old friend," said Kasper.

"Who's that, Pops?" asked Bessie.

"Not a who but a what. Schwarz Boden. Let's take one final walk."

Everyone headed for the door except Rosamund.

"I will clean up."

"I'll help," offered Mama Elsie.

"No, Mama," Rosamund insisted. "You of all people should go and say goodbye to the city. It won't take me long, and I have more packing to do."

"But there's plenty of time," Kasper protested. He placed a hand on her hip. "We don't leave until tomorrow evening."

Rosamund planted a long kiss on Kasper. He'd expected a brief peck, but she held him close for a good ten seconds.

"What was that for?"

"I don't want you to forget my face."

"We're only going for a walk. I'll see you very soon."

Kasper went to the coat rack to retrieve his overcoat, but it wasn't there.

"It's in the office," said Rosamund. "There was a small tear in the collar."

"Really? I hadn't noticed."

"It was very small."

"You didn't have to trouble yourself given... given everything else."

Rosamund's mouth flinched up on the right, an inchoate smile, perhaps. "I'll go fetch it."

Rosamund retrieved the coat and held it for Kasper as he slipped in his arms. She came around and fastened the buttons. She straightened the lapels, which she used to pull him close and plant another long kiss. Kasper opened his mouth to speak, but Rosamund nodded, implying that words would have reduced their love somehow, by defining it, by marking it with linguistic boundaries. She then disappeared into the bedroom. Kasper had the impulse to follow her. He had the unsettling feeling she wasn't just going into another room but heading into another world, a world where he didn't belong and never could be admitted, not even with the best forged papers money could buy.

Don't be silly, he told himself. Nothing more than nostalgia. When you were leaving home for good, the most innocuous things took on deep meaning. The dishrag next to the tea kettle became the finest Chinese silk. The squeak of the hot water faucet handle became the opening draw of the bow from Tchaikovsky's Violin Concerto. The sweet, moldy smell from the radiator became the repository of every stew and dumpling eaten at the table, the sweat in the scarves that had shielded them from the Berlin winters, the breast milk Duke and Bessie had vomited into the rug, and the Bushmills Kasper sloshed on the oak floor during his darker moments. Rosamund's exit into the bedroom was no different. There was no special significance to his lover entering the bedroom. Rosamund had performed this act many times and would repeat it many times in the future.

"Let's go, Pops!" shouted Bessie.

"Right behind you."

Kasper pulled the apartment door shut. He told himself that the latch's click sounded nothing like that final nail he'd driven into Gretel's coffin.

CHAPTER EIGHTEEN

As they ambled through Schwarz Boden Memorial Park, Kasper mentally reinscribed his father's name onto the blank section of limestone. They passed Kimball's toy shop, marveling at a wind-up zeppelin, a red scooter, a child-sized piano, dolls, tin cars, and model ships. No one mentioned that the shop's Aryanization would be completed in a few days. They strolled by synagogues and churches, dry cleaners and department stores, bakeries and butcher shops. Though closed for the evening, these businesses continued to off-gas the distinct odors of old books, petroleum, and baked bread. They walked down Mauer Street to the garment district, which was quiet—dead quiet. Indeed, there was nary a soul in sight. Where was everyone?

On any other November night, Kasper would've welcomed the temperate breeze, but tonight the air was uncomfortably thick and humid. Schwarz Boden seemed to be holding its collective breath, and the stifled respiration was building on itself. Kasper's clothes felt tingly on his skin, as though he'd come down with the flu. He thought, *This must be what a cat senses just before it pounces.* He swallowed hard. *No, it's what the mouse feels just before the cat snuffs out its existence.*

"You okay, Pops?" asked Duke.

"Sure. Fine. Just feeling sentimental. Let's stop in the park."

They played hide and seek among Kiegel Park's dense plane trees, and fooled around on the slide and swings, before venturing to the river. Kasper removed his shoes and waded into the frigid water. Duke and Bessie joined him under the gibbous moon. Kasper put his arms around his children and fantasized that, in some small way, their mother had joined them on their final walk through town. Atomic-sized pieces of Isana were curling around their ankles, reassuring them that a long journey to a far-off place didn't mean the end of things but a new beginning. He bade his deceased wife a silent farewell, saddened she hadn't known Rosamund. In some other reality, they might have become good friends.

"Time to get back," Kasper announced.

The apartment door was ajar, and a panicked female voice was spilling into the hallway. Kasper's heart raced.

"Rosamund?"

A man was sitting in the wingback chair by the radio. Kasper recognized Dieter's head—thin, sandy blond hair swirling around a pinkish pate. The voice wasn't Rosamund's. Heidi Geissmütter was speaking in furtive, breathless sentences.

> Time grows short. They have broken down the door and entered the station. You know who they are. They are easy to recognize in their long black coats and wide-brimmed hats, with their hooked noses and greedy eyes, with their stubby fingers stained with ink from all the Reichsmarks stolen from the Volk. Soon they will be stained with blood, my blood. They have come for me because I dared to speak the truth. They may kill me, but they can't kill the good people of Schwarz Boden, who will step in when I am gone.
>
> (Sound of broken glass and shouting in the background.)
>
> Listen to me, girls, mothers, sisters, daughters. All of you, listen! Look in the mirror. Gaze into the glass of a shop window or the windshield of an automobile. Look at your faces. Witness the miracle, the miracle I witnessed earlier today. Do you see? Yes, you do! We all share the same face, the face of Der Führer. He is in us, and we in him. We are one body, one Volk.
>
> (Sounds of gunshots and yelling.)
>
> They are here. Now, look into the eyes of your new face. These eyes

command you to defend the Volk. Rise up, girls of Schwarz Boden! Shatter the great Jewish lie. All men—all women—are not created equal. We are Aryans! We need not apologize for our superiority. The only crime we commit is remaining a slave to the Jew.

(The sound of a door bursting open, followed by a shout of, "Die, Aryan bitch!")

They're here... Mark the time of your liberation: 11:21...

(A gunshot)

... 11:21...

(Another gunshot)

... 11:21... 11:21...

(Another gunshot and then static)

Dieter flipped off the radio. The sight of Kasper and his family startled him. "Thank goodness. You're back. We need to go."
"What are you doing here, Dieter?" Kasper asked. "What's going on?"
"A riot has erupted across town. It'll reach us soon. My car's downstairs. If we hurry to Lehrter station, we can catch the last Flying Hamburger."
"The ship doesn't leave Hamburg until tomorrow evening."
"I switched the tickets to tonight, just like you'd asked."
"I didn't ask you to do that."
"Rosamund phoned this morning. She said you wanted to leave as soon as possible, before the baby came."
"The baby came last night."
"What? Where is it?"
"She didn't survive."
Dieter brought his hand to his mouth. "Oh my God, Kasper. I'm so sorry. Why didn't you tell me?"
"There was too much going on. I didn't want to trouble you with all the plans you were making for us."
"I should've been there for you and the children. Have you buried her?"

"Yes, this morning."

"Then why would Rosamund tell me she's still pregnant?"

"Because she's completely lost her mind." Kasper looked toward the bedroom. "Rosamund!"

"She's not here."

"Where the hell is she?"

"On the phone, she said she'd meet us at the station after she took care of some personal business."

"What personal business?"

"She didn't say. I'm sorry, Kasper. I thought you knew all this."

There was a ruckus outside—smashing glass, shouts and screams, cars slamming on brakes. The family moved to the balcony to get a vantage on the melee unfolding below. Hundreds of people poured from apartment buildings and alleys, like movie extras responding to the director's cue. Flames licked the sky throughout Schwarz Boden. A smoke plume expanded over the synagogue at the corner. Groups of three, four, or five strode down the street with sledgehammers and axes, smashing in doors and shattering plate glass windows. Other groups carried clubs and shouted, "Juden!" A mob pursued a young couple into an alley. Moments later, the man's female companion screamed. After shouts of "Juden" and "kike," two women dragged the man to the street like a rag doll, his face covered in blood. They dropped him on the sidewalk and then arranged his fractured arms and legs into the shape of a crude swastika.

Kasper shook his head, befuddled. Why were only women on the prowl? Why hadn't the men been inspired to take up arms? Were they clubbing Jews and burning synagogues elsewhere in Berlin? Since when were there sex-segregated riots?

Duke pointed to the man in the moon atop Kimball's shop. The face had been painted with a giant red "J," and a rope had been affixed to the rocket ship in the moon man's eye. An object dangled from the rope. It was a man, dead, neck snapped. The rioters had lynched Rabbi Kimball.

Kasper ushered everyone inside and told them to gather their luggage by the front door.

"Hurry," urged Dieter. "I know a less-traveled route to the station."

Kasper felt his breast pocket for the wishing hat's telltale bulge. It felt off somehow. When he reached his hand into the pocket, his fingers didn't touch warm leather but a woolen scarf.

"It's gone," Kasper muttered. "The hat is gone."

"What hat?" asked Dieter.

"My hat."

"Oh my God," said Mama Elsie, horrified.

"Don't worry about your hat," said Dieter. "You can have mine. We have to go."

"You don't understand. It's not just any hat. It's been in the family for thou—for many years."

"Kasper, if we don't leave now, you may not have a head to put a hat on!"

"Mama, did you put it back in the safe?"

"Why would she keep a hat in a safe?" asked Dieter.

"Do you take me for an idiot?" Mama Elsie objected.

"Sorry. I had to ask. Duke, did you take it?"

"No, Pops."

"So much drama over a silly hat!" remarked an exasperated Dieter.

Kasper recalled Rosamund retrieving his coat from the office, claiming she had stitched a rip. She must have taken the hat and replaced it with the scarf to avoid detection. But why?

"Let's get to the station," said Kasper.

Dieter took Mama Elsie's and Bessie's luggage and proceeded out the door. Kasper and Duke followed with their bags. Neither bothered to switch off the light or close the door behind him.

The vintage of Dieter's car surprised Kasper. Given the number of hat and fabric stores in Dieter's portfolio, surely he could've afforded something newer than a black Lincoln Model L Town Car from the mid-twenties. A used Mercedes, at the very least.

"This thing gonna make it to the station?" Kasper asked.

Dieter was affronted. "I'll have you know this is a very fine luxury automobile. Low mileage. Excellent condition. No sense buying a new one just to be fashionable."

Kasper struggled to fit the luggage into the passenger compartment because a trunk already occupied a third of the space between the two velvet benches. Moreover, despite Kasper's instruction to bring only one suitcase each, Bessie had packed two, one for her and one for her dolls. Had Berlin not been in the midst of a riot, he might've raised a stink. Instead, he directed his irritation at Dieter.

"Maybe you should've emptied out that trunk before picking us up."

"I need it," said Dieter. "I'm coming with you to Bolivia."

"What?"

"I have no choice."

"What are you talking about? With me gone, you're the King of Schwarz Boden."

"This king has been deposed. The Gauleiter noticed my below average flight tax receipts. As of two days ago, he'd nearly connected the dots between the bogus sales contracts, shell companies, and overseas wire transfers. He'll be sending his men for me. It was either Bolivia or Shanghai, and I'd prefer to go where I know someone."

"You're coming with us, Onkel Dieter?" asked Bessie.

"That's up to your papa."

"Oh please, Pops. Let Onkel Dieter come."

Dieter had done so much for them. Kasper could no sooner refuse Dieter than ignore a whimpering puppy. The question was, would he follow them to America?

"Bolivia's a free country, so far as I know," Kasper said diffidently. "I mean, it's not as though you're planning on living with us..."

Dieter didn't chime in.

"Are you planning on living with us?" asked Kasper.

Dieter smiled crookedly. "No. No. Don't be silly."

Kasper eyed Dieter dubiously. "All right, then. You can come."

"Yay!" shouted Bessie as she wrapped her arms around Dieter.

"We should go," said Kasper.

"Of course," said Dieter. "Just one more thing." He stuck small Nazi flags near the headlights and the back bumpers. "Camouflage."

Dieter frequently backed up and turned onto different streets on the way to the station because fights or bonfires blocked intersections. Other streets were covered in broken glass, and Dieter didn't want to risk a flat tire. Thanks to the conspicuous Nazi flags, rioters didn't try to smash the car's windows or open its doors and yank out its passengers. There were two such instances before Teilung Street took them out of Schwarz Boden.

The first involved a Jewish family of four. The mob stopped the car, punched and clubbed the father, and tossed him through a shop window, as his stunned wife and two young daughters looked on. The mob then pushed over the sedan and lit it on fire.

The second instance involved a single man whom the mob hauled from a car amidst shouts of "filthy kike." He insisted he wasn't a Jew but a Protestant. They didn't believe him. Though his nose wasn't big, it was "big enough." And his eyes—they were shifty, just like a Jew's. A woman scooped shards from a broken window while two others restrained him. They pried open his mouth and stuffed it with glass. The rest formed a circle around the man and ordered him to "swallow or die." He swallowed and then collapsed face down. "Looks like he swallowed *and* died!" someone joked, sending the mob into a fit of hyena-like laughter.

"They're mostly women," Dieter marveled.

"They're *all* women," Kasper corrected.

Dieter instructed Duke to cover his sister's eyes, but Kasper said no. He wanted Bessie to witness the mayhem and remember it. Duke's face and fists clenched with anger. Kasper envisioned him opening the door and attempting to intervene. It would've been futile. There were too many rioters. One man couldn't fight an entire town of feral women. Their only objective was to survive.

The violent sights and sounds slowly receded from the rear window. They followed the River Spree in silence until arriving at the train station.

The Lehrter Bahnhof, an elegant French Neo-Renaissance structure wrapped in arched windows, bustled with activity. Helmeted soldiers manned a makeshift checkpoint. A guard with a German shepherd at his heel stood at the wooden gate arm, which was striped like a black and white candy cane. A soldier emerged from the tiny guard booth, also striped in black and white, and approached the driver's window. Dieter produced his passport and identified himself as the Blockleiter of Mauer Street. The soldier was unimpressed. He gestured to the other passengers. They, too, produced their papers. The soldier quickly zeroed in on the large red "J's" emblazoned on the passports.

"Juden," the soldier commented.

"As you see," said Dieter, "they have visas for Bolivia. I must get them to the Flying Hamburger if they are to make their ship."

"We're sending all Jews south," said the guard. "For resettlement."

"These Jews are resettling in Bolivia."

The soldier shot Kasper a steely gaze. Kasper turned his face toward the window. The moonlight illuminated his facial scar, which seemed to gum up the soldier's mental gears. The soldier seemed too overtired, perhaps too underpaid, to sort out the paradox of a Jew bearing the mark of a Nordic god. He handed the papers to Dieter and waved them through the gate.

"Did Rosamund say where she's going to meet us?" asked Kasper.

"She didn't. I assume at the train platform."

Dieter pulled the car to the left of the building. He and Kasper unloaded the trunks and suitcases, and then the family entered the broad central platform separating two sets of train tracks. A soldier stood on a folding ladder, shouting instructions through a megaphone at several hundred Jews huddled near the dingy, third class train cars. He explained that they were being "resettled" to the south for their own safety. They were to leave their luggage on the platform, as it would be loaded onto a special luggage car. Where was this mysterious luggage car, someone asked, given the guards had positioned people outside every train car? It is coming, he assured them. He then ordered them to board the cars, which they did, well beyond capacity. The soldier apologized for the "temporary discomfort," but assured them it was a "small price to pay for permanent resettlement."

Kasper recognized several people boarding the train cars—that is, he recognized what was on their heads. One was a mushroom-shaped hat covered in taffeta and crepe chiffon and trimmed rosettes. Another was a cloche hat; another a homburg. They were his hats, pieces of himself being forced into boxcars destined for a concentration camp. What would become of his hats? Would they end up soaked with the sweat and blood of forced labor? Or would the Nazis confiscate them for their girlfriends and wives (or secret boyfriends)?

Another train pulled into the station. The sleek "Flying Hamburger," painted in a glossy, two-tone pallet of indigo and beige, had antennae-shaped bumpers on the front, which made it look like a shiny caterpillar. When the train stopped, Dieter ushered the family off the center platform, toward the station's west side. Kasper scanned faces as quickly as he could. There was no sign of Rosamund.

Dieter stopped three cars down from the front of the Flying Hamburger, where a guard was checking passports and tickets. He glanced at Dieter's papers and handed them back with an approving head nod. Kasper handed his and the children's papers to the guard, who not unexpectedly announced, "Juden board the resettlement train."

"They have visas for Bolivia," Dieter corrected him. "They're taking this train to the port."

The guard looked back at the papers. "Forgeries."

"No. No. The consular general at the Bolivian embassy gave them to me personally."

"How do I know that?"

"Because that's his signature."

"Could be a forgery."

"As Blockleiter of Mauer Street, I can vouch for their authenticity."

The guard handed the papers back to Kasper. "You may board," he said to Dieter. "The other three must board the resettlement train. Take your luggage."

"This is an outrage!" yelled Dieter.

"Why, because you're a Blockleiter?" The guard spoke the word "Blockleiter" with contempt. "I've taken shits with more backbone than you."

Kasper shook the bizarre metaphor from his head and asked, "What do you want? Money?"

"Leave it to the Jew to bring up money. But now that you mention it, yes, money may help me see things in a different light."

Kasper handed the guard a wad of Reichsmarks.

The guard pointed at Duke and Bessie. "You and you may board."

"What about him?" Dieter asked of Kasper.

"The lighting is very poor in here. I still can't determine if this signature is authentic."

"For God's sake, he's given you all his money."

"I don't think so. He was very quick to hand me that wad."

"You're a shrewd man," said Kasper. He extracted more cash from his pocket. "This means my family won't eat for two days, but if it helps you with your vision..."

The guard held the cylindrical wad to his eye and studied the visa like a jeweler examining a gemstone. "Mmm. Much clearer now. You may board."

Kasper had anticipated such bribes, so had prepared three wads of Reichsmark banknotes. For each wad, he'd wrapped a single one-hundred-Reichsmark bill around 10 ten-Reichsmark bills, making it look like a small fortune. He figured the guard wouldn't bother unraveling the bills, and he'd been right.

Kasper stepped past the guard and leaned against the train, keeping a lookout for Rosamund. He couldn't fathom what personal business she had to take care of, why she hadn't shared her plans with him, and why she would've taken the wishing hat. Who knew how a sick mind worked? She'd always been a mystery. Kasper was attracted to her inscrutability. One moment she'd be as stern and powerful as an army general; the next, weepy and delusional. Always, however, beautiful. Always, those deep green eyes staring into his soul, making him long to dive into the warm sea between her legs, when she'd relinquish her secret pain, free herself, and smile, really smile.

The crowd separated for two gray-uniformed Gestapo agents. They stepped aboard the Flying Hamburger, and within ten seconds, the passengers were filing off. The agents walked down the car and pulled down the window shades. They then stepped off the train and gestured for Kasper, and only Kasper, to board. He obliged, weak-kneed and nauseated.

The train car was empty except for someone at a table at the far end. The stranger was dressed in black, facing the opposite direction. A black patent leather satchel rested against his left leg. Kasper assumed the bag was filled with torture implements—blades, brass knuckles, pliers. He found dubious comfort in the bag's small size, figuring it was large enough to hold a battery and cables to connect to his sensitive body parts. He pulled on the front of his boxers, which had twisted during the commotion to the train station. He then swallowed hard and approached the veiled stranger.

Klaus.

Klaus gestured for Kasper to sit opposite him.

"Herr Mützenmacher," Klaus said in his legendary drone, "do you understand the reason for this meeting?"

"No, I don't."

"I think you do."

Klaus lifted the satchel onto the table between them.

"Please, whatever you think I've done, my family is innocent. Let them board this train."

"Why would you want them to board this train?"

"It goes to Hamburg. That's where we pick up our ship to Bolivia."

"A very long voyage."

"Yes."

"Too long." Klaus popped open the satchel and pulled out the ancient leather sunhat. "This would be much faster."

"Where did you get that? From Rosamund?"

"In a manner of speaking, yes."

"Where is she?"

"Close."

"At the station?"

"Close."

"May I see her?"

"Not possible. She's in the midst of a debriefing."

"About what?"

"Her mission."

"What mission?"

"Isn't it obvious? Rosamund Lux is my spy, one of many. Her mission was to infiltrate your family, learn how you escaped from custody with Fraulein Wandel, and report back. Don't blame her, though. The poor girl had no idea she was working for me."

"That's ridiculous."

"As you well know, the most ridiculous things are often the truest."

"Will Rosamund be joining us after this so-called debriefing?"

"Reliable spies are hard to come by. She has more work to do, much more."

"But she's a full-German citizen. Her travel papers are in order."

"They're forgeries."

"Regardless, she has rights, and she's my wife."

"Your wife?"

"Well, technically we're engaged. We've been living as husband and wife, and—" Klaus raised an eyebrow. *Yes! Yes! I'm a racial defiler.* "What I meant was she's practically a mother to my children. They need her. If you won't release her, then we will remain in Germany."

"Don't be a fool. You spent weeks in a work camp. That was a vacation resort compared to where that resettlement train is headed. Do you want that for Duke and Bessie? For your mother?" Klaus had spoken the children's names with a warmth otherwise absent in his cold, monotonous tone. He cleared his throat. "I might add, this is what Fraulein Lux wishes for you."

"I want to hear it from her lips."

"My lips, her lips—it makes no difference."

Do you even have lips?

"Will you at least give her a message? Tell her I love her."

"Very well."

"And one other thing. I won't give up on her. We'll see each other again. Make sure to say that part, too."

"Why raise false hope?"

"I don't want her to think I abandoned her."

"I meant your false hope, not hers. Tomorrow, she won't care one whit about you. After her debriefing, she will fully recall what she is—my spy. She won't feel love for you or the children because those sentiments were premised on a lie. She will revert to a blank slate, ready for her next mission."

Kasper so wanted to unleash a flurry of fists into Klaus's absurd masked face. "Just tell her." He squeezed his anger into the wishing hat.

"As you wish."

"You saw Isana and me vanish that day, didn't you?"

"I did."

"Then you know what this hat can do."

"I do."

"I don't understand. Why not give the hat to your bosses? Your ilk could take over the world in months, eradicate anyone you want, claim the entire planet for the Greater Nazi Reich."

"Or you could use the hat to save innocents from the concentration camps."

"Are you joking?"

"Let me make it plain for you. You and your family will not be riding this train to Hamburg. You will board the resettlement train and wish yourselves and as many other souls as you can to America."

"Since when do you care about saving Jews?"

"That is my new mission—mine and Fraulein Lux's."

"You just ignited a violent pogrom against the Jews. Why the hell would Hitler now order you to save them?"

"He wouldn't."

"Are you saying you've switched sides?"

Klaus remained silent.

"Have you joined the resistance?" Kasper pressed.

"One day you'll understand. But not now. Not in this time or place."

"Who are you really?"

"I am no one. I am the faceless."

"Everyone has a face."

Klaus was trembling. He seemed vulnerable, at a tipping point. A crazy impulse struck Kasper—a stupid, dangerous, impulse, but he couldn't resist. He reached for the veil. "Show me your face."

Klaus remained still, as if tacitly assenting to his imminent unmasking. But the moment Kasper's fingertips grazed the veil's fabric, Klaus stood and declared, "Our time is up, Herr Mützenmacher. Best of luck in your future travels. Remember, you are to board the resettlement train."

Klaus exited the train. The two Gestapo agents joined him, and they rapidly departed the platform. When Kasper stepped off the train, Elsie, Duke, and Bessie embraced him, relieved.

"Come. We have a train to catch."

Dieter beamed. "Klaus is letting you go? All of you?"

"Yes. Thank you for everything, Dieter. Good luck in Bolivia."

Kasper grabbed two bags, instructed Duke to grab two others, and then began leading his family down the platform.

"Wait," said Dieter. "Where are you going? *This* is the train to Hamburg."

"We're taking the resettlement train."

"Are you insane? You know where it's headed, don't you?"

"I almost forgot. I have something for you." Kasper pulled the chullo hat from his side coat pocket. "Here."

Dieter accepted the hat, not comprehending Kasper's cavalier attitude. "What about Rosamund?"

"Yeah, Pops," said Bessie. "Why isn't Tante Rosamund coming with us?"

Kasper spied Klaus filtering through the crowd like quicksilver, as though sliding on ice instead of walking on stone.

"Klaus says Tante Rosamund must stay here. It's what Rosamund wants."

"Why would she want that?" asked Dieter. "He tortured her."

"Rosamund is not what we thought she was."

"What is she?"

"Does it matter, Dieter? She can't or won't come with us. The only way to assure our freedom is by boarding the resettlement train."

Dieter was crying. "Those trains are headed to the camps."

Kasper put his hands on Dieter's shoulders. "Look at me, Dieter. We're getting on that train, but we are not going to the camps. I don't have time to explain how. You must accept that."

"But it'll take a miracle."

"Yes, it will. You have to abandon your reason and just believe what I'm telling you. Believe it in your gut, with every fiber of your soul. We will be fine. Can you have faith in my words?"

Dieter gazed at Kasper with wonderment. He brushed Kasper's scar with his index finger. "I don't know why, but I can. I have faith. How strange."

"My stunning good looks have that effect on people."

Dieter kissed Kasper's cheeks.

"All right, Dieter. Don't get all sloppy on me."

Dieter's eyes projected the same intimacy Kasper had seen in the boiler room all those years ago. But this time it didn't terrify Kasper. This time he welcomed Dieter's love, even though it was a kind of love he couldn't reciprocate. This time he could embrace this man's heart and tell him without actually saying, "Yes, Dieter, your blood matters very much."

"I love you, too," Kasper added. "We all do."

After bidding farewell to the rest of the Mützenmachers, Dieter boarded the Flying Hamburger. He dried his eyes and took a seat by the window in the second car. He saw Kasper, Elsie, Duke, and Bessie board car 21 on the resettlement train and squeeze among the hundred other occupants. Kasper spoke to Bessie while gesturing to her doll suitcase, which she was supposed to have left on the platform with the other luggage. Bessie remained stone-faced until her exasperated father looked away. She then faced out the dirty window. Upon spotting Dieter, she smiled and waved. Dieter waved back feebly, mustering the semblance of a smile for the daughter he would never have.

The guards shut the car doors, and the resettlement train blew its whistle. Kasper then donned a large black sunhat.

How odd, thought Dieter.

Kasper turned his back and joined hands with Elsie, Bessie, and Duke. A stranger took Bessie's hand, and another took Duke's. Soon, all the car's occupants were holding hands and listening intently to Kasper, who appeared to be instructing them. As the resettlement train pulled away, Dieter felt a rumble, and his ears filled with what sounded like a herd of shrieking elephants. A flash of purple light dazzled his eyes, and after the cacophony dissipated, the third train car from the back was utterly empty.

CHAPTER NINETEEN

After Kasper instructed everyone to exhale, he closed his eyes, thought of Ellis Island, and made the wish. At first, Kasper assumed he'd wished incorrectly, because there was a delay, as though the hat was taking stock of the number of souls it had to transport. Then, instead of the telltale popping sound followed by the feeling of compression and expansion, a deep, melodic rumble shook car 21, like being trapped in the bell of a gigantic baritone sax. The lights in the train car faded, not dimmed per se but lost substance, or perhaps the occupants of car 21 had lost substance. The rumble grew deeper, more strained, like an old man's groan. Could the hat transport this many people? Would it peter out and strand everyone where they'd started or drop them in the middle of the Atlantic? Would they end up trapped in an oblivion of electromagnetic energy?

Everything went black and silent.

Kasper hadn't envisioned a specific location on Ellis Island before wishing but complied with his father's advice to wish for dry land. The hat dropped the train passengers in a relatively secluded location, between the Immigrant Building and the New Ferry House. Because the local time was six hours earlier than in Berlin, the sun was shining. Kasper peered around the building. Activity on the island seemed to be centered around the Main Building, where a few men in uniforms watched the MS New Orleans entering the ferry slip. Kasper and his fellow travelers weren't at risk of immediate detection.

Most of Kasper's fellow travelers were disoriented, doubled over with abdominal cramps, or both. Some assumed they were dreaming. Others thought they were experiencing a delusion caused by the Nazis flooding the train car with noxious gas. Within a half hour, however, everyone had accepted the miracle. One moment they'd been crammed inside a boxcar bound for a concentration camp; the next they were standing on American soil.

The miracle proved bittersweet. Not everyone had survived the journey. A middle-aged man with a heart condition and three of the elderly, including Mama Elsie, lay prone and unresponsive on the macadam separating the two buildings. The collective sense of awe morphed into collective grief. One of the bereaved shrieked and was sympathetically shushed. Others chanted Kaddish, the Jewish prayer for the dead. Others simply wept on the nearest shoulder.

Kasper pushed his grief aside. At that moment, he had to focus on avoiding the immigration authorities. He reconnoitered the nearby buildings—a laundry facility and a hospital. The laundry building was preferable because part of it was under construction and therefore unoccupied. There were no workers, so they should be safe at least until morning. Duke carried Mama Elsie's limp body to the laundry building and set her in the corner. Bessie found a canvas tarp and draped it over her. A moment later, Bessie peeled back the tarp, kissed Mama Elsie's cheek, and then covered her back up. Duke put his arm around his sister and offered her a chocolate bar from his pocket.

Kasper peered through a dust-caked window, trying to figure out how in the hell he was going to get a hundred people legally admitted to the United States. A man approached and introduced himself as Grimsky. Grimsky was tall, well over six feet, but his stooped shoulders rendered him close to average height. He wore a tailored black suit and a starched white shirt with a loose necktie. There were crumbs on his suit coat's left side vent from a bun he'd been nibbling since their arrival. In one hand, he held a scuffed leather briefcase, suggesting he was a professional. In the other, he gripped a homburg hat with a badly torn crown. Kasper instinctively reached for the damaged hat, like a veterinarian for a wounded puppy.

"May I?"

The man nodded. Kasper inspected the crown.

"The guard at the train station wasn't happy with my bribe," Grimsky explained. "Accused me of hiding more Marks in my hat. Put his fat fist right through the crown. I don't know why I hold onto it. It's kaput, like everything else in Germany."

"It's a fine hat. I recognize the stitching. Finkelman's, right?"

"That's right."

"Old Abe Finkelman always uses the heavy gauge thread for his liners. He stitches it twice—once with an elegant feather stitch, and again with a sturdy backstitch." Kasper stared at the hat; he was rambling, waiting for his brain to catch up to the situation at hand. "Think of all the extra pfennigs in materials and labor he spends on each hat, then multiply that by thirty years of making hats. He's wasted a small fortune."

"I'm sure that's the least of his concerns. He was on car 20, right in front of us."

"I'm afraid your homburg is beyond repair."

"As I figured. Just toss it away."

"I will do no such thing. Your hat's life as a homburg may be kaput, but it can become something else. If I may, I have an idea you might like."

"By all means. Speaking of hats, I see no point inquiring how yours works. One second, we are packed like Jewish sardines. The next, you ask us to have faith in your special hat, we close our eyes, we exhale, and then we are here. Truly the stuff of miracles, which I'm sure would require more explanation than we have time for. The pressing question is, how do we avoid deportation back to Germany?"

"I've been thinking," said Kasper. "Did you notice the MS New Orleans? That's a Hamburg-American ship."

"It is."

"There must be a thousand passengers. Why couldn't we all just mingle in, tell the immigration officers we were on board?"

Grimsky nodded and then inhaled like a professor taking in a student's argument before blowing it away with logic and common sense. "We could say that. The problem is, the Americans will expect to see that our papers are in order. I'm afraid they're no different from the Nazis in that regard. The passengers will have nametags pinned to their coats. The tags will have numbers, numbers that correspond to a list on the ship's manifest. The immigration officers will compare the numbers to the manifest."

"We need that manifest. We have to add all our names to it. We'll also need nametags. I could wish myself onto the ship and get them in a flash, if only I knew where they were kept."

"In the purser's quarters."

"How do you know all this?"

"Before the Nazis took away my law license, I was an attorney. The Hamburg-American Line was my client. I reviewed their procedures and schedules."

"How lucky for the rest of us you were on our train car."

"Luck is having a man with a magic hat on your train car."

"I suppose Fate is looking out for both of us." Kasper pulled the wishing hat from his coat pocket. "Well, time's a-wasting."

Grimsky put a hand on Kasper's forearm. "Even if you get the manifest and the tags, there's still the matter of the visas. None of us has permission from the U.S. Consulate to enter the country. We'll need forged documents."

"I know just the person."

"Forgeries will take time, probably all night. Not enough time to join the passengers from the New Orleans. The SS Blücher arrives tomorrow."

"We must remain hidden until then."

"I'll see to it," said Grimsky, "while you and your hat take care of the rest."

Kasper formed a mental image of the Flying Hamburger and then wished, *Take me there.* There was a brief delay before compression, only a few seconds, but unusual for single-person hat travel. The hat seemed to be saying, *I'm so tired. Do I really have to do this? Oh, very well.* Kasper was squeezed to a point and launched at the speed of thought across the Atlantic. As he materialized in the train's luggage compartment, a wind pushed him forward, as though the hat had belched him out of the ether.

Kasper easily located Dieter, because the train had only two passenger compartments and only one tiny man in a Bolivian chullo hat. He knelt beside Dieter and leaned into his ear.

"Dieter," Kasper whispered.

Dieter flinched violently, tearing a page of his Spanish-German dictionary.

"Shh. Relax. Don't turn. Keep looking forward. It's me, Kasper. I don't have time to explain how I'm here or how we vanished off the train. We are all safe, but we won't stay that way unless you help me, no questions asked. Please nod if you can do that for me."

Dieter nodded and then, on request, gave Kasper his master forger's name (Kopnick) and location (Krumm Street). Kasper vanished and then appeared at Kopnick's bedside. He hoisted the startled man in checkered pajamas to his feet.

"What? Who? I paid the money. The check's in the mail. I have a gun!"

"Calm down, Kopnick."

"How do you know my name? Who the hell are you?"

"Shut up and listen. I'm Dieter Daimler's close friend. I require your services for the next twelve hours. I will pay you handsomely, just name your price."

Kopnick climbed back into bed and draped a pillow over his head. "My price is a good night's sleep."

Kasper hauled the man back to his feet.

"Ow. You're hurting my arm."

"This is an emergency. You will help me, or I'll drop you at the peak of Everest."

Kopnick snickered, whereupon Kasper grabbed his arm, exhaled, and made a wish. In an instant, they were standing on rock and snow, breathing thin, cold air. Kopnick vomited the two knishes he'd eaten as a bedtime snack, while a violent wind whipped his flimsy pajamas. Kasper closed his eyes and wished them back to Kopnick's bedroom.

Kopnick was shivering. He fell to his knees. "Wh—what just ha— happened? Oy, I have such a headache."

"You have the bends. I gave you a glimpse of your new home, unless you help me. So how much for twelve hours of your time?"

"What is this madness? You've drugged me."

"I can drop you in a volcano if you'd like more proof."

"No. No. Please. What do you want?"

"First, tell me your price."

"Cash is good. Bearer bonds are even better. Much less bulky than cash and totally anonymous. I'm having a little trouble with the tax authorities, and—"

"How much?"

"Seeing you're Dieter's friend, I'll give you the discounted price of ten thousand Reichsmarks, but I doubt you have—"

"Fine. Where are these bonds kept?"

"At the Reichsbank on Jagerstrasse, but I hardly see how that matters. They're in a vault."

"Is it a walk-in vault?"

"Yes, but I don't know the combination."

"Just tell me the floor and the room number."

After Kopnick gave the information, Kasper vanished. Three minutes later, there was a squeal and a purple flash, followed by Kasper's reappearance in Kopnick's bedroom.

"Holy Hell!" screamed Kopnick. "How do you do that?"

Kasper handed Kopnick five pages of parchment paper, each picturing the Reichsbank Building and the phrase Eintausend Reichsmark. "Are these the bonds?"

Kopnick's eyes widened into tea saucers. "Well, kiss my kishkes!"

"You'll get the other five when your work is finished. Gather your things."

Kopnick collected a Leica camera, rolls of 35mm film, photo chemicals and paper, a portable darkroom, a typewriter, a glue bottle, fountain pens and different colored inks, and twenty blank immigrant identification cards stolen from the U.S. Consulate in Berlin. They needed at least eighty more identity cards. Kopnick told Kasper where to find them in the consulate, and suggested that, while Kasper was there, he might as well swipe the Consul General's signature stamp. That would save Kopnick several hours finalizing the visas. Kasper was gone and back in under five minutes.

Kopnick shook his head when Kasper popped out of thin air. "My God! Are you sure you want to go to America? We could become very rich men, working together."

Kasper ignored the proposition. "Here, hand me the camera, the film rolls, and the glue." He stuffed the items in his coat and pant pockets. "I can carry the portable darkroom and the identity cards, too. Put the pens, chemicals, paper, and the inks in that box there. Set the typewriter on top. You'll carry those. Make sure to hold everything tightly."

"No problem." Kopnick fumbled the typewriter but caught it before it slid off the box. "No problem," he repeated.

Kasper squeezed Kopnick's elbow with his free hand. He exhaled and made the wish. Again, there was a delay before compression, this time six seconds. They compressed slowly. Instead of blinking out, their bodies deflated into nothingness like untied flesh balloons. Seconds later, they appeared in the Ellis Island laundry building. Kopnick fell to his knees and vomited the third and fourth knishes he'd eaten while Kasper had been at the consulate. Kasper felt bad (well, not too bad) about forgetting to tell Kopnick to exhale.

While Kopnick set up a makeshift photography studio, Kasper wished himself into the purser's quarters on the SS Blücher. The purser was fast asleep. The ambient light through the porthole window illuminated the ship's manifest on the desk. The nametags were in a box underneath. Kasper folded the manifest and stuffed it in his coat pocket before grabbing a stack of tags and then returning to Ellis Island. Meanwhile, Kopnick had begun snapping photos for the visas. He taught Duke to develop the headshots in the portable darkroom, which freed Kopnick to add the hundred extra names to the manifest in the purser's (forged) handwriting. He tasked Bessie with writing the manifest numbers on the nametags. Bessie prepared the tags for Mama Elsie and the other three deceased first, so their bodies could be taken to the hospital morgue under cover of darkness. Their loved ones would claim them after passing through immigration. Grimsky then typed the passenger information on the identification cards. After Kopnick finished the entries on the manifest, Kasper traveled back to the purser's quarters, dropped the papers on the desk, and returned. He then wished Kopnick and his equipment back to Berlin and handed over the remaining five bearer notes.

The hat was suffering. Not only was there was a ten-second delay before Kasper vanished from Kopnick's apartment, but the compression stage was painfully slow. More alarming was that Kasper didn't immediately reappear at Ellis Island. Indeed, he didn't think he was going to make it there. For a second, he thought he was appearing over the ocean, far from shore. It would've been a long swim in cold, choppy waters. But then the hat rallied. It surged with warmth and deposited Kasper, intact and dry, to the laundry building. The heat dissipated, and the hat was cool again, like a turtle's flesh.

Though Kasper experienced the cumulative side effects of hat travel—queasiness, buzzing in his ears, a spinning sensation, a blue halo in his visual field—he was relieved "the craving" was not among them. Unlike when Kasper was twenty-two, the hat wasn't forcing him to make wish after wish in order to fill an impossibly deep hunger. If anything, the hat desired less travel, not more. It seemed diminished, weakened, drained of its life-force. He doubted the hat had another journey left in it.

Kasper fished a few dry crackers from his pocket and stuffed them in his mouth. They took the edge off the nausea, until he detected the taste of Kopnick's glue, which he'd foolishly stored in the same pocket.

The SS Blücher arrived at dusk. As thousands of name-tagged seafarers disembarked and clogged the front of the Main Building, the hundred souls from train car 21 filtered into the crowd, a dozen at a time. With their paperwork in order, though a tad smudged from the still-wet ink, they navigated the inspection process without incident.

Twenty-four hours earlier, the Jews of car 21 had been marked for hard labor and starvation. With the help of a divine hat and a common criminal, they'd been reborn as Americans. Grimsky tipped his new hat to Kasper. The hat's brim and two-thirds of the crown were sturdy black felt. The top third was black alpaca yarn with an indigo spiral terminating in a tassel. Kasper had performed the first, and perhaps only, hat graft surgery.

"It breathes much better than my old homburg," said Grimsky. "Do you have a name for this creation?"

"No. Any ideas?"

"The purple swirl reminds me of a spinning top. How about the 'spinning top hat'?"

"That'll do."

"I shall never forget what you did for us. Truly a miracle. Of course, I will not speak of it. No one will, as you've requested."

Only after the immigration officer welcomed Kasper to the United States by name did he realize he was no longer a Mützenmacher. Duke had instructed Kopnick to inscribe the name Leghorn on the ship's manifest and their visas. Kasper liked the name. Leghorn was the Italian city in which his ancestors had settled after leaving Greece and flourished there for a thousand years. Leghorn also was the type of straw from which they'd woven thousands of hats, and from which they'd weave thousands more. Leghorn was the past, present, and future. It transcended time.

On the train to Detroit, Kasper took his renaming to its logical conclusion. "Kasper" was rooted in Germany, and Germany was the past. America was the future, so he should have a totally American name. From then on, he'd go by Cap. Cap Leghorn.

As they neared Michigan Central Station, the orb above the Penobscot Building's radio antenna momentarily eclipsed the moon, winking it out of, then back into, existence. It was as though Fate, standing high above the Earth, had snapped a photograph to document the moment of Cap Leghorn's birth. Cap smiled, because that's what people were supposed to do on joyous occasions, especially those worthy of a snapshot. He then studied the hands with which he'd fashioned thousands of hats in the so-called Fatherland, rested his forehead on the glass, and wept.

Goodbye, Mama.

PART TWO

CHAPTER ONE

1943

Some denounce me as unpatriotic for challenging our feckless Commander-in-Chief during wartime. They label me a Nazi sympathizer, an anti-Semite, and a traitor. I assure you, my friends, no ad hominem attack will deter this man of the cloth from telling you the truth. And the truth is this: A cancer is devouring the very heart of America. I speak of the twelve Federal Reserve Banks that own fifty billion dollars in government debt. That's a fifty-billion-dollar mortgage on our jobs, farms, and incomes. And the debt keeps growing, because the more the government borrows, the richer these banks—and the international bankers who run them—become.

Friends, there are ten million unemployed, two-thirds of families live on an average of sixty-nine dollars per month, and the government has confiscated forty thousand farms. Yet, our President expects them—expects us—to keep fattening the wallets of the international bankers.

These bankers say the debt finances the war in Europe. But that war wouldn't exist but for them. They speak of Nazi atrocities. They spread rumors of vast concentration camps that starve and kill the Jews. But these overblown claims are meant to distract us from the bankers' true agenda—the government takeover of our factories and livelihoods. Their agenda is the communist agenda.

Has history taught us nothing? The very same international bankers, with names like Greenberg, Loeb, and Warburg, financed the Russian

Revolution. Nazism arose naturally, to prevent the same communist fate from befalling the good German people. Decrying communism doesn't make me an advocate of Nazism. Decrying the international banker does not make me an anti-Semite. It makes me a preacher of the cold hard facts.

Friends, our hour is up. Until next time, I am your humble Father Filconi. For my local listeners, Sunday mass at the Shrine of St. Bernardine will begin promptly at 9:00 a.m. The Sacrament of Penance is offered Mondays, Wednesdays, and Fridays at 3:00 p.m. All are welcome to confess their sins.

The sidewalk on Oakland Street wasn't especially narrow or crowded. Yet, the man approaching Cap Leghorn from Grand Boulevard was veering into his path, subtly but steadily encroaching an inch or two with each step. By the time he'd reached Cap, the man's shoulder bone was digging into Cap's left pectoral muscle. The bump spun Cap a quarter turn. The man continued on, as though blissfully unaware of the collision. It could've been an accident. Perhaps the man had been distracted by the car horns or the attractive woman fussing with the mannequin in the dress shop window. Perhaps he'd had more than one "morning nip" at the hundred-foot bar inside Sunnie's Corner. Or, perhaps this was Detroit, and Cap Leghorn was a white man. The stranger with the stray shoulder was black.

The "Arsenal of Democracy" was burgeoning, now that the auto plants had been repurposed to make tanks, bombers, and trucks. The twelve billion dollars in defense contracts had enticed three hundred fifty thousand souls into the city, including Appalachian whites, who'd brought their attitudes toward blacks with them. Despite having the money to live elsewhere, the great majority of blacks were confined to Paradise Valley's crumbling structures, leaky roofs, unsafe stairs, and bad plumbing—where there was plumbing, that is; often, the only toilet was in an outdoor shack mounted over the sewer main. Riots erupted like cold sores. The last major riot had flared in 1942, when blacks were moving into the Sojourner Truth Housing Project. As hundreds of whites blocked roads and unleashed a hail of stones, more than a thousand city cops and sixteen hundred National Guardsmen mobilized around Nevada and Fenelon Streets to protect six black families.

Detroiters knew another riot was imminent. Every evening, it seemed, gangs of older white assembly line workers invaded Hastings Street searching for a black man to rough up. In the meantime, some blacks were expressing their rage by "bumping" whites, knocking into them on the sidewalk or in stores and elevators, although not so overtly or violently that the victim could prove the bump was intentional.

In his youth, Cap (né Kasper) would've horse-collared any man who'd bumped him, thrown him against the building, and brandished his flaming cheek scar. But he was in his forties now. He was a family man. He ran a hat business on that very street. Leghorn Millinery's clients, mostly the black "jitterbug" crowd, lived in this North End neighborhood. He had to be extra tolerant. His clients understood he wasn't a Nazi, despite his German accent. He was known as a "good Kraut" and wanted to keep it that way.

Cap pulled on the shop's front door. It should've been unlocked, because Duke was supposed to have been in early taking inventory.

Duke had been scattered and unreliable since turning eighteen and registering with the Selective Service. The idea he could be sent into battle terrified him, he'd confessed to Cap, and he just couldn't focus on anything else. He'd stroll down Oakland Street, listening to the rustling pear trees and mourning doves. He'd think how tranquil and still things were, while a war raged thousands of miles away. Bombs and bullets were blowing men to smithereens, and they were the lucky ones, because their comrades writhed in agony, clutching exposed bones or futilely gathering their scattered guts. Duke couldn't reconcile the two very different scenes playing out simultaneously, only a divine hat and a wish away from each other—well, theoretically anyway. The wishing hat hadn't worked since Ellis Island, and who knew when it might revitalize, if ever? Cap had vowed to use the hat to rescue more Jews, but not even that noble cause could inspire Fate to breathe life into the tired gryphon leather.

Kasper was disappointed that Duke was practically as comatose as the wishing hat. He'd stumbled through two semesters at Wayne University, picking up and dropping classes, seeing nothing to completion. What was the point of filling his head with knowledge, he'd told Cap, when his brains could be splattered on the cold, hard earth in six months' time? Loaded with facts about the circles of Hell in Dante's Inferno or Kant's categorical imperative, Duke's exploded gray matter wouldn't glisten any brighter in the firelight or quiver any less from the war machines' rumble than the brains of the uneducated farm boy who knew about weaning pigs and heaving hay bales. Gunpowder was the great equalizer. Cluster bombs didn't discriminate, and intelligence was no shield when your skull was in the blast radius.

Instead of going to class, Duke watched ballgames at Briggs Stadium and frequented "black and tans" like Club Zombie and the Royal Blue Bar. He lost himself in the crowd's roar, cigarette smoke, the crunch of peanut shells, and the cornet's wail. Even when he showed at the shop, he wasn't really there. He cut irregular patterns. His stitching was uneven. Twice, his smoldering cigarette butts set the trashcan on fire. Both times, he extinguished them with a Schlitz beer, his breakfast drink of choice.

The door rattled open just as Cap stepped foot in the back.

"Duke? That you?"

"No. It's me, Pops."

Cap returned to the shop floor. "Bessie?"

She was already a woman at sixteen. Though short like her mother, her narrow belted waist, padded shoulders, and thick pompadour hairstyle made her look tall. She set her schoolbooks on the display table for ladies' turbans.

Cap checked his watch. "No school today?"

"Don't you remember? I adjusted my schedule."

"You did?"

"You signed the form. I flipped study hall to my first class, so I can help in the shop."

"When did I sign that?"

"Last week. Jeez, Pops. You never listen to me."

"There's a reason for study hall—namely, studying."

"I don't need that time. Besides, you're shorthanded."

"I've got Duke."

"Really," Bessie said skeptically. "Is he in back?"

"He's not here. Not yet."

"I know. He's passed out on his bed, face down. He's still breathing, though, so maybe he'll wander in here before closing."

"I'll manage. You shouldn't be cutting school."

"I'm not cutting school. I'm helping you."

"It's not your place to help me."

"But it's Duke's?"

"Yeah."

"Because he's a boy."

"You know how the curse works."

"I know what you've told me."

"You don't believe me?"

"I believe that centuries of Mützenmacher and Petasos men have refused to let their daughters run the hat shop when they die."

"Count yourself lucky you're not cursed. Girls can do whatever they want in this world."

"As long as men allow it."

"As long as *Fate* allows it."

"That's a load of bull, Pops. You're prejudiced against women. Rosie can rivet bombers, but Bessie can't stitch a bowler."

Cap's face got hot. "How dare you call me prejudiced."

"Admit it. You'd be thrilled if I had a penis."

"I'd be horrified, and little girls shouldn't use that word."

"I'm a woman, Pops. I know things about penises."

"Stop saying penis."

"It's just a word."

"Yeah... but... it's eight o'clock in the morning," Cap asserted, as though uttering the word in daylight made it highly combustible.

"Penis! Penis! Penis!" she shouted.

Cap's throat constricted. He couldn't formulate any words to quiet his daughter, managing only a peculiar groan. Bessie swiped her books from the display table and left, slamming the door behind her. The ermine fur hat in the window display slipped off the mannequin and fell on its decorative ostrich plume.

"Damn it."

Cap reached into the display area, straining to fish out the hat, which lay just beyond his fingertips. The door re-opened, and someone entered.

"I really don't appreciate your attitude," said a frustrated Cap. As much as he stretched the tendons in his hand, he still couldn't make contact with the fallen hat. "That mouth of yours. Damn it. And exactly what 'things' do you know about penises?"

"This is a hat shop, ain't it?" asked the male voice.

"What the hell?" Cap turned. "Oh, for God sakes. I thought you were someone else."

"That's good. Who?"

"My daughter."

"That's not so good."

Cap abandoned the hat for the moment. "Ahh, forget it." He stepped from the display. "How can I help you?"

The wiry fellow with a pencil tucked behind his ear asked, "Came to see if you want to plunk some change down on a few numbers."

"I'm not a gambling man."

"You're white, and you set up shop in this neighborhood. I'd say that makes you a gambler."

"You don't know me."

"Then allow me to introduce myself. Cyrus Silk."

Cap shook Cyrus's extended hand.

"Cap Leghorn."

"Sure you don't wanna place a bet? Only two bits. Here. I'll give you some numbers on the house. How 'bout 121? No one ever picks that."

Cyrus handed Cap a chit with the numbers.

"Who's running this game?"

"Solly Colton."

"Colton, eh? Sounds like a gangster."

"Solly ran with the Purple Gang back in the day. He's freelancing now. But I don't want you to think I'm a gangster, 'cause I'm not."

"You only work for one."

"Yes... no... well, sorta, but only until I scrounge enough dough to pay off Uncle Henry and buy a house. I'm in the Brewsters right now."

"The Brewsters? Black folks live there, no?"

"That's right. I'm Negro."

"You're awful light."

"Yeah, I get that a lot. Anyway, I ain't gonna be in the Brewsters for long. Got my eye on a place in Highland Park, just off Woodward."

"That's a white area. Are they going to let you buy there?"

"Long as the bank thinks I'm white. They're gonna give me a loan just as soon as I pay my debts to Uncle Henry."

"Is Uncle Henry a mobster, too?"

"Seriously? Uncle Henry, as in Mr. Henry Ford of The Ford Motor Company?"

"Oh, that Henry."

"I got a regular job down at the Ford plant."

"Good, honest work."

"Sure, if 'honest' means a buck-fifteen an hour in stiflin' heat and greasy overalls, or nearly losin' your life two or three times a day, or gettin' dressed down by the foreman for havin' the audacity to break for a bowel movement. Honest Abe's got nothin' on me, 'cause I work at it every day. Know how I do it? I grab a red hot coil spring from the coiling machine, lift it to my chest, turn around, and plunge it in the quench tank, all in about five seconds. I do that 'bout fifteen times a minute for eight hours. They call the job 'mankilling.' A better name would be manhoodkilling, 'cause I just about lose my testicuels at least once every hour."

"Testi-cuels?"

"The family jewels, the gonads, the stones…"

"Ahh, we're back to that topic."

"One day, you'll be drivin' down Grand Boulevard with your honey at your side, and you'll hear a rattle in the shocks, and you'll ask, 'You hear that? Wonder what the hell that is?' I'll tell ya what it is—my testicuels bouncin' around in those coils!"

"Don't worry. I don't have a honey, and I plan on buying a Chevrolet."

Cyrus bugged his eyes and exhaled violently, as though punched in the gut. He slapped his knee and exploded in laughter. "Shit. Chevrolet! That's a good one, Cap." Cyrus rubbed the knuckles of his right hand into his right eye. "Anyway, Uncle Henry fronted me cash for that place in the Brewsters. Also got me a radio, a phone, a sofa. Doesn't leave much in the paycheck for food, let alone a house."

"Are you sure Uncle Henry isn't in the mob?"

"Uncle Henry's a great man, right up there with Jesus. He's done more for our people than any man since Lincoln, at least until he started bringin' up those Appalachians. Don't really get why he feels those crackers need emancipatin'. Ahh. There I go again. Never mind that crackers crack. That's not the way folks where I'm from talk. Well, actually it is. All I'm sayin' is Henry ain't the perfect uncle, but God's got his flaws, too. Look, I gotta be goin'. I'll be back tomorrow and let you know if your numbers came in."

"I'm closed tomorrow. I'll be at the Tigers game."

"I can't tell you the last time I hit the ballpark. Actually, yes I can. May 2, 1939. Gehrig's last game as a Yankee. Helluva trooper, that ole Iron Horse."

"That was my very first ball game."

Cap hadn't known much about America's Pastime before emigrating, but he did follow Gehrig, the son of German immigrants. Gehrig didn't boast like Ruth. He just went out day after day and did his job better than most anybody else. He was the best of what a German could be when removed from the befouled, Nazified air.

Gehrig hadn't taken the field that day. He'd pulled himself from the line-up after playing 2,130 straight games. When he waved to the crowd, Gehrig was a shell of his former greatness. He was sick—dying, in fact—though no one knew at the time what was causing his muscles to atrophy. A darkness had overtaken the gentle giant, sucking his goodness from the world like a black hole ripping light into nothing. Gehrig was Germany, the country plagued with a metastasizing darkness. Unlike Gehrig, Cap had escaped death. He'd been given a second chance in America. Gehrig's demise, Germany's demise, marked Cap's beginning. And Cap immediately felt at home among the crowd of cheering and jeering strangers. That din of the common man, what Tiger broadcaster Harry Heilmann called "the voice of baseball," was almost as good as jazz. Almost. It was the sound of Cap's new Volk, his people.

"Come with me to the game tomorrow," said Cap. "I'll pack some BLTs. Uncle Henry doesn't work you on Sundays, does he?"

"BLTs at Briggs. I like the sound of that. Yeah. Sure thing. How much I owe you for the ticket, Cap?"

"My treat."

Cyrus put two fingers to his temple and gave Cap a mini salute. "See you tomorrow, friend."

CHAPTER TWO

Confession at St. Bernardine was scheduled to end at 4:00 p.m., and it was already 3:45. There were two penitents ahead of Duke: an old, purse-clutching biddy and a middle-aged man in an expensive business suit. Duke had no idea how long confession took. He wasn't Catholic and had been in only one other church, the Cathedral of Our Lady in Schwarz Boden, and then only to use the facilities during Oktoberfest. He assumed there was no set time limit, that the confession's duration depended on what the penitent had to say and the Father's willingness to keep listening.

Five penitents already had entered and emerged from the confessional's indigo curtain; none had gone longer than six minutes, and most had taken only three or four. The businessman constantly checked his wristwatch. He was in a hurry. That was good. He'd spit out his confession and then hail a taxi to an important meeting, maybe with his accountant or the Board of General Motors or the Office of Price Administration. Either way, his final destination wasn't a battlefield. Duke envied him.

Duke was more concerned about the old woman. Outside the church, Duke wouldn't have thought twice about her. Short, bespectacled grannies in frumpy tea dresses and clunky black oxfords were a dime a dozen. But inside this foreign house of worship, she cut a terrifying figure. Her Brillo Pad hair, pulled into a severe bun on the nape of her neck, seemed to be awaiting the command to launch itself onto Duke's face. Her bushy eyebrows, like two rabid caterpillars, would then swoop in to pick off the remaining flesh. Those white-gloved hands concerned Duke most. Why was she gripping her purse like a vice? Were her unconfessed sins threatening to explode out the top? Would the priest be able to triage and treat them, and still leave enough time for Duke? Duke's forehead and hands glistened from worry. His heartbeat raced. The pressure of urine stretched his overfull bladder. He shouldn't have drunk so many beers.

The businessman finished his confession in two minutes. The old woman wasted a good thirty seconds shuffling the twenty feet to the confessional. Still, it was twelve minutes to the hour. Also, Duke was last in line. Surely, the priest would let him confess, even if the woman exhausted all twelve minutes, right? That would be the Christian thing to do, wouldn't it?

Duke scanned the nave for some clue that might bear on these questions. The left wall was all stained glass and smoldering votive candles. The right wall was a parade of fourteen sculptures headed by a guy being laid in a tomb. Duke thought it odd they hadn't removed his hat before laying him to rest. The wide-brimmed hat with the low crown bore an uncanny resemblance to the wishing hat. Was this how Christ had effected his miracles, in which case, why hadn't he just wished himself off the cross? The preceding sculptures gave a clearer perspective on the hat, especially the depiction of the Roman soldier nailing Jesus to the cross. The "hat" was, in fact, a halo. Duke's heart sunk when he noticed the scar on the soldier's face. His cheek bore a mark like the runic symbol for Thor, similar to Cap's. That was a bad omen. Very bad.

"You may go in, young man," said the old lady. "It's not polite to leave the Father waiting."

Her confession had taken less than three minutes.

Duke took a deep breath and approached the ornate mahogany confessional. He parted the velvet curtain and stepped inside. The curtain, weighted at the bottom, swung behind him, sealing him in darkness for the few seconds it took his eyes to adjust. He heard a sliding sound. A man's shadowed profile appeared behind a rectangular grid of octagons. There was a cushioned kneeling pad at the partition's base. Duke wasn't totally ignorant about the process. He knelt on the cushion and uttered, "Bless me Father Philco for I have sinned."

"Welcome, my child," answered the priest. "Please. Call me Father Filconi."

Duke was mortified. He'd called the priest by his popular nickname—Philco, after the brand of radio.

"Sorry, Father."

"Hazards of being a celebrity. How long has it been since your last confession?" The priest's resonant voice filled the confessional. Duke could practically feel the mahogany vibrating sympathetically under his knees.

"I... This is my first."

"At this church? You have an accent. German, is it?"

"Yes, Father. But no, this is my first confession ever. I'm not Catholic."

"I'm sorry. You cannot participate in the Sacrament of Penance. Confession is only for those baptized into the Church."

"On your broadcast, you said, 'All are welcome to confess their sins.'"

"I meant all Catholics."

"Then you should've said that."

"It was implied. What is your religion?"

"I have none. My father is an unobservant Protestant. My mother was a Jew."

"Then by Jewish tradition you are a Jew."

"I don't observe those traditions."

"The Jew's mark is carried via the mother's blood."

"Like a curse," Duke mused.

"What is it you seek?"

"Forgiveness."

"I cannot offer you absolution, only pastoral counseling."

"Fine. I'll take that."

"What troubles you?"

"I'm going to steal something from my father."

"So you have not yet committed this act?"

"No."

"Then it is not forgiveness you seek, for you may not do it."

"Oh, I'm gonna do it."

"What is it you plan to steal? Money? A car?"

"A hat."

"A ha— I see..."

"Not just any hat. It's divine. It belongs to Hermes. He used it to wish himself from place to place, transport souls of the dead, that kind of thing. My Greek ancestor stole it in the fourth century, and my family has had it ever since."

"Do I detect beer on your breath?"

"I don't think drinking's a sin. I'm eighteen."

"I agree. I wonder only whether your judgment is impaired."

"The wishing hat's real. My father transported an entire boxcar of Jews to Ellis Island. The hat stopped working after that. Too many souls to transport at one time, he says. Drained the hat's power. But I checked yesterday. The hat's getting warm again, not warm enough to go anywhere, but soon, I think, it'll hit fifty Celsius."

The priest glanced at his watch.

"My son, the hour is fast approaching, and I'm afraid your 'problem' will require more than the few minutes we have remaining. Perhaps you can return next week, when you're sober. We can meet in my office, face to face."

"Next week's too late, Father. They've called my number. I've got to report to Fort Custer. Well, I'm *supposed* to report."

"What is your intention?"

"I can't go to war. I'll get blown apart in two seconds. I'm gonna wish myself away."

"With this hat, the one that belongs to your father?"

"The hat really belongs to Hermes. Is it a sin to steal what's already stolen?"

"The Seventh Commandment is fairly explicit."

"No exceptions?"

"Only if you have an urgent necessity, say, if you need to steal to provide for an immediate, essential need."

"Does shirking your military duty in wartime count as an immediate, essential need?"

"Not usually."

"Oh."

"But that's assuming your country is in the right. Not all wars are just."

"How do you get more just than fighting Nazis?"

"If they're our true enemy, then yes, it is a just war."

"You're telling me I shouldn't take the hat."

"You should talk to your father before doing anything."

"There's no point. He'll disown me and change the safe's combination. I'll have no choice but to fight."

"I recommend you dry out and then come back when your head is clear. In the meantime, there's a clinic on Beaubien—"

"I'm not a drunk, Father, and I'm not crazy. Ahh, crud. You don't believe me."

"Would you?"

"I figured, as someone who preaches miracles, you'd have an open mind."

"I believe you believe, but the wishing hat is not part of my faith."

"This is not a matter of faith. It's fact. Forget it."

Duke stood.

"Wait, my child," the priest commanded.

Duke felt a rattling in his bones. He froze as though he'd stumbled into a slumbering attack dog.

The priest continued, "I do not turn away anyone who comes with sincerity in his heart. Bring me the hat. Show me this miracle. Then we can discuss the morality of your choice. Now, I must go. My broadcast begins momentarily."

"I will. Thank you, Father. Thank you."

"Peace be with you."

Duke and the priest exited the confessional simultaneously. Father Filconi slid a displaced lock of thin, reddish-brown hair back into place and then acknowledged Duke with an avuncular smile and impersonal gray eyes, which his thick, round spectacles magnified. Duke wasn't sure whether the priest looked at everyone like that or reserved that colorless gaze for crazed cowards carrying "the Jew mark." The priest's black blazer, buttoned tightly around his thick middle, and his slacks, hemmed at the ankle, lent him an overall stubby disposition. He ambled behind the altar and entered the tower.

Duke exited the knave and entered the vestibule. He was desperate to empty his bladder. He turned left without looking and bumped into a table holding a candelabra, which toppled into the holy water font. He fished out the candelabra, wiped it with his shirt, and set it back on the table. The splashing sounds intensified his urge to pee. He turned around and thanked God when he saw the restroom sign.

As Duke relieved himself, Father Filconi's broadcast poured from the church's PA system. Now that Duke had seen the priest in person, the Father's rumbling baritone seemed to have far too much gravitas for such a short, narrow-shouldered man. The priest was the human equivalent of an outboard motor affixed to a toy boat.

> ... The international banker is no friend of the worker and certainly no friend of the working Negro. They call you Schwartzes, a Yiddish term for black, but they might as well be calling you niggers. They hire you as maids. They give you their worn clothing. They extend credit to your stores when no one else will, but don't be fooled. After you have paid him usurious interest for decades, the international banker owns your soul, faster than the Devil himself, who at least waits until you're dead before claiming it...

CHAPTER THREE

Cap peered from the living room of his tidy brick Colonial on Edison Street. His head was pinned to his right shoulder because of the awkward angle he'd been sleeping on the sofa. Bessie strolled up the street, arm-in-arm with a young black man in a purple zoot suit. Cap could've made at least ten hats from the fabric in that suit. What a waste. Beyond that, it was seven in the morning, ridiculously past Bessie's midnight curfew.

Cap flung the door open before Bessie inserted her key in the lock. Her male companion yelped at the sight of Bessie's dad with his head cocked at a zombie-like angle, scarred face, and tattered terrycloth robe most hobos would've rejected. Nonplussed, Bessie hugged her father and thanked him for greeting them. She introduced Marvin, a friend from the art and design program at Cass Technical High School. Marvin had a black eye. Cap grunted a greeting. Bessie's eyes looked strange—definitely bloodshot but also glassy.

"You mind telling me why you're back so late? The swinging club at the school ended eight hours ago."

"We went to the Bizrete after, just like I told you."

"You didn't say anything about the Bizrete."

"I did, Pops. Did you forget?"

"No."

"Just like you didn't forget about the study hall form."

Trying to figure out what he'd forgotten versus what he'd never known but Bessie claimed he'd forgotten made his head spin.

"You must've been the only white girl there."

"Sheila Jordan was singing. She's whiter than I am."

Cap turned to Marvin. "How dare you drag my daughter to that club."

"Marv didn't drag me anywhere, Daddykins. The Bizrete was my idea. I'm sorry you forgot about it. It makes me sad you were up all night worrying."

Bessie hugged her father again, a cheap ploy to melt his anger. It worked, mostly because he still felt guilty about their argument the other day. Notwithstanding Bessie's womanly curves (and professed expertise in all matters penile), she still possessed her girlish ability to manipulate her father like her tea party dolls—the Daddykins doll. Cap was an ersatz father. He played the role of dad, reading a script Bessie authored. She would ask him for permission or, after the deed was done, claim she had asked. Then, she'd say sorry for defying him, all without fear of repercussions because she knew a hug would reduce him to a spineless mass of wool batting. He was powerless. But the same didn't hold for the strange dark boy in the big purple suit.

"You. Marvin. I need to have a word with your father. What's his name?"

"Cyrus, sir," answered the nervous boy. "Cyrus Silk. Do you want his number?"

Cap was never much of a jaw-dropper, but the coincidence was too much even for his vise-like mandible. Somehow, Cyrus was playing him.

"Never mind. He's got mine."

―――◦╎◦◇◦◉◦◇◦╎◦―――

Cyrus arrived at the shop at 11 a.m., an hour earlier than planned, because he was so excited about the ball game. He'd packed a container with six Stroh's beers and Cracker Jacks boxes. He set it on the counter, next to a paper bag imprinted with the words "Goresky's Deli."

"Cap, my man! I came equipped. It's gonna be a hot one, though. Make sure you bring a hat. Been thinkin' about those BLTs all morning. They in the bag here?" Cyrus peered inside and added, "Hey, there's only one. Guess we'll split it. We can get dogs at the game, too."

Cap glowered. "We need to talk."

"Sure thing, Cap. Let's catch up. We got time."

"It's about your son."

"Marvin? You know him?"

"My daughter does."

"Your daught—... Bessie?"

Cap nodded.

"Dang! What are the odds?"

"You're the numbers man, Cyrus. You tell me."

"Why you talking like that? All 'spicious."

"You come by here yesterday asking me to bet on numbers, all the while your son is secretly messing with my daughter. Damn right I'm *'spicious.*"

"Messin' around? Nah. They just friends. She never told you about Marvin?"

"No."

"Oh. Well, now you know."

"Do you realize they were out all night? At the Bizrete?"

"Marvin told me his plans. I trust him. Bessie got home all right, didn't she? 'Cause if she didn't, I'll give the boy a shiner."

"He's already got one. Besides, she's fine."

"So, what's the problem?"

"She was supposed to eat ice cream and listen to the high school band, not hang out with a bunch of… with a bunch of… ?"

"Negroes?"

"People grinding their bodies into each other, drinking booze."

"Marvin don't drink a lick. I've tried sharing a beer with him, even the occasional bourbon shot, but he won't have none of it. Says it's not good for his body. He's funny that way. I been tryin' to man him up forever."

"I don't want him getting funny with my little girl."

"I don't think they're gettin' funny. Between you and me, I wish they would, a little bit."

"That's disgusting."

"I don't mean gettin' nekkid. Nothing un-Christian. Just kissin' and petting."

"Stop talking about my girl that way—like she's a doll you fondle."

"God's sakes, Cap. You're gettin' all worked up."

"Wouldn't you, if you saw a purple Jitterbug sauntering to your front stoop with your daughter at 7:00 a.m.?"

Cyrus scanned the store's merchandise. Half the hats on display were enormous, wide-brimmed hats in bright orange, yellow, and red.

"Yeah," Cyrus said sarcastically, "those damn Jitterbuggers. Oughta be a law against those zoot suits. S'pose the hats are okay, though."

"Just tell your son to stay away from Bessie."

"No."

"No?"

"Marv's a bit of an oddball, but I trust him. He ain't breakin' the law. Can't say the same for Bessie."

"What's that supposed to mean?"

"Never mind. You obviously don't know your own daughter. Can't trust someone if you don't know him."

"I agree. Get out."

"What about the game?"

"Get... out."

"I see. It's 'cause Marvin's a Negro, ain't it? If he were Marvin Horowitz, it'd be all okay. Fine. Forget the damn game. Oh, by the way, your numbers came in."

Cyrus slapped five ten-dollar bills into Cap's hand, grabbed his cooler of beer and Cracker Jacks, and left. A moment later, Cyrus returned, slapped another dollar on top of the fifty, and swiped the Goresky's Deli bag off the counter.

"Buy yourself a dog at the game," said Cyrus on the way back out. "Wouldn't want you goin' hungry 'cause a Negro stole your BLT."

Cyrus slammed the door behind him, causing the picture windows to vibrate.

Cap felt rotten. Cyrus was right. Cap wouldn't have gotten so ticked had Marvin been white. Such prejudice might've had some basis had Cap grown up in a racially divided Detroit, but he'd been a Berliner most of his life. The only prejudice he'd experienced came from folks with skin whiter than his. His greatest fear should've been seeing Bessie strolling up Edison Street with a blond-haired, blue-eyed Norseman. He skipped the ball game.

CHAPTER FOUR

The next morning, Cap descended the stairs and found his son sprawled on the sofa like an unconscious mugging victim. Duke was wearing Cap's favorite (and shabbiest) terrycloth bathrobe. His cheeks betrayed two days of stubble, and his thick black hair was matted into a crude fin on the left side. He reeked of cigarettes and whiskey.

"Christ, Duke."

Duke shot awake, wide-eyed. "I didn't steal it!"

"Steal what?"

"What? Nothing. Just a nightmare."

"I'll say. This is getting out of hand. You're not in school. You're not helping me in the shop. You just smoke my tobacco, drink my booze, and sleep in my clothes. What're you good for?"

"The U.S. government thinks I'm good enough to kill people."

Duke pulled a letter from his robe pocket and handed it to his father. The Draft Board was ordering him to report for induction at Fort Custer.

"They called my number, Pops."

"Says here you've got to report tomorrow. Should be enough time to dry out."

Cap handed the letter back.

"What am I going to do?"

"When your country calls, you answer. It's always been that way in our family."

"You didn't fight in the Great War."

"I had flat feet. They wouldn't take me."

"Grandpa Hermann took your place."

"Who told you that?"

"Mama Elsie."

"Well, I didn't ask him to. And it was a lot easier to pull something like that back in 1916. Bureaucracy's much better these days. Anyway, I wished he hadn't. Fighting would've made me more mature."

"Or more dead."

"You know how evil Hitler is. If Germany wins, America won't be safe. The Nazis will throw you in a camp and work you to death, assuming they don't shoot you first. I'd rather go out fighting. That's why I registered with the Selective Service."

"The 'Old Man's Registration' isn't the same, Pops. You'll never see a battlefield."

"I can't do anything about my age."

"Father Philco... Filconi says some wars aren't just."

"Why the hell would you care what that asshole radio priest thinks?"

"He told me the international bankers concocted the whole thing."

"He *told you*? Personally?"

"Yeah, at confession."

"You're not Catholic, and what the hell would you have to confess anyway?"

"That's privileged."

"Jesus, Duke. Father Philco is no better than the Nazis in Schwarz Boden. You remember them, don't you? The ones who put us on a boxcar to Dachau? You think they were just made up?"

"No, but—"

"Listen to *this* father, your true father." Cap tapped his fingers on his heart. "You get your ass to Fort Custer."

Duke's chin was quivering. He pulled a cigarette and lighter from his pocket and lit it with a trembling hand. Cap sat on the sofa beside him.

"Look, son," said Cap with a tenderness he hadn't expressed since Duke's childhood, "I know you're scared. No shame in that. Courage is pushing on despite your fear. This'll be good for you. You're gonna find out who you really are."

"And who's that?"

"A brave son who'll make his father proud. A true Leghorn."

"I'm gonna die over there."

"Fate wouldn't have rescued you from Kristallnacht only to kill you with a Nazi bullet."

"Fate didn't save Grandpa Hermann in the Great War."

He's right, thought Cap. *Think. Think.*

"Yeah, well, Grandpa Hermann was the older generation, see? I was waiting in the wings to take over for him, just like you'll do for me. Nothing can hurt you. Fate won't allow it."

Right, Fate?

"I guess."

"Plus, you're strong and powerful, thanks to Charles Atlas."

"I haven't done Charles Atlas in years. I'm a weakling."

"Oh, come on. Let me feel that handshake of yours."

Cap took Duke's extended hand.

Jesus, I've held soggy newspapers with a stronger grip.

"Just as I thought," said Cap with feigned enthusiasm. "Like a vice." He extricated his hand and wiped it on his trousers. "I'd better go. I'm already late to the shop."

Please, Fate, bring my son back in one piece. You owe me that much for taking my papa.

The moment Cap opened the store, a heavyset black woman entered and handed him her calling card—Frannie Pickford, President, Housewives League of Detroit. The phrase "Build. Buy. Boost." was printed on the back. Mrs. Pickford had buggy eyes and a buggier ass that seemed out of proportion to her thin torso. In dim light, she'd have been difficult to distinguish from a bowling pin.

Frannie Pickford wasn't in the market for a new hat. She was conducting an inspection. Her inspection didn't involve checking labels to make sure that the hats advertised as wool or silk actually consisted of wool or silk. They did. Nor did she care whether the bowlers, advertised at "Factory-to-You" prices, were in fact priced lower than normal. They were. No, she was interested in the means of the hats' production—namely, whether a Negro had contributed to their creation. Since Cap made all his own hats, the answer was no, although blacks very likely had manufactured some of the materials. That didn't cut it for Mrs. Pickford. She signaled to a throng of black women outside, holding signs with the same "Build... Buy... Boost" slogan. They promptly formed a picket line in front of the store, urging the public not to shop there because Cap refused to employ blacks. That was true only insofar as Cap refused to employ anyone, regardless of color. Mrs. Pickford didn't let that detail stand in her way. The picketers grew louder. Cap was simultaneously mortified at the negative publicity and impressed with the speed with which the boycott had formed. The Nazis had nothing on the Housewives League of Detroit.

Cap was about to retreat to the back of the store, to hide out until the protest died down. But then Cyrus walked in, and Cap saw an opportunity.

"What brings you by, my friend?" asked Cap, all smiles.

Cyrus did a double-take at Cap's warm greeting. "Yeah… uh… I made a mistake yesterday. Your actual winnings were forty, not fifty. If you'd pay me back the ten, I'll be out of your hair forever."

"Of course, I'll pay you, Cyrus. I always pay my employees." Cap made sure he spoke loud enough for Mrs. Pickford to hear. He then made a show of pulling a wad of cash from his pocket and peeling off a ten dollar bill. "There you are, Cyrus. A little advance for you."

Cyrus was flummoxed. "The hell you talkin' about?"

Cap waved to Mrs. Pickford. "I want you to meet Cyrus Silk, my employee."

"You said you had no employees," she answered.

"Which was true at the time."

"Two minutes ago?"

"I just hired him."

Mrs. Pickford slipped on the eyeglasses dangling from her neck and inspected Cyrus. "You sure he's a Negro? He's awful light."

"I am a Negro, but—"

"But nothing," Cap interrupted. "We need to get you to work, Cyrus. That is, unless Mrs. Pickford intends to put us out of business. Is that what you want, Mrs. Pickford? Another unemployed Negro?"

She studied them both closely with pursed lips. Finally, she gave a reluctant nod. "Very well. I'll call off my girls, but I have my eye on you."

Mrs. Pickford exited the store, spoke to the picketers, and then led them up Oakland Street, toward their next target. Cap breathed easier.

"Thanks, Cyrus. You can go now."

"Go where?"

"To work, I guess."

"Apparently, I work *here*."

"I just told them that so they'd go away."

"So if I tell them I don't work here—maybe tell them you just fired me—they'll come back?"

"But you won't do that."

"Why won't I?"

"Because you have a job at the Ford plant."

"Why should I sweat my ass off for a buck-fifteen there, when I'm makin' a cool buck-fifty here?"

"You're not 'makin'' anything here because you don't work here. Anyway, who said anything about a buck-fifty?"

"I'm only clarifying the terms and conditions of my employment."

"Stop this nonsense, Cyrus. There's no job here."

"Have it your way. I'll let the Housewives know."

Cyrus turned toward the door.

"Stop! You win. You have a job."

"At a buck-fifty an hour. That way I can go fully legit, not run any more numbers."

"Fine."

"And time-and-a-half if I go over forty hours. Also, two breaks a day, fifteen minutes each. We can talk about the production standards and the grievance procedure later."

"Jesus, Cyrus. I'm not cranking out Fords. Do we really need a collective bargaining agreement?"

"Well, I s'pose a handshake will do for now."

… just as they financed the Russian Revolution. I have official documents from both the American War Department and the British War Cabinet to prove it. They identify the international bankers by name. Curiously, a majority of the Soviet Communist Central Party membership carry the same names or are married to women who carry those names. I—

Father Filconi was suddenly at a loss for words. One moment he'd been speaking into the microphone, alternating his gaze between his papers and the portrait of Jesus, and the next, Jesus was gone. Well, not exactly gone. Obscured by a man in a floppy black hat. Father Filconi's first thought was that a fanatical Jew—a Twelfth Street Chasid—had snuck into the tower to assassinate him. He should've taken the steady trickle of threats mixed with his fan mail more seriously. He wasn't ready to martyr himself. Not yet. Not with so much more to say. His next thought was, how the hell could this man have appeared out of nowhere? The tower doors were shut, and he would've heard the squeaky hinges had they opened even a crack. The intruder must've been hiding, perhaps in the bell tower.

The closer Father Filconi studied the man's face, the more he suspected he was in no immediate danger. The man wasn't holding a weapon, nor was he poised to pounce. His arms were crossed in front of his body, and he was smirking, and not with an "aha-I've-got-you-now" glare but more of a "see-I-told-you-so" smile. Nor was the intruder wearing the Chasid's traditional black garb but an enlisted man's khakis. The Father recognized the stranger's big nose and broad forehead. This young man had tried confessing to stealing his father's magic hat or some such nonsense. He was a drunk or a lunatic or both.

Father Filconi cleared his throat and continued the broadcast. "Ladies and Gentleman, I don't need to belabor the point. Suffice to say, decrying communism doesn't make me an advocate of Nazism. Let us devote our remaining three minutes to prayerful reflection. I shall return to the airwaves next week. For my local listeners, Sunday mass at the Shrine of St. Bernardine will begin promptly at 9:00 a.m. The Sacrament of Penance is offered Mondays, Wednesdays, and Fridays at 3:00 p.m. All are welcome to confess their sins."

Duke shook his head in disapproval.

"All *Catholics* are welcome to confess their sins. May Christ the Savior be with you."

Father Filconi flipped off the microphone and slid it away. "How the hell did you get in here?"

Duke tapped the wishing hat.

"Don't take me for a fool. Were you hiding upstairs?"

"I wished myself here, Father. I'll demonstrate."

Duke exhaled and then vanished with a piercing squeal and an indigo flash. Father Filconi shot to his feet, startled.

"Jesus, Mary, and Joseph!"

"I believe that counts as taking the Lord's name in vain, does it not?" asked the voice behind the priest.

Father Filconi wheeled around. "What?... How?..."

"You said to come back and show you the miracle."

"It's a trick."

"It's no trick. Here. Take my hand. Where do you want to go?"

"I will do no such thing. Get out of here!"

"As you wish."

Duke exhaled and vanished again. Father Filconi rubbed his temples and shook his head to clear the visual afterimage of Duke's silhouette. Then there was a knock at the tower doors.

"What? Who is it?"

There was no answer, only another knock.

"Oh for Goodness sake."

He opened the doors, and there stood Duke.

"I'm dreaming," said Father Filconi. "I've lost my mind."

"Were the people dreaming when they saw Jesus walk on water? Did the blind men of Jericho lose their minds when suddenly they could see?" Duke extended his hand. "Come with me."

Father Filconi took Duke's hand tentatively.

"Name a place," said Duke. "Doesn't matter where. How about the Vatican?"

"Sure. The Vatican."

"Any spot in particular? Perhaps some place discreet?"

"The Sistine Chapel. It should be vacant at this hour."

"Got it. Exhale the air from your lungs. On the count of three. One... two... three...!"

Duke sat in Father Filconi's office beside the roaring fire. The priest handed him a half glass of red wine and sat in the second wingback chair with his own full glass.

"Communion wine, but it's a good vintage," the Father said sheepishly. "Hopefully, it can do something for this headache."

"Happens to first-timers. It'll go away. I'm impressed you didn't upchuck."

"Thank you, Duke, for sharing this miracle with me. This is proof of God's handiwork."

"A god's anyway. I was right about the hat coming back to life. Hit fifty Celsius this morning. Wished myself right off the Army bus. I'm officially AWOL."

"Pay no mind to that. You have a much more important role to play than as a pawn in the bankers' war."

"You really think so? I'm not a coward? Pops wanted to use the hat for good, to save Jews from the concentration camps. If he knew it was working again..."

"He doesn't know?"

"I know you said I should talk to him, but—"

"No. No, that's good. Your father's right. The hat should be used for good, but not to save the Jews. It doesn't get at the root problem."

"Nazis?"

"Deeper than Nazis. The very reason Nazis exist. The international bankers. They fomented communism's rise. Though I don't agree with the Nazis' methods or their nationalism, their instinct to hate communists is natural. The bankers are responsible for this horrible war. I can talk about them until I'm blue in the face, but the people won't rise up without proof. The hat can give us that proof."

"How?"

Father Filconi handed Duke that day's *Wall Street Journal*. "Page three. The Federal Open Market Committee will be gathering in Washington, D.C. That's the Federal Reserve's Board of Governors and five Federal Reserve Bank heads all in one room! It's a closed meeting, so no one from the public can hear their machinations. No one except the two of us. All we have to do is wish ourselves there. We'll pack a recording device inside something innocuous, like a vase or a cigar box, and expose these financiers for the true evil in this war. One of your people—the late Justice Louis Brandeis—said sunlight is the best disinfectant. Well, we're going to expose their words to the sunlight, Duke. We'll broadcast their confession across the continent. That'll end the war faster than bombs and bullets. We'll cut the money supply to Soviet Russia and starve communism. Without an enemy, the Nazis will come to the peace table."

"You think so?"

"I'm a student of history. I know how these things work."

"So I did the right thing stealing the hat and running from the Army?"

"Absolutely. You're an instrument of God. Both of us are."

"How do you know?"

"I have faith."

"Must be nice."

"Haven't you ever believed in something greater than yourself?"

"Most things are greater than myself."

"I'm talking about something spiritual. Something you can't see or touch. I wish we could switch souls for a second. That's all the time you'd need to know."

"In other words, I'll never know."

"Pull your chair closer. We have much planning to do."

CHAPTER FIVE

Cap secretly thanked Frannie Pickford and her gaggle of marauding housewives, because Cyrus proved to be a fantastic hire. Duke had been unreliable and, in any event, had since departed for the Army. Bessie had stopped volunteering her time, seeing no future in the hat business. Although Cyrus had a tendency to yammer about nothing in particular, he was a quick learner. Within a few weeks, he'd mastered cutting, dyeing, and basic assembly. He and Cap got along well, exploring their mutual interests in baseball and jazz.

Their first serious disagreement was about shoe polish. Leghorn Millinery occupied the former space of Holdsclaw's Shoe Repair. The proprietor, Enoch Holdsclaw, had moved down South in 1938 because he was "no longer attracting the right sort of clientele." At the time, Cap had no idea what Holdsclaw had meant, since it seemed the "right sort" would be anyone with feet. Mr. Holdsclaw had a crate of polishes, dyes, shoe stands, rags, and leather swatches he didn't wish to transport, so he offered it to Cap for ten dollars. Although Cap figured the polish alone was worth twenty, he didn't accept the offer immediately because he was new to America and tended to agonize over even the most insignificant deals while re-establishing the hat business.

Cap had tossed and turned that night, mulling all the reasons he shouldn't buy the crate. There weren't any. The polish tins were full and moist. The leather swatches were supple and clean. Yet, he felt uneasy. He didn't really need the materials. It might've been a good deal for somebody else but not for him. He decided to tell Mr. Holdsclaw no. But Cap never got the chance. Mr.

Holdsclaw left town the next day and had abandoned the crate in the shop. It was the best deal Cap never made.

Cap eventually found a use for most everything in the crate, especially the black shoe dye. The product's racist name (Nigger Head) hadn't registered with him, nor had the "My black don't run" slogan or the caricature of the black man with the oversized white lips. Cap knew it only as that stuff that darkened wool and leather. He'd seen the words and the offensive imagery hundreds of times, but he hadn't consciously read them. Perhaps because he'd witnessed so much racism in Germany, he resisted the notion that the same bigotry also infected his new homeland. There was no malice behind it.

Malice or not, Cyrus demanded that Cap immediately stop stocking the product. Cap argued that he technically wasn't "stocking" the shoe polish, because he wasn't selling it to the public, only using it as an additive in the manufacturing process. Anyway, he agreed the product was offensive and promised not to buy any more once it ran out.

That wasn't good enough for Cyrus. Cap had to throw away the existing stock, arguing that there was no point using it up because that racist dye was despoiling the merchandise. According to Cyrus, Cap's mostly black clientele would've been shocked to learn they were wearing Nigger Head. Cap was insulting them with a subliminal badge of inferiority. If Cap didn't toss the Nigger Head, he had a duty to tell his customers that their hats were made from the racist dye, and let them make an informed choice. If necessary, Cyrus would go on strike per the forty-five-page collective bargaining agreement he'd compelled Cap to sign.

Cap didn't press it further. He dumped the remaining polish and also "paid reparations," as Cyrus put it, by buying a batch of dye from a local supplier pre-approved by Frannie Pickford.

Although racial harmony had been restored inside the shop, Cyrus's battle with the outside world continued to rage. Between higher wages at the hat shop and the one-month advance he secured from Cap's guilty conscience after the shoe polish incident, Cyrus was able to buy a house in Highland Park. Cyrus's former neighbors from the Brewsters accused him of "going white," an accusation Cyrus didn't deny. His response was unassailable. If he wanted a house, he needed financing, but he could get a mortgage only if his house was in a white area. Thus, to buy a house in a white area, he had to be white. And, technically, Cyrus wasn't really "going white." He already was white, mostly. His father had been white, and his mother had skin the color of café au lait, meaning a fraction of white, slave-owner blood ran through her veins, and half that fraction had been passed to Cyrus. That half of a fraction pushed Cyrus across the fifty percent mark separating the realms of Blackness and Whiteness. As a white man, mathematically speaking, Cyrus's purchase fully complied with the covenant that prohibited selling the house to a Negro.

To Cap, Cyrus's purchase was the stupidest idea in the world. Cyrus was going to get himself killed. He suggested he buy a gun. Cyrus didn't like guns, which Cap found ironic given his association with ex-Purple Gang members.

"Just come to the housewarming, Cap. You'll change your tune on the house."

"I'll be there."

Cap was impressed with Cyrus's new house. The porch extended along the entire front of the arts and crafts bungalow, and was sheltered by the projecting attic, which four hulking trapezoidal columns supported. The interior was trimmed in birch, covered in oak flooring, and featured a beamed ceiling in the living room, an elegant cased opening between the hall and parlor, and leaded art glass windows. Cap was pleased that employing Cyrus had enabled him to purchase such a sturdy home. Cyrus earned (or would earn) every penny of that wage, but Cap had made it possible (albeit reluctantly at first), whereas the great Henry Ford couldn't or wouldn't.

The housewarming was a small gathering. Cyrus had many acquaintances from Black Bottom and the Brewsters, but he'd invited only a few close friends, so as not to frighten the neighborhood into thinking there was a black invasion underway. After Cyrus's house tour, Cap stepped onto the porch, where Marvin and Bessie sat in rocking chairs. Marvin looked like he'd just disembarked a yacht, in his blue sport coat, white pants, and pink shirt. He held a bottle of Coca-Cola, while Bessie nursed an iced drink with a few mint sprigs floating on top. Cap wondered whether her drink was alcoholic, but he didn't want to pick a fight. Instead, he asked about the purple marks on the inside of her left arm.

"Just dog scratches," she said.

A white man in his late thirties or early forties leaned against a massive porch column, sipping a beer from his left hand. His head was turned toward the street. He wore a cream double-breasted suit and a matching fedora wrapped with a purple band. His hand-painted tie, also purple, pictured a Clydesdale horse.

Cyrus entered the porch behind Cap. He rolled his eyes at Marvin's attire and warned his son not to travel into Black Bottom dressed like that. Cyrus then pulled Cap aside and identified the man in the cream suit as Solly Colton. Why had he invited a criminal to the housewarming? The day Cyrus had moved in, a few neighbors gave the evil eye to Marvin and his wife. He'd mentioned it to Solly, who, in addition to providing Cyrus a shotgun, offered "protection" services for the housewarming.

"Come on, Cap. I'll introduce you. Solly's not a bad guy. You'll see."

Cap was unimpressed. Solly's face resembled an over-tenderized veal cutlet. Islands of red and purple spider veins pocked his otherwise pinkish-gray complexion. He had a dirty five-o-clock shadow, two chimney brushes for eyebrows, and slick-backed hair, which he'd seemingly brushed on with asphalt sealcoat. His nose was fat and crooked. The fatness was genetic. The crookedness came courtesy of numerous fist impacts and a pop from a Louisville Slugger.

Cap mentally traced a vector from his right-hand's left-most knuckle to the nook in Solly's nose. *How satisfying it would be to rest my knuckle in that nook,* thought Cap. *I bet it'd be a perfect fit.*

Cap shook Solly's hand, heavily calloused from hauling liquor crates during Prohibition. Solly nodded vaguely in Marvin and Bessie's direction, whereupon Bessie launched herself from the rocking chair, pulled a cigarette from a case, and inserted it between Solly's lips. After she lit the cigarette, Solly pulled her against his body and planted a kiss. When Bessie stepped back, she exhaled the ex-gangster's smoke.

Cap became enraged. He fantasized about hurtling his body into Solly's, and then the two of them smashing through the porch railing and crashing into the azaleas below. His violent imagery registered only as a slight shift of weight to his left foot.

Cap's sullenness didn't faze Solly. Indeed, he went out of his way to needle Cap, constantly referring to him as "Pops," even though Cyrus had introduced him as Cap. He called Bessie "Doll," and handled her as though she were stuffed with sawdust, several times yanking her from the rocking chair, spinning her in a little dance step, and setting her back down. Cap couldn't stomach that Bessie was this gangster's plaything. Worse, Solly was brazenly asserting his ownership, openly claiming the right to manipulate her, place her, prop her.

The conversation soon revealed that Bessie had been to the Bizrete more than that one time. She was a regular, in fact. She'd sing a song or two in between sets by the paid entertainment and then sit at Solly's table, smoking Lucky Strikes and drinking mint juleps. Cap was disgusted but also amazed

Bessie had been able to pull A's and B's at Cass Tech. He'd given her freedom, assuming good grades were a proxy for maturity and responsibility. He hadn't questioned the late-night study sessions or the choir rehearsals or "this thing I have to do," which invariably spilled past his bedtime. She was always there in the morning—bleary-eyed, to be sure, but what teenager wasn't? He hadn't contemplated the possibility she was living a whole other life after sundown.

Solly should've shut up at that point. He'd already exposed Bessie's nightly transgressions. Instead, he tried to reassure Cap by saying his "little girl" was in good hands. *Yeah*, thought Cap, *she's in Solly's good, calloused, old man hands*. Solly claimed he was working hard to advance Bessie's singing career. And exactly what other singing careers had Solly advanced? Solly dismissed Cap's question with an "Oh, no one you've heard of." Cap pressed Solly for a few names, but he wouldn't provide even one, claiming "singer-promoter confidentiality."

Cap asked about his contract with Bessie. There wasn't one, not in writing anyway. That seemed unusual for someone who supposedly had launched so many to stardom. Solly puffed on his cigarette, noting, "Contracts are just paper, and paper's good for two things—wrapping tobacco and wiping asses." And what was Solly charging for all his hard work? Bessie interjected. She asked her father to leave it alone. She was an adult and could do what she wanted. But Cap pointed out that she wasn't an adult. She'd just turned seventeen, and Cap would have to give his consent to any contract, whether written or oral.

"Oh, it's oral," said Solly, his tone oozing with depravity. "Definitely oral."

Bessie looked down.

Cap felt the porch giving way. He tried to wipe the nauseating image from his mind and stabilize his stance. While he wasn't looking, his daughter had grown up and fallen in with the wrong sort. She was staying out late, drinking booze, and trading fluids with a man old enough to be her father. She was no longer the innocent little girl who'd held tea parties and lectured her dolls and father on proper etiquette. Cap knew he was to blame. He hadn't paid enough attention during those teas. He hadn't been interested, so she found a daddy who was. But there was still time, wasn't there? He could save his little girl. He could give her the attention she craved, couldn't he? Well, he was gonna damn well try.

Cap grabbed Bessie's arm and announced they were leaving. Bessie yanked herself free and said she was staying with Solly. When Cap grabbed her arm again, Solly stepped close and warned, "The little girl made her intentions clear. Shove off, old man." Cap turned his trembling face toward Solly to expose his pulsating scar. Solly smiled and said, "Nifty scar. I gotta few myself. I've been cut in all sorts of places. I just can't show them all, not in polite company. Ain't that right, doll?"

Cap had been right. His right hand's left-most knuckle fit perfectly in the nook in Solly's nose. Had Solly not careened into the column, he would've flipped over the porch railing. His hat was not so fortunate, and it tumbled to the mulch below. Solly stuffed a handkerchief into his nose to stem the blood flow, which dripped onto his tie and expanded into a red blotch over the Clydesdale's white muzzle. Cap didn't understand why, but the image made him shiver, as though his soul had been impaled with an icicle. He collected his wits and then, once again, grabbed Bessie's arm and began to escort her away. They stopped cold on the porch steps, however, when Solly cocked his nickel-plated Colt .38.

"I'll grant you one free shot—the daddy's prerogative," said Solly, his voice muffled and nasal. "But see, I'm the new daddy in town. Next time, I might not be so forgiving."

Bessie pried her arm away and moved to Solly's side.

"Bessie, where are you—?" asked Cap.

"I hoped to tell you under better circumstances, Pops, but you left me no choice. I'm moving in with Solly."

———o|o-◇◇─⬥─◇◇-o|o———

Cap stewed in the back of the Yellow taxicab. For the first time in decades, he was on his own. He had no lover. Mama Elsie was dead and buried. His son was heading to war, and his daughter was shacking up with a gangster. Had Cap displeased Fate by coming to America? Perhaps he should've stayed in Schwarz Boden, where he would've been close to the Nazis' halls of power, privy to the whispers about the times and locations of military assemblies. Working with the underground, he could've wished himself into Himmler's flat and Hitler's crapper, lit some dynamite, and blown the war up before it really got started. Cap was impotent in America. The hat had stopped working after Ellis Island, and he didn't know if or when it might recharge. Years of daily checks had dwindled to weekly, then monthly, and bi-monthly, checks, until he'd lost faith in the hat altogether. All he could do was pray his adopted country would rescue the Nazis' victims the old-fashioned way—with bullets and bombs.

Someone had left a newspaper on the cab's backseat. The front page reported that the Nazis had declared Berlin "Judenfrei" (free of Jews), the last thirty thousand having been transported "eastward." Eastward meant Poland. In Warsaw, food rations provided only a quarter of the calories necessary to keep a human being alive. Nevertheless, thousands of Jews had mustered the energy to resist turning over their women and children for transport to concentration camps. But they'd lost their battle. Those not executed on the spot had been transported to Treblinka, which, according to Polish reports, was an extermination camp.

How can You let this go on? Cap asked Fate. *Bring the wishing hat back to life. Today. Right this second. Let me save at least a few, dammit!*

"We're here, pal," said the taxi driver, stopping at Cap's house.

"Change of plans. Take me to Oakland Street."

After the cabbie dropped him at the shop, Cap made a beeline for the cutting room. The Lou Gehrig portrait was askew.

What the—?

Cap took down the picture and opened the safe. He was horrified at what he found or, rather, what he didn't find. No hat. No gold Hermes coin either. "Son of a bitch!" Cap left Gehrig propped against the worktable, locked the store, and hailed a taxi to take him to the house of the only person he figured could've emptied the safe—Cyrus.

Cyrus was on the porch when Cap exited the cab. He was vigorously brushing a stubborn hand-shaped bloodstain off the handrail. Solly's blood.

"Hey, Cap. You all right? Sorry for inviting Solly. I feel bad Bessie's mixed up with him. I was hoping Marvin would be able to steer her from trouble. But he ain't got the strongest personality. More interested in lookin' fine than bein' a man. S'pose there's not much he coulda done for her anyway, once she got hooked on the junk."

"What do you mean 'the junk?'"

"You seen the tracks on her arm, right?"

"The dog scratches?"

"Shit, Cap. Those are needle marks."

Cap grabbed Cyrus by the collar and shoved him against the porch post.

"God damn it, Cyrus! What'd you do to my little girl?"

"Nothin'! She fell in with the wrong crowd at the Bizrete. Solly took a fancy to her, made big promises, got her hooked."

"But you've known."

"I didn't know Bessie was your girl until a few weeks ago. Before then, she was just someone Marvin hung with, and I was happy he was hangin' with any girl, even if she was trouble."

"Trouble?"

"Well, *in* trouble.

"You're lying."

"I ain't. You can trust me."

"Then why'd you crack my safe?"

"What safe?"

"Don't bullshit me, Cyrus. Lou Gehrig was crooked. You obviously didn't put him on straight after you emptied my safe."

"I don't know nothing about any safe."

"That's how you afforded this house. You took the gold coin and sold it."

"I ain't no thief. I bought this house with my money, no one else's."

"Says the man who runs numbers and cavorts with gangsters."

"I didn't steal no gold coin."

"What did you steal?"

"Nothing."

"Forget about the goddamn coin, okay? Just give me back the hat."

"What hat?"

"Don't fuck with me, Cyrus! Where are you hiding it?"

Cap swung open the front door and searched the house for the hat. He slid out the sofa in the parlor, scoured the closets, rifled through cabinets, inspected the attic, and ripped open unpacked moving boxes. He worked himself into a furious sweat and strained his back from all the stooping and lifting. Twenty minutes later, he abandoned his search.

"Satisfied?" asked Cyrus.

"You sold it to that piece of shit Solly, didn't you? You have no idea what you've done, what that maniac will do with that kind of power!"

"Christ, Cap, if I didn't know you, I'd say you're the one on junk. You just got some bad news about your little girl, so I get it. You're in shock. You're lookin' for someone to blame, and your friend Cyrus is an easy target. Go home. Cool down for a day and then you'll see you made a big mistake. Then you can focus on fixin' the problem with Bessie."

"The only mistake I made is hiring you. I'm fixing that now. You're fired."

CHAPTER SIX

Father Filconi tightened his black bowtie. Duke hadn't a clue how to fold his—not that bow-tying skills would've mattered. His jacket fit so snugly he couldn't raise his hands above chest level.

"I told you size forty," said Duke.

"You said thirty-four," the Father answered in a testy tone. He adjusted Duke's tie so one end was longer than the other and then folded it over the shorter end.

"I distinctly said forty. Elroy Hirsch wears number 40 for the Wolverines. That's how I remember my jacket size."

"Then have Mr. Hirsch rush you another jacket."

Father Filconi tightened the tie so vigorously that Duke had to stick a finger between his neck and collar to breathe. The tie unraveled.

"Ahh. Hold still so I can finish the bow."

"Finish the bow or finish *me*?"

Perspiration beaded on Father Filconi's forehead, and dampness saturated his underarms. He breathed deeply, exhaled, and recommenced tying.

"This Dick Tracy stuff is exciting, huh, Father?"

Father Filconi ignored the question. He squinted hard at his handiwork, seemingly trying to put the fear of God into the fabric, commanding it to tie itself or else suffer an eternity in sartorial Hell. He then tied an imperfect bow that listed clockwise. He twisted it counter, but the tie refused to level itself. That was the best his anxious hands could do.

Duke stuck both arms forward like a man groping in the dark and then dropped them into a pendulous swing. The sleeves of his white server's jacket rose up and down his forearms with each swing. Even holding his arms straight down, the cuffs ended a good three inches from his wrists.

"I've got baboon arms."

Father Filconi fought the impulse to give Duke a Three Stooges slap on the face. "Forget about the sleeves, will you? These outfits are just to blend in with the staff." He went to the desk and patted the sides of an eighteen- by twelve-inch mahogany box. The top was inlaid with the gold crown emblem of La Corona Habana-brand cigars.

"That cigar box is gonna record everything they say?" asked Duke. "Where's the microphone?"

"Inside."

"How's it gonna pick up the sounds?"

"This is very sensitive recording equipment."

"Where'd you get it?"

"Does it matter?"

"Just curious."

"I borrowed it from the Police Department. They use it for undercover work."

"How's it work?"

"Pressing the crown primes it."

"Since when do you prime a tape recorder?"

"I mean, powers it on."

Duke extended his index finger within inches of the crown emblem. "This button here?" The priest swatted it away. "Ow. Jeez-o-pete, Father."

"Just... just don't touch it. Like I said, the equipment's very sensitive."

"That's it, then? Just press the crown?"

"Yes. It'll start recording once the humidor's opened. And, before you ask, the answer is no, they won't see the recording mechanism. It's hidden in the false bottom, underneath the cigars."

"What makes you so sure they're gonna want to smoke?"

"Fed Bankers are notorious cigar smokers. Every newspaper photo shows them with stogies poking from their crooked mouths. They won't resist these fine Cubans."

"And all I have to do is wish us there and back."

"That's right." Father Filconi checked his wristwatch. It was 12:45. "We'd better go."

Duke fetched the wishing hat off the desk and put it on. Father Filconi picked up the box with great care and, to Duke's surprise, great effort. Duke thought he heard rattling metal.

"You put lead cigars in there?"

"No!" the priest barked. "The recorder's heavy, that's all," he added in a calmer voice.

Duke placed a hand on the priest's shoulder. "Just so I'm clear, we're going to the Eccles Building in Washington, D.C.... the Board Room."

Father Filconi swallowed hard. "Yes, but wish us into the men's restroom down the hall, in case someone's already in the Board Room."

"On the count of three. Make sure to exhale, unless you want to toss your Communion wafers."

"That reminds me. We need to pray first."

"No, we don't. I just wish."

"*I* need to pray... for courage."

"Have it your way."

Father Filconi made the sign of the cross. "O Lord, may our cause be just. May our courage not falter. Forgive us for the wounds we will inflict on our enemies. Should we perish in this struggle, grant us everlasting peace in Your kingdom. Amen."

"You religious types sure love your violent metaphors."

Duke placed a hand on the Father's shoulder and began counting. They both exhaled on two. On three, Duke closed his eyes, imagined the restroom nearest the bankers' boardroom in the Eccles Building, and then thought, *Take me there.*

As far as Cap was concerned, Cyrus had pulled off a masterful scam. While portraying the affable, innocent fellow, Cyrus had insinuated himself into Cap's employment and trust. He then must've discovered the wishing hat by accident, perhaps by knocking into the Gehrig portrait and finding the safe. Or, Bessie might've told him about the safe and its contents. Bessie knew about the hat, and she knew it was in the safe, along with the gold coin. Even if Cyrus dismissed the wishing hat as the product of Bessie's alcohol- or drug-induced fantasy, he would've seen the gold coin as an easy score. Frannie Pickford might've been his accomplice, creating the conditions under which Cap felt he had no choice but to hire a Negro, and then—lo and behold—Cyrus happened to be passing by at that very moment! Although Bessie didn't know the safe's combination, Cyrus probably was acquainted with a safe-cracker or two.

Cap had it all figured out.

Only he hadn't, which he learned during his morning coffee two days later. As he was sorting through the previous day's mail, he came across a letter from the U.S. Army. He felt an electric thrill, thinking the Draft Board had inducted him. But then he remembered the Army wasn't conscripting old men.

Although addressed to Cap, the letter concerned his son's military status. It stated that Duke had reported to Fort Custer and later boarded the bus to Camp Claiborne but didn't arrive in Louisiana. As a result, Duke was facing AWOL charges under the Uniform Code of Military Justice, charges that could be increased to desertion, an offense punishable by death in wartime. The letter asked Cap to report any information on his son's whereabouts to the Military Police and noted casually (but ominously) that aiding and abetting desertion also was a crime. It was signed by Major General William Carey Lee, 101st Airborne Division, United States Army.

Holy shit.

Duke knew the safe's combination, but why take the hat? It was defunct... unless it wasn't... unless it had recharged... unless Duke had been secretly monitoring the hat for warmth. *Oh Jesus.* Cap knew Duke was afraid of heading to war, but *that* afraid? So afraid he'd go AWOL and risk a firing squad? Yet that made the most sense. On the bus to Louisiana, at night or during a bathroom break or a fill-up, Duke probably donned the hat and wished himself far from any battlefield where the hat might do some good. Cap's own flesh and blood, war hero Hermann Mützenmacher's grandson, was a coward. And the topper? Cap had betrayed his only friend—accusing Cyrus of stealing the hat and helping to corrupt his daughter. He felt like puking.

Christ, I gotta say sorry.

―⸺o|o⸺⟨⟩⸺⬬⸺⟨⟩⸺o|o⸺―

No one answered the door at Cyrus's house. When Cap knocked again, a voice spoke from the rocking chair.

"No need to knock when a man's sittin' on his front porch."

Cap gave a start. "Didn't see you there. Look, I came to say I'm sorry. I'm a complete asshole."

"No argument here."

"You didn't rob my safe. Duke did. I got a letter from the Army. He's AWOL."

"My word wasn't good enough? You needed a letter from the Army?"

"That's not what I meant."

"But that's what you said."

"I guess I did. I'm sorry. This whole Bessie business has thrown me for a loop."

"Ain't nothin' to apologize for. In fact, I need to thank you."

"Why?"

"You made me realize something. This afternoon, I'm gonna march over to the head of the homeowner's association and tell him the truth. I'm a Negro. I'm gonna say, 'You've gotta an entire nigger family livin' in your neighborhood.'"

"Cyrus, don't do that."

"And after I tell him, I'll make my demand. Fifteen thousand dollars to buy me out. I paid only five. I'll have to move back to the Brewsters, but better to be a rich Negro than a poor white man. Know what I'm gonna do with all that cash, after I pay back your advance, of course? Start a business. A hat business."

"I was hoping you'd help me run my shop."

"You fired me, remember?"

"I'm un-firing you. I need you. You're a born milliner."

"You're too fickle, Cap. I'm hired. I'm fired. I'm hired. But that's okay. You taught me a valuable lesson. I need to be my own man."

"Well, I can't say I blame you. If you change your mind—"

"I ain't gonna change my mind."

"Where you going to set up shop?"

"I've got my eye on a space on Oakland Street. We're gonna be next door neighbors."

Duke and Father Filconi appeared in the vacant restroom. Despite exhaling before the trip, Father Filconi was overcome with nausea. He jammed the humidor into Duke's chest and then vomited in the sink. The unprepared Duke jostled the box. There was a distinct metal on metal sound as he stabilized it.

"Careful with that," the priest scolded between heaves.

"Sounds like loose parts. Maybe we should open it up and—"

"No! Don't do anything. Don't move a muscle."

Father Filconi removed his spectacles and splashed his face with cool water. He dried himself with the continuous cloth towel, replaced his eyeglasses, and then gestured for the humidor.

"All I was saying is things may have shifted in there." Duke handed the box back. "We should make sure the tape didn't come unspooled or something."

"What tape?"

"The *recording* tape."

"Oh... yes...All right."

Father Filconi set the humidor on the deep window ledge that doubled as a heating vent. He knelt to eye level with the box and then ran his fingers lightly over the crown emblem, which was still flush with the wood. Satisfied, he opened the lid. The false plywood bottom had dislodged, and several cigars had rolled into the mechanism. He set the plywood aside and carefully extricated the cigars. Although Duke was no engineer, he realized the box was not a tape recorder. It contained five steel pipes capped at the ends, and each sprouted wires that converged into a timer. A wire led from the timer to the underside of the box top, terminating underneath the crown emblem. The pipes were surrounded by nails, screws, and jagged metal bits.

"What the hell, Father? What is this thing?"

"It's Divine Justice."

"It's a goddamn bomb, is what it is."

"That, too."

"You didn't say anything about killing people."

"This is a war, Duke."

"They haven't killed anyone."

"They're financing that killing overseas—the killing you're so afraid of, the killing that brought you to me."

"We're only supposed to expose them. Disinfect them, you said."

"We've reached a point where disinfection's no longer possible because it's diseased all the way through. These men are a lethal cancer. You don't go easy on cancer. You pound it with all your might, with every weapon at your disposal. You make it a blitzkrieg."

"You mean, you act like a Nazi."

"Their methods, not their motivations."

"Is there really a difference?"

"If Adolf Hitler walked out of that stall this moment and I handed you a gun, would you shoot him?"

"Hell yes."

"Without hesitation?"

"I hope so."

"Why?"

"Because he's pure evil. He's slaughtered millions."

"Not personally. Not by himself. Legions of officers and soldiers are helping him."

"I guess."

"There's no guessing about it. Businessmen and bankers finance his war machine. Do you think those who buy the metal and gunpowder for Hitler's armies are any less culpable than those who pull the trigger?"

"I... uh..."

"Why hesitate with those fat cats but not Hitler? The men out there are financing communism—financing the very reason Hitler rose to power. They are his oxygen. Strangle them, and you strangle him."

"So, you're saying, those Feds are belligerents."

"Yes."

"No different than if they were firing machine guns."

"Absolutely."

"Then it's not a sin to kill them. It's like self-defense."

"Yes, and it's also God's will."

"I'll have to take your word on that."

"This is a major breakthrough, Duke. You're beginning to have faith."

"I suppose you better put that box back together," Duke said after a pause.

"And you should put the wishing hat away until it's time."

Duke stuffed the hat inside his too-small coat, causing his left lapel to bulge conspicuously.

"Cripes. Looks like I'm smuggling a house cat."

After Father Filconi replaced the false bottom and arranged the cigars back into three tight rows, he carefully closed the lid, and they proceeded to the boardroom. Four waiters in white coats and black bowties were arranging the coffee service and straightening the twenty-five chairs around the long conference table. Duke and Father Filconi didn't exactly blend in, though it had little to do with their uniforms. The wait staff was black. When the oldest waiter eyed them askance, Father Filconi said, "Chairman Eccles asked us to deliver his cigars to the meeting. Ask him yourself." The priest nodded toward the hallway, where a group of middle-aged white men conversed. They all looked alike to Duke, and apparently to the waiter, who merely grunted. Father Filconi set the humidor at the table's center and depressed the crown emblem.

"Come on," he whispered to Duke. "We've got ten minutes. The meeting will be well underway by the time it... you know." Father Filconi breezed through the doorway and filtered through the regional bank presidents entering the room. Duke, however, didn't follow. He hadn't budged from his spot by the conference table. The priest re-entered the boardroom and grabbed Duke's elbow. "What are you waiting for?"

"This is wrong, Father. I know what you said about Hitler's oxygen, but my gut's telling me this is wrong."

"Are you going to have faith in me and God's plan or your gut?"

"I gotta go with my gut."

Duke tried to step toward the conference table, but the priest restrained him.

"What are you doing, Duke?"

"I'm getting the box. Let's go with the tape recorder idea, broadcast their lies on your radio show."

"My show's over."

"Huh?"

"My audience has been dwindling for years. I've run out of money for airtime. I failed to inspire a single soul to act. It's time to shut up and lead by example… like Jesus."

"I'm not up on my Bible. How many people did Jesus blow up?"

"Leave the box and let's wish the hell out of here."

"No."

A banker gestured for Duke to move so he could take his seat. The nameplate identified him as the President of the Federal Reserve Bank of San Francisco. When Duke lifted the humidor from the table, the bank president said, "Hold on, son. I'd like one of those." The banker opened the case but didn't seem to notice the wire running along the lid's underside. He picked a cigar and closed the lid. Duke took the humidor and started to leave.

"I hope you're not walking away with that," said the bank president. "See if my colleagues want one."

As Duke played "cigar boy" for the head of the Cleveland Bank, Father Filconi reached into Duke's jacket and yanked out the wishing hat.

"What the hell?! Give it back," said Duke in a furious stage whisper.

"It's us or them, Duke." The priest donned the hat and added, "Ooh, it's warm." He closed his eyes and said, "Take me to the Shrine of St. Bernardine." Nothing happened. He opened and closed his eyes. His face strained as he repeated emphatically, "Take me to the Shrine of St. Bernardine." Again, he didn't vanish. "Why isn't it working?"

"I'm not telling you that."

"Then die with them."

"No one's gonna die."

Duke slammed the humidor shut as the head of the New York Bank was reaching for a cigar and then brushed past Father Filconi into the hallway. The priest hurried after him.

"What are you going to do, Duke? Hide the box in the bathroom? They've seen you. They'll catch you and put you on trial for treason."

"They'll catch you, too, 'cause you're not going anywhere with that hat."

"Seems we're at a standoff."

"Seems so."

Father Filconi checked his wristwatch. "Tick. Tick. You realize they give the chair for treason."

Duke said nothing as he thought long and hard about what to do. He glanced at the wall clock and then said, "Okay. I give in."

"No funny stuff now."

"Nope. You win, Father."

"*God* wins." The priest gestured toward the boardroom. "After you."

Duke re-entered the boardroom, interrupting the wait staff as they closed the double doors. He set the humidor on the table and exited to the hallway. The irritated staff then shut the doors.

"You've made the right decision," said Father Filconi.

"Let's just get the hell out of here. You need to follow my instructions to the letter, got it?"

"Yes."

"We're going to the Shrine of St. Bernardine?"

"Yes."

"You got it fixed in your mind?"

"Yes."

Duke put his hand on the Father's shoulder and said, "Repeat after me, 'Take me there.'"

"Take—"

Duke ripped the wishing hat from the priest's head before he could utter another word. Father Filconi emitted a muffled shriek and then froze in silence, eyes fixed and wide. Duke put on the hat and then burst through the double doors. The Fed Chairman halted his introduction and turned an ireful face toward the intruder.

"What is the meaning of this?"

"Fire Marshal. No smoking, gentleman. I'll have to confiscate this."

Duke grabbed the humidor and rejoined the entranced priest in the hall.

The Chairman turned to the President of the New York Fed. "Never seen a fire hat like that, have you? And since when do firemen wear bowties?"

After the boardroom doors slammed shut, Duke steadied the humidor on his left hip. He took Father Filconi's limp hand and thought of Briggs Stadium, deep in centerfield.

"Take us there," he said with an exhale.

The Detroit Tigers weren't playing or practicing, nor was the grounds crew tending the field, when Duke and Father Filconi suddenly appeared near the centerfield bleachers. Both collapsed to the grass. Duke's head was swimming like a cheap booze hangover. He left the humidor on the turf and scrambled to his feet. He pulled up the disoriented priest.

"Come on, Father! We gotta run."

Duke draped the priest's arm over his shoulder and half-ran-half-dragged him toward the infield.

"Wh… where are we? What's happening?" asked the befuddled priest.

"It's gonna blow!"

"What's gonna blow?"

"The bo—"

The humidor detonated.

"Get down!"

Duke tackled the priest to the ground, twenty feet from second base. Tiny projectiles whizzed over their heads. Screws and nuts pelted Duke's shoes and skipped off his back. They had too little velocity to cause any serious damage. After the blast's echo faded, they sat up. Other than grass stains on their white jackets and the Father's bloody nose, they'd come through unscathed—at least physically. Father Filconi shook his head. He scanned the sky, confused, and then locked eyes with Duke.

"What did you do?"

"I didn't kill anybody, that's what, and I saved our asses."

"You did something to me." He put a hand on his abdomen and squeezed. "Something's missing."

"You lose your lunch?"

"I'm empty… in here, in my gut."

"Let's grab a bite, then."

"It's not hunger, dammit! Back there, when you ripped the hat off me, something tore inside my head. Like you carved out a piece of my brain."

"That's ridiculous, how could…?"

Duke recalled the story Cap had told him about great-great-great grandfather Ludwig's wishing hat mishap. Ludwig spent the rest of his life sharing consciousness with his equine companion.

"I'm lost," the priest continued. "I haven't felt like this since I was a boy, since before I had faith. You took it."

"Took what?"

"My faith."

"Calm down, Father."

"Where is it? Give it back!"

"I have no idea."

But Duke couldn't deny it. Something was lodged in his center, something amorphous, intangible, and foreign. Images of Jesus on a cross and Communion wafers flashed in his mind. Although that sensation was uncomfortably intimate, a soothing warmth also flooded his gut.

"Yes," said the priest, "it's inside you. I see it on your face."

"You're nuts, Father. I'm outta here."

Duke marched toward home plate.

"Wait, Duke. We must unbind ourselves."

"Even if that were true, how the heck do we untangle two souls?"

"I have no idea. Maybe do whatever you did but in reverse."

"That could make it far worse, believe me, kill us even."

"We have to try. Our souls belong to God. He won't let me into His eternal kingdom with a partial soul."

"I'm sure it'll grow back."

"You fool. The soul isn't a lizard's tail."

"Well, the Big Guy'll cut you a break under the circumstances."

"I cannot take that risk."

Duke tore his arm away and broke into a trot.

"Duke! Don't leave me like this!"

Duke closed his eyes and envisioned the Book Cadillac Hotel's lobby. He'd hang out there until he figured out his next move.

"The Book Cadillac?" asked the priest. "Is that where you're going?"

Duke stopped and looked at him quizzically.

"I saw it in your mind's eye," said the priest. "There's no point in running. As long as a piece of me is inside you, I'll always know where you are."

"Doesn't mean you can catch me."

Duke envisioned a new place, a place very far away, across a vast ocean.

Take me there.

Cap hadn't seen or heard from Bessie in three days. He couldn't take it any longer. He didn't know where Solly Colton lived, and Solly wasn't the type to be listed in a telephone directory. Cap was too proud to ask Cyrus. Instead, Cap parked himself in front of Cass Tech High in the afternoon, hoping Bessie still had the good sense to finish out her junior year.

Bessie emerged with the other students. Cap didn't recognize her right away. He initially thought her a faculty member because she moved like an older woman, someone carrying the weight of adult burdens. Her eyes were puffy and tired, her cheeks sunken. She'd gotten so thin her clavicle bones bulged from her dress. Two girls trailed in her wake. They'd been Bessie's friends for years, one the daughter of a Ford executive, the other the child of a restorer at the Detroit Institute of Arts. They looked child-like behind Bessie. They inhabited a world of bobby socks and soda jerks, while Bessie was wading through a cesspool of needles and booze.

Bessie breezed by.

"When are you coming home, Bessie?" asked Cap, running to catch up to her.

"I have a new home with Solly."

Cap swallowed his anger. Blowing up wouldn't do any good.

"You need help."

"You don't know what I need."

"Then you tell me."

"It's too late."

"Why?"

Bessie looked at Cap fiercely. "I needed you to believe in me, respect me. You never did. You always preferred Duke."

"Only for the hat business, and that's only because of the curse."

"So you say."

"I didn't make up the curse. You've read Lorenz's letter."

"Yeah? Where'd Lorenz get his info?"

"I have no clue."

"And that's exactly your problem."

"Please. I saw the tracks on your arm. Let me help you get clean. That junk is gonna kill you."

"I guess that's my curse."

"Screw it." Cap grabbed Bessie's wrist and dragged her toward his car. "Let's go."

"Get off me, Pops!"

"You obviously don't know what's best for you."

Bessie slapped and punched at Cap's thick forearm, but he didn't let go.

"Help! Help!" Bessie shouted to two burly man-boys in varsity letter jackets.

The boys hurried over, grabbed Cap's arms, and plucked him off Bessie like a pawn from a chessboard.

"What's the problem, old man?" demanded a boy with a massive chin and Vitalis-saturated hair. The football patch with the "C" on his varsity jacket indicated he was the team captain.

"It's not what it looks like. Bessie is my daughter."

"Dad or not, you're acting like a bully."

"He is a bully," said Bessie. "He beats me all the time."

The boys squeezed Cap's arms more tightly.

"That's not true. She has a problem, a medical problem. I'm taking her to the doctor."

"Ha!" Bessie mocked. "He's lying. He's gonna lock me in my room and whip me with his belt."

Bessie rushed down Grand River. Cap futilely tried to extricate his arms.

"Easy, old fella," said the football captain.

After Bessie turned the corner, the two meatheads warned Cap not to show his face again unless he wanted it shoved up his ass. Cap reddened. His cheek scar swelled, which disconcerted the football captain. He released Cap's arm, and his teammate followed suit.

Cap's scar was so good at driving people away. It had worked hundreds of times over the years. He'd have gladly ripped it off his face for one chance to bring his children back.

CHAPTER SEVEN

A few weeks later, around 5:00 p.m., a pudgy man in a black suit coat and ascot cap accosted Cap as he was locking up the shop.

"Are you Mr. Leghorn, the proprietor of this establishment?"

"I am. And you are...?"

"I have questions about your son, Duke Leghorn."

"You know him how?"

"The U.S. Army has placed him in AWOL status."

"Yeah. I got a letter about it. What's it to you?"

"I'm investigating his whereabouts."

"Last I knew, he'd left Fort Custer on a bus for Louisiana."

"He hasn't called or written?"

"No."

"He hasn't reached out in some other way?"

"What, like a telegraph?"

"For instance."

"No."

The man scratched his red stubble. "Do you have any idea where he might have gone? Perhaps to a relative or a vacation home?"

"We don't have much extended family. None in the States. We've got distant relatives in Ireland, but I doubt he went there."

"Where in Ireland?"

"County Antrim, near the Bushmills factory."

"Do they go by Leghorn?"

"No, but like I said, he—"

"Any second homes? A log cabin somewhere?"

"Just the house on Edison Street."

"Should you hear from him, call me at once."

The man handed Cap a plain business card with a phone number.

"Who should I ask for?"

"Just leave your name with my service." He tipped his cap and added, "Thank you for your time." He turned and headed briskly down Oakland Street.

"Wait," Cap called out. "Will you let me know if you find him?"

The stranger turned the corner. Cap wondered why the man hadn't been in uniform. He also looked overweight for a military man. And since when were ascots standard issue? Perhaps the Army had hired private detectives to track down AWOL soldiers. Cap stuffed the card in his shirt pocket.

Cap fished the keys from his trousers, just as a cloud of cigarette smoke drifted into his nose. Cyrus was smoking in front of the defunct Cecile's Centennial Wigs, now home to Hats by Silk.

Cyrus's decision to locate his business right next to Leghorn Millinery had irked Cap. He'd hired Cyrus against his will, paid him above market wages, and trained him, only to have him become a direct and proximate competitor. Soon, however, Cap realized he had little to worry about from a competition standpoint. Cyrus knew how to make a few styles of hats; he had no idea how to run a business. During his opening week, Cyrus had run various promotions to stimulate customer traffic—door prizes, a jazz trio playing out front, Sander's ice cream for the children. They worked. Bodies filtered in and out of his store, but none was a paying customer.

By far, Cyrus's worst idea was a raffle for a brown velvet fedora. The raffle tickets were free, but to entice folks into the store, he also offered free Stroh's beer. Most of the takers were former Ford co-workers getting off their shifts in the afternoon. Forty of the lugs, stinking of sweat and furnace fire, packed themselves into Cyrus's shop, each downing three or more beers. Cyrus went to Wrigley's three times to re-stock. He must've spent thirty bucks on beer, plus another five on the materials for the fedora, not to mention his labor in making the hat. Otis Franklin, a two-hundred-fifty-pound man who worked Cyrus's old job, won the raffle. The hat looked like a fungal growth emerging from his enormously fat head.

After floundering for two weeks, Cyrus steadily established a clientele who didn't significantly overlap with Cap's. Whereas Leghorn Millinery catered to the Jitterbuggers, traditional businessmen, and fashion-forward women,

Hats by Silk attracted a more casual crowd, who preferred fedoras, panamas, and Leghorn straw boaters, their crowns circumscribed with strips of cream or brown silk. Indeed, their two businesses complemented one another. If a customer couldn't find something he liked at one store, he generally found it at the other. Cap's grudge dissolved, and, although he and Cyrus still weren't on speaking terms, Cap acquiesced to Cyrus's success.

A blue, torpedo-bodied Cadillac parked outside Cyrus's shop. It was Solly Colton's car. Solly visited Cyrus most days, usually in the late afternoon. Cap had no idea why, although with Solly it couldn't have been just a social call. Still, those visits were Cap's only source of information about Bessie. Solly usually would crack open Leghorn Millinery's front door and announce that Cap's "little girl was just peachy" and not cutting school. It was cold comfort, but Cap had nothing else to cling to as long as Bessie refused to see him.

Solly and his two men exited the car and hovered around Cyrus. Solly nodded to Cap and said Bessie was "doing swimmingly." He then nodded to his thugs. One swatted the cigarette from Cyrus's mouth, while the other hauled him to his feet and inside the shop. This was the first time Cap had seen Solly getting rough with Cyrus. Cap crossed Oakland Street, so he could keep an eye on things. He took a table at the Albert's Diner front window, from which he had a clear view into Cyrus's shop.

Solly pulled a bulging leather wallet from his suit coat and handed it to Cyrus. Cyrus held up his hand, trying to refuse it. Solly then stuck the wallet in Cyrus's chest. Cyrus still wouldn't take it. Solly's men grabbed Cyrus and held him, while Solly slapped him across the face with the wallet—left, right, and left. He paused and then struck Cyrus once more on the right cheek, presumably to fulfill a warped sense of sadistic symmetry. He dropped the wallet on the counter and left the store with his men.

Cap sipped coffee for a couple hours and peered across the street until Cyrus locked up and walked to the streetcar. He appeared to be out of danger.

Only he wasn't.

Cap paid his tab and stepped outside, just as Cyrus's shop window shattered. Then, there was a loud pop, followed by billowing smoke. A car raced away. Cap ran into the street to catch the license plate, but he was too late. The air reeked of rotten eggs.

A telephone rang. He assumed it was Cyrus's phone. Was this how the mob operated? Smash a window, detonate a stench bomb, ruin all your merchandise, and then follow up with a phone call to make sure everything went off without a hitch? Customer service in the gangster underworld. But the ringing wasn't coming from Cyrus's store. It was Cap's phone. He fumbled for his keys and quickly unlocked the shop.

Bessie bawled into his ear. She apologized for treating him so badly. She said she'd been a bad daughter, and she just wanted to hear her father's voice before she died. Cap reassured her she wasn't dying, only experiencing the initial stages of withdrawal. And she wasn't a bad daughter. He was a bad father. She'd turned to the needle because he wasn't there for her. He'd make it right. He'd bring her home, and they'd recover from this nightmare together.

"Where are you, Bessie?"

"Outside Goresky's."

"Wait for me. I'm coming."

"Hurry, Pops."

Cap temporarily closed the shop to nurse Bessie through her withdrawal. He applied cold towels for her flop sweats, but there wasn't much he could do for her bouts of cramping, anxiety, and restlessness. The only sustenance she'd tolerate was hot Vernor's ginger ale. As a child, she'd detested the drink's intense gingery fizz, which was more Listerine than soda pop. Bringing it anywhere close to her nose would induce nausea, followed by a coughing fit. But in the throes of withdrawal, Vernor's was her elixir of life.

Cap's home phone rang constantly that first day. There was always silence at the other end. Cap figured Solly was trying to reach Bessie. After the eighth such call, Cap spoke to the silence. He said he knew it was Solly and threatened to report him to the police for corrupting a minor. The calls stopped.

After a week, Cap spent the mornings with Bessie and re-opened the store in the afternoons. He was friendly with the projectionist at the Norwood Theater, who let them watch as many films as they wanted before opening to the public. They could even help themselves to the day-old popcorn. They watched newsreels about the war, Three Stooges shorts, Abbott and Costello and Spencer Tracy movies, and an Ethel Waters musical. The movies distracted Bessie from the intense itching on her scalp, the latest withdrawal symptom. She'd already worn away a half-dollar-sized patch. Since she tended to scratch with her left arm, Cap sat on that side, where he could pin her arm on the rest. They enjoyed *The Wizard of Oz* and *Casablanca* the most, watching both a dozen times. They talked about how Dorothy's ruby slippers worked like the wishing hat, only worn on the opposite end of the body, and how *Casablanca* also involved the wishing hat's close kin. To escape French North

Africa, Victor Laszlo planned to use stolen "transit papers" that permitted their bearer to travel unmolested, anywhere in Europe.

Is Duke traveling unmolested through Europe? Is he doing any good with the hat?

"I'm tired, Pops," said Bessie, as Rick Blaine told Captain Renault about the beginning of their beautiful friendship. Bessie rested her head on her father's shoulder and closed her eyes. "I'm so, so tired."

In the taxi, Bessie's slight, insubstantial body reminded Cap of a long-ago horse-drawn carriage ride through Kiegel Park. Then seven, Bessie had spent hours climbing the park's plane trees and rolling down the hills with Duke. Rosamund had purchased a box of apple strudel from Flagler's. The strudels were for dessert, but the children were too hungry from all their activity. Bessie ate two and then reached for a third, when Rosamund cut her off. A minute later, Bessie was sound asleep against Kasper, sporting a crude apple filling mustache.

Bessie had been so innocent then. She'd known nothing about Nazis or gangsters or heroin. Her life had centered around dolls, which she controlled and manipulated to her heart's content. But now she was being controlled and manipulated. Solly Colton had shackled her to his table of former Purple Gang degenerates, and was serving her cups of addiction. If only Cap could go back in time and find that precise moment when Bessie drifted off course. If only he could materialize before his daughter and say, "Don't go in there. Stay. Drink tea with me."

If only there were a hat for that.

After putting Bessie to bed that evening, Cap dug out her old dolls. When he opened the box flap, Melinda greeted him with her pouty mouth. She looked freakishly alive, albeit frozen, in the dusty light. Cap resisted the urge to fling Melinda across the attic, because her porcelain head, which dated from the 1880s, likely would've cracked. But if Melinda appreciated Cap's mercy, she certainly didn't show it. That fixed pout made her look both spoiled and petulant. She inspired irritation, even fantasies of mild violence. No wonder Bessie used to scold her so often.

Cap found three other dolls like Melinda, with bisque heads and jointed wood bodies. He didn't know their names. One had indigo eyes, straight blonde hair tied with a bow, and dimples deep enough to hold a water droplet. She looked pleasant enough. Cap speculated her name was Vivian. The second doll had a deformed, V-shaped head. The upper portion was far too wide relative to the chin, rendering the doll's eyes tiny islands in a vast sea of forehead. Also, her features were androgynous. Replace her silk dress with a two-piece suit, and she could've passed as a boy. Cap called her Lenny. The third doll bore an eerie resemblance to Bessie as a child. She had a plump face, orchid red lips, skeptical blue eyes, and a mass of dark ringlets. She was trouble, that one. Cap named her Nessie.

Cap didn't know the cloth doll's name, which was the only doll he'd ever gotten Bessie (not counting the Gretchen doll Bessie had bought with proceeds from the embezzled jazz records). She was much smaller than the bisque dolls and dressed less elegantly. She was wearing an ethnic costume with a puffy sleeved blouse and a burlap skirt, a lace-up vest, and laced boots. The gigantic painted-on eyelashes, sloppy red lips, and raised eyebrows gave her a furtive expression. This doll was definitely the oddball—small, poorly dressed, and obvious—compared to her upper-class companions. She also couldn't articulate her arms and legs—a severe disability in the doll universe. She reminded Cap of an over-the-hill prostitute named Hildi, who'd begun servicing Schwarz Boden's red light district before automobiles invaded the city. Hildi was passable from a distance, but when you got within ten feet, the harsh arc lights revealed cracked pancake makeup and a frayed corset, which seemed to be the only thing keeping her aged bones upright. Cap named the cloth doll Hildi, in honor of the old prostitute.

Cap surmised Melinda had made these teas especially uncomfortable for the decrepit Hildi. That little snot. Poor Hildi.

Cap retrieved the child-sized dining table, chairs, and a tiny tea set, which he'd bought shortly after their arrival in Detroit. He set them up in the living room. There were six chairs, which meant there were spots for the five dolls and one live human being. Cap dusted the dolls, straightened their clothes, primped their hair, and propped them in the chairs. He boiled hot water for Darjeeling tea and poured a cup for each setting. He didn't have fancy tea cookies in the house, so he made peanut butter and jelly sandwiches, cut off the crusts, and quartered them. He brought over two candlesticks and lit them. He tuned the radio to classical music, which wasn't his favorite, but he thought it more appropriate than jazz. His preparations complete, he sat in the open chair and waited for Bessie to arise.

Cap grew restless. He went to the stairs and listened for movement from Bessie's room. He sat back down. He surveyed his guests. He'd set Hildi to his immediate right, figuring the others would behave better if she were closest to the master. Nessie sat on Hildi's right as a further buffer. Melinda was at the table's opposite end. Cap wanted her as far away as possible. The problem was, he had a clear view of Melinda's face. He switched indigo-eyed Vivian to the end and moved pouty-faced Melinda to the far left corner. Anvil-headed Lenny sat to his left.

Cap glanced back toward the stairwell. There was still no movement upstairs. The tea was getting cold. Hildi suddenly was slouching to the left. Due to her inability to bend at the waist, she had only three contact points with the seat (her head and two boot heels), which lacked sufficient surface area and adhesiveness to grip the smooth, oaken surface. He got up and straightened Hildi as best he could and then struck up a conversation in the haughtiest tone he could muster.

"Please help yourself to the tea sandwiches. What's that, Melinda? Oh, I see. You're watching your figure. No, I don't have any caviar. How silly. You don't have caviar at a tea.

"Now, Lenny, you've taken three sandwiches. Just start with one.

"What's wrong now, Melinda? You're out of tea? Already?

"Lenny, why are you taking more sandwiches? That makes five. Where do you store all that food? Probably in that trapezoidal head of yours.

"Is everyone all set now, because I'd like to sit down. For God sakes, Hildi, sit up straight. Is it any wonder the others despise you?

"Listen, how would you all like a special treat? I'm going to fetch it from the cabinet. Here we go. Have any of you had Bushmills? No, Nessie. It's not tea. It's whiskey. Ha. Yeah, 'whiskey' is a funny word. Hold out your cups, please. Ahh. Now isn't that better than any tea? Slow down, Lenny. Don't gulp it.

"God damn it, Hildi! Sit up straight. Lenny, put down that goddamn sandwich!

"Hildi? Where'd Hildi go? She's under the fucking table? That's just great.

"Hey, where's that sandwich? Don't deny it, Lenny. The peanut butter is smeared all over your man-lips.

"Well, this tea has turned into a perfect disaster. We're done. Back to the box with you, Melinda. Stop struggling, you little shit!"

"Pops?"

Bessie was sitting halfway down the steps. Her face was contorted, her hair disheveled, and she was scratching her scalp.

"You're up!" Cap blurted out. His face was deep red, and his eyes were wide and brimming with madness.

"I heard shouting. Are you choking Melinda?"

"No. No, just putting her back."

"Why was she out?"

"It was supposed to be a surprise for you. Like old times."

"I'm not seven."

"I know. It's just that... well, I wasn't very good at playing tea party when you were younger—"

"You haven't improved."

"I don't know what I was thinking. That's not true. I do know. Second chances. I wasn't there for you. I mean, I was there but not there. I want to try again."

"We can't go back, Pops."

Her words sent Cap hurtling toward a dark mood. He flailed for something to grab, anything to halt his plummet into despair. He groped backward for a rich memory of Bessie's childhood in which to lose himself and then forward for an unexploited possibility that, if actualized, might transform him into a better father and her into a thriving daughter. He came up empty-handed. There was only the eternal now, with all its imperfections and pains and uncertainties, the inescapable present that condemned fallible men to reap and re-reap the consequences of their paternal neglect.

Cap glimpsed the moonrise through the window. It was reflected light, to be sure, but light nonetheless. Its source remained invisible but would reveal itself in time. It always did. Not even Fate could prevent that.

"Hey, I have an idea. How about we go listen to some live music? There's gotta be something going on at Club Zombie or the Paradise Theater."

"I'm not feeling up to it."

Bessie clawed at her scalp.

"Careful with that scratching."

"I can't stand it. It's like my brain's itching."

"Come here. Let me see." Cap parted the coarse thicket on her head. "Jesus, Bessie! You're bleeding again. All this from your fingers?"

"Mostly... and the barbecue brush."

"You ran metal bristles across your scalp?"

"It really itches."

"The bald patch is the size of a pancake. You look like a monk."

"I'd happily live in a monastery if that would stop the itching."

"You just need a distraction. When I was battling my addiction, I got busy with my hands. I made hats. Let's go down to the shop."

"I haven't worked on hats in months."

"You don't lose the skills. It's like riding a bike."

"What skills?"

"You have incredible talent, Bessie."

"I do?"

"Absolutely."

"You really think so?"

"I was going to wait until you're feeling better, but what the hell. I want you to work with me in the hat shop. One day, you'll take over."

Bessie smiled crookedly.

"Don't worry. It'll be a long time from now. Years."

"Would you be offering if Duke was here? You always say the curse doesn't allow it."

"I'm not gonna lie. Had Duke not run off, we probably wouldn't be having this conversation. But I've thought about it. Nothing written says our daughters can't carry on the hat-making tradition."

"Lorenz's letter."

"His letter says only that women haven't run the hat shop, not that they're prohibited. That tradition is just a habit, like smoking or shooting heroin. It can be broken. The fact is, our hat shop would've gone under were it not for Mama Elsie. My father stunk at millinery. Same with Duke. Screw Fate. I did wrong by you, Bessie, but this is your opportunity. Save yourself. Save me. Save this family."

"Okay, Pops."

Cap hugged Bessie tightly. "I can't tell you how happy this makes me. First thing in the morning, we'll hit the shop and put you to work."

The phone rang. Frank Horowitz, the elderly owner of the wig store across the street from Cap's shop, was calling to report that Leghorn Millinery was in flames.

"I've got to go," Cap said in a panic.

"What's wrong, Pops?"

"Something at the shop I have to take care of."

"You look worried."

"It'll be fine." He blew out the candles on the table. "Please. No more scratching while I'm gone. Tomorrow, we'll make hats. We'll also find a doctor to help with the itching. Should've done that in the first place. I'm a terrible father."

"You were there for me when I called." She kissed his cheek. "When you get back, let's have a proper tea. No dolls."

"I'd like that."

"I can't wait for tomorrow."

"Me, too." Cap did a double-take at the Melinda doll, which was dangling on the edge of the box as though caught mid-escape from her cardboard prison. "Do me a favor. Put Melinda away. She gives me the creeps."

Cap figured Solly had set the fire because of his threat to go to the cops. Well, Cap didn't care about the store, as long as Bessie was free of him. He had insurance. The equipment and material could be replaced. No adjustor could assess Bessie's value, nor compensate Cap should he lose her. Solly had made his point, but he didn't have Bessie, and that was all that mattered.

Cap arrived to find his store intact and undisturbed. Cyrus's store was smoldering. The billowing smoke must have confused Mr. Horowitz about which store was burning. Fortunately, the firefighters had arrived promptly and extinguished the flames before they spread.

Cyrus was picking through singed straw hats, broken stands, and shattered glass for anything salvageable, which was next to nothing. For the first time in a month, Cyrus spoke to Cap. He revealed that, in the flurry to sell his house and open the store, he'd forgotten to buy insurance. He hadn't sold his house for as much as he'd expected. Several folks in the homeowners association didn't believe Cyrus was black, despite his insistence otherwise and the fact he'd married a black woman and had a black son. Yes, Cyrus spoke like a black man, but, then, many blue-collar men sounded alike from spending so much time together on the assembly line. They forced Cyrus into a demeaning demonstration of his Blackness, which proved much more difficult than he'd anticipated. His wife and son's word carried little weight. He couldn't locate his birth certificate, which would've listed his mother's race. An old letter with a canceled stamp and a Black Bottom address was somewhat persuasive, but when asked about his schooling, Cyrus admitted he'd attended Bishop School, where most students were Jewish at that time. Nor could Cyrus resort to the basest racial stereotypes. He couldn't dance a lick to demonstrate he was "one of the musical people," nor would he drop his trousers to reveal the black man's "natural gift." Although Cyrus had convinced a majority of his Blackness, a vocal minority threatened to delay the negotiation until conducting a more thorough search for his birth certificate. The final offer: Cyrus could take two-thousand dollars more than he'd paid or nothing at all. He took the deal, but after closing costs, moving, and re-renting his old place in the Brewster's, he'd barely broken even.

In order to finance his own store, Cyrus needed a partner. Solly Colton was the only man he knew with sufficient resources. As a condition of his investment, Solly required Cyrus to launder the proceeds from his illegal lottery and growing drug trade. Solly began delivering Cyrus piles of money, which Cyrus recorded on his books as hat sales and deposited in his business bank account for later disbursement to Solly. But Cyrus got cold feet. He didn't want to participate in a criminal enterprise. He just wanted to sell hats. He offered to pay Solly back on an accelerated schedule and end their business relationship. Solly refused. A deal was a deal. When Cyrus said he wouldn't do it anymore, Solly got rough. Cyrus "shaped up" after the stink bomb incident but later told Solly he was done. Flames ensued.

"You going to be all right, Cy?"

"Oh, yeah. Sure. Just a little hitch."

"Well, if you need anything..."

"I'll be fine, Cap. I can get along myself. That's been my problem. Gotta stop puttin' faith in anyone but Number One."

"Listen, I gotta check on Bessie. You know where I am if you need me, right?"

Cyrus nodded noncommittally.

Cap left Cyrus among the soaked rubble and hopped on the Clairmount streetcar. He'd left Bessie alone for more than an hour. Trying to will the streetcar to move faster only increased his anxiety and accentuated his impotence. He should've taken a cab. Shit. He should've bought a damn car by now. He was living in the Motor City, for Chrissake! If only he'd had the wishing hat, he could've been home in an instant.

Cap dismounted at Byron Street and ran the long two blocks home. He burst through the front door and shouted Bessie's name. She didn't answer. Cap realized he hadn't unlocked the front door before entering; he was sure he'd locked it before leaving the house. More disturbing, that day's mail was strewn across the foyer. The desk was in disarray too. Although Cap was no neatnik—he hoarded years' worth of bills, invoices, and correspondence—he kept his papers in tidy stacks on the left and right sides of the desk, leaving two square feet of clear space in between. Now the stacks were toppled over. The correspondence stack was utterly decimated, as though someone had flipped through and then discarded the letters one by one.

"Bessie!"

"Huh?" came the stuporous response from the shadows.

Bessie was sitting at the table with her dolls. Hildi sat upright in the chair. Lenny's face was free of peanut butter and he, like the other dolls, had one cookie on his plate. Cap sat in Melinda's vacant chair.

"Jesus, Bessie. You scared the hell out of me. How come you didn't answer?"

"Sleeping... I... guess," she slurred.

"What's wrong with you?" Cap felt her forehead. "You're cold. Look at me."

Bessie gazed up from her teacup, head swaying, eyes swimming in their sockets. Her pupils were two pin pricks. She'd re-lit a candle, and next to it was a spoon with a shallow puddle of brown residue. She was resting her right elbow on the table, revealing raised indigo tracks running four inches down her forearm. A glass syringe rested across the teacup's mouth, the needle pointing directly at Cap.

"Christ. You used. Solly was here, wasn't he?"

"No... I swear."

"The front door was unlocked. There are papers all over the floor. You let somebody in."

"Not Solly."

"Who?"

Bessie closed her eyes and swayed in her chair.

"Who?!" Cap repeated.

Bessie's eyes shot open and settled at quarter mast. "Fat man... red beard."

"What fat man with a red beard?"

"Looking for Duke... called ambulance... prayed."

"What the hell kind of criminal breaks in and prays? It had to be Solly's henchman. He brought you the dope, right?"

Bessie's eyes closed. Her head fell back. Her jaw went slack.

"Bessie. Bessie, wake up!"

Cap smacked her cheeks lightly, but she didn't rouse. He shouted in her face. He shook her shoulders and then carried her limp body to the sofa and lay her down. She was little more than skin and bones with frizzy hair.

Flashing lights illuminated the front window.

"Oh God. Oh God. Oh God," Cap incanted as he ran to greet the ambulance.

Bessie wasn't dead. Not yet. Officially, she'd die twenty minutes later at the hospital. By the time Cap returned home, the candle on the table had melted into a puddle. Its yellow wax had mixed with the brown residue in the spoon and hardened into the shape of a red, lifeless orchid.

CHAPTER EIGHT

There was no body to bury, as Bessie's corpse had been promised to the medical school at Wayne University. The memorial was a small affair at the old Carlton mansion, assembled on short notice and attended only by a few of Bessie's school friends, Dr. Kennedy, the projectionist from the Norwood Theater, Frank Horowitz, and Cyrus, his wife, and Marvin. Cap spoke a few words, played *Mood Indigo* on his cornet, and then gestured to the five banana cream pies—Bessie's favorite food—that Goresky's had donated for the occasion. He didn't take a bite. He didn't deserve to. He was too angry to eat, anyway. What he craved was violence.

Cap had been in many fights as a young man, not counting his university swordplay. In all but one he'd used his fists. The sole exception involved a stale Kaiser roll. Cap (then Kasper) had been thirteen. His victim, Max Fenster, was eighteen. Fenster was beating another boy, Jaime Fellender, with a tree branch, calling him a fairy and a *fagala*. Jaime was face down, hands shielding head, waiting for Fenster to tire or the tree branch to break. Kasper grabbed the nearest implement, which he'd thought was a stone but was actually a renegade bun from a long-ago picnic, and then cracked Fenster's head open. (A decade later, Kasper and Jaime would form their Friday night jazz appreciation group, Mooch's Minions.) In sum, Cap had inflicted bruises, bleeding, and even buns on other men but had never killed a soul. That was going to change. Though Bessie could've been hoarding a syringe and vial of heroine, Cap was convinced Solly Colton had delivered it to her during the fire he'd set at Cyrus's shop. So, after Bessie's memorial service, he would kill Solly.

Solly usually took his breakfast at Goresky's Deli. Cap would've preferred killing him in a less public place, but Goresky's was no stranger to death. Former Purple Gang enforcer Larry Shullman was shot in the head at Goresky's in 1937. Cap wouldn't use a gun, though. He came armed only with his cornet, which was more than adequate to crush a man's trachea. Solly was in a booth with his two thugs, stuffing a shmeared bagel in his mouth. In one swift motion, Cap sat next to Solly and pinned him against the window. He punched Solly in the face, dazing him, and then put him in a headlock and pressed the cornet's mouthpiece into his throat. The men across the table pulled their guns, but there was nothing they could do. Solly was a human shield.

Cap roared his accusations in Solly's ear—"Murderer... arsonist... cradle-robber... pervert..."

Solly kept calm. He'd grown numb to such precarious situations. Over his dubious career, he'd been shot, stabbed, burned, half-drowned, left naked in sub-freezing weather, and dragged for a half-mile on Woodward Avenue. An angry cornetist was little more than a nuisance. He nabbed a paper napkin from the holder and wiped a cream cheese splotch from his upper lip. He then calmly denied any role in Bessie's death. He could only speculate Bessie had kept a hidden stash of heroine. That's what junkies did. In any case, Solly had an alibi. He'd been at the Bizrete during the fire. He'd been there all night.

"You ordered your man to do it," accused Cap. "Some thug with a red beard."

"I never hire fellas with beards. Not hygienic, you know?"

Cap eyed the two fat-faced, clean-shaven thugs across the table.

"I don't believe you."

"Believe what you want, but Bessie... she didn't really matter to me. Just another strung-out girl. She was nothing."

"She wasn't nothing, you bastard. She was my little girl. You got her hooked. That's killing in my book."

"She got herself hooked. I gave her booze, but I didn't stick a needle in her arm. I said it would ruin her. She wanted to do it anyway."

"She was just a child."

"You know, I asked about her papa when I first met her. She told me she'd been emancipated because her dad beat her."

"That's a stinking lie!"

"Her lie, not mine."

As tears rolled down Cap's cheeks, he loosened his hold on Solly, who extricated himself and shimmied away. He picked up his partially eaten bagel as his men trained their guns on Cap's head.

"Go ahead," Cap dared with a dry-throated croak. "Do it."

Solly shook his head, and the men holstered their guns.

"What the hell are you doing?" Cap demanded. "I told you to shoot. Kill me!"

Solly finished chewing and sipped his coffee. "Sorry, Pops. Much as I'd like to, there's no angle in killing you."

"Please," Cap begged. "Consider it a public service."

"I ain't in the givin' mood."

"And you call yourself a gangster?"

"I don't. I'm an independent contractor. Unlike you Krauts, I ain't big on bendin' a knee to chumps who think they're better than me. Now, if you don't mind, I gotta bagel to finish."

Cap was leering at him.

"That means scram, Pops."

Cap slid from the booth.

"For what it's worth," added Solly, "your girl had a helluva voice. Coulda been another Ella."

Cap left Goresky's with the cornet dangling from his index finger. He wandered Twelfth Street in his black suit, fedora, and grim face, looking like a backup musician for an all-star mafia musical revue. He inhaled the noxious soup of car exhaust, factory smoke, and smoldering bonfires. The foul air had caused the elm leaves to prematurely yellow and curl, while acid rain had peeled the bright colors from storefronts painted only a few months earlier. This pollution was choking the people too, constricting their lungs and turning their skin sickly and sallow. Soon, Cap surmised, Detroiters' flesh would slough right off, leaving behind their empty, skeletal cores. Would that finally stop them from driving their shoulders into each other? Probably not. Cap doubted they'd even notice their missing skin, muscle, and organs. The instinct for violence was so all-consuming and powerful, so ingrained in the marrow, that not even death could kill it.

A news kiosk confirmed that the lust for violence was a worldwide epidemic: *Girl, 12, Murdered in West Side House. Twelve Dead after Scorned Man Sets Fire to Black Bottom Residence. Surge in Stabbings Plagues American Cities. Death for Ration Fraud in the Nazi Reich. Mysterious Mass Deaths on Ellis Island: Foul Play Likely.*

Not even Cap's dark mood could quell his morbid curiosity over that last headline. Twenty corpses had appeared on Ellis Island, nineteen adults and one young girl, arranged in a circle between the Immigrant Building and the New Ferry House. The victims were dressed in striped burlap shirts and work pants. They were painfully thin, and their forearms were tattooed with numbers. Investigators speculated the victims had been inmates in a German concentration camp, yet they puzzled over how this emaciated group could've escaped a camp, traveled hundreds of miles over land, avoided Nazi checkpoints, and secured transport to America, only to perish simultaneously on freedom's shore. The harbor police's working hypothesis was that a German U-boat patrolling near the shore had offloaded the corpses as a form of psychological warfare, to unsettle New York City's substantial Jewish population. According to the article, the only certainty was "an outside force had manipulated and posed these poor souls like raggedy dolls."

So true.

People were dolls. Outside forces—whether Nazis, gangsters, or random chance—were constantly manipulating them. It didn't matter that a "person" doll had a heartbeat and a functioning brain, whereas a toy doll didn't. Neither had control over her position at any given moment. The person doll merely deceived herself into believing that was the case. Toy dolls were fools by design. People dolls were fools by choice.

Cap was no exception. His father had taught him to believe his life had meaning grounded in an ancient curse about a stolen magic hat. The curse was a burden, that was true, but it also defined him. It bound him to hundreds of generations of Mützenmachers and Petasoses before him, and it would bind him to hundreds of generations going forward, starting with his own children. How could his father have been so wrong? Bessie was dead, and Duke had fled like a coward, taking the hat with him. Cap was alone, with nothing and no one to live for. Outside forces had manipulated and posed him into the form of a pitiful old man.

Cap stiffened his spine. He refused to be a doll any longer. He was leaving the toy tea table and quitting the game. There was one thing this doll could control—whether to live or die. There was no need to bloody his wrists, put a bullet in his head, or hang himself until his tongue swelled and his bowels evacuated in his trousers. He wouldn't step in front of the first car whizzing by, which would've been an especially selfish way to go, etching the sight of his sad sack face in some innocent driver's memory (and windshield). No, a plunge into the Detroit River would be fast and clean, rendering him a much better specimen for the medical students at Wayne University who'd eventually dissect him. He gave himself an hour to get to the Ambassador Bridge.

After twenty-five minutes, Cap somehow was back at Goresky's Deli. He must've gotten turned around somewhere. He knelt to the curb and adjusted his right sock, which had lost its elasticity and was creeping down his calf. He'd become progressively cheaper in his older age and had purchased the low-quality nylon socks at the Woolworth's instead of paying three times as much at Hudsons. That was the last time he'd buy dress socks at the dime store—rather an empty vow, given he was a half hour from his death plunge, and corpses tended not to fuss over flaccid socks.

When Cap rose, he spotted Cyrus through the window. Cyrus was still wearing the skinny black suit he'd worn to Bessie's memorial service. A distraught Marvin sat across from him. Cyrus pounded the table and wagged his finger. He snapped his fingers below Marvin's nose as his son stared sullenly at the table. When Marvin didn't look up, Cyrus slapped his face. Customers at the surrounding tables briefly turned toward the sound and then resumed their lunches. At a place where men were stabbed or shot while stuffing hot pastrami sandwiches in their mouths, a face slap didn't hold their attention for long. Marvin got up and walked away. Cyrus gestured for his son to get his ass back to the table, but Marvin was already out the door and heading down the sidewalk. He bumped Cap's shoulder, though it wasn't a racial thing. Marvin was looking down, no doubt contemplating how his father had failed him. Maybe poor parenting was catching.

Cyrus spied Cap and waved him inside. Cap checked his watch. He was down to thirty-three minutes. If he spent no more than five minutes with Cyrus, he could still make it to the bridge by his deadline. Fine. He'd go in.

As Cap stepped toward the entrance, a black man bumped him. Cap dropped the cornet, denting the bell. He considered shouting at the man, but he didn't have the will to fight any more battles. Cap figured he'd made the world a slightly better place by absorbing some of that stranger's racial rage.

Cap joined Cyrus in the booth. He told him he was on his way to the bridge to kill himself and had a schedule to keep. Cyrus played it cool. He nodded as though Cap had just said he had a manicure appointment. Cyrus beckoned the waitress for two slices of banana cream pie.

"I don't have time for pie, Cy."

"There's always time for pie."

"Not today."

"Today of all days, I'd think. You didn't take one bite at Bessie's funeral."

"I'm not eating."

The waitress set the slices on the table.

Cyrus pulled Cap's plate toward him. "Guess I'll have to eat your piece."

"What's going on with Marvin?" asked Cap. "Is he okay?"

"The boy's like this pie. Soft. He needs to man up."

"What's that mean?"

"It means he needs to stop dressin' like a clown and get himself a girl. It means he needs to be jitterbuggin' on the gridiron instead of the dance floor. He needs to stop actin' so damn funny."

"I don't know, Cy. I've come around on Marvin. He's a good kid, you know? He looked out for Bessie as best he could."

"I s'pose."

"Does he get in fights?"

"I wish."

"Because I've seen him with bruises from time to time."

Cyrus stuffed a forkful of pie in his mouth.

"Sons can be hard to figure out," Cap continued. "I tried to toughen Duke up for the longest time, but it just seemed to make him weaker, more afraid. It was the wrong approach. Some guys have gentle souls. They'll never be fighters. It's the way they were made. Kind of like, however much you try, you'll never make a bowler into a top hat. And if you keep trying, if you keep cutting and snipping at it, you'll destroy the fabric and have no hat at all."

Teardrops were falling into Cyrus's paper napkin.

"Hey, pal," Cap said softly. "I'm sorry. I shouldn't have butted in. It's none of my business."

"He likes boys, Cap. He's a fucking fairy. It's bad enough he got his momma's dark skin but a faggot as well? Where'd the hell that come from?"

"Who knows where anything really comes from? We've just gotta deal with it."

"Like by jumping off a bridge?"

"All I'll say is I've known men who've loved other men, and women who've loved other women. I don't begin to understand it, but some folks don't ever get to love anyone. What good is being a regular guy if that's your fate?"

"So you're sayin' I'm an asshole."

"I'm saying you're lucky your son is still around."

"In other words, I should stop bein' an asshole."

"Love doesn't care about color or religion, whether you're a beauty or a beast, or what's between your legs."

Cap grabbed a fork and carved a morsel of pie from Cyrus's plate. He stuck it in his mouth and then reached across and grabbed a more substantial bite.

"Careful there. Don't give yourself a cramp. Might not make it to the bridge."

Cap fed himself another heaping forkful and then asked, "What are you going to do about your store?"

"What store? It's in ashes. I'm broke. Guess I'll go crawlin' back to Uncle Henry."

"Take Leghorn Millinery."

"I couldn't do that."

"I won't need it where I'm going. They'll probably just board it up. You could keep it running." Cap reached into his coat pocket. "Here." He tossed the keys on the table.

"You're giving me the store? Without a contract? No payment? Not even a handshake?"

"Good point. It's not official if there isn't an exchange of consideration. Tell you what, you let me finish this slice of pie, and we'll call it even. Deal?"

Cap extended his hand. Cyrus shook it.

"Deal," Cyrus confirmed.

"Least I could do for my only friend in the world."

"We are friends, ain't we?" Cyrus realized.

"Always. So, what great plans do you have for the shop?"

"I'm pretty good with straw, as you know. I'll probably head more in that direction."

"Makes sense. Go with your strengths. Though Mrs. Goldnick likes her green felt porkpies. Hopefully, you can see clear to make her one every year."

"Sure. Sure thing, Cap."

"And Dr. Kennedy. He's that bigwig from Hutzel Hospital. He was at the funeral. Every spring he buys a herringbone fedora."

"Got it. Green felt porkpie, herringbone fedora."

"Now I can plummet to my death knowing my customers will be taken care of."

"Absolutely."

"I almost forgot. I'm supposed to make four pink slouch hats for the Dundee wedding. I'd hate to lose their business."

"You're gonna jump off a bridge. You'll lose everyone's business."

"Still, I'd hate for people to think Cap Leghorn bowed out without fulfilling his obligations."

"Fine. Fine. I'll make the slouch hats. Is this my business or what?"

Cap peered at his watch. "Course it's your business… in twenty-five minutes. I want to make sure you take care of it."

"If I don't, you'll be none the wiser."

Cap pointed to Cyrus's half-eaten piece. "You gonna eat the rest?"

Cyrus slid the plate to Cap.

"I'm gonna miss this pie," Cap mused.

"That's just it, Cap. You ain't gonna miss a thing."

"True."

"You don't sound like a man who's gonna kill himself."

"Oh, I'm gonna do it."

"Uh-huh."

"Just maybe not in twenty-five minutes. I'll definitely be walking slower after all this pie. Crap!"

"What's wrong?"

"I didn't show you how I keep the books or give you my suppliers' names."

"I'll figure it out."

"Yeah, but it'll slow you down. Come on. Let's go to the shop, and I'll walk you through everything."

"You got only twenty-five minutes."

"Twenty-four now. Shit. Well, right after I show you, I'll take a cab to the bridge. Shouldn't delay things more than fifteen minutes."

"Just admit it, Cap. You're not gonna kill yourself."

"No, I'll do it. In thirty-nine minutes, I'll be floating face down in the Detroit River."

"Bullshit."

"There's no point in living. I've lost my children. I've been a terrible father. I have nothing to give this world."

"You sound like a man trying to convince himself otherwise."

Cap grabbed the shop keys. "Know what, Cy? Forget the shop. Let it die with me."

"Hey. We had a deal. I gave you pie. We shook on it."

"It's a long-term deal, Cyrus. It's gotta be in writing. Haven't you ever heard of the Statute of Frauds?"

"No, but if it's like any other law on the books, it's probably designed to screw Negroes. Enjoy the rest of your life—your lonely-ass, banana-cream-pie-mooching, hat-store-reneging life!"

Cyrus got up.

"No. Wait, Cy. Sit down."

"Why?"

"This is all wrong. I mean, I'm all wrong. You're right. I don't want to die.

As horrible as I feel, what makes me feel the absolute worst is I want to live. I'm a selfish son of a bitch."

"No argument here."

"God damn it, I'm not gonna let Bessie's death mean nothing. I'm gonna change right here and now. I need you, Cyrus. You're my friend. I love you. That's right, pal. I love you. I'm not ashamed to say it. Nothing funny about brotherly love."

"Cain and Abel were brothers too."

"Be my partner for life."

"I'm a married man, Cap."

"*In business*. Let's show this city how whites and blacks can work together before we all kill each other. We'll be fifty-fifty partners. I'll have my lawyer draw up the papers and make it legal."

"How's that legal? Didn't you say every contract needs consideration? I'm broke."

"You saved my life, Cyrus. That's gotta be worth something."

CHAPTER NINE

Serendipity struck in Leghorn Millinery's cutting room a few months later. While fashioning a straw fedora, Cyrus inadvertently wove in a parasisal braid he'd dyed with black Kolor-ol. The dye bled into the virgin leghorn straw, creating the effect of a tiger stripe wrapping around the crown. Cyrus tossed the hat in the trash, but Cap saw opportunity.

A week earlier, Gabby Olhauser, an up and coming catcher for the Detroit Tigers, had left the store empty-handed because he found Cap's wares too staid. Cap was sure that Gabby would like the tiger-striped fedora, and he was right. Gabby's eyes lit up when Cap presented it to him during batting practice at Briggs Stadium. His teammates also wanted one. Suddenly, Cyrus was crafting twenty-eight more hats. Detroit Free Press beat writer Wallace "Waxy" Spokes subsequently mentioned the "Tiger Fedoras" in a lifestyle piece accompanied by a photo of Gabby Olhauser, Dixie Parsons, and Stubby Overmire. The next day, the Tigers' business office forwarded three hundred fan requests for Tiger Fedoras. By mid-summer, hundreds of Tiger Fedoras dotted the heads of white and black fans.

So pleased was the Tigers organization, it planned a hat day for late August, enough for two thousand fans. The Tigers gave Cyrus a vintage pine crate, engraved with an Old English "D," in which the team had stored baseballs, gloves, cleats, and extra spikes during the Ty Cobb era. After completing a batch of fifty hats, Cyrus would load them into the crate and deliver them to Briggs Stadium.

Cap focused on the non-straw hat side of the business, so Cyrus could devote all his energies to the Tiger Fedoras. Cyrus worked fourteen-hour days, sustaining himself on chicory coffee, Camels, and Goresky's banana cream pie. He was determined to meet the quota. He wouldn't fall short by a single hat and give ammunition to the white folk that he wasn't up to the task. To that end, he demanded that Marvin spend every spare moment in the cutting room with him.

"How ya' comin' on those crowns, Marv?" asked Cyrus.

"Got one done."

"I need five."

"I've been working only a half hour."

"I do five in a half hour."

"You've had a lot more practice."

"You gotta work faster, ya hear?"

"Yeah, Pa." A pause and then, with trepidation, "Hey, Pa?"

"What?"

"Did you get around to writing that check?"

"What check?"

"The application fee... for Parsons School of Design."

"Hand me that wad of plaiting, would ya?"

Marvin grabbed a wheel of braided straw and extended it to his father but dropped it before Cyrus gripped it.

"God damn it, Marvin! It's gonna unravel."

Marvin stomped on the spool so it wouldn't unwind.

"Jesus, you crushed it!"

"Just the very end. You can cut it off." Marvin scooped up the spool and handed it to his father. "Sorry, Pa. I thought you had it the first time."

"You thought wrong."

"You got it now?"

"Yeah. Let go."

Cyrus fed the plaited straw into the sewing machine and pressed the foot pedal. The needle rattled to life. He began turning the braid on itself, forming the crown's embryo. He took his foot off the pedal and looked at Marvin.

"You'll be registerin' for the Service soon. Can't very well fight the Nazis if you're at that parsley college of yours."

"It's *Parsons*. Anyway, I don't have the makings of a soldier."

"Be a man and fight for your country. Men don't do fashion."

"You and Cap sew hats."

"Hats ain't dresses."

"Oh," said Marvin, unconvinced.

"When you turn eighteen, you're gonna enlist. After you get back from Germany or Japan, you can apply to the parsley school or the carrot academy or rutabaga university. I don't care which."

"No."

"No?"

"No."

Cyrus yanked a yardstick off the pegboard. Imprinted with "Ford Factory Engineered Parts," the yardstick was the only tool from his automotive career with practical application to millinery. When it came to his son, however, Cyrus didn't use it for measurement but discipline. The yardstick's ten evenly spaced holes substantially reduced air friction, enabling Cyrus to deliver a hard swat with minimal effort, which he demonstrated on Marvin's shoulder. Marvin winced and then brought his hand to the impact site.

"You can beat me to a pulp, Pa, but my answer's gonna stay the same. If I don't get drafted, I'm going to college. If you won't pay the application fee, I've got my own money. Professor Glass—he teaches at Parsons—he says there might be scholarship money, too."

Cyrus lowered the yardstick and sat against the cutting table.

"I once worked with this fella at the Ford plant. He tried to get funny with some guys. Know what they did? Dumped oil in the quench tank while he wasn't looking. When he plunged the hot coil, flames burned half his face off. And he was lucky. If he'd been Negro, they would've burnt both halves."

"Why are you telling me this?"

"It's a dangerous world for 'funny' people."

"The word's gay, not funny. That's what I am. A gay man."

"Keep your goddamn voice down. We got customers. Whatever you call it, it multiplies being Negro by ten. You won't get a job, or you won't be able to keep it."

"That's not the way it works in the fashion world. Professor Glass says—"

"Marvin. Son. We live in a cruel, cruel world. You might be fine with those fashion folks for a time, but don't fool yourself. You'll get complacent. You'll let your guard down, and the next minute you're lynched in Times Square."

"At least it'll be me getting lynched, not a pretender."

"What's that supposed to mean?"

Marvin shook his head. "Nothing. Forget it. I'll see ya."

"Don't walk away. You calling me funny? You calling me funny?!" Then, he added, defeated, "Come back, Marvin. I need you."

Leo Tipton purportedly ignited the riot when he climbed on the stage at The Forest Club and announced to the seven-hundred-plus dancers that several whites had thrown a black woman and her baby off the Belle Isle Bridge. Tipton's claim came on the heels of skirmishes between white sailors and black youths on Belle Isle. That fighting poured over the bridge and onto East Jefferson Avenue. Meanwhile, whites began passing their own rumor that a black man had raped a white woman. Blacks flooded Paradise Valley, smashing the windows of white businesses, especially Jewish-owned shops. They bolted down Woodward Avenue with briskets, salamis, and corned beef slabs tucked under their arms. Southern whites converged on Woodward from the west, looting stores, overturning cars, and mauling any black person in their way. An elderly black man stepped off a city bus and was promptly beaten in view of four indifferent policemen. Another mob pulled a trolley from its wires and tipped it over, pummeling anyone with dark skin who emerged. White middle-aged foundry workers, practiced in beating up black men on Hastings Street as an after-work ritual, whipped Vaseline-haired teenagers into a frenzy, spewing racist venom, handing them clubs, chains, and knives, and then backing to a safe distance to appreciate the morbid music of cracking skulls, crumpling jaws, and angry howls.

Cap and Cyrus were working late, trying to make a dent in their backlog of Tiger Fedoras. They broke at 11:00 p.m. Cap poured each a whiskey shot and flipped on the radio. He was searching for jazz, but none of the stations were playing music. The announcers were talking about rampant fighting and looting. They warned listeners to lock their doors and stay inside because a race riot had erupted. Although the North End was quiet for the moment, trouble was coming. Frank Horowitz daubed white paint on the window of his wig shop, spelling out the word "Colored." He advised Cap to do the same in order to prevent looting by blacks. Cap was incredulous. He wouldn't participate in this sick twist on Kristallnacht. Anyway, Frank Horowitz wasn't even close to black. He was as Jewish as they came. He closed on Saturdays, his clientele were primarily Orthodox women with shaven heads, and he'd nailed a mezuzah to the doorway. Frank Horowitz hoped the looters would see the "Colored" label and move on.

Angry blacks filtered onto Oakland Street. Cyrus suggested they mark the store "Colored." Cap refused. He wasn't "colored," nor was he a Jew or a German or, for that matter, a white man. He was a goddamn American, and so was Cyrus. If Cyrus wanted to mark the store window with anything, he could paint an American flag.

Cyrus didn't want to be a foolish patriot. He begged Cap to make their store "colored" store for one night. It wouldn't be dishonest. After all, he and Cap were partners, which made the store at least half-colored.

That made no sense to Cap. Which half of the store was colored? Each of their fingerprints dotted every square foot. Each had inhaled and exchanged every cubic inch of air. Each had had a hand in producing their inventory. They could no more divide the shop into colored and non-colored halves than a tiger could separate its striped and non-striped halves. And who knew how the riot would play out? Although the growing crowd was black at that moment, what if the whites were to come and push them out and then inflict special damage on the stores marked "Colored"? Paint a flag or nothing at all was his ultimatum. If the shop was destroyed, it would be destroyed as an American shop.

Cap felt so damn patriotic, he could've crapped in red, white, and blue. The fact that he'd just updated his business insurance policy also bolstered his intestinal fortitude.

"I got another idea," said Cyrus.

To that point, they'd manufactured four hundred fifty Tiger Fedoras. Cyrus suggested they distribute them to the crowd for free, figuring with so many folks in the same hat, they'd be less inclined to turn on each other, just like at the ballpark. Cap agreed. If the likely alternative was the store going up in flames, they might as well give the hats away.

Within a half hour, hundreds of the fedoras dotted the crowd, which still hadn't turned violent or destructive, even when the whites arrived. But then Kristallnacht's ghost surfaced. A white man stuffed a pamphlet in Cap's hand and vanished into the crowd. The pamphlet depicted a stooped man looking up with sinister eyes, furrowed brow, and long, hooked nose. He was stepping on a black man's throat. The text inside recounted the Hebrew tribes' enslavement of the Negro race, citing Biblical sources. Then came the disembodied shouts of the pamphleteer. He told his "brothers" to rise up against the Jewish conspiracy to keep down the Negro. The fedoras didn't symbolize equality, he claimed, but subservience. "The whites wear it only to mock the Negro," asserted the voice. "The Jews must be taught a lesson!"

A flaming spiral soared over the crowd and landed at Cap's feet. Someone had ignited the straw fedora and tossed it like a Frisbee. In seconds, the crown burnt to nothing, leaving an empty space surrounded by the brim's charred remains. Another spiraling flame landed near the smoldering hat, then another, and then another. Soon, hundreds of burning hats were colliding with store windows and parked cars. A glass bottle broke somewhere. Or was it a window? It didn't matter. The shattering sound resonated in the mob's soul. That fractured music was its oxygen. Men kicked in windows, sent bricks through others, and smashed more with baseball bats. Wave after wave of glass shards washed over the sidewalks like tides of dislodged teeth.

Cyrus stepped in front of Turk Watson, who had his eye on the shop's last intact window.

"I'm a Negro! I'm a Negro! Like you," Cyrus pleaded.

But Turk had as much capacity for independent thought as the pipe wrench in his fat paw. "The store ain't marked 'Colored.' And you ain't no Negro neither. Step aside, whitey."

As Turk reared back with the wrench, Cyrus launched into his torso, sending both to the abrasive beach of glass. The wrench skittered away. Turk flipped Cyrus to his back and whaled on him with his fists. Cap was powerless to help because the crowd had formed a tight circle around the skirmish. Cyrus took punch after punch. His left eye swelled. His bottom lip got fat and bloody. He likely would've died, had the bystander in indigo pants not worked himself through the throng and yanked Turk off him. It was Marvin. He staggered Turk with an uppercut and then decked him with a right hook.

"This is my Pa!" Marvin screamed over the vanquished Turk. "He's a black man, and this is his fucking store!"

Marvin lifted his father to his feet as two squad cars pulled up. The policemen had no idea what had transpired. They saw only a furious black man dragging a bloody white guy. They didn't ask questions. A cop struck Marvin across the right scapula with his nightstick. Marvin wheeled around and caught the policeman in the face with a left cross. That cop went down, but not the other three. They beat Marvin to the street, cuffed him, and threw him in a squad car.

The riot ended a day and a half later. It took five hundred fifty billy clubs, eighteen hundred arrests, thirty-four deaths, two hundred tear gas canisters, and a cavalcade of Army troopers with their truck-mounted machine guns, but it ended. The cops booked Marvin for disturbing the peace and assaulting a police officer. He spent four days in jail. Each morning, the officer he'd struck brought him to an interrogation room and posed questions to Marvin's face using a form of full-contact sign language. Cyrus wasn't allowed to post bail for his battered son until the fifth day. To avoid a trial and more beatings, Marvin pled to a battery charge and was released with time-served. Parsons School of Design later rejected Marvin's application because of his criminal conviction.

Whereas white supremacists had burned Frank Horowitz's wig shop to the ground, Cap's shop had incurred little damage, other than the broken windows and the incinerated fedoras. Ten days later, the Michigan Mutual Insurance Company sent him a reimbursement check; unlike after Kristallnacht, the government hadn't confiscated insurance proceeds to pay for the cleanup.

Also in the mail was a large envelope bearing strips of German and British censor tape, purple pencil marks, the word Lisbon, an ink stamp with the letters TC/S, and canceled Nazi, British, and American postage stamps. The document inside was stamped with the red seal of the Nazi's Office of Racial Research and imprinted with bold black letters. Kasper Mützenmacher's request for racial reclassification had been granted. In a fiat of serological alchemy decreed by a few magic words and undersigned in a madman's ink, Kasper was, once again, "of pure German blood."

Cap was befuddled. Why would Hitler have done this for an American, and how had he known the former Kasper Mützenmacher had emigrated to Detroit? Surely, the Nazis had better things to do than keep tabs on a self-exiled hatmaker. Cap flipped over the envelope. The return address wasn't a government office building but the family's old apartment in Schwarz Boden. Whoever had championed Cap's reclassification request had sent it outside normal channels. It must have been Rosamund. But why? Was this her subtle way of telling him that she was thinking of him, that she still loved him? Klaus had said Rosamund wouldn't care about Cap after her "debriefing." Was that a lie to mollify Kasper's conscience, to make it easier to leave Rosamund behind?

What other lies had Klaus told? Maybe Rosamund hadn't been his unwitting spy, after all. Maybe she'd accepted her mission for Klaus with open eyes. Maybe she'd volunteered and then executed it flawlessly, insinuating herself into Cap's life and assuming the roles of lover and mother to Hollywood perfection. Maybe she'd been Klaus's lover the entire time. After Rosamund had given birth to Gretel, Cap had attributed her outrageous paternity claim to post-partum delirium. But maybe she'd been confessing, truly confessing. As she'd said, who other than the Stealer of Faces could've spawned a faceless child?

It all made sense now. Guilt—not love—had motivated Rosamund to pursue the racial reclassification. Guilt over soiling the bedsheets with her betrayal. She should've known, however, that it was a meaningless gesture. Rosamund had betrayed Kasper Mützenmacher, not Cap Leghorn. She'd hurt a different man, a man who'd Cap had laid to rest on Ellis Island. Cap carried that fellow's memories but not his psychological obligations and burdens. It had to be this way. He couldn't be two people at once. No one could.

Cap stuffed the certificate in the envelope, struck a match, and incinerated the letter in the kitchen sink.

CHAPTER TEN

1946

Duke showed up at Cap's front door holding a two-year-old boy's hand. In his fury, Cap didn't immediately notice the knock-kneed toddler with the bulbous nose. He accused Duke of cowardice for stealing the wishing hat to avoid the war. He claimed Duke was single-handedly responsible for the deaths of thousands of Jews whom the hat could've rescued. How dare he show his face, Cap roared. Oh, and by the way, Bessie was dead, and he'd missed her funeral.

Cap was panting by the end of his rant. When Duke was sure his father had nothing to add and wasn't going to pop a blood vessel, he introduced the boy.

"His name's Lukas."

"Whose name?" asked Cap as though Duke were a crazy person with an invisible rabbit friend named Harvey.

Duke gestured to his three-foot-tall companion. The boy was wearing a heavy worsted wool sweater with two lower patch pockets and a zippered pocket at the breast, where an adult might store cigarettes, but where he'd stuffed a quarter bar of Bonomo Turkish Taffy. With the silk tie around his neck and the straw boater on his head, he needed only a tiny pipe in his mouth to be a one-half scale version of Bing Crosby.

"Where'd he come from?"

"He's been here the whole time, Pops. His name is Lukas. 'Lucky' for short."

"Lucky's not shorter. Got the same number of letters. Who is he anyway?"

"Your grandson."

Cap stared at Duke, unblinking. He then noticed that Duke's forehead and neck were dotted with cherry red papules.

"What's wrong with your skin?"

Duke tugged on his shirt collar. "Just acne. Pops, can we come in?"

Cap was at a loss. He produced a grunting noise that sounded vaguely like permission to enter.

"Lucky, you go have a seat on the sofa there. Pops and I have to talk. You have your train?"

Lucky nodded in an exaggerated fashion and then pulled a model train from his front right patch pocket. The shiny toy replicated the Flying Hamburger's every detail, right down to the two-tone pallet of indigo and beige and the antennae-shaped front bumpers. He sat on the tweed couch and ran the train along the arm while producing a spittle-laced engine sound.

Cap sat in the armchair next to the sofa and folded his arms, glowering at Duke. "So?"

Duke sat on the sofa's edge. He wouldn't allow his full weight to sink into the cushion. He tensed his thigh muscles, ready to launch himself through the roof, if necessary, should things go awry. He crossed and uncrossed his legs at the ankles, twice. He stopped himself the third time and settled both feet on the floor. He took a deep breath and let it go. His head and hands shook with a mild tremor. Cap hoped whatever ailment Duke had acquired overseas wasn't contagious.

"I'm waiting," said Cap.

Finally, Duke spoke. He said that shortly before he was due to report to Fort Custer he'd discovered the wishing hat was warm, not warm enough to work, but soon, he'd figured. He reported to Fort Custer with the hat in his duffel bag. By the time he'd boarded the bus to Louisiana, the hat had gotten much warmer. Duke wished himself away when they stopped for a meal break.

"I didn't remember the rush being so intense when you wished us to Ellis Island. I just felt sick then. But I got used to the nausea after a few more wishes. Each trip was more incredible than the last. I was a human radio wave, traveling at light speed!" Duke caught his father's cold gaze and abandoned his reverie. "But I should've been using the hat for good. I was a coward."

"Damn right you were."

Duke went on. He said he wished himself to a Polish concentration camp. He initially planned to appear inside a barracks and wish away the occupants, as Cap had done with the train car. He was unsure, however, whether there was enough power in the hat to transport so many souls, so he started small.

He appeared in a supply closet inside the camp's medical barracks. Upon exiting the closet, Duke stumbled across a sleeping female prisoner. She would be his first rescue. He didn't rouse her, figuring she'd scream bloody murder and attract the guards' attention. Duke touched the woman, formed a mental image of their destination (Belle Isle woods), and made his wish. Nothing happened. He tried again, wishing harder. Again, nothing. The hat, it seemed, was powerless.

The woman stirred. Duke closed his eyes and concentrated hard on Belle Isle woods. Suddenly, he felt the sensations of hat travel's initial stage—the compression, the floor falling away, the ceiling expanding. The sensations fizzled. Then the woman awoke and recoiled from the hovering stranger. Her mouth morphed into a silent scream.

Footsteps approached. Duke had to escape, but there was only one door, and getting there meant walking toward the footsteps. He tried one more wish—this time somewhere closer, one that wouldn't require a transoceanic leap. He closed his eyes, made a wish, and they vanished.

The hat went cold after they arrived in Lauterbrunnen, Switzerland. A sympathetic vintner gave them a room in his house. With a moribund wishing hat, and a trip to America by traditional means out of the question, Duke and the woman, Francesca, remained on the vintner's farm for the war's duration. They fell in love, and Francesca gave birth to Lukas in 1944.

After a long silence, Cap remarked, "So that's your story."

"That's what happened, yeah. I'm sorry about Bessie, but I was trapped in Europe. How'd she die?"

"Heroin overdose."

"Jesus."

"Your kid looks pretty big for two."

"He's closer to three."

"Where's my daughter-in-law, this Francesca?"

"She died of influenza last year."

"Last year?"

"Lucky was a sickly baby. As soon as he was strong enough to survive transatlantic travel, I brought him to America. Look, Pops. I did a shameful thing, chickening out of the war. But I tried to make it right. There just wasn't enough power in the wishing hat to rescue more than one inmate. It petered out for good after that last trip to Switzerland."

"Yet you wished yourself here," Cap accused.

"No, we came by steamship."

"Transatlantic steamships don't dock in Detroit."

"We docked in New York and took the train from there."

"Can I see your steamship tickets?"

"I threw them out."

"The train tickets, then."

"Same. I tossed them."

"The immigration folks didn't arrest you at the port? You went AWOL. You're a wanted man."

"I entered with a false identity and a forged passport."

"There should be a stamp on it showing entry into New York, right? Let's see it."

Heat welled in Duke's face. He adjusted his shirt collar. "I told you how we got here. A ship and a train. Not the wishing hat."

"I know what you're telling me. I want proof."

"How about having some faith in your son?"

"You're lecturing me on faith? You've never been true to anything longer than five minutes."

"Are we really going to have this argument now?"

"Maybe my grandson can shed some light on this. A steamship and a train is a big deal for a little kid." Cap turned to the child. "Hey there, Lucky."

The boy didn't look up from his train.

"I said, 'Hey there, Lucky.'"

The boy remained entranced in his toy.

"Does he speak?"

"Yeah."

"Is he deaf?"

"Just shy with strangers."

Cap studied his son, smiling ambiguously. It could've been the beginning of a joyous expression. More likely, a sign of contempt.

"What are you not telling me, Duke?"

"Nothing."

"You left something out, or you're lying your ass off."

"Why can't you just believe me?"

"Because you're an addict, and addicts lie."

"I am not an addict, Pops."

"You sure look it. You're thin as hell. Sunken eyes. What's your poison? Booze? Heroin?" He eyed Duke's left lapel, which was bulging. "No, none of those things. You have it on you."

Duke flushed. "Have what on me?"

"The wishing hat."

"The thing doesn't work. Why would I carry it around?"

"So, where is it?"

"In my trunk out at the curb."

"Go get it."

"Fine. I see where your priorities are." Duke rose. "Keep an eye on Lucky, would ya?"

Cap launched himself from the chair and intercepted Duke before he hit the front door.

"Wait. I'm coming with you."

Duke pushed Cap back. He stumbled into the telephone table, causing the ringer to vibrate. Lucky glanced up at the commotion.

"Why can't you trust me, Pops? Why is everything a fight?"

"It doesn't have to be, son. Give me the hat, and I'll forgive you."

"I told you I was getting it."

"I know what you said."

They locked eyes.

"You don't give a shit about me or forgiveness."

"That's not true. I love you."

"Sure, Pops."

Duke opened the door and stepped outside.

"Don't leave."

"I'm just going to the curb."

"Don't you dare run away again. Fate isn't kind to those who stray from the hat business."

"That bullshit again? You can't scare me into carrying on your legacy. I fucking hate hats."

"Then forget about hats. Let me help you get clean."

Duke trembled, and his cheeks reddened, as though Cap had caught him with his pants down.

"I don't know what the hell you're talking about."

"Come on. You've got the shakes and those sores on your forehead."

"They're not sores."

"I'm confused about one thing, though. My hat addiction ruined me in a few weeks. The cravings were too strong. How have you managed to keep it together for three years?"

"Go to hell."

Duke slammed the door shut. Seconds later, there was a piercing squeal. Cap flung the door open.

"Duke!"

There was no one on the walkway or the sidewalk. There was no one on his lawn or his neighbors'. There was no trunk at the curb or a taxicab in the street. There was no one as far as the eye could see.

Cap closed the front door and went to the living room, where a diminutive creature was making choo-choo sounds on the sofa. The child bore a strong resemblance to Duke at the same age—the bulbous Petasos nose, the gangliness, the waves of dark curls. Only his eyes were different. Green to Duke's blue.

Cap sat on the sofa and contemplated the boy's name. "Lucky" didn't sit right. Lucky was the name of a gangster or a dog. That name was asking for trouble, baiting Fate to prove he wasn't lucky. Men weren't born lucky any more than a Brahman calf was born with juicy ribeyes, tenderloins, and briskets clinging to its bones. Men had to grow into their luck from whatever scraps Fate tossed their way—the occasional choice cut but more often organ meat, gristle, binders, and fillers. A man had "sausage" luck, at best.

"Hey, boy. Look at me for a second."

Lucky stared at the ruddy-faced man with the deep scar and the big nose.

"Good. You're not deaf," said Cap. "Listen, your daddy's gonna be away for a while. Not sure how long, but I'll watch you until he comes back. I'm your grandpa. You can call me Pops, okay?"

The boy nodded.

"If it's all the same to you, I'm gonna call you Chance. Chance isn't presumptuous like Lucky. Oh, I bet 'presumptuous' is a pretty big word for a tyke. It means going beyond what you should do, like if your train decided it wanted to fly like an airplane. That'd be presumptuous. Whereas Chance... well, every man deserves a chance. Even Fate has to concede that much. Should a man seize his chance and turn it to his advantage, then, and only then, might we call him lucky. A man's gotta earn his luck. Does that make sense?"

The boy nodded again.

"You're a smart kid. So, Chance it is?"

"Sure thing, Pops," said the boy in his elfin voice.

"Ahh, you talk, too," Pops said with great delight. Cap slid next to the boy, removed his boater, and playfully touched his nose with his index finger. "Know what, Chance?"

"What, Pops?"

"I think this is the beginning of a beautiful friendship."

—o╂o—◇◇━●━◇◇—o╂o—

"Who sleeps in here?" Chance asked that evening.

"Used to be Bessie's room. She would've been your aunt. Died a while back."

"Was Bessie nice?"

"Very."

"I'll never know my nice Aunt Bessie."

Cap swallowed the nascent lump in his throat. "Pick a book from the shelf. I'll read it to you."

"Sure thing, Pops."

Chance chose *A Mad Tea-Party*, an early reader's adaptation of the tea party scene from *Alice's Adventures in Wonderland*. Cap sat Chance on his lap in front of the old three-mirrored vanity. The mirrors were framed with fluted mahogany molding, which morphed into spirals at each corner. Chance started shaking.

"You cold?" asked Cap.

Chance turned his face into Cap's chest. "Can we read somewhere else?"

"Are you scared?"

Chance nodded.

"Of what?"

"The Lolos."

"The *Lolos*? What are they?"

Chance pointed out the split nautilus shells carved into the mirrors' frames.

"Why do you call them Lolos?"

"That's what their name is."

"I see. Why do the Lolos scare you?"

"They spin and spin and spin, and they're empty."

"Empty?"

"In the middle."

"Well, these Lolos are a different kind."

"There are different kinds?"

"Sure. These here only *look* empty in the middle. In fact, they're filled to the brim."

"With what?"

"With whatever you want. Depends on the person. For me, Duke Ellington's orchestra is inside that spiral. Trumpets, trombones, grand piano, bow-tied musicians, the whole nine yards. You probably see something different, right?"

Chance squinted. "Nope. Nothing."

"Use your imagination."

"Like pretend?"

"Sort of."

"So the Lolos really aren't full in the middle. You're lying."

"Lying is a pretty strong word for it. More like dreaming. You have dreams, don't you?"

"Yep."

"There you go. Fill those Lolos with a dream. You pick. Just make it a pleasant one. Can you do that?"

"Okay, Pops. I'll try."

"Good boy. We ready to read now?"

Chance nodded. The book contained few of Lewis Caroll's original words, so Cap filled in the details, using the illustrations as a guide. He explained how the March Hare and the Hatter fussed about the tea's temperature and insufficient room at the table. Meanwhile, they jockeyed for prime elbow position on the snoozing Dormouse. Then, who should happen by—*uninvited*—but Alice.

"Look," said Chance, pointing to the illustration of the Hatter. "His scar is like yours, Pops."

Indeed, the pen sketch depicted a sideways-hat mark on the Hatter's left cheek.

"That's not a scar. Probably a wrinkle, or the illustrator made a mistake."

"So all hatters don't have scars?"

"Only the crazy ones."

"Are *you* crazy?"

"The crazy hatters always have scars, but a hatter isn't crazy *because* he has a scar. You get the difference?"

"Like the moon has a face, but having a face doesn't make you a moon."

"Dang, you're smart."

"Wish I had that scar."

"And ruin that beautiful face?"

"It didn't ruin yours."

"Aw, that's nice of you to say, but you're too young for scars. Look, you have my nose, see? And my forehead. That's one big forehead. Lots of brains behind there."

"I guess," said Chance, unpersuaded.

"Tell you what." Cap slid open the vanity's drawer. He fished through lipstick canisters, compacts of powder, pancake, and rouges, and three cold cream canisters in various states of depletion. "Good Lord. You'd have thought your Aunt Bessie was in the circus, there's so much makeup. Ahh. Here we go." Cap held up a black eye pencil. "Turn your head to the right. Good." He drew a vertical line on the boy's cheek and then a triangle resting on the line's right side. "There. Now you have a scar like mine."

Chance smiled. "Wow! And it didn't even hurt."

Chance brought his hand toward the mark, but Cap intercepted it.

"Careful. It'll smear."

Chance's smile faded. "Does yours smear?"

"No."

"Because it's real. Mine is fake."

"Why do you want a scar so badly?"

"So when I look in the mirror, I'll see you."

"Why would you want to see my silly mug? Your face is much nicer."

"So I can see you even when you're not around... when you go away."

Damn it, Duke. This is what happens when you abandon your kid.

"I'm not going away."

"But you'll die someday, like my nice Aunt Bessie."

"Not for a long, long time. You'll be all grown up."

"You'll still be gone."

"True. But I'll still be around."

"Like a ghost?"

"Not exactly." He thought for a moment. "You and I come from a very special family. We've got sixteen hundred years of history behind our faces. Know how many faces that is? Hundreds. Thousands! Remember that every time you look in the mirror. It's not only your face. It's your father's face and mine, my father's face and his father's, and his before him, stretching back through time. You'll never be alone because you've got a thousand fathers behind your face."

Chance ruminated on Cap's words. The worry lifted from his brow.

"Feeling better?"

Chance nodded and then asked, "Pops?"

"Yeah, Chance?"

"How many of those thousand faces had scars?"

"You sure ask a lot of questions." Cap set the book on the vanity. "Let me ask you one. How much do you know about the wishing hat?"

"What's a wishing hat?"

"Your daddy didn't wish the two of you here?"

"We took a steamship and then a choo-choo train."

At least that much of Duke's story was true.

"He didn't tell you about a hat that takes you anywhere you wish?"

"Nope."

"Get comfortable, boy. I've got a story for you. Tomorrow, I'll show you the hat shop. We're gonna be spending a lot of time there."

CHAPTER ELEVEN

1951

One seasonable day in May, Cap cranked open the living room window and oriented the radio outdoors, so he and Chance could take in the Tigers game. Word was Harry Heilmann would be sitting in for a few innings to call the game with Ty Tyson. The name Heilmann translates to "healthy man," which was ironic because Harry was dying of lung cancer. Like Gehrig, he was another German-descended baseball great knocking on death's door.

Cap stuffed a baseball glove in Chance's gut and announced they were playing catch. Chance's fingers were raw from a solid month of clipping wire and twisting the strands into one-piece frames, as well as practicing millinery's "ten critical stitches." Even so, he jumped at the chance to do something with his grandfather that didn't involve hats. They headed to the narrow, grassy patch between their house and the street. Cap slipped on his glove and tossed an underhand throw to Chance, ten feet away. The eight-year-old boy misjudged the lob, and the ball smacked his forearm before falling to the turf.

"Keep your eye on it, son."

As Chance gripped the baseball, he thought about the poor slob who'd stitched it together. That guy probably spent long days feeding red thread through the tough horsehide. His hands must've been a twisted heap of bones and callouses. Chance's hands suddenly didn't hurt as much. He threw the ball back stiffly, using only his wrist and elbow. The ball landed at Cap's feet and dribbled another six inches.

"Put your shoulder into it next time. Try again."

Cap tossed the ball back, an overhand lob. Chance fared no better on the second attempt. He moved in too close, and the ball pinged off his chest. He rubbed his smarting right pectoral muscle and fetched the ball. This time he overemphasized the shoulder motion and sent the ball straight down into the grass. He picked up the ball and tossed it to his grandfather, forgetting to use his shoulder again.

"We've got work to do. You don't want to be throwing like a girl."

"Why not?"

"'Cause it's not the right way."

"In gym class, Gloria Templeton throws farther than any other boy. I want to throw like her."

"She must throw like a boy."

"If she threw like a boy, she wouldn't be the best."

"Never mind about Gloria Templeton. Focus on Chance Leghorn, okay?"

"Sure thing, Pops."

"Now, try it again, and put your body into it. Don't be afraid to twist your back. Throwing isn't just an arm thing."

Chance threw much harder the next time. Although Cap had to pivot five feet to make the catch, the throw had zip.

"Much better! But you're side-arming it. Bring your hand over your ear as you release."

Cap tossed the ball back, and Chance caught it one-handed in the glove's webbing. He set his feet, reared back, and threw a heater (well, a seven-and-a-half-year-old's version of a heater), which made a satisfying "thuck" sound in the meat of Cap's glove.

"That's what I'm talking about, son! You feel the difference?"

"Yeah, Pops. That was swell."

"You've got lightning in that arm. Let's try some grounders."

Cap sidearmed the ball onto the turf. It skipped, landed, and bounced again. Chance flinched and turned away from the ball, attempting to field it backhanded. The ball scooted under his glove's webbing.

"You've got to square your body to the ball and squat." Cap demonstrated. "Make yourself the biggest target possible. Then, when the ball comes, you put your glove down. Even if you misjudge it a little, even if it rolls up your glove or hits you in the chest, the ball will stay in front, and you can make the play at first base."

Chance tossed the ball back. Cap wound up but stopped mid-throw.

"Get yourself ready, son. You look like you've got no knee joints. Bend your legs. Good. Keep both hands in front of you. That's right."

Cap threw another grounder. It bounced once, twice, and on the third hop, skipped off a patch of hard packed soil. The ball smacked Chance's sternum and then chucked him under the chin. The impact made his nose tingle and fill with a coppery smell. He picked up the ball and make a hard throw to Cap.

"Nice!"

Chance rubbed his chin and dabbed his nostrils. No blood.

"You okay?"

Chance nodded.

"You caught a bad bounce there, but you did the right thing by staying down and keeping the ball in front. Good life lesson. You can't predict all the bad bounces, but if you keep them in front, if you don't turn away, if you face them like a man, you'll be okay."

Chance was dubious. The lesson just as well could've been, "Don't field life's grounders. Let the ball settle to a predictable path or, better yet, let it come to a dead stop and then pick it up." Although Cap's approach might get the ball to first base faster, did it really matter if the price was a cracked chin or broken nose? On the other hand, the risk of a fractured bone was more tolerable than a grandfather's disappointment. In fact, thought Chance, maybe he could parlay this baseball thing into more freedom from the hat shop. He'd seen a flyer at school for the Black Bottom Bombers, a Little League team that practiced after school two days a week. Chance fielded a few more grounders and threw hard back to Cap.

"You're a quick learner."

"You think I'm good enough to play on a team?"

"Sure."

"'Cause the Bombers practice after school, and they've got spots."

"Oh... well... I'm not sure if that'll work. You're at the shop after school."

"Practice is only two days a week, and the whole season's like three months, I think."

"That adds up. You'd miss four hours a week in the shop, multiplied by twelve. That's forty-eight hours, not even counting games. And that's only this year. If you stick with it, you'll go to three practices a week, plus more games, and tournaments. In high school, you'd practice every day. We're talking thousands of lost hours. You won't be prepared to take over the hat shop. You'll have to sell factory-made hats. Customers won't stand for it.

You'll run the business into the ground. You'll get desperate. Maybe try gambling, but you're no good at it, and you lose your shirt. You'll need a loan to stay afloat, but no bank will loan you money because hat sales are so bad. So you turn to a loan shark who charges you a thousand percent interest. But you can't even keep up with the interest. He breaks your right leg one week and the left leg a week after. Then your hands. You turn to booze, which you drink through a straw because you've got two broken hands. You destroy your liver and die young of cirrhosis. All that because you wanted to have a little fun on the diamond."

Chance scratched his head with his glove. "So you're saying no?"

"Play ball, if that's what you want to do. Far be it from me to stop you. I'm just giving you the facts. You decide. All right. Let's try a pop fly."

Cap heaved a high-arcing throw. He was pumped from his diatribe and put too much juice on the ball. It sailed over Chance's head and into the neighbor's white oak. The ball flitted through the leaves before ricocheting off a broad branch and dropping in the street. Chance took off for the ball before it rolled away.

"Chance! No!" Cap yelled.

Chance froze in the street as a Ford pickup barreled toward him. The driver slammed the brakes and stopped short of him. The ball continued to roll, and it was picking up steam. Chance resumed the chase.

"For God sakes, Chance. Get the hell out of the street!"

The ball raced alongside the chain of parked cars, bouncing off tires and bumbling through potholes, opening up a good twenty-yard lead. Chance was ready to kiss the baseball goodbye when the driver's side door of a green and yellow Checker taxi opened. A man stepped out and barehanded the renegade ball.

"Thanks, mister," said a breathless Chance.

"Been in your shoes many times," answered the cabbie. He was a stocky fellow with a chubby face, red beard, and a black ascot cap. "The trick with grounders is keeping your glove down."

"It was a pop fly."

The man flipped the ball in his hand.

"For those, make sure you play deep enough. Easier to run in than turn tail and chase after it."

"You play baseball?"

"Back in the day. Now I just coach."

"For the Tigers?"

"No," the man laughed. "Little League. Kids about your age."

"The Bombers?"

"Another team."

"Which one?"

The man stopped flipping the ball and rubbed the cab's side panel with his other hand. "Oh, well. We're called the... the Checkers. Anyway, I was watching you and your pa up there. You've got some skills. What team are you on?"

"I'm not."

He moved closer, blasting Chance with chocolate breath. "You should join the Checkers."

"Really?"

"Heck yes."

"My grandpa won't let me. I have to work in his hat shop."

"It's important to help the family business."

"It is?" asked Chance, disappointed.

"But it's also important to have fun. You have only one childhood, you know?"

"Yeah, I know."

Chance eyed the baseball, as the man tossed it hand to hand.

"If you'd like, I'll have a word with your grandpa."

Cap yelled from up the street. "What's the holdup, Chance?"

"Thanks, mister, but forget it."

"Probably not the best time. Work on him. Tell him there's nothing more American than baseball. It's one thing that separates us from the Reds."

"What's wrong with Cincinnati?"

"Not those Reds. I'm talking about Commies."

"Chance!" Cap yelled.

"I really gotta go... Uh, the ball?"

The man looked at the baseball in his hand with surprise. "Sheesh. Forgot I still had the thing. Here."

Chance took the ball, but the man didn't let go right away. He pulled the ball and Chance toward him. The grimace beneath his brownish-red beard caused Chance's heart to skip a beat. But then the cabbie smiled broadly and released the ball, adding, "Wasn't sure you had it. See ya around, kid."

Cap's face looked sour as Chance approached.

"Who were you talking to?"

"A cabbie."

"You shouldn't be talking to complete strangers when you're alone."

"He's all right. He knows a lot about baseball."

"And Hitler knew a lot about art. How'd that work out for us? Come on. Go inside and wash up for dinner. I gotta get the water boiling."

After washing his hands, Chance worked a gob of thick hand cream into his fingertips and wiped the excess on his pants. The Tigers game was over. They'd lost... again. It was going to be a long season.

He turned the radio around and tuned to a show called Chandu the Magician. According to the teleplay, Chandu had mastered teleportation, among other superpowers, solely through the power of thought. Although Chandu wore a turban, he didn't require any kind of hat, wand, device, or spell. He needed only will himself to a place, and there he'd go.

"Is that possible, Pops?"

"Dunno," said Cap as he poured milk into two glasses. "Come to the table. Dinner's ready."

Cap scooped a pile of nutrient-starved, canned green beans onto Chance's plate. He clanked the spoon with too much enthusiasm, and two beans infiltrated Chance's spaghetti pile. Cap immediately took Chance's plate and doled out a new pasta pile for his grandson, because (in Chance's view) the beans had indelibly stained the other pasta, rendering it inedible. This had been Cap's modus operandi since 1950, when he'd accidentally bumped the table and dislodged a brussels sprout from Chance's "sprout pyramid." Though the wayward sprout had barely grazed Chance's fish, he refused to eat it, even the untouched portion. Thus commenced a three-hour staredown, after which Cap threw out the cold filets as well as the apple pie he'd let burn in the oven rather than concede defeat to his grandson.

"If Chandu can travel just by thinking, why do we need the wishing hat?"

Cap twirled the noodles in his spoon.

"Chandu's made-up. The wishing hat's real." He stuffed the mass of pasta in his mouth.

"How do I know it's real?"

Cap stopped chewing.

"What do you mean? I've told you those stories a million times."

Chance nodded and then thought for a while. "The Chandu story's on the radio. Millions of people listen to it. Wouldn't that make him real, too?"

"No, that's ridiculous."

"But you just said telling something a lot makes it real."

"No, I didn't."

"You did."

"I did?"

Chance nodded up and down in a showy way.

The boy's logic was unsound, but Cap couldn't figure out how to articulate the flaw. "Your spaghetti's getting cold."

Chance forked two noodles into his mouth.

"The difference is, my stories are true," Cap continued.

"Why aren't the Chandu stories true?"

"A writer invented them. He sold them to the radio stations. All those ads you hear—for Camel cigarettes or Gold Bond powder—companies pay the stations to run them during Chandu. The stations then pay the writer for more Chandu stories. Get it?"

"Yep. If it's on the radio, it's not true."

"No. No, most stuff on the radio is true."

"Like the ads?"

"Right. The ads."

After a pause, Chance announced. "I should smoke Camels."

"What?"

"Most doctors smoke Camels. The man on the radio said that."

"That's malarkey. Come to think of it, you can't really trust ads."

"What then?"

"The news. That stuff's true... well, usually true. They get some things wrong, like that 'Dewey Wins' fiasco. I know. The weather report—no, they're wrong half the time on that, too. Ahh, I got it. Ball game scores. Those are true. Stock market reports. That kind of thing."

"But not Chandu, 'cause someone got paid to make him up."

"That's right."

"If you get money to say something, you're a liar."

"Well, no. Not necessarily. You really have to look at the source. Who's telling you what? What's their angle on the thing that might make them lie? What proof do they have?"

"The wishing hat is true because you told me it's true."

"Exactly."

"You didn't get paid to tell me that."

"Nope."

"Pops, do you have an angle?"

"You think I'd lie to you?"

Chance shrugged.

Cap was mortified. "You don't know?"

"You might have an angle I don't know about."

"But I don't."

"Do people tell each other their angles?"

"Lots of times angles are secret. And before you ask, the answer is no, I don't have a secret angle."

"Okay, Pops. That's good."

"Glad we got that settled."

"Pops?"

"Yeah, Chance?"

"Do you have any proof of the wishing hat?"

Cap banged his fist on the table. "Now, see here—"

A Checker cab zoomed by the living room window and honked its horn. When Cap turned his head, his cheek scar squirmed atop his masticating jawbone like a caterpillar trying to bust free of its cocoon. Chance pictured the scar leaping from his grandfather's face, coiling around his weak little neck, and cinching his windpipe until he face-planted on his meatballs. Cap turned back to Chance and smiled.

"Hey, after dinner, you wanna head to Goresky's for a slice of pie?"

"Sure thing, Pops."

―――o|o―◇◯◇―o|o―――

As Chance waited for the streetcar the next day, the sounds of a pick-up baseball game from the back of the school made him bristle. A bat smacked a ball. Someone shouted for a cut-off throw. Someone else shouted, "Safe!" Chance didn't want to hear it. He hummed. He kicked at the sidewalk. He coughed. Then a Checker taxi pulled up. The driver greeted Chance through the open passenger window.

"Hey, slugger," said the bearded stranger from the other day. He was gnawing on a Bonomo Turkish Taffy bar.

"Oh. Hey, mister."

"Where you off to?"

"Pops' hat shop."

"Don't sound too happy about it."

Chance shrugged.

"You keep working on your old man. He'll come around."

"Do the Checkers have practice today?"

"The who?"

"Your team. The Checkers."

"Yeah, in a little bit. Too bad you can't join us."

"Yeah. Too bad."

"Want a ride?"

"I don't have any money."

"No worries. It'll be on the house. Oakland Street's not that far."

"How'd you know I'm going to Oakland Street?"

"The streetcar line. I just figured."

"Pops says I shouldn't talk to strangers. I don't think he'd want me riding with one either."

"Do you know the fellow's name who drives the streetcar?"

"No."

"So he's a stranger."

"I guess."

"You ever take the bus alone?"

"Sometimes."

"And who drives the bus?"

"I don't know."

"So you'll get in a streetcar or a bus with a stranger but not a taxicab. How does that make sense?"

"I guess it doesn't."

"Come on. Get in."

Chance headed to the rear passenger door. As he grasped the door handle, the streetcar squealed to a stop a block away.

"Looks like I won't need that ride. Thanks anyway, mister."

"Suit yourself. Maybe I'll see you tomorrow."

The same sequence replayed the next day, only this time, the fat, bearded stranger didn't invite Chance into the cab. He got out of the car, grabbed Chance's arm, opened the right rear passenger door, and stuffed him inside. Chance was too stunned to resist. Before he could react, the man had slammed the door shut, and the taxi was zipping away.

"Stop the cab! Let me out."

"In due time, my boy."

The man's voice had changed. He spoke less nasally and more formally. He didn't sound like a working stiff anymore.

"Pops is expecting me. If I don't show, he'll come looking. He'll call the cops."

"As any good grandfather would. But the search will take hours, even days. I don't need that much time."

"Time for what?" Chance snorted back his burgeoning tears. "You gonna kill me?"

"No. Of course not. Here." He offered Chance a handkerchief. "That would be a mortal sin."

Cap warily eyed the hankie's mysterious brown stains and then opted for his shirt cuff. "And kidnapping isn't?"

"I do not do this lightly. Your father has left me no other choice. He stole something very valuable. Priceless. Now I have stolen something priceless from him. All I want is a fair exchange."

"I haven't seen my dad in five years. He doesn't write or call. I don't know where he lives. He's not even gonna know you took me, if he's even alive."

"He'll know, and I assure you he's very much alive."

"Is he here? In Detroit?"

"He's halfway around the world."

"Then how's he gonna come for me?"

"He has the means, believe me."

The man pulled off East Grand Boulevard and entered the Packard Plant complex, winding through a grid of roads before parking the car in an alleyway between two warehouses. He cut the ignition. The only sounds were the cabbie's labored breathing and the distant rumble of machinery.

"Now what?" asked Chance.

"Now we wait."

The man unwound a string of prayer beads from the rearview mirror. He kissed the silver Crucifix, made the sign of the cross, put his thumb and forefinger over one bead, and began speaking Latin. Gradually, his thumb and forefinger moved up the rosary as he uttered more Latin words. Chance was comforted by his kidnapper's religiosity, figuring if he were truly devout, he wouldn't hurt a boy. Then again, if he were truly devout, why had he resorted to kidnapping? After prayers, the cabbie plopped his doughy hand on the giant candy wrapper pile next to him. He offered Chance a Hershey Bar, which he refused. The cabbie tore open the wrapper and devoured the candy like he hadn't eaten in weeks.

"What did Duke take from you?"

"A piece of my soul."

A piece of his soul? That was crazy talk. Chance recalled that adults often spoke about things obliquely when they felt too uncomfortable to say them straight out. Like the time Mr. Gilman threatened to "sue Pops' ass off" after the wire frame in his hat burst through the fabric and lacerated his forehead.

"No," Cap had assured the then-six-year-old Chance, "Mr. Gilman does not literally want my buttocks, nor will a judge order me to give them to him." Mr. Gilman had used an expression—"a metaphor," Cap had called it. In the same way, the cabbie couldn't have meant that Duke had stolen part of his soul. Like in those Philip Marlowe radio stories, Duke must've taken something dear to the cabbie, something sentimental, maybe a family heirloom, or maybe Duke had gotten mixed up in a love triangle, and the woman chose Duke over the bearded man.

"Why would Duke want your soul?"

"It was an accident."

"Can't he give it back?"

"He can, but he won't."

"Maybe you should sue his ass off."

The cabbie raised an eyebrow. "The law can't help me. A chunk of my soul's inside him. That's why I see what he sees, and he sees what I see. We're linked."

Chance wasn't so sure the stranger was speaking in metaphors. He seemed to be an actual loon, and now he was a crying loon. Chocolate-tinged saliva dribbled from his mouth. He squeezed the Crucifix in his fist and pressed it to his forehead. Grown-ups weren't supposed to cry, especially kidnappers, thought Chance. They were supposed to have everything under control.

"Hey, mister. Maybe you just think he has a piece of your soul, but it's been inside you all along. You ever consider that? One time, I was sure I'd lost my George Kell rookie card, but then it turned up in my underwear drawer."

"My soul is not a stray sock. Your father stole it. I must get it back if I don't want to spend eternity in Purgatory."

"But it's not your fault."

"It doesn't matter."

"God's not gonna blame you."

"Believe me, I'm an expert on the human soul. I went through years of training and self-sacrifice. I forsook the pleasures of the flesh. I was ordained to hear confessions and consecrate the bread and wine as the body and blood of Christ."

"Boy, I had no idea it was so hard to become a cabbie."

"I'm a priest."

"Priests drive cabs?"

"I *used to be* a priest... before your father ripped my soul apart. I've spent years trying to find him, but he always knows I'm coming. He vanishes before

I get there. He must come to me."

"I'm sorry Duke hurt you. He hurt me too. He dropped me on Pops' doorstep and that was that. He's never once checked on me. He doesn't love me, so you may as well take me home."

"He cares about you deeply. He'll come. He has to."

Hours passed. The machinery fell silent. After sunset, Chance lay down and fell asleep. Father Filconi was asleep, too, dreaming a black, silent dream. He hadn't had an actual dream since the day Duke abandoned him in Briggs Stadium. When Duke ripped away that piece of his soul, he'd broken the priest's link to his unconscious mind.

The boy in the backseat wasn't so debilitated. Chance dreamed he was standing on second base and Duke was on the pitcher's mound. The priest was taking practice cuts outside the batter's box, only he wasn't holding a baseball bat. A Louisville Slugger rested on the mound, next to Duke. Cap was umping behind the catcher. He had no ass—just a torso and legs. A man in the stands behind home plate shouted, "Play ball!" He was wearing a giant Mad Hatter's hat with a tag marked, "11/21," and his forehead was bleeding.

The sky turned dark indigo. Blue and red police lights flashed on top of a tiny cop car. The car parked in the aisle, next to the Mad Hatter, who asked, "What's the charge, officer?" The cop pointed underneath the Mad Hatter's seat and said, "You're not supposed to have that. Give the man back his ass." Resigned, the Mad Hatter reached under the seat and pulled out a large hatbox with a lid shaped vaguely like buttocks. He stood and then bolted onto the diamond. Cap ripped off his ump mask and yelled, "Don't just stand there, Chance. Save my ass!" Chance, however, ran away from the Mad Hatter, toward deep centerfield. "Figures," said Cap, disappointed. "Saves his own ass first."

The outfield bleachers were empty except for a blonde woman eating banana cream pie. She brought a forkful to her mouth, only she had no mouth, just a twisting vortex of folded skin with an empty center. *It's the Lolo*, thought Chance. *I have to stop running toward it.* But he couldn't slow down. Each stride turned into a long, floating leap, as though he was tethered to a hot air balloon. The Lolo woman was pulling him closer and deeper into her gravitational well. "Get out, Chance!" Cap yelled. "Get out!"

Chance awakened to the priest hauling him from the backseat.

"Get out! Get out!"

"Wha—? What's going on?"

Blue and red lights flashed from the alley's end. A voice broadcasting on a megaphone announced, "We know you're here. Surrender yourself." The priest pushed Chance against the warehouse wall and then quickly got back in the cab and pulled away, disappearing into the darkness. Chance ran toward the lights and waved down the squad car patrolling the grounds. Another car trailed closely behind it. Cap's Chevy screeched to a halt, and Cyrus exited the driver's side. Cap got out on the passenger side, ran to his grandson, and embraced him.

"Thank Fate you're alive! Are you okay?"

"He didn't hurt me. Hi, Uncle Cy."

"Which way'd he go, kid?" asked one officer.

Chance pointed into the alley.

The squad car made a sharp right turn and zoomed down the alley.

"How'd you find me?"

"Duke called a half hour ago. Said a guy in a Checker cab had you at the Packard Plant."

"How'd he know?"

"The cabbie was blackmailing Duke to get the wishing hat. I assume he called Duke and told him where—"

Cyrus interrupted, "Lot of crazy folk out there, kid. Glad you're okay. Had your pops awful worried."

"Thanks for driving me, Cyrus."

"Couldn't let you behind the wheel in that state."

"Pops, the cabbie said Duke stole something—a piece of his soul. What did he mean?"

"He said that... a piece of his soul?"

"Yeah."

"That explains how Duke knew."

"Is he coming home?"

"I don't know. He hung up so fast. Stayed on long enough to reverse the charges, though. Gonna cost me a small fortune."

"Duke could've been here in an instant if he had the wishing hat, right?"

"Yeah. Sure."

"But he didn't come."

Cyrus frowned. For years, Cap had been regaling him with tall tales about the wishing hat. Cyrus didn't believe them, but they were damn entertaining. Once, Cyrus had suggested that Cap might be setting up his gullible grandson for a huge disappointment later on, like Santa, the Tooth Fairy, and the Easter Bunny all wrapped into one and multiplied by a thousand. Cap warned Cyrus to mind his own business. After all, Cap didn't question Cyrus's belief in Jesus and the Devil. Fair enough, Cyrus had conceded. It wasn't his place to challenge another man's faith. Still, he couldn't help worrying about the boy.

"Ahh, jeez," said Cap. "Don't feel bad. Duke's got a sickness, an addiction. It colors his thinking. He doesn't trust anyone. He thinks they'll try to steal the wishing hat. He's in no condition to be anyone's father. Hey, you still got me and Uncle Cy. We're not exactly chopped liver, are we?"

Another metaphor. No, they were nothing like chopped liver, although that wouldn't have been so bad, since Chance liked chopped liver, especially at Goresky's, where they smeared it on Jewish egg bread.

"Can we go eat?" asked Chance.

CHAPTER TWELVE

1954

Dr. Simon Finkel, a University of Michigan astronomy professor, spoke to Chance's fifth-grade class about sending monkeys and mice into space, and suggested a man might go someday. Bernie Levin asked if there was a "monkey toilet" inside the rocket. Professor Finkel's answer: No, the flights were very short. If the monkey got desperate, he'd go in his spacesuit—which prompted Louis Marshall to yell, "Just like you on the school bus, Bernie!" Then Gloria Templeton raised her hand. She was one of the few black girls in the school. Her father was a bigwig in the NAACP's local chapter. But if Gloria's minority status bothered her, she never let on. She wasn't shy about going up to the chalkboard and correcting her white peers' mathematical and grammatical errors. Nor did she back down in class activities that touched on race, like the moot court on public school integration.

Gender was the only area where she showed vulnerability. It bugged her that the school principal and vice principal were men, while all the teachers were women. Although she always showed respect toward her white teachers, she was known to grimace at, and, on occasion, bump the administrators in the hallway. Gloria's mother, who'd earned a law degree, had died in an alcohol-related car accident. The rumor was, she was driven to drink after all the white law firms refused to hire her because of her race, and the black firms refused to hire her because of her sex. With that emotional baggage in tow, Gloria asked Professor Finkel why he'd said someday soon a "man" would travel to space. Why not a woman? The answer: Laughter. First, from her fellow students; then, from the professor; and finally, the teacher, Miss Mathis. Only Gloria and Chance weren't amused.

Chance felt bad for Gloria. That the professor and the teacher would mock her serious question was a horrible injustice, especially in light of Bernie's idiotic question. Chance's intense crush on Gloria multiplied his indignation a hundredfold. Her face reminded him of an ebony-wood statue of an African girl at Mooch Records, where his grandfather occasionally bought jazz albums. The similarity wasn't in the color—Gloria was much lighter—but in her plump cheekbones and full lips. Whenever Chance thought about Gloria's lips, he'd get a tickly feeling in his gut. At that moment, Chance wanted Gloria to turn and meet his eyes, so he could convey his emotional support, albeit telepathically. Most of all, he wanted to see those lips and get that tickly feeling. Alas, she didn't look his way.

During the Oreo cookie reception that followed, Chance mustered the courage to ask Professor Finkel about the wishing hat. Chance was savvy enough not to ask directly whether travel by a divine wishing hat was scientifically possible. He kept things vague, asking whether the professor knew if anyone was working on something that could transport someone from one spot to another in an instant.

"Like a time machine?" asked the professor.

"No. Just from one place to another."

"A teleportation device."

Chance got excited. "Yes. Has anyone built one?"

The professor gave an avuncular laugh and answered, "I don't think such a thing is even possible."

"I've read stories where a scientist breaks a person into atoms and sends them through an electric wire to somewhere else, where they're put back together."

"Just stories."

"But someday do you think they may be more than stories?"

"Very unlikely. Probably impossible. The human body has a staggering number of atoms. Trillions. Quadrillions. More than quadrillions. The power required to atomize someone would exceed the energy of a million atom bombs."

"What if the hat works differently?"

"Did you say hat?"

"No… Never mind."

"If you'll excuse me, I must get to the cookies before they're all teleported away."

Later, at the hat shop, Chance reported to his grandfather what Professor Finkel had told him: that the wishing hat was a scientific impossibility.

"I don't know what to tell you, Chance. I'm sure there's a scientific explanation for the wishing hat, just not one we understand yet. Maybe the hat has nothing to do with atoms or patterns. Einstein says space is like fabric, so maybe the wishing hat works like hat-making. Cut some fabric out, sew the pieces together, and Voila! You're there. I don't know. The point is, the wishing hat's real, and it works. We wouldn't be alive without that hat. The Nazis would've killed us sixteen years ago."

Chance fell silent. He wished he shared his grandfather's faith in the divine hat. Then again, faith was easy for Cap because he'd supposedly experienced hat travel. Chance had only Cap's words—*sincere* words but words nonetheless—and a letter written by a long-dead relative in the 1600s. More words.

Chance watched his grandfather bind yarn to felt. It unsettled him, as though he were witnessing a twisted alchemy. The smooth, sturdy felt didn't belong with the undulating, malleable yarn any more than paper with water, or fire with bone. He was grafting opposing media, creating an abomination of fashion, if not physics.

Cap made a few of those strange hats every year. He'd butcher a perfectly good black homburg, cutting away the crown's upper third, and then transplant a disk of woven alpaca. A tight indigo spiral wound around the disk like a record's grooves, with an indigo tassel capping the apex. He'd then ship it to a fellow named Grimsky in New York. Always Grimsky. Chance had no idea whether Grimsky was the man's first or last name, or what this one-named fellow needed with so many of the same strange hat. Did he wear them out? Did he give them away as gifts? Perhaps Grimsky was insane or demented and kept forgetting he'd ordered the hideous hat. That was the simplest explanation, which usually was the right one.

Cap set the packing tape on the cutting table, creating a puff that sent a piece of paper fluttering to Chance's feet. The paper was a list of names, all with the last name Lux.

"What's this, Pops?" asked Chance.

"Research for the curse. If we're gonna break it, we have to work with the Luxes. A few live right here in Detroit."

"The water nymph ladies? But we can't help them without the wishing hat."

"We should prepare for the day we get it back."

"But we won't. You said Duke's addicted to hat travel."

"That's right."

"So what makes you think he'll bring it back?"

"Just a gut feeling."

Chance's stomach growled with a sound like *Why, oh why, oh why, oh why?* Cap frowned, unconsciously blaming the boy's gut for its contrarian borborygmi.

"I'll do some reconnaissance tomorrow while you're at school, try to narrow down the list."

The next day, just before lunchtime, Ms. Mathis announced to the class that the U.S. Supreme Court had decided *Brown vs. Board of Education*. She read this quote from the opinion: "Segregation with the sanction of law, therefore, has a tendency to retard the educational and mental development of negro children and to deprive them of some of the benefits they would receive in a racially integrated school system." Bernie Levin snickered and then muttered "retard" under his breath. Chance glanced at Gloria. If she'd heard the comment, she hadn't reacted.

At recess, Gloria sat alone on the swings, probing the swale of eroded dirt with the tips of her black and white saddle shoes. She seemed lost, dangling and twisting to gravity's whims, the breezes, and her toes. Chance sat on the swing next to her. He mimicked her dangling and probing motions. When the chains of his swing squeaked, Gloria looked over.

"So that's good news about *Brown*," said Chance.

"Doesn't really affect me."

"It affects a lot of people like you."

"You think there are a lot of people like me?"

"No, I meant only—"

"I know what you meant. My skin. Yeah, it's a big deal. But at the same time, it was inevitable. That's what my daddy said."

"But he didn't know, not for sure. A lot of people—judges—had to agree."

"He said all the signs were there. It was just up to Fate to decide when."

"Your daddy believes in Fate?"

"Fate… Jesus… God. It's all the same, best I figure."

Bernie Levin approached with Fred Stinson and Louis Sokowitz, two rough kids who sat in the back of the class. Fred and Louis towered over everyone else, and Louis already was sporting a nascent mustache. Fred and Louis came from Catholic, blue collar families. The only reason they hung out with Bernie

Levin, a scrawny Jew with an optician father, was because he'd give them Lucky Strikes snatched from his mother's purse.

"Look," said Bernie to his thug friends, "It's the 'retard.'"

"Shut up, Bernie!" Gloria yelled back. "You're so immature."

"Least he's not a nigger," said Louis.

"You probably don't even know how to spell that word," said Gloria.

"N-I-G… uh, crud. Fred, it's two g's, right?"

Gloria cackled. "Now who's the retard?"

Louis pushed Gloria in the chest. She fell backward off the swing and hit her head on the compacted dirt.

"Ow!"

"That'll show you," Louis taunted.

Fred laughed. Bernie backed away.

"Guys," said Bernie. "You really shouldn't…" He then turned and ran across the playground.

"Where ya goin', Jew boy?" Louis called after him.

Chance hopped off the swing and knelt beside Gloria. "You okay?"

"No, she's not," said Fred with mock concern. "Her skin's a funny color."

Fred and Louis burst into laughter.

"Shut up!" Chance yelled. "You two are in big trouble."

"Oooh. Tough guy," said Fred. "You gonna tattle? Maybe we should bust his arm, Louis."

"Chance," said Gloria, rubbing the back of her head. "Just forget it. It's not worth it."

"You're worth it."

"Hear that, Fred?" asked Louis. "Chance has a boner for the nigger girl."

"Shut the hell up, Louis! Stop talking like that."

"What? You don't like the word boner?"

"You know what I mean."

"Oh, you mean nigger. But that's what she is, ain't she?"

"I swear, Louis. One more time and—"

"And what?"

"Chance," pleaded Gloria. "Let it go."

"And you'll regret it, that's what."

Louis stepped within inches of Chance, blocking the sun like a giant before it squashes a bug. He repeated, "Nigger," and then, before Chance could react, kicked him in the ribs with his combat boot. Chance fell into a fetal position. Inspired (and wearing the same russet-colored boot in a larger size), Fred kicked

Chance in the back. Louis then knelt and ground Chance's face into the dirt.

"Leave him alone!" shouted Gloria.

Fred and Louis each pounded Chance on the back twice.

"That's good, Fred," said Louis.

"How 'bout we smoke one of them Luckys?"

"Good idea."

After they left, Chance rolled to his back. He wiped the dirt from his forehead and pressed his gut where Louis had kicked him. Fortunately, he hadn't struck rib, only knocked the wind out of him.

"What the heck were you thinking, Chance?"

"I... I wanted to help."

"It's not your fight."

"Seemed like it at the time."

"Well, it's not."

"Sorry."

Gloria moved close to Chance, hovering her face over his. Her lips were moist and full. Her perturbed expression had faded.

"No one's ever fought for me. I mean, you didn't do much fighting. You were mostly a punching bag. But you're a good punching bag." She leaned in and pressed her lips to his for a second. "Thanks."

Chance felt a surge in his crotch. He propped himself to an elbow and gazed into the deep brown wells opposite him. He thought about his fate. He didn't care what the future held, as long as Gloria was in it. And, once he had the wishing hat, he could wish Fred and Louis to the other side of the Earth.

He swallowed hard. "I can be more than a punching bag, you know."

"Better hit the gym, then."

"I don't need big muscles. I have a wishing hat."

"A *what* hat?"

"A wishing hat. You put in on, wish to go to a place, and the hat takes you there."

Gloria ran her fingers through Chance's scalp, pressing on random spots.

"What are you doing?" Chance asked.

"Feeling for bumps. You're loopy."

"I'm serious. Pops said my family has had the hat for, like, two thousand years. It came from the god Hermes."

"Right. And my family has a magic mirror that changes skin color, and we thought it'd be fun to be brown."

"It's real. You'll see."

"Show it to me."

"I don't have it."

"Ha!"

"But I know where it is. My dad took it."

"The dad who abandoned you."

"Well, yeah. So?"

"So, your grandpa invented a story to make you feel better about your dad being a deadbeat."

"No. He wouldn't do that."

Would he?

Gloria stood and dusted her backside. "All right. I'm done joking around. We gotta get back to class."

"Come home with me after school. Pops'll tell you the whole story—much better than I can."

"I ain't going anywhere with you. I'm not your fool."

Chance grabbed her hand. "Wait."

Gloria trembled with rage. "Let go, or I'll smack your head to yesterday."

Chance let go. The outdoor bell rang, signaling the end of recess. When Gloria swung her head toward the school, her tight braids whipped Chance in the face. He rubbed his smarting cheek and then turned and ran the other way.

CHAPTER THIRTEEN

Cap was munching on a sandwich in the kitchen when Chance burst through the front door. He checked his wristwatch.

"Chance? That you?"

No answer.

"School let out early?" Cap didn't wait for a response. He looked down at his list. "I narrowed the names down. Bernard Lux turned out to be an old Jewish guy. Lives alone. No daughters. Francine Lux changed her name when she got married. That leaves only Winifred Lux." Cap looked up. Chance stood before him, eyes seething with fury, forehead scratched and bruised, and shirt stained with a grassy boot print. "Jesus!"

"You're crazy, Pops. There aren't curses or wishing hats."

"What happened?"

"I got my ass kicked. I told Gloria Templeton I could protect her with the wishing hat, but she didn't believe me. You know what? She was right not to. It's a stupid, ridiculous myth you invented to make me feel better about Duke."

"I've warned you against blabbing about the hat."

"Because someone might try to steal it?"

"Yeah."

"They can't steal something that doesn't exist."

"It exists. Duke has it."

"When will you stop lying?"

"It's the goddamn truth is what it is! Ask anyone on car 21. They'll tell you."

"Who are these people, Pops? I've never met one."

"They don't live in Detroit. New York, mostly."

"They'd call or write you, wouldn't they? I mean, if you really saved them with a magic hat, they'd at least send a Christmas card."

"They're Jews. Besides, we reached an understanding."

"Is Grimsky one of them? The crazy guy who orders those ugly yarn hats?"

Cap was hurt. "You think they're ugly?"

"Get him on the phone."

"I don't have his number. Plus, it's long distance."

"Then write to him. Tell him your grandson wants to talk to him."

"We all agreed not to talk about it, not even to each other. I didn't want the scrutiny. I couldn't risk someone trying to steal the hat. The Nazis took it, but I got it back, remember?"

"I remember you telling me that."

Cap's voice got louder and shriller. "And that was the truth!" He poked Chance's chest for emphasis, as though a deep indentation in the boy's left pectoral muscle would convince him. Cap brushed aside a lock of Chance's hair that had fallen over his left eye. "Go get cleaned up."

Chance swatted his grandfather's hand away.

"Easy!"

"I'm not going back to school, Pops."

"Right. You're coming with me to Winifred Lux's house."

"Go to hell."

"What did you say?"

"Go to hell!"

Cap slapped the boy's face. Hard. Chance backed away, trembling head to foot, and then ran out of the house.

"Chance! Come back. Please." Cap looked up. "Oh God. What have I done? What have I done?"

Chance dodged a Chevy turning onto Edison Street and then hung a right on Hamilton. The avenue was blocked to car traffic due to the Lodge Freeway's construction. Soon, there'd be a highway only steps from their front door. Progress. He ran past Kiefer Hospital, where, a month earlier, he'd participated in the polio trials. He didn't know whether he'd gotten the actual vaccine or a placebo, only that the shot had felt like a brass knuckles punch to the arm. A half mile later, Chance passed Ford Hospital. All these hospitals were making him nervous, so he picked up the pace.

Chance planned to follow the train tracks out of town. He crossed Grand

River Boulevard and entered the hardscrabble wasteland the locals called "Drunkard's Doom" due to the winos who stumbled into passing trains with some regularity. Alcohol and trains were never a good mixture, but even a sober man could perish in this area if he wasn't careful. A massive berm shielded the curved track and approaching trains and reflected their sound backward. Worse, conductors didn't consistently blast their whistles before the berm, which apparently was acceptable in a community where the victims tended to be alcoholic loners.

The tracks appeared hobo-free. Not surprising at that early afternoon hour. Chance followed the tracks toward the winking globe atop the Penobscot Building's radio antenna until his foot knocked a booze bottle. He picked it up. The label said it held ten-year-old Irish whiskey. He pressed the bottle to his lips, hoping its former owner had left him a birthday present to make up for the worst day of his life. All he got were a few drops of rainwater mixed with gravel dust. He punted the bottle away—a line-drive into the rails. The bottle ricocheted and somersaulted and windmilled, coming to rest in a lazy position against the rusty rail. The pain on the top of Chance's foot vibrated to his sole and then seemed to travel through the railroad tie and emerge in his other foot. He stepped toward the bottle menacingly and grabbed it by the neck.

"Screw you, Pops! I hate you."

Chance reared back, preparing to wing the bottle but stopped when he noticed a man crossing Grand River waving his arms and shouting something indiscernible. Chance assumed it was his grandfather. He saw two options: turn and run, or stand his ground and fight. He dropped the bottle, stepped off the tracks, and put up his fists.

"Let's go, Pops," he said to himself. "We'll settle this like men."

The man was closer now. He wasn't Cap.

"Train! Train!" the man was screaming.

Chance caught only a gray blur in his peripheral vision before a rush of wind pushed him flat to the gravel. He could barely breathe, gasping dust and diesel for thirty seconds as the train cars buzzed by. His bones rattled so badly, he thought he might shatter. Then, as quickly as the train had come upon him, it had zoomed past with a blast of its whistle. Ten seconds later, dead silence.

Chance took stock. One split lip, two skinned elbows, and a dozen pock-sized contusions on his face and chest to accompany the pre-existing bruise on his back. He'd also wet himself a little. But he was alive. He couldn't say the same for his bottle-friend. It had vanished from the tracks, probably exploded into a million shards.

Strange hands reached under Chance's armpits and yanked him to his feet.

"What the hell were you thinking, kid?!"

The stranger was a skinnier, younger version of Cap, except for the deeply sunken eyes. Vascularized papules dotted his forehead, cheeks, and neck.

"Duke?"

"You've gotten tall, son." Duke dug into a shoulder bag, pulled out a soccer ball, and stuffed it in the boy's gut. "West Germany scored with that very ball during the World Cup match in Switzerland. Happy Birthday."

Fashioned from stitched leather strips, the ball resembled a swollen brain more than athletic equipment.

"I thought you'd be at school. They're looking all over for you, you know."

"How'd you find me?"

"I overheard Pops telling Cyrus you ran this direction. I've never seen him so broken up."

"Really?"

"He's worried as hell. Something up with you two?"

Chance rubbed his cheek. "Nothing I can't handle. Did you talk to him?"

"Only overheard him."

"Are you back for good?"

"Just came to wish you a happy birthday."

"Take me with you."

"Can't."

"Why not?"

"Wandering the world is no life for a kid."

Chance eyed Duke's hatless head.

"You have it with you?"

"Have *what*?"

"The wishing hat."

"What?" Duke laughed. "There's no such thing."

"Pops says otherwise."

"He's still spinning those stories?"

"They're not true?"

"'Course not."

"How do you know?"

"When I was ten, I looked in the safe where he supposedly kept it. Wasn't there. Just the coin and Lorenz's crazy letter."

"The coin's gone."

"I hocked it. Needed the cash."

"But you didn't take the hat 'cause it wasn't there," said Chance tentatively, sounding out the logic of the situation. "The hat wasn't there 'cause it doesn't exist. Pops made it up."

"That's the sum total of it."

"How'd you, Bessie, and Pops escape the Nazis?"

"We got visas, took a train, and then a steamship. Nothing magical about that."

"Pops didn't wish a hundred people from that train car?"

"Hell no!"

The left breast pocket of Duke's pea coat bulged.

"What's in your coat?"

"A hat. A *wool* hat."

"Can I see it?"

"I gotta get going. I don't want things to get awkward, if Pops should—"

"You can't spare five seconds for the son you haven't seen in eight years? Unless you're lying about what's in your coat."

"Why would I lie?"

"You might have a secret angle."

"What secret angle?"

"You don't want me to take it from you."

Duke scowled at his son like an Old West gunfighter. After a beat, he broke into a sheepish smile. "You got me, kiddo. I was lying. It's not a wool cap. It's a leather pouch." He scowled again. "Know what I keep in it? Pill bottles."

Duke reached into his coat pocket and pulled out a vial, which he handed to Chance. The label read, "Lithium Bromide."

"What's this?"

"You probably noticed your old man's not gonna win any beauty pageants. I'm sick. Picked up a weird bug in that Nazi camp I saved your mother from. There's no cure, but these pills help. What I got's contagious. That's why I've stayed away. I didn't want you suffering my fate. That makes me a rotten father, but at least you're alive."

Chance was awash with guilt. "Jeez. If I'd known—"

"You got nothing to be sorry for, son. I'm the one who's sorry. I bet you hate my guts."

"No, I..."

"You should. I want you to hate me. Better yet, forget me altogether, so you don't become anything like me."

"I see you every time I look in the mirror."

Duke studied the boy's features, illuminated by the late afternoon sun. "Yep. You got the Petasos nose, all right. Forehead, too. And... Jesus Christ! Your eyes... Oh God."

"What's wrong?"

Duke turned his face, looking sick to his stomach. "I gotta go."

"Wait. What's wrong with my eyes?"

"Nothing. My pills have side effects. I see things."

A car door slammed on Grand River. A man rounded the front bumper. Duke seemed to recognize him.

"Shit."

"Who's that?"

"A guy."

"Who?"

"I took something of his."

"So give it back."

"Bye, kiddo."

Duke stepped over the train tracks and broke into a fast walk. Chance followed.

"Will I see you again?"

"I don't know. Gotta keep moving."

The man was running toward them.

"Shit. Shit. Shit," said Duke, as he broke into a sprint.

"Wait!" shouted Chance.

Chance fell farther and farther behind. He glanced over his shoulder at the stranger, who was closing in. He knew this man. Although his black ascot cap was dirty and scuffed, and his red beard was overgrown and unkempt, there was no doubt he was the cabbie-priest who'd once kidnapped him. He'd put on fifty pounds at least. His eyes were ablaze, and he was wheezing in deep, low growls. Yellowed teeth poked through a crooked smile, and dry, white saliva caked the corners of his mouth. The former cabbie/priest had gone feral.

Chance didn't notice the stray trash in his path, and he stepped awkwardly on a long-abandoned dress shoe. His ankle buckled. He stumbled and fell forward into the unforgiving earth. A moment later, the priest's plodding footsteps crunched near his ear. Dust filled Chance's eyes, and he felt a searing pain in his left cheek. He'd landed on a glass shard. He wiped the grime from his eyes with his shirttail and dabbed his cheek, which was bleeding profusely.

"Go, then!" Chance shouted toward Duke. "Don't come back. Not ever. You hear? You hear?!"

The only response was a distant squeal, probably train wheels resisting the direction the tracks wanted to take them. Chance puzzled over how Duke had eluded him so quickly. For a sick guy, Duke seemed to have superhuman speed.

Chance pulled himself to his feet. He didn't know what to believe about the wishing hat, but this much was true: Although his grandfather's words about curses and wishing hats were fiction, at least he'd uttered them sincerely, every day, without fail. The boy had come to count on those dubious words, just like he depended on the neighbor's terrier to bark at the milkman and wake him in time for school. That kind of consistency was damn annoying, yet he couldn't function without it. He ran home.

—o╂o-◇◇-●-◇◇-o╂o—

Pressure alone wouldn't stem the blood pouring from Chance's cheek wound, so Cap phoned Dr. Kennedy. According to Edna, his wife, Dr. Kennedy would be home from the hospital in ten minutes and would be happy to take care of Chance. Cap gave Chance a fresh rag before they climbed into the Chevy. All the way there, Cap kept shooting glances at the passenger seat, irrationally worried that his grandson might up and vanish from the moving car. His hands shook nervously on the steering wheel, forcing him to grip it more tightly, which only transferred the jitters up his arms and into his shoulders. He didn't relax until turning onto leafy Boston Boulevard, a wealthy enclave of Italian Renaissance, Prairie, and English Revival mansions.

"What did I say his address was?"

"1921 Boston Boulevard," answered Chance.

"Ahh, that must be it up there."

Cap parked behind a barricaded section of the street undergoing sewer work. Chance exited onto the sidewalk in front of a shabby Italianate-style house. Numerous ceramic roof tiles were cracked or missing. A second-floor shutter dangled from its hinges, and the stucco was crying out for a good patch and paint job. The roots of a leafless, wizened tree had caused the front walkway's flagstones to buckle, while overgrown azalea bushes obscured the first-floor windows. Ivy had overrun the rose beds and raced up the pines along the property line, forming a massive, evergreen tidal wave that looked as if it was about to swallow the old house.

"We're going in *there*?" Chance asked, creeped out.

"That's 1919. Dr. Kennedy's next door."

The bespectacled Dr. Kennedy greeted them warmly and then escorted them to his study, where he cleaned Chance's cheek with gauze and iodine. As he threaded a curved needle, he half-joked through his thick black mustache that Cap should suture the wound since he was more accomplished at sewing. After Cap politely declined, the doctor cinched the gash with ten interrupted stitches and then handed Chance a mirror. Between Chance's yellow-brown-stained skin and the railroad track sutures, it looked like the doctor had grafted a miniature football onto his face.

"Will it leave a scar?" Chance asked the doctor.

"Hard to predict. There's a good chance."

"Will it look like my Pops' scar?"

"That angry beast of a thing? No, don't worry about that."

"Oh," said Chance, disappointed.

Dr. Kennedy was quick to add, "But if it does leave a scar—and there's always a chance—it'll stretch and grow as you grow. It might end up bigger than your grandfather's."

Chance flashed a brief smile.

Dr. Kennedy winked at Pops. "We're all done."

"I can't thank you enough, Doctor. How much do I owe you?"

"No charge. Professional courtesy—one stitcher to another."

"Well, we're in your debt. Maybe Chance can make it up with some chores. There's a heckuva lot of ivy spilling over from your neighbor's house."

"Don't worry about that. Old Winnie Lux sold the house to a builder. He's going to knock it down, clear out the mess."

"Did you say Winnie *Lux*?"

"Yes. The Luxes were one of the original families on Boston Boulevard. You know her?"

Cap pulled a slip of paper from his shirt pocket and read the name and address: Winifred Lux, 1919 Boston Boulevard. He folded it and stuffed it back in his pocket.

"I knew a Lux in Germany. They could be related. Do you know the family well?"

"We both summer at Pointe Aux Barques... you know, up in the Thumb area. Very matriarchal family, the Luxes. Excellent athletes. Natural born swimmers. Winnie's the one who told me about this house when it came on the market in '45."

"Do you still talk to her?"

"Not since she moved in with Figgie, her daughter in Grosse Pointe. She's taking care of her. Winnie got pretty senile. Kept babbling about Greek gods or some such nonsense."

"Gods? Which ones?"

"Does it matter?"

"No. No, I suppose not."

Cap looked at Dr. Kennedy for a good five seconds in silence. Chance bit his lip anxiously.

"Thanks again, Doctor. We'd better go."

Chance made a beeline to the car. Cap meandered, looking far too contemplative for Chance's tastes. Cap unlocked the driver's side door, but he didn't get in right away.

"Chance, come here a second."

Chance froze. "Why?"

"I just realized something about the wishing hat."

Chance dragged his feet as he rounded the front bumper.

"I know what you're gonna say, Pops."

"Do you now?"

"Yep. You're gonna get the Luxes' address from Dr. Kennedy. Then we'll drive to Grosse Pointe and have a chat with Winifred's daughter about breaking both curses once Duke returns the wishing hat."

Cap put his hands on Chance's shoulders.

"You got me all figured out, huh?"

"Yep."

"Well, you're wrong. All I want to say is, if Duke hadn't stolen the wishing hat, you'd have never come into my life. That's the only damn miracle I care about. All that other stuff is bullshit."

Cap gazed into the boy's eyes, projecting the love of a thousand fathers. Chance smiled. Cap smiled back, but then his expression faltered. There was something oddly familiar about the boy's eyes. The way the setting sun brightened his deep green irises and then, for a fleeting moment... He shuddered. He tilted Chance's chin to recapture the sunbeams just so, but they didn't cooperate. The boy's eyes were pure green.

"You okay, Pops?"

"Just a chill." He clapped his hands with gusto and announced, "How 'bout banana cream pie at Goresky's?"

"Sure thing, Pops."

"We can talk about what you might want to do with your life."

Chance smirked. "What's there to talk about?" he asked dejectedly. "I'm gonna take over the hat shop."

"It's high time the men in this family branched out. You're good at arguing, like the Marshall fella who won the *Brown* case. Maybe you could be a lawyer."

Chance brightened. "Yeah. The law might be cool."

CHAPTER FOURTEEN

1969

Although Lila's All Night Delicatessen was only four blocks from Leghorn Millinery, venturing there on foot had been treacherous ever since the tank treads and bullets of the '67 riots transformed the sidewalks into a gantlet of buckling concrete and invasive tree roots. Half the buildings in between—not counting the charred out hulks—were boarded-up havens for drunkards, junkies, and squatters. The remnants of legitimate commercial activity were a "chemist" specializing in herbal colon cleansers, a podiatrist/orthopedic shoe emporium, and three wig shops (there would've been four, but for the lightning strike on Zorba's Wig Palace in 1968). The area was a bizarre version of 1945 Berlin, overrun by constipated zombies with bunions and bald heads. Cap drove the three blocks. The entire trip took forty-five seconds. It normally took thirty-eight seconds, but he had to idle for seven seconds at Heidelberg Street while a gimpy streetwalker fetched her bouffant wig blown into the street.

Lila's made a hearty clam chowder so thick with clams, shrimp, bits of sole, and potatoes that Lila really should've advertised it as a fish stew. Cap would serve it for dinner. Chance was coming with his girlfriend, Shirley. It would be the first time Chance brought a girl home. It was about damn time, too. Chance was already in his third year at law school. Maybe Cyrus would stop asking Cap whether his grandson was "funny."

"How about a banana cream pie to go with the soup, Mr. Leghorn?" Lila asked. "It's the best in the city."

"Thanks, Lila, but no." Cap patted his belly. "Gotta maintain my girlish figure."

That was a lie. Cap already had picked up a banana cream pie from Goresky's. Lila's pie was good, but it didn't hold a candle to Goresky's. Cap didn't see the point of sharing his preference with Lila. The old-timers who'd been keeping Goresky's afloat were dying off or fleeing to the suburbs in droves. With a dwindling customer base, Goresky's was open only a few days a week, sometimes just for a few hours. In six months, a year at the outside, it would close for good. Then, and only then, would he sample a different banana cream pie.

Cap drove back to the hat shop, making great time because he didn't have to swerve around any wayward wigs. Cyrus was sitting out front, dragging on a cigarette. Cap had considered inviting Cyrus to the dinner. His friend could provide moral support in case things got awkward with Shirley or the conversation fell off a cliff. But Cyrus was still raw from Marvin abandoning his wife and young son and moving to San Francisco with his new "man-friend." Seeing Chance with a woman might upset Cyrus, and when Cyrus got upset, he tended to overindulge on booze, which made him loud and handsy. Cap feared the evening might unfold something like this: During introductions, Cyrus would slosh his Schlitz beer on Shirley's breasts, inspiring a comment about how well she fills out her dress. During salad, he'd make a wink-and-a-nod remark to Chance about pre-marital intercourse, recommending "good, old-fashioned petting for the young lovers." After soup and his fourth Schlitz, Cyrus would squeeze Shirley's thigh under the table. After his fifth, he'd squeeze Cap's thigh. Then, while Chance and Shirley cleared the dessert plates, Cyrus would gulp his second and third shots of cooking sherry (because he already would've drunk all the Schlitz, and Cap would've hidden the Bushmills). Cyrus would belch, grab Chance's ass, and declare, "God created this here for a woman! Right, Shirl?"

At times like these, Cap wished he had a wife or at least a platonic ladyfriend. How pitiful that Cyrus was the closest thing he had to a romantic companion.

Cap shut the car door with his hip and then rounded the front bumper holding a giant paper bag with the massive clam chowder container inside. He planned on storing the soup in the cutting room's small fridge until closing time.

"Hey ya, Cap," said Cyrus with a puckish smile.

"Cy," Cap responded suspiciously.

Cyrus wagged a finger in mock accusation. "You been holding out on me, friend."

"How's that?"

"You got yourself a lady."

"What the hell are you talking about?"

"She's inside, waiting for you?"

"Who?"

"Your lady."

"God damn it, Cy. I don't have a lady."

"We chatted. Well, we tried to chat. Her English ain't so good, and my German's a tad rusty."

"German?"

"She said you two share history in the Old Country. Least I think she said history. Come to think of it, she might've said herpes. Ha! Only yankin' your chain, pal. Rosamund don't strike me like that kinda gal."

Cap shivered. "Rosam..." Goosebumps raced from his lower back to his skull. "Rosamund's inside?"

"Yep."

"In our hat shop?"

"Yeah. You all right there? You're shaky and a lot whiter than normal. You gonna be sick?"

"No, I'm okay. I'll... I'll just go on in."

"Want me to go with you—you know, for moral support?"

"Jesus, no!" A pause, and then, "Thanks, Cy. I've got this."

Cap pushed open the shop door. *Holy shit.* There she was, thirty years older. Her hair was more white-gray than blonde, and she wore it loose instead of tightly braided. Her face was fuller, as was her mid-section. Cap liked the extra heft. He remembered the sensation of rolling across her naked body after sex, wishing she had a few more millimeters of flesh to insulate her pointy hip bones. Some things hadn't changed—her arched eyebrows and severe green eyes, the black pearl pendant around her neck.

Rosamund hadn't yet noticed Cap. She was concentrating on the display table devoted to hat styles that Cap deemed too faddish to warrant separate displays—a hodgepodge of African-style kufi caps, cowboy hats à la Jon Voight in *Midnight Cowboy*, hand-crocheted cloche hats, mink dome hats, snap brim hats, and aussie hats. There was a flurry of movement as Rosamund relocated the red cloche hats to the display's center, the cowboy hats to the three o'clock position, and the aussie hats to nine o'clock. She stepped back and contemplated the new arrangement, prompting her to switch the kufis and the mink dome hats. She stepped back again and sighed with reluctant satisfaction. For the moment, Cap forgot that he hated her guts.

"Too cluttered for your tastes, I assume," he asserted in clipped German.

Rosamund turned and met Cap's eyes. She betrayed no emotion, as though they'd been apart only thirty seconds, not thirty years.

"The arrangement is more balanced with the cowboy hats and aussie hats opposite one another, and the red cloches are the only spot of color in the whole collection, so they fit best in the display's center. Don't you agree? Yes, of course you do. By the way, why did you leave the center empty?"

"It wasn't intentional."

"Perhaps not a conscious intention. Perhaps you secretly wish your customers to imagine their heads in that empty center, with the choices circling around them like—"

"Like planets around the sun?"

"Yes. Exactly."

"That's one hypothesis. Or maybe there's a simpler explanation. Maybe this morning I sold the blue suede bowler that used to occupy the center. But I wouldn't expect you to know that, since, by the looks of it"—Cap gestured to the Samsonite suitcase at Rosamund's feet—"you only recently arrived."

Rosamund flashed a crooked smile and stepped toward Cap. He stayed put.

"Kasper, I—"

"I go by Cap now," he said coldly.

"Oh, Cap. Yes. Very American."

"That's me. And you? Are you still very German?"

"West German."

"Why are you here?"

"I have a brief layover. My flight for Buenos Aires leaves in a few hours."

"Argentina? A little vacation?"

"Work. Always work."

"So you figured you'd pop into my life, rehash the good times, and then catch your plane?"

"You're angry. You have every right."

"Is Klaus traveling with you, or is this a solo mission?"

"Klaus is gone. He has been for some time. Since the end of the War."

"That's... that's a lot of years."

"I've been very busy."

"With work. Right. I understand. The hat shop keeps me incredibly busy. You realize I've been wearing these same trousers since 1952? I won't have a free minute to change them until 1972—'71, if I play my cards right."

"My work doesn't keep me in any one place for very long. I hunt Nazis, mostly in South America. I give their whereabouts to the Israelis."

"Do the Israelis know you used to work for Klaus?"

"They know."

"I'm surprised they didn't send a hunter after you."

"Maybe they will."

"What do you want, Rosamund?"

"To confess, Kasper."

"Cap," he corrected her, this time irritated.

"Cap. Sorry."

"You have nothing to confess. Klaus explained everything when he returned the wishing hat. You were his unwitting agent at the time you insinuated yourself into my life, into my bed. Completely ignorant you were his pawn, a Nazified automaton, is how he described you. Any 'love' you expressed was a lie."

Rosamund shook her head. "No. No, my feelings for you, for the children, were genuine. They still are."

"Klaus said they were 'debriefed' out of you."

"He said that to discourage you from trying to rescue me as you once rescued Isana."

"I see. Well, I have a hat shop to run, so if you're not going to buy anything, I'll have to ask you to leave."

"Please hear me out. You don't know all the facts."

"Maybe it's better I don't. Maybe they should stay buried, just like I buried you long ago, just like Gretel."

Rosamund's chin quivered. "If that is what you want."

"It is."

She picked up her suitcase and made for the door. "Goodbye."

Cap grabbed Rosamund's arm as she passed. "Wait. Damn it. I don't know what I want. Jesus, Rosamund. You show up here out of the blue… Yes. Fine. Tell me what you have to say."

Rosamund set down the suitcase.

"Not here," said Cap. "Cyrus can mind the shop."

Despite the strong afternoon sun streaming through the picture window, the greenhouse effect couldn't arrest Cap's chill. He slid on a cardigan and sat next to Rosamund on the sofa. He pulled the afghan from the couch arm and draped it over his legs.

"My mother died in 1911," Rosamund began. "I was ten when the owner of the beerhall where she'd worked dropped me at my father's farm. General Friedrich von Tannenberg's farm."

"Holy shit. That asshole was your father? Are you sure?"

"I'm certain. I found his diary when he deployed to France. It told a very different story than *Face of the Fatherland*."

Indeed, it did.

In 1888, Friedrich von Tannenberg had been a lowly musketeer in German South-West Africa, the soldierly equivalent of a sickly flea on a decrepit donkey's ass. He'd planned to resign at year's end, return to Munich, and work his father's farm. A biting midge infected with "African Horse Sickness" had other ideas. In the ensuing delirium, Friedrich had a vision of an angel, who commanded him to go to the desert. Like a good soldier, he obeyed. Friedrich snuck from the hospital without provisions—no horse, no water or food, not even a hat.

After days of aimless wandering in the Namib Desert, dehydrated and sunburnt, Friedrich was rescued by a nomadic tribe called the Yomeva. The Yomeva were an agglomeration of conquered tribes melded into one nation. Instead of killing or enslaving their enemies, the Yomeva assimilated them through a mesmerizing ritual that stripped away the old allegiances to tribe and family. The result was a culturally diverse, yet spiritually united, society. So enthralled was Friedrich, he asked the chief to induct him into the tribe. Just as the chief began the ritual—speaking in a low, tranquilizing drone while working his fingertips into the base of the skull—Friedrich again heard the angel's call, this time commanding him to return to civilization, telling him he was destined for greatness. Again, he obeyed.

Friedrich quickly advanced from musketeer to general, though not because of his battlefield competence. Rather, employing the Yomeva's mind control techniques, Friedrich and his groping fingertips "persuaded" a string of lieutenants, captains, and majors that he was a misunderstood military *Wunderkind*. He imprinted in their minds the vivid image of a wise, intrepid soldier—so vivid they couldn't see the numerous reports of insubordination, cowardice, and general stupidity that littered his dossier. It was the same psychic blindness that, decades later, he'd inflict on the tribunal members contemplating his court martial for the Perdeau Valley massacre.

Not that death and destruction marked the entirety of the general's life. There was one glaring exception. That dalliance with a Munich barmaid, his first and only act of sexual intercourse. It happened in 1900, during a brief leave from Africa to bury his parents. He engaged in the "dreadful act of carnal congress" because, as someone who regularly ordered men to their deaths, he felt obliged to have some insight into the ultimate creative act. After paying Tesse Lux the equivalent of two weeks wages, he completed the deed in forty-five seconds, after which he shrugged, she shrugged, and then he promptly returned to Africa and ordered more men to their deaths.

Rosamund's voice got shaky. "The very day I arrived, the general locked me in a bedroom. He let me out once for supper and again to use the outhouse. The next day, or maybe the day after, he burst into my room, smiling like a raving lunatic, brandishing a pair of shears. He grabbed my arm and yanked me close. His breath was repulsive. It reeked of turpentine, and his mustache like rancid beeswax. I thought he was about to slit my throat, but instead he cut my hair to the scalp, while muttering nonsense about an angel and a prophet. He ordered me not to laugh, not to smile, not to speak with lilt or inflection—ever. He took me to the river, forced me to stare at my reflection and imagine it fading away. He wrapped a veil over my face. I'd have to wear it all the time, he said—everywhere, even while I bathed or slept. That was the beginning of my training."

"Training for what?"

"He said that from then on, I'd live as a boy. A boy named Klaus."

Cap stared blankly at Rosamund. He'd heard her words but not their meaning. Finally, he blinked. "What?"

"Yes."

"You're Klaus?"

"Yes."

"The Führer's veiled prophet? The Stealer of a Thousand Faces? The engineer of the Schwarz Boden pogrom?"

Rosamund nodded.

"You can't be. It's impossible. You and he—you're different sexes, different people. He tortured you."

"Only different personalities of the same person."

Kasper's eyes searched the floor. "No. I remember you saying you had a cow named Bessie that squirted milk all over you. You rode a horse named Chess. Klaus wouldn't have done those things."

"Yet he did."

"So you were pretending to be two people the whole time we were together?"

"I know this is hard to believe, but I didn't know I was Klaus, not until Gretel's death. That's when it all came flooding back."

"How could you not know?"

"The general smothered the life out of me. Out of Rosamund. I completely forgot her for years. I thought and dreamed as Klaus: without color, without imagination, without warmth."

"But you were still a female, biologically speaking."

"I didn't see myself as male or female. I was a blank. I was Klaus."

Cap rubbed his temples, his face fixed into a wince.

"Should I go on?" asked Rosamund.

He couldn't answer.

"I'll go on. A horse, a Clydesdale, showed up in the barn when I was fifteen. He belonged to the neighbors. He'd broken out of their barn. Wandered through the woods and onto our property. The general refused to return the horse, possession being nine-tenths of the law, or some such nonsense. Those poor Jewish farmers didn't stand a chance against a decorated general. The police, the courts, wouldn't do a thing, so they let the matter go. The general told me to care for the horse, ride it if I wanted, but not to wander too close to the woods. The *verboten* woods."

"And you named the horse Chess. Why?"

"I overheard the Jewish neighbor when he was begging for the horse back. I got only bits and pieces. At one point, he said the name Chess. I thought that was the horse's name. Turned out, Chess was the horse's sibling. Anyway, the horse was a welcome respite from the general's monotonous training. Chess was the closest thing I had to a friend. And I'd need him, because the training would get far worse."

The Great War forced the general from retirement in 1916, so when he returned to the farm after the 1918 Armistice, he intensified Klaus's training to make up for lost time. He taught Klaus methods of sensory disorientation, psychological trickery, and the inculcation of dread, to enhance a person's susceptibility to suggestion. The general's ultimate goal, however, was not merely to enable Klaus to hypnotize men but to metamorphosize them—that is, to erase their faces. That required practice on live subjects.

The general lured destitute men to the farm with promises of employment and then locked them in the barn with Klaus. Klaus easily broke their will with his voice and subtle neck palpations. But no matter how much time he spent with them, no matter how much he denied them sleep and water, no matter how much they begged to do anything—anything!—to stop the torture, Klaus couldn't erase their faces, not so much as a dimple. Oh, the men swore they couldn't see their cheeks, noses, and lips, but Klaus easily detected their desperate lies and continued their interrogations. The men would relinquish more sweat, more urine, more vomit, but never their faces.

In 1919, the general's housemaid wandered into the barn to coax a squirt of milk from the decrepit cow. Thinking she was another test subject, Klaus subdued the maid, and for the first time, he had success. Three days later, the half-starved housemaid bolted from the barn, eyes aflame with madness, ranting about the blank in her face. And so it went with the other women the general subsequently enticed to the farm. Yet, whenever he reintroduced male subjects, Klaus fell short. He could dazzle men, disorient them, bend them to his will, but he couldn't blind them to their own faces.

"Why not?" asked Cap.

"I don't know. I think, unconsciously, I didn't want to fulfill the general's sick fantasy. I was secretly hoping he'd give up. Let me be."

"Be what?"

"Rosamund Lux."

"Was that possible?"

"I thought it was, once."

Klaus usually rode Chess while the aging general took an afternoon nap. After a half mile, Klaus would break the cardinal rule and unfasten the veil to clear his nostrils of the barn stench. The fetidness stemmed from a toxic admixture of animal and human secretions, bacteria, and despair. The general's lone cow, Bessie, was decaying from the outside (foot rot and mange) and the inside (gut worms and cancer). Also, the offgasses and effluent from Klaus's fifteen male and twenty-four female victims had seeped into the rafters and the hard-packed dirt floor. Add in the leaky roof and poor air circulation, and the barn had become a fertile biome for an invisible, yet blindingly pungent, redolence.

Learning to steal faces wasn't exactly growing tulips.

One day, Klaus was riding close to the *verboten* woods when he spotted a girl, also on horseback. When Klaus tried to reaffix the veil, he fumbled it, and a breeze blew it in the river. The girl dismounted, fished out the nondescript, black fabric swatch, and handed him what she'd likely assumed was a handkerchief. She petted his horse and remarked how it looked a lot like her missing horse Checkers. She then asked the horse's name. "Chess," Klaus answered flatly. The girl was astonished, because her horse also was named

Chess. She asked Klaus's name, and to his surprise, he answered, "Rosamund." Even stranger, he'd spoken in a different voice, a voice with lilt and color. *Her* voice. Rosamund had resurfaced.

"The girl's name was Isana," said Rosamund. "Isana Wandel."

"Isana? *My* Isana?" asked Cap.

"She wasn't your Isana—not then. This was years before you met."

"That's a helluva coincidence."

"You should know by now, there are no coincidences."

"I was afraid you'd say that. I need a drink. You?"

"I want to keep my head clear."

"That makes one of us. Go on."

Rosamund and Isana met the next afternoon at the river, by a sprouting laurel tree. They waded in the water. They shared Isana's grandfather's Kiddush wine until their lips turned a deep crimson, the color of red orchids. All the while, Rosamund marveled at this strange creature, who was nothing like the ugly, hook-nosed Jews the general spoke about with such vitriol. Her nose was small, like a seashell, and her fingers weren't stained from handling money. They were clean, her nails neatly trimmed and decorated with red polish. But Isana was no delicate flower either. She had a bellicose laugh. She was irreverent and immodest. She pulled down her top to soak the sun into her bosom. She prattled on about her small breasts, proclaiming their superiority to large ones, which inevitably sagged with age. She described boys she'd seen naked, both circumcised and uncircumcised. Drunk with laughter and hormones, Rosamund pressed her lips to Isana's.

"Huh. My second wife kissed my first wife before I did. How many man can say that?"

"We never married."

"I always considered us husband and wife, didn't you?"

"Yes. Of course." She shifted positions and then looked at the ceiling briefly before continuing. "Anyway, after leaving Isana, I was so happy I forgot myself on the way back to the farm. Although veiled, I was singing a Gershwin song, *There's More to The Kiss Than the Sound*. I was making puckering sounds, like in the song, when I entered the barn, and guess who was there waiting for me.

"The general wasn't angry. Not at first. He actually seemed giddy. He was holding a medical journal with a title I'll never forget. *Jahrbuch für sexuelle Zwischenstufen*. He flashed me this crazed smile and said, 'A Berlin doctor, a Herr Doctor Magnuson, has been experimenting with a radical procedure that can cure you. I'm sure of it.' That's when he got angry. He asked where the hell

I'd been. I didn't answer, which I expected to infuriate him even more, but, instead, he softened his tone and spoke to me like a concerned parent. He said he'd been searching all over to tell me the good news. A second later, though, he was raging again. 'Where the hell have you been? Where the hell have you been?' he kept asking, though he knew the answer. He revealed he'd been on the roof with a telescope, and he'd spotted me without my veil, 'kissing that foul Jewess.'

"I thought for sure he'd beat me within an inch of my life, but he became calm again. He said he understood why I'd transgressed. I had a congenital defect, you see? I'd been born female, and no amount of brainwashing could eradicate this 'affliction' that made me fundamentally weak and hopelessly deferential to men. That's why I couldn't steal a man's face. It was a biological impossibility. But Dr. Magnuson's procedure had given us hope. Modern medicine would eradicate my womanhood. Of course, it carried substantial risks—bleeding out on the table, post-operative infection, untested injections, brain trauma that could render me a complete imbecile. But I had to embrace those risks for the sake of the Volk."

"A sex change?" asked a horrified Cap. "You told him to go to hell, of course."

"I just nodded. That's what he'd trained me to do. Not to reveal myself. He then said he'd wired Berlin to set up a consultation with the doctor. We'd leave in two days. I nodded again. As he walked away, I said the Jewish girl had nothing to do with my transgression, I was entirely at fault, and I'd never see her again. He said it was all right and I shouldn't give her another thought.

"A gunshot sound woke me up that night. I couldn't see anything out the window—it was a moonless sky—except for a vague orange glow from the Wandels' land. The glow expanded into a raging inferno. Fifteen minutes later there was another shot, this one from our barn. A figure emerged. I couldn't see the face, but I recognized the general's stiff gait. An animal was moaning in the barn, crying out in pain.

"I waited for the general to come back in the house and return to bed so I could investigate. But he didn't come inside. He sat on the porch and smoked his pipe, all the while that animal in the barn moaned and moaned. Something shiny—a Mauser, I determined—lay across the general's lap. I was scared if I tried to sneak out, he'd shoot me. Finally, by sunrise, he'd fallen asleep. I crept from the house and went to the barn. Chess was down, eyes wide open like two dull opals. The white swath that spilled to the tip of his nose was stained crimson around the bullet hole. If the general had possessed even a shred of mercy, he would've fired another shot and made sure Chess was good and dead. Instead, he'd left him moaning in his own blood the whole night.

"Then I remembered the fire at the Wandels. I ran the mile to the smoldering house. I stopped short when I saw Isana dragging two charred bodies to the front of the barn. Her grandparents, I'd assumed. There was one other corpse, this one lying half in-half-out of the barn. Chess's brother also had taken a bullet to the brain. Isana had a rag wrapped around her right hand but otherwise looked fine. Well, fine physically. I couldn't imagine her grief, and I was too much of a coward to tell her I was responsible.

"The general wasn't on the porch when I got back, so I went inside. There were breakfast smells. Eggs. Sausages. The general gestured for me to sit at the kitchen table, which I did, and he set a plate before me. He didn't remark on my puffy, red eyes. He didn't scold me for being late to breakfast. He said nothing about the prior night's arson or the four murders (two human, two equine). He merely instructed me to pack my things for the journey to Berlin.

"That night, when I was sure the general was fast asleep, I bound his wrists and ankles to his bedposts. I plucked his pipe from the bedside table, stuffed it with tobacco, and lit it. The sweet, pungent smoke roused him. He asked what the hell I was doing. I grabbed his beeswax tin and liberally anointed his mustache and his nose, lips, cheeks, and forehead. Then I fingered a crude, thick line down to his nightshirt's second button. I reaffixed my veil and set the pipe on his belly. His desperate breaths caused the pipe bowl to tip over, igniting the line of beeswax. After a minute, I couldn't make out his features, though he still had a mouth because his screams were quite distinct. Probably the only honest thing ever to emerge from his mouth."

Rosamund fell silent, her eyes fixed on nothing in particular.

"Why did you stay as Klaus? You were free of the general."

"No, he was free of me. I was his monster. I'd tortured those men, stolen those women's faces. He killed Isana's grandparents and her horse. Rosamund couldn't live with that, but Klaus could.

"I walked through the forbidden woods, along the stream, past the dead laurel tree, and then continued on to Munich. There I joined the German Workers' Party. Two years after that, I moved to Berlin, having completely forgotten the other half of myself, the half that had fallen in love with Isana. Rosamund hadn't forgotten, as I'd later learn. In the meantime, I started stealing faces."

In 1923, Klaus received word of a female agitator who'd bamboozled a group of drunken SA into marching on the Reichstag. Isana. She conceded nothing during the interrogation. Indeed, Klaus made concessions, as the

Rosamund personality rose like a phoenix from the ashes of their shared subconscious. Not only did Isana seem vaguely familiar, but Klaus was developing an inexplicable affection for the diminutive Jewess. On the third day, as he was assessing whether Isana could see her face, Klaus's infatuation exploded into love. He left the interrogation room to gather himself.

Upon his return, a man in a strange black hat was embracing her. Who was he, and how had he gotten into the fortified compound? Why was he holding her that way? He seemed to love her. Jealousy. That was a new feeling. Klaus blinked and, like that, the couple was gone. How? Klaus could make a woman's face disappear but not an entire body, let alone two. Anyway, Klaus didn't literally remove a face, only her capacity to see her own face, and that process took days. But here, in an instant, this black-hatted man had disappeared himself and Isana entirely.

Klaus quickly identified Kasper through his surveillance of Isana. He tracked their movements over the next four years. His agents kept detailed notes on the customers who entered the hat shop, Kasper's Friday evening gatherings with Mooch's Minions, his regular stops at the Schwarz Boden war memorial, the jazz records he bought at Alberti's, his weakness for apple strudel at Flagler's Bakery, and Isana's first pregnancy. Nothing suggested that Kasper was a skilled spy or a master sorcerer. He was a hatmaker with a facial scar, a dubious academic record, and a penchant for jazz and Bushmills whiskey.

Klaus decided he would reinterrogate Isana. He waited until she delivered her second child, when she would be exhausted and most vulnerable. Klaus disguised himself as a hospital nurse, sported thick, round eyeglasses, and assisted in Bessie's delivery. When Kasper went for fresh air, Klaus moved Isana to the quarantine ward. Upon Kasper's return, Klaus told him Isana was gravely ill and likely infectious. He advised Kasper to return in the morning. Kasper didn't question the voice behind the nurse uniform, and left. Klaus then slipped back into his black garb, affixed his veil, and returned to Isana.

Klaus fired question after question about her escape. Isana's answers confused him. Her husband had used a "wishing hat"—a divine teleportation device once owned by the god Hermes. She had to be lying, delirious, or both. Frustrated, Klaus injected her with a psychoactive chemical, which induced hallucinations. "I'm coming," Isana told her imaginary horse. She then repeated the name Rosamund, over and over, before her eyes rolled back. Isana's body seized into an arch. She stopped breathing. Her skin went pale and cold, her lips from red to indigo. Klaus commanded her to breathe, to live.

She didn't comply. Her body relaxed. She released a long exhale and then she was dead.

Klaus ordered Isana's cremation and created false records stating that an infection had killed her. He commanded his lackey to pose as a doctor and tell Kasper the sad news. Then, he walked to the river. He didn't know why he felt compelled to go there. Instinct, he'd supposed. Or was it conditioning? He gazed at his reflection, expecting to see only the blank space the general had cleared for his mad experiment. Instead, he saw the face of a woman with a delicate nose and rich red lips. Oh how he loved that face. It was forbidden, but he did. No amount of sadism or self-flagellation would purge Isana's visage from his reflection. The more Klaus stared into the River Spree and strained to make that face disappear—the more he whipped his body with a cat o' nine tails and repeated the mantra "I am Klaus. I am Klaus"—the deeper Isana's face burned into that blank space like a branding iron.

One October day in 1934, that heat hit a critical temperature. Klaus collapsed and fell into a mental oblivion.

Minds, like the physical world, abhor a vacuum. Rosamund resurfaced and filled the space Klaus had vacated. She didn't remember much—confused fragments about a horse and a farm, bits and pieces about her mother, stories about a god lusting after a water nymph. She also saw flashes of a concentration camp and a windowless room, where Klaus had questioned female prisoners and performed some kind of surgery on them. Amputations. Psychic amputations. He'd sliced off faces with his saberesque voice and deft touch. Rosamund heard his questions echoing off the concrete walls, all spoken in that monotonous, hypnotic drone. She smelled sausage and the dry, metallic-scented heat of incandescent lights. And when Rosamund looked in the mirror, there was only a blank. The only logical conclusion was she, too, was Klaus's victim.

She was free but terrified. No home. No family. She owned only the clothes on her back, a few Reichsmarks, and a cheap Bakelite radio. She didn't even have identity papers. What should she do? Where should she go?

She wandered Schwarz Boden until spotting the big-nosed man at the window of the Mauer Street hat shop. She felt exhilarated. This man, Kasper Mützenmacher, would be her salvation. She didn't know how she knew this, but she was sure of it. It was Fate.

Although Klaus was trapped in Rosamund's subconscious, permanently out of the face-stealing business, he'd already set his plan for Kristallnacht in motion. He'd accumulated all the faces he needed. He'd distributed radios to the thousands of women he'd interrogated. He'd pre-recorded radio programs under Heidi Geissmütter's persona and peppered them with subliminal messages. He'd labeled the tapes of Heidi's broadcasts sequentially, so the station manager at Radio Schwarz Boden would know exactly when to play them. He'd forged all the links in the causal chain, and, in a few short years, that chain would smash Schwarz Boden into a million shards.

Not that Klaus quietly accepted his exile. For years he grasped at Rosamund's feet, tugging her downward, toward madness. She couldn't kick him away or overwhelm him with the restorative power of Kasper's love. She couldn't fry him with electrotherapy. She couldn't blow his brains out with a Mauser without killing herself.

Klaus resurfaced at Rosamund's weakest moment, when Gretel died on the eve of Kristallnacht. This time, however, Rosamund didn't retreat. She stood her mental ground. But now when she looked in the mirror, two faces stared back, overlaid like a double-exposed film image. With one eye closed, she'd see only Klaus's fanged maw. When she closed that eye and opened the other, she'd see a face from her childhood—her true face—only all grown up. At last she comprehended what she was—two identities within a single, conscious mind. He/She was both a sadistic stealer of faces and a water nymph who'd loved a woman, a man, and that man's children. She/He was both Rosamund and Klaus. *My God. What the hell had they done?*

Cap stared at her, mouth agape.

"This was why I couldn't leave Berlin with you," said Rosamund. "I owed it to my victims to stay and fight the Nazis from the inside."

"But they weren't *your* victims," said Cap. "They were Klaus's. He wasn't you, not the true you."

"What is a person but the sum of her actions? *Their* actions. Torture doesn't hurt any less when the tormenter acts involuntarily. I couldn't join you in Detroit, not that I wasn't tempted every day for the last thirty years. The only way I could bear the guilt was to continue the fight."

"So why come now?"

"This is my last mission. I'm dying, Cap."

"What?"

"Pancreatic cancer. I have a couple months. Before you say it, the answer is yes, I've been to the best doctors."

"Then spend your final days here. Let me care for you."

"I have a lead on a former commandant at Bergen-Belsen. If I don't go—"

"Have someone else nab him."

"It has to be me. Only I can bend his will, make him turn himself over to the Israelis. Otherwise, he'll sense he's being hunted and disappear for good."

Cap hugged Rosamund tightly. "Oh God, Rosamund. I wish I could take back my cruel words and my crueler thoughts. I never stopped loving you. I never will."

A car honked its horn.

"My taxi is here. I have to go."

"Stay until the morning, at least. My grandson is coming for dinner with his girlfriend. You should meet him."

"I'm sorry. I can't."

She extricated herself from Cap's arms and stood. He saw that arguing would do no good. Resigned, he threw off the afghan and grabbed Rosamund's suitcase. He led her outside and down the walkway. The cabbie put the suitcase in the trunk and then opened the rear passenger door.

"By the way, have you made any progress on the curses?" she asked. "Did you contact my Lux cousins?"

"No to both."

"I suppose you've turned that responsibility over to your grandson, now that he's grown up. Does he have your hat-making skills? How do you two get along in the shop?"

"He's a lawyer."

"But the curse—"

"Screw that miserable curse. I want him to be happy."

"So Lukas is a happy boy?"

"Yes. Very. But he goes by Chance now. Wait. How'd you know his birth name?"

"I... I must have read an announcement somewhere."

"There was no announcement, unless Duke placed one in a Swiss paper, which I highly doubt."

"Then someone told me."

"Who?"

"I don't remember. The post-War years were a hectic time. I really do have to go."

As Rosamund turned to get in the cab, the sun illuminated her evergreen irises and the distinct indigo flecks inside them. Cap grabbed her arm for a closer look. He felt as though Rosamund had stabbed his gut with an invisible knife. A clammy sweat broke out on his forehead, and he became woozy. Rosamund reached for Cap, to help stabilize him. He waved her off like a pesky housefly.

"How could you do it, Rosamund?"

"Do what?"

"He was my flesh and blood. He was a son to you."

Rosamund opened her mouth but no words followed. Disgusted, Cap stuffed her in the cab and slammed the door. Rosamund groped for the handle, yelling at the cabbie to unlock her door. Cap, however, didn't need to hear more words. Rosamund's eyes had made a full confession. He smacked his hand on the driver's window.

"Get the fuck out of here! Now!"

The startled cabbie slammed the car into drive and punched the accelerator. The rear tires squealed for a good three seconds before the treads locked onto the asphalt and pushed the car forward, enveloping Cap in a black, rubber-tinged cloud. He squeezed his head in agony, as though red-hot barbed wire had been torn from his brain. His psychic scar had ripped open, and something was clawing at the rent.

Fate had liberated the beast.

Chance had met Shirley Markov during law school. All students in his Psychology of Litigation class were required to volunteer as test subjects at the Institute for Social Research. Chance signed up for an experiment that purportedly would explore the relationship between memory and hydration. Shirley, the lead researcher, informed Chance he would have to drink eighteen ounces of water and then take a reading comprehension test for thirty minutes. He would increase his water intake by two ounces on each succeeding day for two weeks. After concluding the instructions, Shirley pushed up her librarian glasses and added, "Understand there will be no bathroom breaks. Therefore, you are to void your bladder *before* taking the test. Can you comply with this requirement?"

Chance hesitated. He lacked faith in his peanut-sized bladder. He considered signing up for another experiment, but Shirley Markov was a stunningly beautiful woman. Even obscured by the formless lab coat, her curves were obvious. Due to the room's chilliness, her nipples struggled to poke through the starched white cotton. And, all of a sudden, her librarian glasses were *naughty* librarian glasses. Her question—"Can you comply with these requirements?"—resonated in Chance's brain like a command. No doubt, this was a standard question for her subjects, but she may as well have had a riding crop in hand and a spiked heel to his naked throat. Chance also had a funny feeling in his chest, as though she'd stabbed his left ventricle with a knitting needle. It hurt but in an overstimulated, sweet tooth sort of way. He hadn't had that sensation since Gloria Templeton in the fifth grade.

Chance told his bladder to suck it up. He would comply with any and all of Shirley's demands. He nodded like a compliant bank hostage. His engorged penis attempted to nod as well, but it couldn't move. Chance subtly shifted in his chair to stave off gangrene.

The experiment ended two weeks later. Chance figured he'd never see Shirley again, but then she appeared, unannounced, as he was exiting the men's room in his law dorm. Before he could mumble a hello, she was pressing her lips to his mouth and grinding her pelvis into his crotch. Chance relied on his ass to navigate a tight corner and the twelve-and-a-half steps to his room. During the coital afterglow of Shirley's ferocious lovemaking, Chance puzzled over how he'd retrieved the key from his pocket and unlocked the door, for he was quite certain he'd kept one hand on her breast and the other on a butt cheek the entire time. It had to be a minor miracle. Then again, his ass already had manifested unprecedented orienteering skills. Perhaps he'd taken the next step in human evolution and mutated an opposable cheek able to grip tools and dorm room keys.

The next few weeks were a blur. Between sex in Chance's dorm room and other, non-standard locations (labs, library stacks, a computing center), Chance learned Shirley was finishing her Masters in Applied Mathematics, combining the study of actuarial science with cognitive psychology. Her pet project was a model to predict human behavior, which incorporated thousands of variables drawn from the results of blood, urine, and fecal samples, physical and emotional stress tests, mood surveys, cognitive performance measures, caloric intake, height, weight, and (of all things) the labor supply's elasticity relative to short-term interest rates. After performing a complex regression analysis (it took weeks for the monstrous IBM ES9000 computer to run the calculations), Shirley could forecast an individual's "inflection points"—critical future events with a high probability of occurrence... or so she claimed. She'd map these points on a line graph and plot a regression line. She overlaid points that remained uncertain, and therefore, unpredictable, with indigo circles. By factoring in more variables, however, she could reduce the circle's diameter, enabling her to predict the contours of the corresponding inflection point with "actionable specificity." In a sense, she promised that, with enough information, she could divine someone's fate and, by extension, change it. Chance didn't mind that none of this made sense to him, because whenever Shirley tried to explain it, she'd get so worked up by his befuddlement he invariably got a raging boner.

Chance was in love. The feeling was mutual. In addition to copious intercourse, Shirley proved her love by committing to shrink Chance's outsized indigo circles of uncertainty to mathematical irrelevance. That meant adding more variables to the equations, which meant gathering much more invasive information. Chance spent two days in a salt water isolation tank, exposed to different light patterns, while sensors tracked his respiration, heart rate, alpha wave emissions, and the number and duration of his erections. He slept three days in the sleep lab hooked to an EEG, as a speaker played snippets of music and cacophonous sounds. Again, his erections were cataloged.

Shirley also ordered Chance to Health Services for a complete physical examination, blood panel, stress test, and stool test. She arranged for the medical school to conduct a colonoscopy, a relatively new procedure at the time. Two days later, the gastroenterologist reported an anomaly—a hat-shaped polyp in the large intestine, which he'd excised. Otherwise, Chance's colon was the healthiest he'd explored in weeks, an opinion shared by the fifty medical students who'd observed the procedure. It took the IBM ES9000 three weeks to do the math, sufficient time for Chance's puncture wounds to heal, missing hair patches to regrow, and sensitive orifices to uncinch.

Most self-respecting men—indeed, most mindless lab animals—would have fled from Shirley long before she'd ordered the insertion of a long tube up his rectum. The thought had crossed Chance's mind in the isolation tank, the sleep lab, and as he evacuated his innards in preparation for the colonoscopy. But just when he'd conclude Shirley was a mad scientist, she'd perform an act of unprompted generosity. She'd give half her uneaten sandwich to the homeless guy lingering outside Drake's, comfort a lost toddler in the Kresge's, or interrupt their dinner date to corral a stray dog on the sidewalk and bring it to the pound. She wouldn't perform a complex calculation before acting, nor did she debate whether to inconvenience herself. She'd just do it. When someone or something was in need, she was decisive. She went with her gut. There were no indigo circles hovering over her inflection points. Chance envied her.

—o|o—◇◇—⬬—◇◇—o|o—

Cap was preoccupied the evening that Chance brought Shirley home for dinner, and was not very talkative. To fill one of the many silences, Shirley brought up a "hot" issue in actuarial science—the controversial use of sex-segregated longevity tables to calculate the annuity amounts that male and female employees should receive upon retirement. On average, women live longer than men. Therefore, she argued, it made perfect actuarial sense to require women to contribute more toward their retirement in order to receive the same annuity benefit. Alternatively, women could contribute the same amount while working and then receive a correspondingly smaller benefit on the assumption that they, on average, will collect for more years than their male colleagues.

Cap broke from his melancholy stupor to disagree vehemently. He argued that Shirley was advocating discrimination.

Shirley agreed but added, "The entire basis of insurance is efficient discrimination." Sex, like race and other genetic factors, is statistically correlated with risk of loss. Women should pay less for auto insurance because they have fewer accidents but more for health insurance because they use more medical services. Blacks typically live six or seven years less than whites, so they should pay more for life insurance, and whites should pay more for annuities.

Cap dropped his spoon in his clam chowder. It may have been an accident. His voice's escalating volume was not. He couldn't argue statistics or efficiencies with Shirley, but he did know right from wrong. Life expectancy, he argued, is a group characteristic. It's a matter of averages. Shirley was letting the group define the individual.

Shirley waved off Cap's argument. "Sentimentality is not an efficient way to allocate societal resources or spread the risk of loss. The group always reigns supreme."

Cap's face reddened. His scar pulsated purple. His German accent got thick, which often happened before he blew his stack. "You sound like the monsters we left behind in Germany. They, too, said the group reigns supreme. Only thing was, not everyone could be part of the group."

"Pops," Chance tried to interject.

"The Nazis didn't single out the Jews for economic reasons," said Shirley. "It was racism."

"Not true. It was all about economics. Nazi economics. They 'Aryanized' the economy. Can't get more efficient than gassing all the Jews."

"It's quite a stretch from group-based risk models to the gas chambers."

"That's what we thought in 1930. A decade later, those stripped naked and stuffed into the showers had a much different opinion." Cap noticed Shirley's empty bowl and added gruffly, "You need more chowder." He picked up the ladle from the tureen. "Bring your bowl closer, would ya?" When Shirley picked up the bowl, her spoon handle slid halfway around the lip and made a raking sound. Cap winced and then dropped the ladle in the tureen.

"You okay, Pops?" asked Chance.

"Did you hear that?"

"Hear what?"

"A bird, I think. Jesus, it was so damn loud. How could you not hear it?" He looked at the ceiling and listened.

"I don't hear anything, Pops."

Cap pressed his palms into his temples and then got up from the table. "I'm gonna lie down for a few minutes."

"Pops?"

"Clear the table when you're done, would ya? I'll join you for dessert. I got your favorite. Goresky's banana cream pie."

"Didn't Goresky's close?" asked Shirley.

"Yeah, it did," said Chance. "Pops, did you mean Lila's?"

"I did not mean fucking Lila's! You want to see the goddamn receipt?"

"Take it easy, Pops."

"Sorry. I'm tired," he said on his way to the bedroom. He closed the door behind him, flipped on the jazz station, and then cranked it as loud as it could go.

CHAPTER FIFTEEN

Six Months Later

Chance broke into a sweat the second he stepped through the double doors separating the dry, frigid outside from the chlorine-laced mugginess of the Wayne State University natatorium. Cap's cryptic note didn't explain why they needed to meet at the Soggy Mitten Invitational, only that it was "urgent." A high school swim meet was not where Chance should've been the day before his wedding. He still had to finalize the food arrangements with the Stage Deli up in Oak Park and then deliver the alcohol to the federal courthouse's ceremonial courtroom, which was all the way back downtown. Ostensibly, Shirley could've handled one of these tasks, but she was hell bent on finding a white silk hat to match her skirt suit. (In a moment of ill-timed spontaneity, she'd permitted the stylist to shear her fountainous coif into a pixie cut, which would've looked great on Mia Farrow but was positively Herman-Munster-esque atop Shirley's prominent forehead.)

Chance had little difficulty spotting his grandfather in the stands. Per his note, Cap was wearing an indigo beret, a millinery beacon among the hundreds of cheering parents and siblings. Dark, puffy bags hung under his eyes like tiny, old luggage. He'd been complaining of poor sleep for months.

Extreme fatigue hadn't slowed Cap down. Just the opposite. He worked longer and longer hours at the hat shop. He also busied himself with house projects—installing extra hose bibs, building shelves, and knitting covers for the armchair and sofa. After tackling the living room furniture, he covered the chairs in the dining room and kitchen. He then moved onto more questionable objects, shrouding the toilet seats in Shetland wool, the doorknobs in Angora, and every faucet handle with cashmere. At times, Cap didn't even seem conscious of his handiwork. He'd spent an hour on the phone explaining to Detroit Edison that he hadn't paid his light bill because the utility hadn't mailed it or the Postal Service hadn't delivered it. After hanging up, he discovered a "bouquet" of unpaid utility bills arranged in an Argyle-covered vase on the kitchen table. Whatever was troubling him had invaded his dreams, too. The previous evening, his hands were frenetically miming a sewing motion as he dozed in the armchair. He flinched awake and announced, "It's torn again."

"Pops, what are we doing here? What was so urgent?"

"Sit down."

Cap had a bag of yarn between his legs. He was embroidering a gryphon image into an oven mitt.

Chance wiped his eyes. "Jesus, do they chlorinate the air in here too? How can you stand it?"

"It's the screeching that gets to me."

"What screeching?"

Cap glanced at a program. "She's up next."

"Who?"

"Diana." Cap gestured to the pool's far side, where eight white-capped girls positioned themselves on their respective starting blocks. "She's in lane four."

Diana was puny compared to her seven competitors, barely over five feet tall and a hundred pounds. The other girls—nascent women, really—were shapely, with rounded hips and breasts. Diana was a flat-chested stick figure, a human Gumby. The swimmers crouched in preparation for the starter's pistol. Everyone but Diana placed her feet side by side; she put one behind the other like an Olympic sprinter. The others dangled their arms, while Diana gripped her platform's edge with every finger and both thumbs, as though expecting the platform to tear loose from its moorings. Her tense posture revealed a musculature that Chance hadn't detected when she'd been standing upright. Her lats bulged through her red, white, and blue swimsuit, and her triceps were like taut hemp ropes.

When the shot fired, Diana uncoiled, threw her arms forward, and launched herself over the water. Though six inches shorter than the other swimmers, Diana's hands landed more than a foot beyond anyone else's. The pool betrayed no obvious splash, creating the momentary illusion that Diana wasn't so much swimming across the pool as soaring over it. Her butterfly stroke was so fluid and efficient, she raced to a lead before the first turn. After propelling herself from the wall, she was ahead by a good three feet. Her swimming was effortless, as though the pool had dedicated an exclusive current for her, and all she had to do was coast, while the others labored through Jell-O.

Chance sensed his grandfather's gaze in his peripheral vision. He turned toward Cap's devilish smile.

"What are you not telling me, Pops? Who is this Diana girl?"

"Diana *Lux*."

"Oh Jesus God. You're stalking teen girls now?"

"Only teen water nymphs. You remember. Back in Fifty-Four, I figured out there was a Lux family in Detroit who could be related to Rosamund. That was Winifred Lux's family. Diana is Winifred's granddaughter. Look at her. She's only thirteen or fourteen, going up against sixteen- and seventeen-year-olds."

"I see. So every swimming phenom named Lux is a water nymph. Makes sense."

"Don't take me for an idiot. We'll ask her after the meet."

"Are you out of your mind?"

"Worst she can say is no."

"The worst she could say is, 'Call the cops.'"

"You worry too much."

"And you don't worry enough about the curse. I'm not gonna live forever, you know."

"Pops, there is no curse. There are no nymphs. There never was a wishing hat. You admitted that when I was ten."

"I never admitted that," Cap growled. "I just let you off the goddamn hook because I didn't think we'd get the hat back."

"You were the one who suggested I forget the curse and become a lawyer. Do you admit that much?"

"Biggest mistake of my life."

"What would you have me do? Hound the poor girl until Apollo tries to rape her? I'd get arrested for attempted pedophilia. Anyway, Shirley and I live in another city. I have a full-time job."

"Keep the communication lines open, that's all. Exchange phone numbers, addresses, so you can be ready to act."

"Does she even have a twin sister?"

"I haven't seen any sign of one."

"Christ, Pops! Have you been spying on that family?"

"Not spying. Reconnaissance."

The race ended. Diana touched the wall a full second ahead of everyone else. She'd tied the meet record set in 1960 by future Olympic medalist Naomi Thomas.

"It doesn't matter anyway. You don't have the wishing hat."

"About that." Cap fished his winter coat from under the bench and pulled out a golf-ball-sized rock. "This came in the mail."

Chance plucked the rock, black and pock-laden, from Cap's fingers. "What's this, a wishing rock?"

Cap handed Chance a slip of paper. "This was with it."

The note read, "Tired of running. She wasn't there. Forgive me. D-----."

"Who's 'D-----'?"

"The writing's awful shaky, but it's definitely Duke's."

"Why would Duke send you a rock? And what the hell's he talking about? 'Tired of running' from what?"

A memory of the railroad tracks and the crazy priest flashed in Chance's mind. It had been his worst birthday ever. His tenth.

"He's tired of running from his destiny, that's what," said Cap.

"Then who's the 'she,' and where was she supposed to be?"

"Isana."

"My grandmother?"

"Duke was so young when she died. Trying to explain death to a kid—shit, what did I know? I told him she was far away, too far away to see. As far away as the moon. Never crossed my mind he'd take me literally, that he'd fantasize his mother had set up camp on the dark side. One time, he suggested we wish ourselves there. I told him it was suicide, but I think he finally went through with it."

"You think Duke wished himself to the moon."

"I wouldn't put anything past him when it comes to his mother."

"Huh?"

"Never mind. The return address was a law firm in Cape Kennedy, Florida. That's where Apollo Eleven launched."

"Pops, think a second. Volcanic rocks are a dime a dozen. Every science museum sells them. And do you think Duke could survive a trip to the moon? There's no air."

"If it was a quick trip, there and back... maybe. Would've blown his lungs out something awful, without a spacesuit. One thing I know for sure, he's dying. My son..."

Cap's eyes turned glassy, but he held his tears in check. Although Chance was sure Cap was speaking nonsense, his grandfather's anguish was authentic. He awkwardly placed a comforting arm around his shoulder.

"Hey... Pops. Come on. You're overtired."

"That's not it."

"Then you're feeling sentimental because I'm getting married, leaving the nest. Don't worry. You and I are still gonna see each other. You're coming to D.C. in the spring, and I'll be up for Michigan games in the fall."

Cap winced and then shook his head. "Ach. That damn screeching."

"What screeching?"

"We need to get to Florida."

"Sure. Next Christmas, when I've earned more leave."

"Tomorrow. After the wedding."

"I have a honeymoon."

Cap's scar pulsed like an angry earthworm. "Damn it, Chance. We've got to get the wishing hat before Duke dies, if he's not already dead. If it falls into the wrong hands—"

"You're not listening. I have a life."

"Don't you want a life with great purpose?"

"I do, at the Federal Trade Commission. I protect consumers from snake oil salesmen. I fight for the scientific method."

"Jesus. You must think I'm the biggest fool in the world."

Not the biggest.

"No."

"I mean, shit, I believe in Greek gods and wishing hats. So did my father and his father, all the way back thousands of years. How does your scientific method explain that?"

"Dr. Lippman calls it an intergenerational delusion, a folie en famille."

"Who the hell's Dr. Lippman?"

"A physician."

"A head shrink?"

"A psychiatrist. He's brilliant. He developed Achromatic Therapy."

"Acrobatic... what?"

"A-chromatic, as in the absence of color. He says a healthy mind is a lens that focuses the internal and external worlds without distortion. People, objects, events, feelings, thoughts—they should resolve in the mind's eye with perfect clarity. But biases and neuroses warp the lens, put a fringe of color around everything, a color that doesn't belong there, a color that's not real.

Dr. Lippman suspects that my discoloration tends toward the spectrum's bluer end. We're making a 'corrective lens' together. That's Dr. Lippman's metaphor for therapy."

"It sounds like the word 'doctor' is his metaphor for 'crackpot.'"

"I'm not doing his theory justice. He's written a book on it. I'll send you a copy."

"You think I'm bonkers, too?"

"Don't get defensive. That's not what I meant."

"You didn't get your problem from me, I promise you that. Must've been that mother of yours. Her kind are always off-kilter."

"How would you know? You never even met Francesca."

"True… True. But I know her kind… Italians."

"Whatever. I don't blame you for my condition." *Even though you're one hundred percent at fault.*

"What's wrong with you that you need a shrink?"

"Trouble sleeping."

"Take a sleeping pill."

"It's more than that. Every so often, I have this delusion, the same one. You remember the Lolo?"

"That swirly shape from when you were a kid? You outgrew that."

"I guess it didn't outgrow me. It hovers above the bed, like an angry purple vortex. Like it's gonna suck me inside. Not every night but often enough I get anxious at bedtime. The anticipation's worse in a way."

"So the Lolo just floats there?"

"And makes a sound. Like this." Chance hummed.

Cap nodded. "B-flat."

"And it sings, 'Go back. Go back.'"

Chance nodded. "A warning."

"About what?"

"The curse. Go back to the hat business or else."

Chance rubbed his forehead. "Pops."

"When did this start?"

"Halloween night."

"Anything significant happen that day?"

"Yeah. I got my Bar exam results. I officially became a lawyer."

"And the next day, that bus hit you. I remember our phone call. You said Fate was no fan of lawyers. Your words, not mine."

"First off, the bus barely grazed me. Second, that line about Fate was a joke."

"Fate's no comedienne. Wait a second. That incident with the space heater. At Thanksgiving. Did you see the Lolo before that?"

"Let me think." *Yeah, I did.* "I don't remember. Maybe."

"Uh-huh."

"What do you mean 'uh-huh'?"

"This is Fate's way of telling you to go into the hat business."

"Pops, two coincidences don't prove anything."

"If it's only two."

Four coincidences don't prove anything either.

"Plenty of bad things have happened to Leghorns who stayed in the hat business. Nazi Germany wasn't exactly a walk in the park."

"I know damn well what Nazi Germany was. Had we been doctors or lawyers, had we forgotten about the hat, we all would've died in Dachau!"

Chance stood.

"Where you going?" asked Cap.

"I've got stuff to do."

"We've got to get to Florida."

"You're a big boy. Fly down yourself."

"I've never been on a plane."

"Air travel's extremely safe. Safer than wishing hats, I hear. Which reminds me. You might as well buy a one-way ticket. If Duke has the wishing hat, you'll save yourself a couple bucks on the return trip."

"Don't be a smart-ass. This is your goddamn heritage. Show a little respect. You already weaseled out of the hat business. Least you can do is escort an old man to see his dying son."

"You know what? Fuck you, Pops! Don't you dare burden me with this inane curse just because you won't face the reality that you failed your children!"

Cap looked utterly defeated. The man who'd fought with swords for fun, stood up to Nazis, saved his family from a concentration camp, and survived three riots might as well have died a thousand years earlier. He was a mummified version of his former glory. An empty shell. Hollow.

Chance backpedaled. "Pops... look... I'm sorry. I didn't mean that."

"No, you're right. I failed Duke. I failed Bessie. And there were others. Isana. My father. He made only one demand—to pass on the hat, and I couldn't even manage that. Fuck me."

"Come with me to the Stage Deli. We'll talk in the car."

"Goresky's is better."

"You keep saying Goresky's is open, but every time I call there's no answer."

"You're not calling at the right time."

"When's the right time?"

Cap tapped his right temple. "I've got the store hours in here. All you got to do is ask. But I expect you wouldn't trust my information. That would require faith."

"Well, I've already placed the order with the Stage. So, you coming?

Cap's fixed his gaze toward the pool. "Nah. You go ahead. I'm gonna stay a little longer."

Chance stood in silence. This wasn't how he wanted to leave things.

"We can't even be sure Duke sent you the rock and the note."

"Not many sure things in this world."

Chance scratched his head in frustration. "I'll make some phone calls this evening, see if Duke or anyone fitting his description has checked into a hospital down there. Isn't that a more reasonable approach than hopping the next plane to Florida?"

Cap shrugged.

"Then I'll see you this evening, okay?"

"Sure thing, Chance," Cap answered forlornly.

Chance set the lava rock on the metal bleacher. As he slid it toward Cap, it made a squealing sound. Cap flinched but checked himself from turning. Then, Chance did something he hadn't done since childhood. He kissed Cap's cheek. In a moment of magical thinking, he believed a kiss would keep his grandfather from slipping away.

CHAPTER SIXTEEN

Cap wasn't home after Chance dropped the three crates of Bushmills whiskey at the courthouse. Shirley hadn't seen Cap since morning. Cyrus hadn't seen him either. Calls to the hat shop went unanswered. By eight o'clock, there still was no word. Chance asked Cyrus to meet him at the hat shop and, if necessary, unlock it.

The interiors of the shop windows were covered in black fabric. The door was closed tight but not locked. Something was holding it shut. Chance drove his shoulder into the door. There was a ripping sound, and the door opened enough for Chance to wedge his body inside. He pushed against the door's edge, using his back as leverage. Yards of black velvet fell on his head. Someone had stapled the fabric over the doorframe.

"Pops!"

At least twenty hats in various stages of construction formed a sinuous path to the cutting room. That was where Cap lay face down, his right hand gripping a shears he'd driven into a black hat shaped like a gryphon.

Cyrus looked at the ceiling. "Aw, Jesus, why you gotta take my best friend in the whole wide world? Why'd you need him so soon? You got the rest of eternity with him. We had big plans, fancy designs in the works, but now..." Cyrus buried his face in Chance's shoulder.

The coroner would later confirm that Cap had died of a massive stroke.

After a somber wedding ceremony the following afternoon, Chance made the funeral arrangements and placed notices in several newspapers. Two days later, Cap was buried next to Bessie. Several hundred people showed up for the non-religious service that Dr. Kennedy volunteered to officiate. Cyrus stood closest to the head of his dead friend's casket, accompanied by his grandson Martin. A short man in a South American chullo hat stood next to Cyrus. Word was he was a German ex-pat fighting for gay rights in Bolivia, of all places. The remaining mourners surrounded the plot in a ring that spiraled deeper and deeper with bodies. They wore the eclectic range of hats that Cap had produced over the last thirty years.

What a spectacular sight the mourning doves had from their perch in the nearby chestnut tree. The color spectrum was well-represented—swatches of red and orange velvet, brocaded silk of yellow, green, and gold, and earth-tone wool. Most of Cap's designs were simple bowlers, panamas, homburgs, berets, and fedoras (including the straw "Tiger" variety), but there were a few ornate creations encrusted with pearls, woven with silver thread, or decorated with brooches, peacock plumes, or ostrich feathers. Most striking (assuming doves appreciate such things) was the indigo streak winding through that millinery whirlpool. Many hats bore at least a hint of indigo—a silk ribbon or bow, a tassel, a dyed feather, dried violet petals. Even hats lacking the obvious indigo accents appeared indigo because Cap had incorporated an iridescent white organza into the designs, such that indoors these hats emanated a warm pearlescence, but outside they reflected the indigo light waves, rendering them as cool and detached as a clear blue sky.

The indigo splashes weren't confined to any one demographic. Young and old, rich and poor, black and white donned indigo in equal proportions. Without fanfare or force, Cap had imposed his singular color on a multichromatic cross-section of Detroit.

A Greyhound bus pulled up the drive and parked. The door opened and a stream of people emerged, all wearing the same strange hat. Chance assumed they were Rotarians or Masons paying their respects to a deceased brother, until the line of fifty souls began snaking toward Cap's burial site. When they got closer, Chance discerned the homburg-chullo hybrid hats with indigo tassels. The assembled mourners widened their circle, allowing the late arrivals to form three new interior rings around the plot. Leading the cavalcade was a tall, slender man with stooped shoulders and gray hair. His necktie was loose and askew, and his jacket's left side vent was tucked into the pocket, the opening covered with crumbs from the dry crackers he'd been nibbling on. He introduced himself to Chance after the ceremony.

"Grimsky."

"Nice to meet you. I finally know what became of my grandfather's weird hats."

"Your grandfather made the first spinning top hat—that's my name for it—on Ellis Island. Over the decades, I placed orders for the others."

"The others?"

"Survivors, like me, like your grandfather."

"It was very nice for you all to make the trip."

"It was our obligation. He saved us."

"How exactly?"

"He never told you the story?"

"He told me many stories."

"This one would stand out from the rest."

"Humor me."

"We agreed not to talk about it."

"You're saying he actually wished a hundred people in a boxcar to Ellis Island?"

"I'm saying nothing, and even if I did say, I sense you would not believe me. It would require a leap of faith you are not prepared to make."

Instead of a two-week, Hawaiian honeymoon, Chance and Shirley remained in frigid, overcast Detroit to tie up loose ends. When Chance wasn't consoling Cyrus or conferring with the accountant to wind down his grandfather's share of the business, he was cleaning out Cap's house in preparation for sale. The day he and Shirley left town, they stuffed old photos and a few lamps in their car. The movers already had picked up the bed sets, dining room table and chairs, sideboard, and armoire. Chance had instructed them to leave Bessie's vanity behind because he "never liked the damn thing."

Chance sat in the driver's seat. He checked his watch, reached into the glove compartment, and removed a bottle. He flipped the cap and dumped a pill in his hand.

"Why don't you go back inside and get some water?" asked Shirley.

"I just want to get the hell out of here."

Chance popped the pill and forced it down. He started the car and shifted into drive. They hadn't moved a foot before a postal truck zipped around the corner and parked within inches of their front bumper, forcing Chance to hit the brakes. The postman hopped from the truck and rolled up the back door. He removed a box and headed to Cap's front door.

"Honey, your grandfather has a delivery. It might be a wedding gift. I'll fetch it."

Chance shifted into park. Shirley greeted the postman and signed for the box. Chance leaned into the passenger seat and rolled down the window as the postal truck pulled away.

"Is it for us?"

"Weird. It's really warm."

The box was imprinted with the words "Lux Toilet Soap" and "Lux Radio Theater." One side featured a caricature of Cecil B. Demille.

"Is that a soap box?"

"Yeah," said Shirley. "It says, 'One hundred beauty bars.'"

"Why the hell would Pops order so much soap? Bring it over here."

Chance pushed open the door, and Shirley set the box on the passenger seat. The box had been sent from Ricardo Sanchez, Esq. of the Law Offices of Rosen and Sanchez, Cape Kennedy, Florida. It was addressed to "Mr. Chance Leghorn, sole heir to the estate of Duke Leghorn, care/of Cap Leghorn."

"Oh honey. I think your dad may have died."

"I don't have a dad. Put the box back at the front door."

"Why?"

"Mark it 'Return to Sender.' I don't want anything from that asshole."

"There might be something valuable inside."

"Like my lost childhood? Probably his damn worthless ashes. Put it back and get in the car."

Five Days Earlier

As he slipped in and out of consciousness at Cape Kennedy Hospital, Duke took stock of his poor choices, most of which involved his father—expressing embarrassment over the Mützenmacher nose, making lousy hats, denouncing Kasper to the Gestapo, stealing the wishing hat... and that other thing. How the hell had he let it happen? At what point had he veered onto that twisted path? When had he made that first, irreversible turn? Had he known it would lead to "that other thing," would he have done it anyway?

Duke closed his eyes. When he reopened them, a morbidly obese man with a scruffy red beard sat beside him, wheezing from the pressure of adipose tissue cocooning his lungs, his flesh and folds spilling from the faux leather chair.

"I don't have it, Father."

The priest already knew that Duke had entrusted the wishing hat to his attorney. That wasn't why he'd come. No, Father Filconi had accepted that in all probability he'd exit this world with a partial soul. He just wanted to be there when death compelled Duke to relinquish the stolen piece, on the off chance it would then return to him like a long-lost dog. But that same hope also made the priest anxious. He couldn't predict how the chunk of soul that had stayed with him—the loyal portion—would react to its wayward sibling. Would it sniff the psychic fragment and welcome it back to the fold, or would it snarl, treat it as a feral interloper, so corrupted and deformed from its futile attempt to assimilate into another man's soul as to be unrecognizable? Would it attack? This was uncharted territory.

"I have to confess something," said Duke.

Father Filconi's religious training, the decades of prayer and practiced ritual, hadn't prepared him for this situation. Though the sacrament was only for Catholics, Church rules hadn't contemplated a penitent like Duke. Surely Duke was at least a "little bit" Catholic, because a piece of the priest was inside him. That would be sufficient in God's eyes, wouldn't it? Again, uncharted territory. Father Filconi would have to make a leap of faith—a leap he couldn't feel but that logic told him must exist.

The priest slipped on a purple stole, made the Sign of the Cross, and rested a hand on Duke's head.

Duke didn't know where to begin. As soon as he'd settle on one event and declare, "There! That's where my downfall began," he'd discover that event was merely an effect of other, earlier causes. He'd reflect further backward—to his childhood, to his first memory (crawling toward the radio), and then to things he couldn't possibly recall—his birth, his conception, Lorenz Mützenmacher, Faustus Petasos, the first homo sapiens—all the way to the Big Bang. It devolved into a pointless, self-delusional exercise.

Father Filconi mulled Duke's dilemma. He acknowledged that confession was necessarily a subjective exercise, fraught with bias, clouded recollections, and enshadowed in the regret-laden penumbra of impending death. Yet subjectivity was the whole point. Whereas a man's choices defined his contours to the external world, his self-definition—his true form, which only he could see, reflected in the mind's eye—rested on his ability and willingness to weigh those choices, prioritize them, and pick the one on which he could hang his soul—even a half soul—and then call it day… or an eternity, as it were.

That made sense to Duke. He settled on 1943. After inadvertently swiping a piece of Father Filconi's soul, Duke wished himself to a place the priest couldn't easily follow, the Tower of London. In the shadow of the Waterloo Barracks, Duke vowed to set things straight. Well, not all things. Not the thing with Father Filconi. That was too risky. Rather, Duke would square things with his real father. He'd use the wishing hat for a noble purpose and make him proud. He would follow his father's example by rescuing Jews from the Nazis. He'd begin with a small number, maybe ten or fifteen, so as not to drain the hat's life force, and then gradually increase his quota. He would save thousands by the end of the war!

Duke wished himself to Auschwitz's medical unit, where twenty inmates were recovering from (or dying of) starvation and dysentery. He whispered instructions into their puzzled ears: gather at the center of the ward, hold hands, and, when instructed, exhale. Most were too weak and half-asleep to protest, let alone register surprise at the black-hatted specter giving them strange commands. A few patients had enough energy to walk to the ward's center, where Duke had instructed them to sit. Duke wheeled the gravely infirm and sat them in a circle with the others. One inmate, a young girl, was so frail and light, Duke carried her to the circle. He sat with her in his lap and reminded everyone to hold hands and exhale on the count of three, which they did. Duke thought of the place and then made the wish. A moment later, they arrived on Ellis Island, at the very same spot Duke and a hundred others had landed five years earlier.

As Fate would so cruelly remind Duke, travel by wishing hat was not for the weak. Everyone but Duke was dead. The horror! Duke pulled his hair and tried to cry out, but he couldn't fill his lungs with enough air to utter more than a feeble squeak. He looked beseechingly at the moon. "Why, Mama? Why did this happen? Why didn't you stop me? I'm no better than the Nazis."

Duke was overcome with homesickness. Home, however, wasn't his father's house in Detroit. Home was back in time. Home was his childhood in Schwarz Boden. He needed to warn his younger self, "Be proud of your big fat nose. Listen to your father. Make hats."

Please. Take me there. Please. Please.

And it did.

Duke appeared outside the front door of the family's old apartment in Schwarz Boden. Had the hat granted his wish? Was his younger self inside? If Duke entered the apartment, would things look exactly like they'd looked back then—the Telefunken radio in the den, the silver samovar from which Grandma Elsie served black tea, the moon maps labeled with his mother's potential location on the dark side? The family lore hadn't said anything about time travel, so Duke braced himself for disappointment. He expected a stranger to answer the door or no one at all. But when he knocked, someone did answer, and she wasn't a stranger. She welcomed him inside. Once, this woman had been his almost-mother and his father's almost-wife.

A black cloak with Nazi insignia hung over a dining room chair. A black veil was spread on the table like a puddle of cotton ink. Duke went to his old room, curled up on the bed, and tried to sleep, but the cold permeated his bones. He couldn't stop shivering. The woman huddled next to him for warmth. Later, she broke out a bottle of Bushmills that Kasper had left behind. They passed the bottle back and forth until they forgot themselves, until they were just two lonely strangers. Then, they lay closer. So much closer.

Duke awoke early the following morning. He'd had a vile nightmare, which he attributed to the spent bottle of whiskey. He'd dreamed of Rosamund. He'd embraced her naked flesh, and she his. The dream was so vivid he could practically feel the press of her hip bones into his back and the scratchiness of her pubis. He shuddered. The body next to him shuddered sympathetically.

Duke scrambled out of bed, grabbed his pants and shirt, and didn't look back. He ran to the kitchen and vomited in the sink. He slipped on his clothes and then fetched the wishing hat from the dining room table.

Switzerland. Take me there.

Although Duke had escaped Rosamund, he couldn't escape the shame, nor could he extinguish the ember of desire. Every few weeks, he wished himself to the apartment's front door, each time losing the will to knock. Six months passed, until Duke could no longer resist. He wished himself inside the apartment, to Rosamund's bedroom.

She'd transformed in the interim. He placed a hand on her abdominal bulge and left it there until she woke up. They didn't speak about their night together. They didn't discuss their feelings or the future. They scrupulously avoided touching one another or even standing near each other. They cohabited until the birth, which was quick and far less alarming than the Allied bombs raining around the hospital. Rosamund dressed and left the hospital while Duke was observing his son in the nursery. Duke didn't find her at the apartment. Her black cloak and veil were gone as well. The note she'd left didn't mention her whereabouts. She'd written only one word: Lukas.

Duke finally had something to live for other than himself. He was a father. He vowed to become the greatest father any child would ever know. Instead of wallowing in regret over the circumstances surrounding his son's conception, he'd revel in the miracle of creation—*his* creation. Fate had smiled upon him. Finally, he was lucky, and so was his son. But Duke hadn't anticipated that, by 1946, Lucky would resemble a miniaturized Cap Leghorn.

That round face. That bulbous nose. Jesus, the kid was a walking, talking reminder of his betrayal. Duke wasn't lucky at all. He was cursed. He was cursed because he was a thief, and he'd stolen something far more precious than a divine hat.

So ended Duke's confession.

"I absolve you from your sins in the name of the Father, the Son, and the Holy Spirit. Amen."

"I don't deserve absolution after what I took from you, but thanks."

"I'm glad you took it, Duke. That's right. Glad. You saved me from doing a horrible thing, killing innocents. I should've seen that a long time ago. That was my sin."

"But what about Heaven? The Big Guy's not gonna let you in, right?"

"I don't know."

Duke began to weep. He spoke to the ceiling. "I let you down, Pops. I was weak. I should've had faith in you, in the curse that kept our family together for all those centuries. But it's not too late for Chance. You'll see. Soon. If only I could see your faces when he…" Duke turned to the priest. "I'm scared, Father."

The priest took Duke's hand. "Don't be afraid, my son. Wherever we're headed, we're going there together."

"Really?"

"Absolutely. All we have to do is hold hands."

Duke smiled beatifically. "Just like the wishing hat."

"Yes, just like that."

Father Filconi rested his head on Duke's abdomen. As the priest's eyelids grew heavy and his breathing slowed to a shallow rasp, a surge of warmth filled his gut—probably just acid reflux from the "Secret Sauce" on his Jack in the Box burger. Then again, this was a pleasant warmth, something he hadn't felt in years, unlike indigestion, which occurred daily. This was faith, pure and simple. But how? He could think of only two possibilities: a delusion generated by his oxygen-starved brain or the gift of divine grace. And then he had his answer.

Their hearts stopped simultaneously. The time was 11:21.

After they left Cap's house, Shirley placed her hand on the back of Chance's.

"Your hand's so warm," he remarked.

"From the box."

"Hey. How about we hit Goresky's before hopping on I-94?"

"I thought we figured out Goresky's closed after the riots."

"I've been mulling it over, and I think Pops may have been right."

"Unlikely. He was really losing his marbles toward the end."

Chance smacked the steering wheel with his palm. "Goresky's is open! Right now. This very moment. I know it in my gut. I just know it. Have a little faith in me."

Chance's head was trembling, and he was biting his lower lip to contain the inhuman howl that seemed to be bobbing at the back of his throat.

"Okay," said Shirley with the same assuredness she'd convey to a lost puppy dog. "Goresky's it is."

Chance swallowed hard. He turned left at the next block and then left again.

"Goresky's is the other way, hon."

Chance parked by his dead grandfather's trashcans. He trotted to the front door and inspected the Lux soapbox, which was way too light to contain a hundred soap bars. It was warm, too. So damn warm. Chance carried the box to the car and popped the trunk, which was packed full except for one empty spot in the center. A perfect fit. How lucky.

ACKNOWLEDGMENTS

I would like to thank my writing colleagues for their blunt, but constructive, feedback as the novel evolved, including Jennifer Hawkes, Andrea Franco Cook, Richard Agemo, and the members of Trey Ellis's workshop at the 2015 Yale Writers' Conference. I also am grateful to Julie Miesionczek, Lisa Gus, and Mark Woodring for their developmental editing wisdom, and Eugene Teplitsky for the fantastic cover art. Further, I owe a debt of gratitude to the writers and teachers who have mentored and inspired me over the years, including Trey Ellis, Meg Wolitzer and the faculty of the Stony Brook Southampton Writers Conference, the faculty of The Writer's Center in Bethesda, Maryland, and Dr. Charles Fremuth of Detroit Country Day School, who, with Socrates' assistance, taught me that the unexamined life is not worth living. Finally, I could not have written this novel without the support and encouragement of my trusted readers, who provided invaluable feedback with virtually no arm-twisting: Will Ducklow, Christine Lee Delorme, Tom Kane, my parents Raylene Fenton and Dr. Stuart Fenton, and, of course, the most important reader of all, my wife Laura.

ABOUT THE AUTHOR

When not sporting my fiction writer hat, I practice consumer protection law in Washington, D.C. Rest assured your tax dollars are hard at work as I battle marketers of "modern miracles" like weight-loss earrings and penile enhancement herbs. (Please let me know if you spot an ad for penile enhancement earrings.)

I graduated from the University of Michigan with a degree in philosophy, which, surprisingly, did not qualify me for gainful employment, so it was on to graduate school. Well, almost. I spent a year touring with a professional comedy troupe, writing and performing sketch comedy at colleges in the Mid-Atlantic States. After that frolic and detour, life became a blur of law school, falling in love, cats, marriage, a dog, children, a fish, more dogs, another fish, a chinchilla, guinea pigs, and an assortment of uninvited rodents that have since burrowed through the foundation. Storybook.

Thank You for Reading

© 2016 **Keith R. Fentonmiler**

http://www.keithfentonmiller.com

Please visit http://curiosityquills.com/reader-survey to share your reading experience with the author of this book!

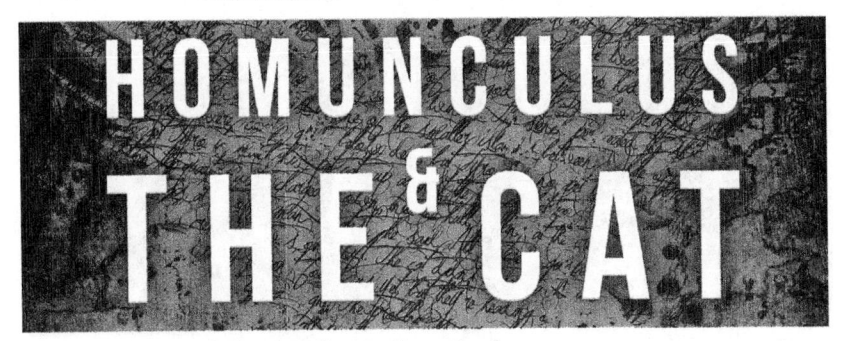

PLEASE VISIT CURIOSITYQUILLS.COM FOR MORE GREAT BOOKS!

Homunculus and the Cat, by Nathan Croft

In a world where every culture's mythology is real, Medusa's sisters want revenge on Poseidon, Troy is under siege again, and the Yakuza want their homunculi (mythological artificial humans) back. Near Atlantis' Chinatown, a kitten and her human campaign for homunculi rights. Against them are Japanese death gods, an underworld cult, and a fat Atlantean bureaucrat. The main character dies (more than once) and a few underworlds' way of death is threatened. Also with giant armored battle squids.

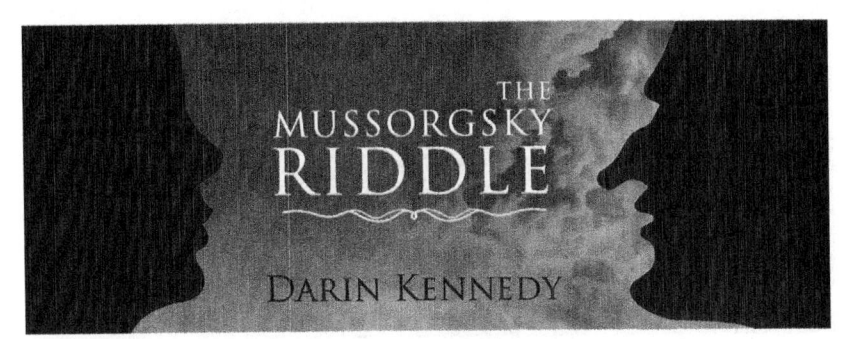

The Mussorgsky Riddle, by Darin Kennedy

The Mussorgsky Riddle is Alice in Wonderland meets Law and Order. Called in to awaken an autistic boy left catatonic after witnessing a grisly murder, psychic Mira Tejedor is pulled into young Anthony's mind and discovers the cause of his strange malady. The crime has left his fragile psyche shattered into the various movements of composer Modest Mussorgsky's classical music suite, Pictures at an Exhibition. Mira must help heal the boy's fractured mind and unmask the murderer before the killer can discover the secrets hidden in the boys mind and silence both of them forever.

The Outs, by E.S. Wesley

Memory-stealing blackouts push a seventeen-year-old honor student into kidnapping a little girl to keep her safe from the creature in her room, but the new voice in his head may be worse than any monster in the dark. Now it's up to a disabled comic book fangirl to save them both before the girl he stole unravels everyone's future.

Unhappenings, by Edward Aubry

When Nigel is visited by two people from his future, he hopes they can explain why his past keeps rewriting itself. His search for answers takes him fifty-two years forward in time, where he meets Helen, brilliant, hilarious and beautiful. Unfortunately, that meeting has triggered events that will cause millions to die. Desperate to find a solution, he discovers the role his future self has played all along.